A ROYAL PASSION

When he first laid eyes on the imperious Matilda, William did not know if he loved her, yet he swore to take her for his own. When she spurned his base blood, she had not reckoned on the devil within him.

What sort of man was he, who dared enter her father's house and publicly whip her? Even when, chastened, she faced him on their wedding night, fear and awe besieged her as she asked: "My lord, have you taken me for love or for hatred?"

THE CONQUEROR

A stirring novel of love and valor
in the time of the Norman Conquest.

Bantam Books by Georgette Heyer
Ask your bookseller for the books you have missed

BEHOLD, HERE'S POISON
A BLUNT INSTRUMENT
CHARITY GIRL
THE CONQUEROR
THE CORINTHIAN
COUSIN KATE
DEATH IN THE STOCKS
DEVIL'S CUB
ENVIOUS CASCA
FALSE COLOURS
FREDERICA
LADY OF QUALITY
NO WIND OF BLAME
PENHALLOW
REGENCY BUCK
ROYAL ESCAPE
THEY FOUND HIM DEAD
THE UNFINISHED CLUE

The Conqueror
Georgette Heyer

BANTAM BOOKS · TORONTO · LONDON · NEW YORK

*This low-priced Bantam Book
has been completely reset in a type face
designed for easy reading, and was printed
from new plates. It contains the complete
text of the original hard-cover edition.*
NOT ONE WORD HAS BEEN OMITTED.

THE CONQUEROR

*A Bantam Book / published by arrangement with
E. P. Dutton & Company, Inc.*

PRINTING HISTORY

*Dutton edition published October 1966
2nd printing .... October 1966*

Bantam edition published February 1968

2nd printing .. February 1968	5th printing .... March 1970
3rd printing .... March 1968	6th printing .... March 1972
4th printing .... March 1969	7th printing ... January 1973
	8th printing .. December 1974	

Bantam Books are published by Bantam Books, Inc. Its trademark, consisting of the words "Bantam Books" and the portrayal of a bantam, is registered in the United States Patent Office and in other countries. Marca Registrada. Bantam Books, Inc., 666 Fifth Avenue, New York, New York 10019.

PRINTED IN THE UNITED STATES OF AMERICA

CONTENTS

PROLOGUE
(1028)

"He is little but he will grow."
Saying of Duke Robert of Normandy.

There was so much noise in the market-place, such a hub-bub of shouting and chaffering, that Herleva dragged herself to the window of her chamber and stood peeping down through the willow-slats that made a lattice over the opening. Market days brought a mob of people to Falaise from all the neighbouring countryside. There were franklins with slaves driving in the swine and cattle for sale; serfs with eggs and furmage spread on cloths upon the ground; great men's stewards and men-at-arms; knights' ladies on ambling palfreys; burghers from the town; and young maidens in troops of four or five together with little spending-silver in their purses, but full of exclamations for every novelty that met their eyes.

Wandering pedlars with their pack-horses had tempting wares to show: brooches of amethyst and garnet; bone combs; and silver mirrors burnished until one might see one's face in them as clearly as in the beck that ran below the Castle. There were stalls piled high with candles, and oil, and smear; others with spices from the East spreading an aromatic scent: galingale, cloves, cubebs, and sweet canelle. Hard by, the food-merchants had set up their shelds, and here could be bought lampreys and herrings, fresh caught; such rare stores as ginger, and sugar, and pepper; jars of Lombard mustard; and loaves of wastel-bread, each one bearing the baker's seal. Beyond these a chapman with copper-pots and chargeours for the table plied a brisk trade among the housewives; while near at hand an apothecary tried to catch the women's attention with his salves for bruises, his dragon's water, and angelica-root, and even, slyly whispered, his love-philtres. His mild voice was

1

drowned by the shouts of his neighbour, who spread length upon length of falding and sendal over his stall, and bade every passer-by see and feel his fine cloths.

But the crowd was the thickest round the foreign pedlars, who had stranger merchandise to offer. There was jet brought from outremer which would drive away serpents if one heated it; finer cloth than falding held up by the Frisian merchants; cunningly wrought cups and jewels shown by dark Byzantines; orfrey, embroidered by Saxon women in England; and any number of trinkets, and ribands for the binding of one's hair.

As she caught sight of one of these bunches, invitingly held up to a knot of maids below her window, Herleva lifted the heavy plait that lay over her shoulder, wondering whether a scarlet riband would look well twisted round it, and whether my lord Robert would think her pretty decked out in red. But nobody, not even so hot a lover as my lord Count, could think her pretty just now, she reflected. She was heavy with child, very near her time, and my lord Count was away in Rouen, waiting upon the pleasure of his father, good Duke Richard of Normandy. She wished that her pains might start, and the birth be soon over, so that she might ride up the steep hill again to the Castle that crowned one of its crags, and call upon the men-at-arms to open: open to Herleva the Beautiful, daughter of Fulbert, burgess of Falaise, and mistress of my lord Count of Hiesmes. Involuntarily her eyes turned towards the Castle, which she could just see, high above the squat wooden houses of the town and half-hidden by the trees that climbed its hill.

She thrust out her lower lip a little, picturing to herself the haute ladies of the Court at Rouen. She felt ill-used, and had begun to dwell upon her fancied wrongs, when her attention was diverted by a troop of minstrels who had begun to play quite near the house. They had come to the market on the chance of a few coins from the younger and lighter-hearted of the crowd, and perhaps a bite of supper afterwards in one of the rich burgher's halls. The harper started to sing a popular chanson, while the juggler in his train cast up plates and balls into the air, and caught them all one after the other, faster and faster, until Herleva's eyes grew round with wonder.

From the window Herleva could see her father Fulbert's sheld, with the furs hanging up in it, and her brother Walter haggling with burgher over the price of a fine rug of marten-skins. Close beside was a chapman who held up trinkets before the eyes of several envious maidens. If Count Robert had been there he would have bought his love the bracelet of hammered gold which the pedlar kept on showing, thought Herleva.

The remembrance of my lord Count made her discontented, and she moved away from the window, already weary of the bustle below it.

At the far end of the room a wooden door gave directly on to the twisting stair that led down to the hall, the principal dwelling-place of the house. No doubt her mother was busy preparing supper for Fulbert and Walter, but Herleva had no mind to go down to help her. The mistress of the son of the Duke of Normandy, she thought, had nothing to do with cooking-pots and greasy patins.

She crossed the floor with lagging steps, pushing the rushes with her feet, and laid herself down on the bed of skins against the wall. It was a bed for a Duchess, truly, made of good wood, and covered over with a bearskin which Fulbert had said grudgingly was more fit for Count Robert than for his *mie*. Herleva snuggled her cheek into the long fur, and smoothed it with her little hot hand, thinking of Count Robert, and how he called her, in his extravagant way, his princess.

Outside the sun was sinking slowly behind the heaths that lay beyond the town. A beam of gold came in through the willow-lattice, and struck the foot of the bed, making the brown hairs of the bearskin glint to an auburn glow. The hum of chatter, and the noise of the horses' hooves, the occasional sharp sound of a voice raised above the general hubbub still continued in the market-place, but it had grown less with the sinking of the sun, and would soon cease altogether. Peasants from outlying villages were departing already from Falaise to reach home in the safe daylight; the chapmen were packing their bundles; and a stream of mules and sumpters was wending its way under the window towards the gates of the town.

The measured clop of the hooves made Herleva drowsy; she presently closed her eyes, and after some restless twisting and turning upon the bed, dropped off into an uneasy slumber.

Gradually the shaft of sunshine disappeared, and with the deepening of the shadows the noise in the market-place died away. The last pack-horse was led slowly past the

3

house; and the merchants who lived within the town were all busy fastening up their shutters, and comparing each his day's fortune with his neighbours'.

The light faded quite away; the cool of the evening stole into the chamber; Herleva shivered and moaned in her sleep, troubled by strange dreams.

She dreamed that as she lay a tree grew up out of her womb, spreading steadily till it became a giant among trees, with great branches stretched out like grasping arms. Then she perceived, in her dream, that Normandy lay before her gaze, even to the remotest corner of the Côtentin, and the far outpost of Eu. She saw the grey, tumbling sea, and was afraid, and cried out. The cry was muffled in her sleep, but beads of sweat started on her brow. Land lay beyond the sea; she saw it plainly, and knew it for England. And while she lay sweating in a strange terror she saw that the branches of the tree stretched out further and further till they over-shadowed both England and Normandy.

She screamed, and started up on the bed, pressing her hands to her eyes. Her face was wet with her fright; she wiped away the sweat with her fingers, and dared at last, as she realized that she had awakened from a nightmare, to look about her.

Her mother, Duxia, was standing in the doorway with a rushlight in her hand. "That was a great shout I heard you make," she said. "I thought the pains had come upon you, and here I find you sleeping."

Herleva found that she was very cold. She pulled up the bearskin round her shoulders, and looked at Duxia in a boding way. She said in a low voice:—"I dreamed that a tree grew up out of my womb, mother, and no babe."

"Yes, yes," Duxia replied, "we have all our fancies at these times, daughter."

Herleva clasped the bearskin closer round her, with her hands crossed between her breasts. "And as I lay," she said in a hushed voice, "I saw two countries spread before me, and these were our land of Normandy in all its might, and the land of the English Saxons, over the grey water." She let go one hand from the bearskin and pointed where she thought England might be. The bearskin slipped back from her shoulders, but she seemed no longer to feel the chill in her flesh. She fixed her eyes upon Duxia, and in the flickering rushlight they glowed queerly. "And the tree of my womb put forth huge branches that were as hands that would seize and hold fast, and these stretched out on either

4

side me till Normandy and England both lay beneath them, cowering in their shadow."

Duxia said: "Well, that's a strange dream indeed, but meanwhile here is your father sitting down to his supper, and if you don't bestir yourself the pottage will be cold before you come to it."

But Herleva still sat motionless upon the bed, and Duxia, coming further into the room, perceived that she had a strange look in her face as of one who sees marvels beyond ordinary folks' vision. She laid her hands suddenly about her middle and said in a voice that had grown strong and clear: "My son will be a King. He shall grasp and hold, and he shall rule over Normandy and England, even as the tree stretched out its branches."

This seemed a great piece of nonsense to Duxia. She was just about to make some soothing remark when Herleva gave a cry of pain, and straightened her body, with her muscles stiff to meet the sudden hurt.

"Mother! Mother!"

Duxia began to bustle about her daughter at that, and both of them forgot all about the dream and its meaning. "There, child, that is nothing. You will have worse pain before you are better," Duvia said. "We will send out to summon our neighbour Emma, for she's a rare one at a lying-in, and I warrant has helped more babes into the world than you will ever bear. Lie still; there is time enough yet."

She had no leisure to think any more about Herleva's prophecy, for Fulbert was calling for the boiled meats downstairs, and at the same time Herleva was clinging to her with both hands, very much afraid, and expecting every moment to undergo another such agony. Duxia found that she had her hands full for the next hour, but presently Emma came into the hall, and after she had seen Herleva and said that they might look for nothing for some hours yet, she helped Duxia clear away the dirty platters from the table, and directed the serfs how they should place the straw and the skins for the master's bed.

Fulbert was fond of Herleva, but he was a sensible man, and he had a hard day's work before him on the morrow, so that he thought he would be a great fool if he lost his sleep for nothing more serious than a lying-in. Moreover, he had never quite liked his daughter's position, and though none of the neighbours considered it anything but an honour for Herleva to be the mistress of so puissant a siegneur as my lord Count of Hiesmes, he still could not feel at ease about it. As he made himself ready for the night, he felt that he would have been better pleased if the child to be born had been the lawful son of an honest burgher instead of a noble bastard.

When everything was set in order in the hall, and all the household disposed round the master for sleep, Duxia and Emma went off up the stairs to the room where Herleva lay whimpering upon her fine bedstead.

Emma was the wisest woman in Falaise. She knew the signs of the stars, and she could read omens, and foretell great happenings, so that presently as the two women sat on stools by a small brazier of charcoal Duxia was minded to tell her of Herleva's dream. The two coiffed heads drew close together, and the red glow from the brazier showed the lined faces intent and knowing. Emma nodded, and clicked her tongue in her cheek. It was very likely, she said, and she went on to tell Duxia of other such visions which she had seen happily fulfilled.

An hour after midnight the child was born. A cock in some shed not far away, perhaps catching sight of a star through a chink in the door, crowed once, and then was silent.

There was a pallet of straw in a corner of the room near the brazier. Emma wrapped the babe loosely round in a cloth and laid him down upon this pallet, where he would be safe while she turned back to Herleva. When Duxia presently went to pick up the child she found that he had thrust his arms from out of the cloth, and was clutching the straw on which he lay in both his fists. She was glad to see that he was so lusty an infant, and called to Emma to admire his strength. Perhaps the prophecy was running in Emma's head, or perhaps she had never seen a newborn child so vigorous. "Mark what I say, Duxia!" she exclaimed, "that child will be a great prince. See how he takes seisin of the world! He'll grasp everything that comes in his way and out of it, you see if he doesn't."

Her words reached Herleva, who seemed to herself to be sinking leagues deep into a heavy swoon. She said faintly: "He will be a King."

As soon as she was well enough to think and plan again Herleva sent for Walter, and insisted that he should ride to Rouen to tell the Count of the birth of his son. Walter was too fond of her to resent her imperious ways, but Fulbert, who needed him to dress a couple of otter-skins, thought it a great piece of nonsense, and was very near to forbidding him to go.

When Walter came back from Rouen Herleva was up and about again, and he had scarcely set foot inside the hall when she pounced on him, asking a dozen questions at once, and wondering how he could have been away so long.

"It was not easy to come at my lord Count," Walter explained, in his patient way. "There are so many great seigneurs about him in the Castle at Rouen, and the pages would not let me pass the doors."

"But you saw him?" Herleva said eagerly.

"Yes, I saw him at last as he was on his way to a great hunting of deer."

At that Herleva broke in to ask how my lord had looked, and what spirits he was in, and what he had said when he heard the news. Walter answered all these questions as well as he was able, but he could only say that my lord looked much as he always did, which Herleva considered no answer at all. Then he fished out of his wallet a girdle of gold links set with matrix, and gave it to his sister, saying that my lord had sent it as a token of his love for her, and had bid him tell her to keep the child safe against his coming.

But after all it was not until some time after the child's baptism that Count Robert came back to Heismes. Word was brought to Herleva that he had ridden into Falaise and up the Castle hill at the head of a great train of followers.

At once Herleva and Duxia fell into a flurry of preparation, redding up the hall, strewing fresh rushes, and sweeping up the grey wood-ash that was blown over the floor from the fire of pine-logs in the middle of the hall. Herleva dressed her babe in a robe woven by her own hands, and when that was done she chose a blue robe for herself, which she drew in round her hips with my lord's girdle. Even Fulbert was moved to change his leather tunic for one of fine wool, and he sent Walter outside to see that enough wine and barley-beer lay in the cellar for the Count's refreshment.

These preparations were hardly completed when a great clatter of hooves and jingle of horse-trappings announced my lord's approach. Fulbert and Walter ran out to receive him, and found a calvacade at the house-door, my lord, in his boisterous humour, having brought several noble seigneurs along with him, and a great many servants.

The lord Count bestrode a black stallion. He was a fine man, with close-knit limbs, and a small head set proudly on

7

his neck. He wore a mantle of royal purple, clasped on his right shoulder with a large ouch of onyx. He carried his sword at his side, and his tunic, which showed where the mantle fell away, was red, purfled with a design dancetté. Gold bracelets, each more than an inch broad, encircled his arms. The hood of his mantle was thrown back, and his head was uncovered. His hair was cut short, Norman-fashion, and was as black as a crow's wing.

He swung himself down from his horse, and Walter, who had knelt to receive him, jumped up to take the bridle. My lord Count clapped him on the shoulder in the familiar way he used towards men whom he trusted, and spoke a jovial word of greeting to Fulbert. Then he turned to the lords who had dismounted with him, and called out:—"Come, seigneurs, you shall see my fine son of whom I hear so much! In with you, fair cousin; I will promise you a right welcome." He caught the man he had addressed by the arm, and swept into the hall with him.

The house seemed dark after the bright sunlight in the market-place. My lord Count halted on the threshold, blinking in the smoke of the fire, and looking about him for Herleva.

She came to him with a quick step, and at once he let go his cousin's arm, and gripped her round the waist, lifting her off her feet in his hardy embrace. Some soft lovers' talk passed between them, too low to be heard by the men who stood behind the Count.

"Lord, you shall see your son," Herleva said, and she took Count Robert by the hand, and led him to the cradle in the corner where the babe lay.

Count Robert, whom men called the Magnificent, seemed to fill the hall with his splendour. His mantle brushed the rushes into little heaps as he passed, and the jewels on his arms glittered as the firelight caught them. Still holding Herleva's hand he stood beside the cradle and looked down at the child of his begetting. There was some eagerness in his eyes, as he bent over the cradle, and a chain which he wore round his neck slipped forward, and dangled above the child. The babe stretched out clutching hands towards the treasure, and as though wondering whence it came he lifted his eyes to Count Robert's face, and gave him back stare for stare. It was seen that the two pairs of eyes were much alike, and that the child had the same dogged look in his face that all the Norman Dukes had had as their birthright since the time of Rollo. A kinsman of the Count, young Robert, the son of the Count of Eu, whispered as much to the black-avised man at his elbow. This was William Talvas, Lord of Belesme. Talvas, peering over the Count's shoulder at the child, muttered something that sounded like a curse, and upon young Robert of Eu looking at him in surprise, he tried to turn it off with a laugh, saying that he read hatred in the child's eyes, and saw therein the ultimate ruin of his house. This did not seem very likely to young Robert, and he suspected that the Lord of Belesme had drunk too deeply of the barley-mead up at the Castle, for whereas the babe before them was a landless bastard, William Talvas held lands in France and in Normandy, and was accounted an ill man to cross. He looked so blankly that Talvas coloured, and moved away, himself scarcely understanding the meaning of his sudden outburst.

Count Robert was delighted with his son. "Why, this is very bone of my bone!" he said. He turned his head, and once more addressed the man whose arm he had taken outside. "Edward, tell me if I have not bred a noble son!"

The Saxon Prince moved forward, and looked smilingly down at the babe. In contrast to these Normans he was very fair, with long, blond ringlets, and a pink complexion. His eyes were of northern blue, rather weak, but very amiable. His younger brother, Alfred, who stood now in the doorway, was of the same type, but he had more purpose in his face, and he did not smile so easily. Both bore themselves proudly, as indeed they had a right to do, being the sons of the dead King Ethelred of England. One day, when Cnut, the Danish usurper, was safe under the sod, they meant to go back to England, and then Edward would be a king. Just now, as he looked up at Count Robert, he was an exile, a dependant of the Norman Court.

"You shall swear to love my son well, all of you," Count Robert said, with a challenging yet genial look round. "He is little, but he will grow, I promise you."

Edward touched the child's cheek with his finger. "Indeed, I will love him as mine own," he said. "He is very like you."

Count Robert beckoned up his half-brother, and made him take the child's hand. "You shall honour your nephew, William," he said laughingly. "See how he grabs at your finger! He will be a mighty fellow."

"It is always so with him," Herleva said softly. "He grasps

as though he would never let go." She would have liked to have told the Count of her dream, but in the presence of these nobles she did not care to speak of it.

"A fierce boy," William said, jesting. "We shall have to look to ourselves when he is grown."

Count Robert pulled his great sword from its sheath. "A warrior, if he is a true son of mine," he said, and laid the sword down beside the child.

The flash of a jewel on the hilt caught the babe's eye, and he left stretching his hands to the necklace round Count Robert's neck, and at once grasped the sword by the cross hilt. Duxia, who was hovering in the background, quite overcome by such a noble assembly in her house, could scarcely restrain an exclamation of horror at the sight of the gleaming steel within the child's reach. But Herleva looked on smiling.

The babe had one of the cross-pieces of the hilt fast in his hands, whereat there was much laughter from the watching barons.

"Said I not so?" Count Robert demanded. "He will be a warrior, by the Face!"

"Has he been received into the Church?" Edward asked gently.

He had been baptized a month ago, Herleva said, in the Church of Holy Trinity.

"What name is he given?" inquired Robert of Eu.

"He is called William, lord," Herleva answered, crossing her hands on her breast.

"William the Warrior!" laughed the Count.

"William the King," Herleva whispered.

"William the Bastard!" muttered the Lord of Belesme beneath his breath.

Herleva slipped her hand in my lord Count's. They stood looking fondly at their son, William, who was called Warrior, King, and Bastard, and the child crowed with delight at his new plaything, and twined his tiny fingers about the heavy sword-hilt.

PART I
(1047—1048)

THE BEARDLESS YOUTH

"Thus from my infancy I have been embarrassed, but by God's mercy
I have freed myself honourably."
Speech of William the Conqueror.

CHAPTER I

Hubert de Harcourt gave his youngest son a sword upon the
day that he was nineteen. "Though I don't know what you
will do with it," he said in a grumbling voice.

Raoul had worn a sword for several years, but not such
a one as this, with runes on the blade, inscribed there by
some forgotten Dane, and a hilt wrought with gold. He
twined his fingers round the cross-pieces, and answered
slowly:—"By God's grace, I will put it to good use."

His father and his half-brothers, Gilbert and Eudes,
laughed at that, for although they were fond of Raoul they
thought poorly of his fighting power, and were sure that he
would end his days in a cloister.

The first use he found for the sword was to draw it upon
Gilbert, and that not a month later.

It fell out very simply. Gilbert, always turbulent, and,
since the days of his outlawry after Roger de Toeni's rebellion, more than ever a malcontent, had picked a quarrel
with a neighbour not long before, and between these two a
rather one-sided warfare raged. Raoul was too well-
accustomed to such happenings to pay much heed. Raids
and pillages were everyday occurrences in Normandy, and
barons and vavassours, lacking a strong hand over them,
behaved very much as the old Norse fighting blood directed
them. If Geoffrey of Briosne chose to come in force and
ravage Harcourt lands, Raoul would put on his battle-
harness to defend them, but Harcourt owed fealty to the
Lord of Beaumont, a haut siegneur, and Geoffrey, who held
his land of Guy, princeling of Burgundy, was disinclined to
risk an engagement.

It was hardly a month after his nineteenth birthday that

Raoul rode out one afternoon on his horse Verceray to the small market-town not many leagues distant from Harcourt. His errand was to buy new spurs for himself, and it pleased him on his return to take the shorter road which led him across a corner of Geoffrey de Briosne's land. Some thought of the enmity between Geoffrey's house and his flitted across his mind, but it was growing late in the afternoon, and since he hardly expected to meet any of Geoffrey's men-at-arms at this hour, he thought he might well trust to his new sword and Verceray's swift hooves to guard him from any sudden danger. He was unattended, and wore nothing over his woollen tunic but a cloak to keep him warm in the chill spring evening, so that it would probably have gone hardly with him had he chanced on any of his enemies. But it was not an enemy whom he was destined to meet.

The sun was setting when he turned aside from the rough track to follow a footpath that ran beside some freshly ploughed fields on Geoffrey's land, and the level rays made the curves of sod glow redly. An evening quiet had fallen, and now that the town had been left behind, everything was very silent. To the west the river Risle ran between sloping banks, and to the east the ground stretched undulating to some low hills in the distance that were now fading in the blue evening mist.

Raoul rode along at a gentle pace, picking his way. As he rode he whistled between his teeth, and mused on this pleasant country of the Evrecin, thinking it would be a good place for a man to live in and cultivate, if only he might be sure that his harvest would not be seized by a hungry neighbour, or his house burned by pillaging soldiery. This thought was in his mind when his attention was caught by a red glow a little way to the east of him, behind some trees that grew in a dell beyond the ploughed lands. There was a smell of burning carried on the light wind, and as he looked more closely he saw the quick leap of flames, and thought that he heard someone scream.

He reined Verceray in, hesitating, for he was not upon his own ground, and it was no concern of his if a serf's hut caught fire. Then it flashed across his mind that perhaps some men of Harcourt might be responsible, and impulsively he set Verceray at a canter across the fields that separated him from the vale behind the trees.

As he drew nearer he heard again, and this time unmistakably, that tortured scream. It was followed by a confused sound of laughter which made Raoul fold his lips tightly together. He knew that brutal laughter; he had heard it many times in his life, for men laughed thus wildly when they were drunk with bloodshed. He spurred Verceray on, never pausing in his indignation to consider what he should do if he were to find himself suddenly in the midst of foes.

The flames were roaring fiercely as Verceray thundered down the slope, and in the hellish light Raoul saw a cottage burning, and men in leather tunics brandishing torches. A pig ran squealing from out the burning house into the garth; one of the soldiers rushed after it shouting a hunting cry, and drove his lance through its back. Tied to a sapling by his wrists was a peasant, obviously the owner of the ruined cottage. His tunic was slit from neck to girdle, and his back was bleeding. His head rolled on his shoulder, and there was foam on his grey lips. Two men-at-arms were flogging him with their stirrup-leathers, while another stood by holding a dishevelled woman by her arms. She seemed half demented; her dress was torn across her shoulders, and her hair, escaped from the close cap, streamed about her in wispy strands. Just as Raoul came crashing down into the middle of the group she shrieked out for God's sake not to kill her good man, for she would fetch her daughter, even as the noble seigneur commanded.

She was allowed to go, and a man who sat astride a great roan destrier, cold-bloodedly observing all that was going on, shouted to his servants that they need not finish their victim off yet awhile if the woman kept to her word.

Raoul reined in Verceray so hard that the big horse was wrenched back almost upon his haunches. He twisted round in the saddle to face the man on the roan destrier. "What beastly work is this?" he panted. "You dog, Gilbert! so it is you!"

Gilbert was surprised to see his brother. He made his horse move towards Verceray, and said with a grin:—"Holà, and where did you spring from so suddenly?"

Raoul was still white with his passion. He pressed up to Gilbert, and said in a low voice:—"What have you done, you devil? What reason had you? Call off your hounds! Call them off, I say!"

Gilbert laughed. "What business is it of yours?" he said contemptuously. "Holy Face, but you are in a rare temper! Do you know where you stand, you silly dreamer? That's

13

not one of our men." He pointed to the bound serf, as though he had satisfactorily explained his conduct.

"Let him go!" Raoul ordered. "Let him go, Gilbert, or by God and His Mother, you shall rue it!"

"Let him go, indeed!" repeated Gilbert. "He can go when that old slut brings up his daughter, perhaps, but not before. Have you gone moon-mad?"

Raoul saw that it was useless to bandy more words to and fro. In silence he wheeled Verceray about and rode up to the captive, pulling his knife from his belt to cut the rope that bound the man.

As soon as Gilbert perceived that he was in earnest he stopped laughing and cried out angrily:—"Stand back, you young fool! Hands off my meat! Here, you! pull him off that horse!"

One of the men started forward to obey the command. Raoul's right foot left the stirrup and shot out, to crash full into the man's face, knocking him clean head over heels. No one else made any movement to come at him, for although these men were Gilbert's own bullies they knew what respect was due to Hubert de Harcourt's other sons.

Seeing that no one else was advancing upon him Raoul leaned over in the saddle and sawed quickly through the rope that bound the serf's wrists to the tree. The man was either dead, or swooning; his eyes were shut, and his face grey under the flecks of blood. As the last strands parted he fell in a heap on to the ground, and lay there.

Gilbert had spurred angrily after Raoul, but the shrewd kick that had stretched his servant flat brought back his good humour, and instead of storming and swearing as he usually did when crossed, he clapped Raoul on the shoulder, and sang out:—"By the Rood, that was neatly done, cockerel! I swear I didn't know you had it in you. But you are all wrong, you know. The dirty bondman has been hiding his daughter from me this past week, and I've been obliged to beat him till he's three parts dead before I could learn where the wench was hid."

"Keep your foul hands off me!" Raoul said. "If there were justice in Normandy you would hang, you hound!" He slid down from Verceray's back, and bent over the peasant. "I think you have killed him," he said.

"One lousy knave the less, then," said Gilbert. "Not so free with your tongue, Brother Priest, or maybe I'll school you a little as you won't like." The scowl had descended on

14

his face again, but at that moment he caught sight of the woman who had gone off to fetch her daughter, and he forgot Raoul's audacity. "Aha!" he cried, "she was not so far away!" He jumped down from the saddle, and stood waiting with a flushed face and hot gloating eyes for the two women to come up with him. The elder woman was dragging her daughter by one wrist, but the girl cried, and hung back, turning her pretty face away as though she were afraid to see the lustful eyes that watched her so greedily. She was very young, and frightened, and she kept calling in a fluttering voice on her father to aid her. Her startled gaze fell on his inert body, and she gave a whimper of horror. Gilbert caught her and pulled her close up to him. His eyes devoured her while she stood shivering, and he brought up one hand to her throat, fondling it. She shrank away, but his grip on her tightened, and his fingers closing on the neck of her gown tore it away suddenly from her shoulder. "Well, my shy bird!" he muttered thickly. "So you come at last, do you? I have a mind to you, my girl, I think."

There was a movement behind him. Gilbert jerked up his head, but was too late to fend off Raoul's blow. It took him unawares, a tremendous buffet that knocked him clean off his balance. He and the girl went down in a sprawling heap. The girl scrambled up in a moment, and ran to where her father lay, but Gilbert stayed propped on his elbow, glaring up into Raoul's face.

Raoul's sword was out, and shortened for the thrust. "Lie still!" he snapped. "I have something to say before I let you up."

"You!" Gilbert spluttered. "You nithing! you insolent whelp! God's belly, if I do not crack your skull for this!"

"That's as may be," Raoul retorted, "but for the present you will be very ill-advised to move a finger. You can tell that scum you keep for bodyguard to stand still until I have said my say." Then, as Gilbert only swore at him, he added in a matter-of-fact voice:—"It will be better for you to do as I bid you, for by the Cross I am in a mood to stick you like a pig with no more ado!"

"Stick me? Why—why—Holy Virgin, the whelp is bewitched in good sooth!" Gilbert gasped. "Let me up, you young fool! God's eyes, if I do not flay you for this!"

"First you shall swear to let the wench go," said Raoul. "Afterwards it shall be as the better man decides."

"Let the wench go at your bidding? Ha, now you provoke

15

me!" Gilbert cried. "What traffic have you with the girl, Master Saint?"

"None. Do I kennel with serfs? I shall certainly slay you if you don't swear. I will count up to twenty, Gilbert, and no more."

At the eighteenth count Gilbert left blaspheming and growled a reluctant oath. Raoul drew back his sword then. "We will ride home together," he said, keeping a weather-eye on his brother's sword-hand. "Mount, there is no more for you to do here."

Gilbert stood hesitating for a moment, his fingers gripping the hilt of his sword, but Raoul clinched the matter by turning his unarmed back to him. His first blind fury having had time to abate, Gilbert knew that he could not draw steel upon a young brother who was not expecting it. Astonishment at Raoul's conduct again consumed him, and as one in a bewildered muse he got upon his horse, trying to puzzle it all out in his slow brain. His roving eye caught sight of the sly grins upon the faces of his men, and flushing angrily he rasped out an order to get to horse. Without waiting to see what Raoul would do next he clapped his spurs into his destrier's flanks, and set off at a canter through the trees.

The serf had recovered his senses, and lay moaning at Raoul's feet. The women, kneeling beside him, looked up in some alarm at the young knight. That he was nobly born they knew, and they were at once suspicious of him, finding it hard to believe that he could have intervened for them in a spirit of pure chivalry.

Raoul pulled his purse from his belt, and let it fall beside the peasant. "Here is something to pay for the house," he said awkwardly. "You need not be afraid: he won't come back, I promise you."

He caught Verceray's bridle, and vaulted into the peaked saddle, and with no more than a nod to the older woman, rode off in the wake of Gilbert's cavalcade.

When he came in sight of the donjon of Harcourt the first stars were winking overhead, and the light had grown dim and grey. The drawbridge was still down, and the gate-keeper was on the watch for him. He rode into the bailey, and leaving Verceray to one of the grooms, went to the main building, and ran quickly up the outside stairway to the door that opened into the great hall.

As he had expected, Gilbert was there, angrily recounting

all that had befallen to his father, and to Eudes, who sat astride one of the benches, and roared with laughter. Raoul slammed the door shut behind him, and unclasped his cloak from his shoulders, tossing it into a corner. His father looked at him frowningly, but more in perplexity than in wrath. "Well, here is a fine piece of work!" he said. "What have you to say, boy?"

"This!" said Raoul, coming into the circle of light thrown by the candles on the table. "I have sat at home idle too long, shutting my eyes to what I could not cure." He glanced at Gilbert, fuming on the other side of the table, and at Eudes, still chuckling to himself. "Year after year such beastliness as I chanced upon to-day happens, and men like Gilbert there, and Eudes, ravage Normandy for their lusts, caring nothing for the weal of this Duchy." He laughed shortly to see Eudes staring at him with dropped jaw, and turned his eyes back to his father's puzzled face. "You gave me a sword, father, and I swore that I would put it to good use. By God, I will keep that oath, and wield it for Normandy, and justice! Look!" He whipped the sword out of the scabbard as he spoke, and holding it flat between his hands, showed them the runes inscribed on the blade. The candle flame quivered in the draught, and the light flickered along the steel.

Hubert bent to read the runes, but shook his head over the strange writing. "What does it mean?" he asked. "I have never known."

"Brother Clerk will surely know," mocked Gilbert.

"Yes, I know," Raoul said. "In our tongue, father, it reads thus: *Le bon temps viendra.*"

"I do not see much to that," said Eudes, disappointed.

Raoul glanced across at him. "But I see a great deal," he said. He slammed the sword back into the scabbard. "The good time will come when men who conduct themselves like robbers are no longer allowed to go unpunished."

Hubert looked in a startled way at Gilbert. "God's feet, is the boy mad? What sort of talk is this, my son? Come, come, you have no need to be in such a heat over a parcel of bondmen! I won't say that Gilbert is right, but as I understand it you drew steel upon him, and that is a bad business, and gives him some cause to complain of you."

"As to that," Gilbert growled, "I am very well able to take care of myself, and I don't bear malice against a silly stripling, believe me. I'm glad enough to see the whelp has

17

blood in his veins, instead of the water I always thought ran there, but for the future I'll thank him to keep his hands off my affairs."

"For the future," Raoul said, "you will keep your hands off that wench, Gilbert. Let that be understood!"

"Ah, shall I indeed?" Gilbert said, beginning to bristle again. "And do you think I am very like to heed your words, you eft?"

"No," replied Raoul, with a sudden smile that was like sunshine after storm, "but I leave for Beaumont-le-Roger at daybreak, and mayhap you will heed my lord instead of me."

Gilbert's hand flew to his knife. "You tale-bearing cur!" he stuttered. "So you would get me outlawed, would you?"

Hubert pushed him back. "Enough of that!" he said. "Raoul will tell no tales, but if these raids of yours come to Roger de Beaumont's ears you will get short shrift. There must be an end to this wild work. As for the boy he is enflamed, and will be the better for his supper."

"But what is all this talk of justice, and of leaving Harcourt?" demanded Eudes. "What did the boy mean by that?"

"Nothing," Hubert said. "It is not so serious that he need leave his home, and when they have eaten, they will clasp hands and think no more of this day's doings."

"With good will," said Raoul promptly. "But by your leave, father, I shall go to Beaumone-le-Roger tomorrow."

"To what end?" asked Hubert. "What will you do there, pray?"

Raoul did not answer for a moment, but stood looking down at the flickering candles. Presently, he raised his eyes to his father's face, and spoke in a different voice, serious and hesitating. "Father, you and my brothers there have always laughed at me for being a dreamer. Perhaps you are right, and I am fit for nothing else, but my dreams are not so ill, I think. For many years I have dreamed of law in this Normandy of ours, law and justice, so that men may no longer burn and slay and pillage at will. I have thought that perhaps some day a man might rise up, with the will and the power to bring order into the Duchy. I would like to fight in his cause." He paused, and looked rather shyly at his brothers. "Once I hoped it might be our Lord of Beaumont, for he is a just man; and once I thought perhaps it would be Raoul de Gacé, because he was Governor of Normandy. But of course it could not be these. There is only one man who has power enough to curb the barons. It is his service I would enter."

"This is bookish talk," said Eudes, shaking his head. "Poor stuff."

"Holy Cross, what fancies a boy will get into his pate!" exclaimed Hubert. "And who may this fine man be, my son, of your grace?"

Raoul's brows lifted. "Could it be any other than the Duke himself?" he said.

Gilbert burst out laughing. "The young bastard! A lad no older than yourself! Foh, here's a piece of wool-gathering! If he keeps his coronet even it will be a strange thing, I can tell you that."

Raoul smiled a little. "I saw him just once in my life," he said. "He rode into Evreux at the head of his knights with Raoul de Gacé on his right hand. I saw his face for a minute as he passed me, and the thought came to me then that here was the man I had dreamed about. I don't think that that one will lose—anything."

"Silly talk!" Hubert said impatiently. "If a base-born lad of nineteen is to work his will on Normandy it will be a more marvellous thing than anything you ever dreamed about. There has been trouble enough for him already, while he was still in ward, but if it's true he has turned off his guardians now we shall soon see a lively state of affairs in the Duchy." He shook his head, and went on grumbling to himself all about the folly of making a by-blow Duke of Normandy, and the child no more than eight years at that; and how he had known from the first, when Duke Robert the Magnificent made up his mind to go on that disastrous pilgrimage, what would come of it. Normandy would not be ruled by a beardless youth, and if Raoul wanted peace— which was every honest man's desire—he had better look for a new Duke, and one more acceptable to the barons.

Eudes broke in on this monologue to ask Raoul whether he was fool enough to try and join the Duke's court at Falaise. Raoul did not answer at once, but when he did he spoke so earnestly that even Gilbert forgot his anger in surprise. "Bastard he is," he said, "bastard and stripling, even as you have said, father, but since the day that I looked into his face I have wanted to follow him, perhaps to great glory, perhaps to death." The lashes veiled his eyes suddenly. "You don't understand. Maybe you have not seen him. He has that look in his face which draws me. A man might put his whole trust in him and not fear to be betrayed." He stopped, and seeing how they stared at him, coloured up, and said more humbly: "Perhaps I shan't be allowed to serve him. I thought my lord would be able to tell me."

Hubert banged his fist down on the table. "If you want to serve a great seigneur, serve Roger de Beaumont!" he said. "God knows I have nothing against young William—no, and I would not join Roger de Toeni against him, as your brother Gilbert was fool enough to do!—but it does not take a sage to know that the Bastard's days will be short in Normandy. Why, you silly boy, from the day that Duke Robert—God rest his soul!—died on his pilgrimage there has been no peace in Normandy—and all on account of the base-born child who was set up to rule the Duchy! What has happened to his guardians? Alain of Brittany was the first, and a rare end he made of it. You were no more than a babe yourself then, but Alain died, poisoned at Vimoutiers, and the King of France marched into the Argentan, and seized the border stronghold of Tillières which he holds to this day! Was there peace then? Was there peace when Montgoméri slew the Seneschal, Osbern, in the Duke's own chamber? Was there peace when Thorkill died, and Roger de Toeni fought the ducal troops? Will there ever be peace while a mere lad holds the reins of government? Why, you are raving to think to find glory in the service of that ill-starred boy!"

"Am I so?" Raoul retorted. "Yet will you say that our Duke has made so ill a beginning? You speak of his childhood, but I seem to remember that when Toustain Goz dared to hold the castle of Falaise against him not so long since my lord Duke had a short way with the rebels."

"Bah, De Gacé took the castle by storm on the Duke's behalf!" said Gilbert scornfully. "It seems to me that you have filled your head with silly imaginings, and would be the better for a sound trouncing."

"Try it!" Raoul challenged him. "I am ready for you, I promise you."

"No more of that!" Hubert interposed. "The boy will soon find his mistake. Let him take service with the Duke, if my lord can so arrange it for him. If I am right and he comes back disappointed—well, there will be a place for him still at my board. If he is right, and the Duke is a man even as his father was before him, why, so much the better for us all! But now you shall clasp hands, and think no more of this quarrel."

20

Hubert's word was law at Harcourt when he spoke it in just that tone. Across the table Gilbert and Raoul clasped hands with as good a grace as they could muster. Eudes still sat pondering over the talk, with his brows knit and his gaze abstracted, until, presently, having unravelled it to his satisfaction, he looked up, and said portentously: "I see what it is. Raoul looked upon the Duke, and finding him comely enough, he has taken it into his head he would like to serve under his gonfanon. Boy follows boy."

"So be it," said Hubert. "I see little good, but no harm. Let boy follow boy."

CHAPTER II

The hall of the Castle of Falaise was rush-strewn, and hung with tapestries; at the dinner-hour trestle-tables were set up, with benches and stools for the Court to sit upon. Only the Duke used a chair with carved arms and a high back; his nobles had each a stool, but the knights and the squires crowded on to benches at the tables that ran down the length of the hall. There was a fire of logs on a pile of wood-ash, and beside this a couple of huge alaunts lay stretched out, blinking at the hot glow. The other dogs roamed among the table-legs at will, waiting for chance scraps of meat, and wrangling over the bones tossed to them by their masters.

The hall seemed crowded to Raoul, still, after three months, unaccustomed to life at Court. The hangings shut out the draught, and the place was stuffy, with a mingled smell of dogs, smoke, and roast meats on the air. Up at the high-table the Duke sat in his great chair, and between the courses his minstrels played and sang, and Galet the Jester cut capers, and told lewd stories which made the barons about the Duke shout with laughter. The Duke smiled sometimes, and once he frowned a quick menace when Galet cracked a jest at the expense of the new King of England's chastity. This was Edward, the son of Ethelred, until two years before a guest of Normandy, and the friend of the young Duke. But for the most part the Duke's attention was all for his haggard, which he had taken from her perch behind his chair on to his wrist. She was a fierce bird, with talons that dug into his hand when he teased her and bright cruel eyes above her hooked beak.

"A rare hawk that, beau sire," Hugh de Gournay said. "They tell me she never misses."

William smoothed the hawk's feathers with his finger. "Never," he answered, without turning his head.

A flourish of trumpets at the end of the hall heralded the coming of the boar's head, the same animal that had been stuck by the Duke in the Forest of Gouffers two days before. The head was carried on a great silver chargeour, and brought up to the high-table. One of the stewards began to carve it, and the servers ran with the slices on long spits to offer to the Duke's guests.

There was a considerable noise of talk at the far end of the hall, where the lesser people sat. The talk was all of the Duke's projected visit to the Côtentin. He was going to Valognes to hunt bears in the forests there, and would take only a small retinue with him, since the dwelling to be set aside for his use would hardly accommodate even so meagre a Court as this held at Falaise.

Some of his barons would go with him, and a bodyguard of knights and men-at-arms under Grimbauld du Plessis, a dark, saturnine man with a lip twisted by a scar received in some past combat. He was of the Duke's personal retinue, and sat next to Raoul now at the table near the door. Raoul had heard of two lords only who meant to accompany the Duke, and these were Humphrey de Bohun, whose lands lay on the Côtentin border; and Guy, younger son of the House of Burgundy, who sat now at the Duke's right hand.

Guy was a little older than William, whose cousin he was, but he had been brought up with him at the palace of Vaudreuil. He was a handsome youth, but too much aware of his charm. Raoul thought his long-lashed eyes womanish, and found that his smile soon cloyed a man's stomach. He was graceful and indolent, set much store by his own importance, but made it his business to be accessible to all men. Raoul preferred a sterner, less affable prince, whose favour was not so easily won. He looked away from Guy, and allowed his gaze to rest on the Duke's face, once more pondering this silent young man to whom he had sworn allegiance.

Although he had been in his service for three months he had scarcely come into contact with the Duke, and knew no more of him than was shown to all the world. It was impossible to guess what thoughts lurked behind William's eyes. These were set well apart, and were not unlike the eyes of the haggard he fondled, only that they were so dark that they looked sometimes almost black. They held a hidden gleam, as though they watched even when they seemed most abstracted. Their gaze was direct, and often disconcerting. Raoul thought that whatever a man might wish to conceal from the Duke would surely be betrayed under the ordeal of that hard stare.

Springing between the eyes the Duke's aquiline nose was at once haughty and masterful. His mouth was clearly defined, its lips well curved, and the expression a trifle sardonic. It could smile with unexpected good humour, but in repose it had a grim look. He kept his lips firmly pressed together, as though he guarded his secrets, but in anger the corners of the mouth were observed to quiver. One saw then what passion the man had in him, curbed nearly always, but apt to leap up under provocation and sweep everything before it: kindness, justice, policy.

In person William was sturdily built. His father's height was curiously combined with the stockiness of his mother's burgher blood. There was a thickness to his body which did not come from Robert the Magnificent, and his hands, although the fingers were long and tapering, were square in the palm: powerful, workman-like hands, Raoul thought.

Already, and young as he was, he possessed great strength and endurance. Fatigue never seemed to trouble him; he could out-ride the hardiest of his knights, and the shock of his charge in a mock combat had been known to unseat even Hugh de Grantmesnil, one of the finest warriors in Normandy. He was passionately fond of hunting, and hawking, and every form of knightly exercise. Raoul had seen him nock an arrow while he rode at full gallop, and it was said that no one but himself could bend his bow.

A voice intruded upon Raoul's wandering attention. He turned his head and found that a man seated opposite to him was inquiring whether he was to be one of the few bound for the Côtentin. He answered diffidently that he believed the Seneschal, FitzOsbern, had spoken his name as one of those to accompany the Duke.

"You will have rare sport there, I dare say," said the other, wiping a morsel of cocket-bread round his platter.

It seemed to Raoul that Grimbauld du Plessis looked up rather sharply at this remark. A cackle of laughter came from behind his chair, and he started round to see the jester cuddling his bauble. "Rare sport for the Duke's knights," grinned Galet. He held his bauble to his cheek. "Oh, my little one, praise the saints you will be safe in Galet's girdle!"

Grimbauld's face darkened; he shot out a hand to grasp the jester by one thin arm, and jerked him to his knees beside him. "Ha, fool, what is that you say?" he growled.

Galet postured and whined at him. "Do not harm poor Galet! Rare sport, I said; oh, rare sport at Valognes!" He peered up into Grimbauld's face, and gave again his silly laugh. "Will you hunt a noble hart, cousin, in brave company? Nay, but you will find it a cunning beast."

"Go, you are a knave!" Grimbauld struck him aside, and he fell sprawling on the rushes. He twisted his deformed limbs grotesquely, and howled like a dog. One of the pages, hurrying down the hall, tripped over him, and came down with a crash of the silver dish he carried. Galet shook his big head at him, and groaned: "Why, here's a brave company overset by the poor fool!" He grovelled for the scraps of the boar's head that were scattered over the floor, and went limping off to the fire at the end of the room.

"The fool lacks a whipping," Grimbauld said, and turned back to pick over the meat on his platter with his thick, short fingers.

Raoul's eyes had followed the jester to the fire, watching curiously how Galet threw himself down beside one of the hounds, and murmured his nonsense into a cocked ear. Galet shook the bells in his cap, and muttered, and glanced about him with many odd grimaces, and a hunching of his crooked shoulders. When he saw Raoul looking at him he grinned his sad, half-witted grin, and began to rock himself about, hugging his body in his arms. Raoul wondered what clouded thoughts troubled the fool's brain. He tossed a scrap of meat to him, and jester and hound fell on it together, wrangling each one alike with growls and bared teeth.

A stir at the high-table made them all look round. The Duke had risen, and was on his way to the twisting stair that led to the gallery and the rooms above. He had paused to listen to his cousin of Burgundy, who had intercepted him with a hand on his shoulder in the familiar way he always used. He still held his haggard on his wrist, and still absently smoothed her plumage with his finger, but his glance was on Guy's face, impassive and unsmiling. A shaft of sunlight slanting down through a window set high up in the wall touched with gold his crisp black locks, and glinted on a ring he wore upon the stroking finger. His uncle Walter, a solid

24

man of middle years, stood a little on one side, waiting for him to finish with Guy.

"See the noble tanner's son!"

The softly spoken words just reached Raoul's ears. They had been uttered by Grimbauld, and as Raoul looked quickly round at him he saw the scarred lip twisted into a sneer. It was of no use to pay any heed to such whisperings. Ever since he had come to Court Raoul had heard them, covert jibes directed at the Duke's base kindred: Walter, the tanner Fulbert's son; Walter's son William; and, not less, the Duke's own half-brothers, Robert and Odo, children born to Herleva by her marriage with Herluin, knight of Conteville. They were both present now: Robert a few years younger than the Duke, a heavy boy with a dogged, open face; and Odo, his junior, brighter-eyed, and readier of tongue. They waited beside their father at the bottom of the table, but the Duke had spoken with them on their way to the stair, and again Raoul had caught a vague murmur of dissatisfaction, so faint that he could not locate whence it came.

Still standing by the bench he watched the Duke walk to the stairway, and go up it, with Walter following him. Guy of Burgundy lounged back to his place at the table, and called to a server to fill up his cup.

There had been silence while the Duke was on his way out, a puzzling silence fraught with some emotion Raoul could not understand. Up at the Duke's table two barons exchanged fleeting glances as they resumed their seats. Again Raoul knew an instant's feeling of unrest, as though in that quick enigmatic look he had seen danger. A gleam in Grimbauld's narrowed eyes that were fixed so intently on the Duke made him catch his breath. Something in the concentration of Grimbauld's gaze made him feel uneasy, afraid of a danger he could not see.

Two days later the hunting-party was on the road, the Duke riding at the head of his cavalcade, with the Burgundian beside him. He had business at Bayeux, so that the first day's ride was to the north, and short. They swept into Bayeux at the dinner hour, and were received by the Bishop, by Ranulf de Bricassart, Viscount of Bressin, and by several other lords of the district. Once more a disquieting feeling stole over Raoul. As he slid down from Verceray's back, and saw the Duke walk forward between strangers to the door of the palace, he could have sworn that danger lurked in the air. So acute was this premonition that he was almost uncontrollably urged to run after the Duke with an absurd warning to him not to stop in this grey town with its twisted streets, and furtive corners. He fought back the impulse, and just as he had satisfactorily argued away his fears, there was Galet bestriding his mule, and grinning at him as though he knew what suspicious thoughts had crossed his mind.

"Fool, you haunt my footsteps," he said irritably.

Galet slid down from the mule's back. "Why then, I am as good as your conscience, cousin, and thereafter more fool than I knew. Where is my brother William?" He saw the Duke in the doorway of the palace, and laughed shrilly. "Propound me this riddle, Cousin Raoul: which is the wolf, and which the sheep of those yonder?" He pointed to the group about the Duke, and twisted his face into a leer.

Raoul looked where Galet pointed. "Truly, you are right," he said. "They have a very wolfish look, those men."

" 'Oh what a clever boy is mine!' cried your mother when you tried to grasp the candle-flame. Brother Raoul, Brother Raoul, did you ever hear the tale of the wolf that put a sheepskin over his shoulders?" He poked his bauble at Raoul's ribs, and went off after the Duke with another of his empty crows of laughter.

At Bayeux the Duke's retinue was quartered in the palace for the one night they were to stay in the town. When supper was over, and the trestles were cleared away, pallets were spread on the floor, and all but the nobler lords lay down to sleep there. The horn-lantern at the foot of the stairs cast a feeble glimmer of light over the bottom steps; where Raoul lay the red glow of a dying fire lit the floor of the hall.

Waking from an uneasy sleep in the quiet of the night he saw a shadow on the stairs, and jerked himself up on his elbow. In the dim light he could see the hump of a man's shoulder, the outline of the head laid on a folded cloak. Someone at the far end of the hall was snoring; the man next to Raoul shifted on his pallet with a grunt and a sigh. The shadow on the stairs moved again, and the lantern-glow faintly illumined the face of the jester. He sat huddled against the wall, and as he moved his head into the light Raoul caught the gleam in eyes that were very wide awake.

Raoul threw back the cloak that covered him, and rose up cautiously in his shirt and hose. He had to grope with his foot to save himself from treading on sleeping forms as he crossed the hall, but he made no sound and woke no one in his stealthy progress towards the stairway.

Galet hailed him in a whisper. "Do you find your pallet hard, brother?"

Raoul stood with one foot upon the stair, gravely looking down at him. "Why do you watch?" he asked. "Is your pallet so hard you cannot sleep?"

"Nay, nay, Galet is a good dog," the fool answered. He clasped his body in his long arms and looked up at Raoul with an expression half sad, half roguish.

Raoul glanced over his shoulder, as though he expected to see someone standing there. He dropped down on to his knee on the stair, and brought his lips close to the fool's ear. "Speak! What is it you fear?" he whispered.

Galet smiled, and rocked himself sideways. "Not you, brother." He put out his hand and touched Raoul's knee with his bauble. "Take my bauble, fool. 'I will not be afraid of shadows,' quoth the goat when he saw a wolf lurking in the thicket."

Raoul grasped at his shoulder, and shook him. "Speak out, fool! What danger threatens?"

The fool rolled his eyes, and lolled out his tongue. "Nay, do not shake poor Galet's wits out of him. Go and sleep, brother: what danger should threaten such a lusty calf as you?"

"None. But you know something. Who means ill towards the Duke?"

The fool gave a mocking laugh under his breath. "There was once a peacock, brother, lived in a noble lord's park, and when men exclaimed continually at the beauty of his plumage he grew vain, and fancied himself greater than the lord who fed him, and imagined, in his folly, that he could drive out the noble lord and rule over the park in his stead."

Raoul nodded rather impatiently. "Stale talk, fool. All Normandy knows that the Burgundian grows large in his own mind. No more?"

Galet threw him a sidelong look. "Plots, plots, brother: dark deeds," he said.

Raoul glanced up the stairway. "Can you speak no word of warning, you who sit at his feet?"

The fool showed his big teeth in a mirthless grin. "Did you ever warn a heron to beware the hawk, brother?"

"The heron needs no warning," Raoul said, frowning.

"Yea, yea, my little William is a sage heron," crooned Galet, and began to play with his fingers like a half-wit. "Yet he bears a hooked beak. Can a heron do so, Cousin Raoul?"

"I am sick of your riddles," Raoul said. He stood up, chilled by the night air striking through his shirt. "Watch on. Four eyes may see further than two." He went creeping back to his pallet, and began to dress himself. The rings of his mail tunic clinked as he pulled it over his head, and the man beside him stirred and muttered in his sleep. He buckled on his sword, and wound the bindings up his legs over the loose hose. When he picked his way to the stairs again he was fully clothed even to the helmet on his head.

"What a brave knight is this!" chuckled Galet. He made room for Raoul to pass him. "William my brother, you are well-served." He watched Raoul go up the stairs. "Sleep sound, William," he muttered. "He has a keen nose, your new watchdog."

When the dawn-light stole into the castle it showed sleeping forms on the floor, harsh faces softened in slumber, and swords lying beside straw pallets. Upon the stairs the jester was curled up with his head pillowed on his arm, dozing uneasily. Outside a shut door that opened on to the gallery above a young knight stood with his hands folded on his naked sword. He stood very still, but when some slight noise reached him from below he turned his head to listen more intently, and his fingers closed tighter on the sword-hilt.

The light grew warmer, and with the rising of the sun new sounds broke the stillness. Scullions began to move about in the kitchen, and from outside came the stir of the waking town.

With a sigh, and a stretching of weary limbs, Raoul left his post. Down in the hall the men still slept, but Galet was awake, and patted him between the shoulders. "Good dog Raoul!" he chuckled. "Will he throw a bone to his two hounds, our master William?"

Raoul yawned, and rubbed his hand across his eyes. "Fool, in the clear daylight I ask myself, am I also a fool?" he said, and passed on out of the hall into the sunlight.

On this second day's ride they struck westwards along the coast until the rivers that separated the Bessin from the Côtentin were forded. The way led northwards after that over wild country, and through many straggling forests. Adulterine fortalices looked down from every hill, each one a potential menace to the peace of Normandy. Unfriendly this land seemed, unlike Raoul's own province of the Evrecin.

Valognes itself lay on the edge of a forest, and the dwelling set aside for the Duke's use was scarcely more than a hunting-lodge, easy of access, and with no fortifications. Besides the hall it possessed one or two solars built in the thickness of the wall upstairs, and round the main building, in a rude court, were a cluster of ramshackle wooden houses. In one of these were quartered the few men-at-arms; another accommodated the Duke's scullions, cooks, valets, and huntsmen; and there was a third, somewhat larger, which was used as a stable for the destriers. Horses belonging to the less fortunate were haltered under a thatched roof supported on posts. Here Raoul had to see Verceray bestowed. As at Bayeux, the knights made what shift they could in the hall of the main building for sleeping-room, but Raoul, whose suspicions had not been lulled by what he had seen of the country and the people of the Côtentin, snatched what rest he could by day, and every evening when the torches were quenched, and the household slept, he took up his post outside the Duke's door, and remained there throughout the night. He felt an odd pleasure in these vigils. This was service, and even though the Duke neither knew of his devotion, nor ever noticed him above his fellows, he was content, and felt through the long, still hours a queer bond tightening between him and the young man who slept, secure because of his watch, behind the shut door.

The Duke hunted the beasts of the forest and the warren, and flew his hawks at the brook and at the heron, and conducted all the business that had brought him into the Côtentin with the firmness and dispatch that was as yet strange to his nobles. His grip on affairs seemed to be masterly; little escaped him, and he left little to chance. Yet if he saw so much, Raoul wondered, how could he be blind to the signs of hostility all round him? No one could misread these signs: the barons of the district held aloof; of his own attendants men whispered in corners, and when he went abroad he was accompanied by fewer knights than those who crowded round the handsome Guy of Burgundy.

One might have thought that this smiling prince was the ruler of Normandy. His train of satellites was numerous; he swaggered it royally in velvet and jewels, and used towards William an affectionate manner that was not untinged by the patronage of an elder cousin. The knights hung round him, and because he laughed gaily, and scattered largesse with a lavish hand, the common people always raised a cheer for him when he passed.

Raoul hated him. When he saw him charming William's knights away from him, when he heard him impudently usurping ducal privileges or acknowledging homage that was due to William, he raged inwardly, and wondered with a kind of sick disgust why the Duke bore with him, and never seemed to notice his graceful insolence. It was almost as though the stronger character dominated the weaker, but no man looking at the two faces could think William the weakling of the pair.

Here, at Valognes, Raoul's dislike for the Burgundian grew, and into it crept distrust. It was no secret that Guy had pretensions to the throne of Normandy, but until now Raoul had not imagined that these were anything more than the grumblings of a dissatisfied young man. So many seigneurs had objected to their base-born Duke, and there had been so many who asserted greater claims to his coronet that it was nothing extraordinary to hear murmurings amongst Guy's court that it was he and not William who should be the ruler of Normandy.

But now Raoul's suspicions were stirred, and he began to watch Guy. There were secrets abroad; he had seen a note slipped into the Burgundian's hand by one who seemed only to pass him on the stair, and once he had run against a stranger in the dark passage upstairs. The man had come out of Guy's room like one who did not wish to be observed, and in the torch-light Raoul had seen dust of hard travel on his clothes. Later he had met him at supper, when it appeared that the stranger was come to Valognes on quite innocent business. But why, Raoul asked himself, had he been closeted with Guy of Burgundy; and why did he look confused when he had stumbled on Raoul in the passage?

There befell an incident in the forest which kindled all his suspicions to a flame. In company with Guy, De Bohun, Grimbauld du Plessis, and some few knights and huntsmen, the Duke had gone out after bear. Raoul was in his train, staying as close to him as he dared, for the thought darted across his mind, when he saw of what doubtful men the party was composed, that if treachery were meditated this gloomy forest would be no such bad place for the execution of a dark deed. All the morning they had followed the hounds on a hot trail, under the shade of giant trees, and through dense thickets, further and further into the lost heart of the forest. The hounds had led them to their quarry, a big surly brown bear, and while they bayed and worried him the huntsmen stayed on the edge of the clearing, only the Duke, by his own desire, ready to run in to deliver the spear-thrust that would end the combat.

The hounds were all around the bear, slashing at his flanks and heavy quarters, bewildering him, and rousing him from sulkiness to a massive rage. He fought them with his teeth, and his great paws. One of the bitches went over and over with a broken back; a rache, running in unwarily, crawled away dragging his hind-quarters and leaving a trail of blood in his wake.

William was eagerly watching his moment. Raoul had hardly ever seen him in so animated a mood. His eyes sparkled, and he urged on the hounds continually, shouting out hunting cries, and chafing for an opportunity to run in and engage with the infuriated beast himself.

When the opportunity came he advanced quickly, grasping his spear, and struck with all his might where the neck joined the shoulder. It was an admirable thrust, but the bear had swung suddenly away, lunging at one of the hounds with a murderous rake of his forearm, and the spear was deflected slightly, and struck the shoulder. As the head went home there was heard the snap of a breaking shaft. A sort of sigh went up from the group of watching men. The Duke let a great oath, and sprang back, casting the broken shaft away from him. A fallen tree-branch lay across the ground, and caught his heel. He fell heavily, and the bear, shaking himself momentarily clear of the pack, came at him in a lumbering rush.

In that dreadful moment, and even as he raced across the clearing to cut the bear off from William, Raoul realized that not one of the men behind him had made a movement to go to the Duke's rescue.

He ran desperately. A hound, darting in, had closed his fangs on the bear's shoulder, but though he checked he could not turn the brute. The instant's respite allowed Raoul to fling himself between the beast and the man. William had leaped to his feet, and was tearing the fleshing-knife from his belt, but it was Raoul who struck the final blow, a true thrust, deep and sure.

"Back, beau sire! back!" he shouted.

The bear seemed to lurch forward, and fell with a crash, and a gush of blood at nostrils and mouth.

Others came hurrying up. Had they really hesitated, or had he only imagined that they held back? Mechanically wiping his spear, Raoul watched Guy of Burgundy clasp William affectionately, and heard him say: "Cousin, cousin, why would you not let another man take that risk? Christ's wounds! if the brute had reached you!"

Raoul felt an insane desire to laugh. He moved away from the group round the Duke, shaken by the shock of having seen his master helpless before a horrible death, and out of breath from his own headlong rush to the rescue. He wiped the sweat from his face with an unsteady hand, angry with himself for being so easily discomposed. Then he saw William put the Burgundian aside, very much as a man might push away a troublesome puppy, and walk with his quick, yet deliberate step towards him.

He was beside Raoul before Raoul could move a step to meet him. "My thanks to you, Raoul de Harcourt," he said. He held out his hand in a gesture of friendliness, and while his gaze scrutinized Raoul's face, his stern lips curled upwards in a smile.

Words choked in Raoul's throat. He had dreamed often of what he would say if ever the Duke noticed him above his fellows, but now that the moment had come, he found that he could not say anything at all. He looked quickly up at William; then, letting fall his spear, he dropped on his knee, and kissed the Duke's hand.

William glanced over his shoulder, as though to be assured that no one was within earshot. He looked down again at Raoul's bent head. "You are the knight who guards my sleep," he said.

"Yes, beau sire," Raoul muttered, wondering how he knew. He rose to his feet, and spoke the thought that was foremost in his mind. "Seigneur, your spear—should not have snapped."

William gave a short laugh. "A fault in the shaft," he said.

Raoul whispered urgently: "Beau sire, I pray you have a care to yourself!"

His eyes encountered the Duke's keen look, and for a moment the glance held. Then the Duke gave a brief nod, and walked back to join the group that watched the skinning of the bear.

After the bear-hunt Raoul began to feel an added hostility in the air, hostility now directed towards himself. Men looked scowlingly at the marplot; he had the dubious satisfaction of knowing that the plotters—if plotters they indeed were, and he had not allowed his imagination to deceive him—considered him a danger to the safe carriage of their plans. He went abroad thereafter with ears on the prick, and his dagger loose in its sheath. When an arrow sang past his head one day at a hunting of deer he thought only that someone's aim was badly at fault, but when he tripped at the head of the stairway in the dark, and only by the veriest chance saved himself from falling headlong down, he began to realize that some man or other had good reason for wishing him out of the way. A log of wood had been laid on the second step, and it rolled over when he trod on it. That it had been meant for him he was reasonably sure, and he guessed from it that his ill-wishers were aware of his nightly vigil. He was always the first man to descend the stairway in the morning, and if he had not paused upon the top step, warned by an intuition of danger, he must certainly have pitched down the stair, and broken, if not his neck, at least a leg or an arm.

He was not surprised therefore when Galet whispered a warning to him one evening before the supper-hour. Galet sat cross-legged on the floor, juggling with some sheep's bones, and as Raoul passed him he said softly without raising his head or moving his lips: "Do not drink tonight, cousin!"

Raoul heard, but gave no sign. He contrived at supper to empty the contents of his drinking-horn on to the rushes under the table at a moment when all eyes were turned towards the jester, who was performing contortionist feats with his ungainly limbs. Afterwards he pretended to drink from the empty horn, and watching under down-dropped eyelids he thought that he detected satisfaction in the face of Grimbauld du Plessis. A pulse began to beat unpleasantly hard in his throat; he had a feeling of apprehension that was almost a sickness, and the palms of his hands felt damp and cold. He shivered, and blamed the chill draught that swept through the hall. The candles guttered in the sudden gusts of wind, and threw odd shadows. Men's faces appeared sinister in the uncertain light; all at once Galet's caperings became macabre, and his shrill voice eldritch. Raoul wished that he would stop, for calamity seemed to brood over the sombre house. He set his teeth, and forced himself to join in the talk at his table, disgusted to find that he was so little the cool intrepid man he would wish to be.

The Duke went up to his chamber after supper with Guy's arm thrown round his shoulders. Guy's light laugh sent a shudder through Raoul; he stared after them, his fingers tightening unconsciously round the narrow end of his drinking-horn. Thus, surely, traitors laughed.

His right-hand neighbour was yawning. His eyes looked heavy with sleep; he complained in a thick voice of the hard day's hunting, and lolled over the table like a drunken man. Looking round Raoul saw others similarly mazed. His throat felt parched suddenly. Grimbauld du Plessis was watching him across the room. Raoul got up with a lurch and a stagger, and went with unsteady steps to the stair.

Grimbauld stood in his path, smiling at him. "Watch well, you Friend of the Friendless," he mocked.

Someone sniggered. Raoul blinked owlishly, and put up a hand to rub his eyes. "Yes," he said stupidly. "Watch—watch well. I will—watch well, Grimbauld—du Plessis."

Grimbauld laughed, and stepped aside to let him pass. Raoul went stumbling up the stairs with his hands on the rope.

At the top, and out of sight, he gave a quick look to right and left of him. No one was in the gallery, but he could hear voices in William's chamber, and knew that Guy of Burgundy was still with the Duke. He went to the edge of the gallery and peeped down through one of the vaulted arches at the hall below. Men were gathering into small groups. Some were dicing, some talking in low voices, and others drowsing with their heads on the table. The servers were still busy clearing away the trestles, and spreading pallets; and presently the Duke's valet came up the stairs and went into William's chamber. From the ambry leading into the hall came a muffled clatter of patins in the wash-tub; outside in the court the men-at-arms were still moving about. Raoul wondered whether their mead had been drugged, or whether they, too, were in the pay of the conspirators. There was no sign of Galet; he must have slipped away when the Duke went upstairs.

Guy came out of the Duke's chamber, calling over his shoulder: "Sweet dreams, dear cousin."

"Judas!" Raoul thought, hating him.

Guy shut the door, and paused for a moment, looking about him. Raoul saw him go to the edge of the gallery, and lean over. He made a sign to someone below, and went away to his own chamber at the opposite corner of the building.

Raoul listened to his retreating steps. Should he go to the Duke, and warn him? Warn him of what? He bit his lip, feeling himself a fool. What could he say? That he thought the wine had been drugged? That he misliked the look of Grimbauld? It was of no use to carry such vague suspicions to a young man who only gave a laugh, and seemed to look right through one. He drew his cloak closer about him, and leaned rather disconsolately against the wall. When the household slept he might be able to find Galet, and hear what he had discovered. Then, if treachery stalked abroad indeed, perhaps between them they could contrive to smuggle the Duke away.

A stir below drew him to the side of the gallery again. Humphrey de Bohun was going out, wenching, Raoul guessed. There was nothing unusual in that, for many of the Duke's men preferred a night spent snugly in the arms of some loose bordel-woman to one on a hard pallet in the castle. Several of the knights went out with Humphrey, and the noise in the hall died down. The valet came out of the Duke's chamber, and quenched all but a single torch at the other end of the gallery. He went clattering down the stairs, and across the hall to the kitchens.

Men had tumbled on to their pallets without troubling to remove their tunics or their chausses. Only Grimbauld and some half a dozen others still sat at a table that had been pushed up against the wall. They were talking in whispers, all but Grimbauld and one Godfrey of Bayeux, who seemed absorbed in a game of chess. A sleepy scullion came out of the kitchen to put out the candles. Grimbauld and Godfrey played on in the light of a horn-lantern.

There were still faint sounds of movement in the castle, but soon these ended, and nothing broke the stillness except the stertorous breathing of the sleepers, and once, coming from the world outside the castle, the long, far-off howl of a wolf.

There was a click of ivory as Grimbauld gathered the

chessmen together. He stood up, and said something to one of the men beside him, and picking up the lantern went towards the foot of the stairs.

Raoul's heart began to race. He drew back quickly to the Duke's door, and sat down on the floor, holding his sword across his knees, and letting his head fall forward on his chest as though he slept. A glimmer of light shone on the bend of the stair; Grimbauld came into sight, holding up the lantern.

If he means to slay me now, Raoul thought, I can at least make a fight for it, and shout to warn the Duke. God and His saints aid me!

But Grimbauld, although he bent over him, closely scrutinizing his face, made no movement to touch him. After a moment or two he seemed satisfied that Raoul indeed slept, and went away again as stealthily as he had come.

A light sweat had broken out on Raoul's forehead. He lifted his head, frowning into the darkness. If Grimbauld meant to slay the Duke, why had he not stepped over the apparently drugged man at the door, and gone in to do the foul deed at once? There were six men to answer to his call; he surely ran no risk. But the scullions and the men-at-arms were within hail: Raoul had forgotten them. They could not all have been drugged, and if an alarm was given some at least would run in to the Duke's rescue.

He got to his feet suddenly. Why had Humphrey de Bohun gone out with his knights? And what connection with all this dark business had had that dust-stained stranger whom he had seen coming out of Guy's chamber before the day of the bear-hunt? Guy must be implicated in this, and Guy would not move unless he had a strong following at his back. Some foul treachery was afoot, more serious than he had guessed. He tiptoed to the side of the gallery again, and strained his ears to hear what was being said below. The low voices were hushed; he could distinguish no words, but as he watched he saw the men draw their cloaks round them, and follow Grimbauld to the door.

Raoul licked his lips; his hand clenched unconsciously on his sword. Grimbauld was unbarring the door. As it opened a cold air spread over the hall. The cloaked men went out one by one, and the door was softly shut behind the last of them.

The single torch was still burning at the end of the gallery. Raoul pulled it from its socket, and went down the stairs, holding it high above his head. He bent over a sleeping form in the hall, and tried to shake honest Drogo de Saint-Maure awake. Drogo only groaned, and fell back on to his pallet.

The torch flared in the still darkness; the smoke from it rose in a thin spiral to the rafters. Raoul thrust it into a niche in the wall, and went silent as a ghost to the door. As his hand grasped the heavy latch he heard a sound behind him, and turned sharply to see Galet slink into the hall from the kitchen.

Galet was breathing hard, and his face shone with sweat in the torchlight. He flung out his hand to check Raoul. "Nay, nay, brother!" he said in a shrill whisper. "You can do nothing there. They are gone to open the gates. There is a great company assembled not a league from the town, and at the appointed hour they will be here to seize our heron." He caught his breath on a laugh, and flitted to the stairs. "Come! and remember that a peacock may screech alarm. Oh, William my brother, now is the time!"

Raoul drew his sword with a hiss of the steel against the scabbard. "Do you warn the Duke," he said. "I must saddle two horses. If I am seen—why, maybe I can lead them astray while the Duke breaks through."

"The Duke has a new fool," Galet said, jeering at him. "Alack, what will become of me? The horses are tethered beyond the walls, brother fool."

Raoul stared at him. "By the Bread, I think I am indeed the fool. You have been at work while I stayed wondering."

"Yea, yea, you are a child, cousin Raoul." The jester slipped up the stairs.

Raoul snatched the torch from the wall, and followed hard on his heels. No sound came from the room at the far end of the gallery where Guy slept. Raoul's lips curled back in something like a snarl as he looked towards that shadowed doorway. "Judas will lie close until his cut-throats have finished their work," he whispered. "If not—why, by the Face, I shall not be amort!" He lifted his sword, and the light shimmered on the blue steel and threw the runes on it into relief.

"Nay, does the jackal kill the lion's prey?" Galet lifted the latch of the Duke's door and went in.

The torchlight showed William sleeping on a bed of skins, with his cheek on his hand. Raoul closed the door softly behind him, and held the torch up so that the glare of it fell on William's face. William's eyes opened, blinking at the

37

sudden light. They rested on Galet and grew wide awake in an instant. He raised himself on his elbow, frowning a question.

Galet struck him on the shoulder with his bauble. "Up, up, William, you are a dead man else!" he mouthed. "Soul of a virgin, wherefore do you sleep? Your enemies are arming all around you. Little brother, if they find you here you will never leave the Côtentin alive!"

William sat up, thrusting him aside; he looked straightly across at Raoul. Light sparkled in his eyes; of alarm there was not a trace.

Raoul said urgently: "Beau sire, the fool speaks the truth. They who mean your death are gone to open the gates, and your men lie drugged below-stairs. Seigneur, rise! There is no time to lose."

William threw back the rug that covered him, and stood up in his shirt and short breeches. He began to pull on his long hose. "So!" he said, with a certain harsh exultant note in his voice.

A queer lump rose in Raoul's throat. This was a man to die for, even as he had dreamed in those far-off days at Harcourt. He caught up the Duke's sword-belt and buckled it round his waist.

"Haste, haste, brother, and follow the fool," Galet said, opening the door. "The horses stand ready."

William swung his mantle over his shoulders. "I am well served," he said gaily. "Lead on, fool."

"Yea, you are well served, my son, who have a fool and a child to guard you." Galet stole to the stairs and went down them with William and Raoul close behind him. As they rounded the last bend the torch showed the sleepers lying like dead men on the floor of the hall. Raoul heard William give a laugh under his breath.

The moon had risen, and a pale light crept in at the windows; Raoul thrust the torch into the dying fire, and left it there. Over the sleepers they picked their way to the door into the kitchens. William trod boldly, and once his foot spurned an inert form as he passed. The drugged man moaned in his sleep, and again Raoul heard the Duke laugh.

There was no one in the kitchen. Across one of the windows the wicker-lattice had been torn away. Galet pointed silently towards it.

William nodded, and stepped forward, but Raoul was before him. "Beau sire, I will go first," he said, and climbed on to the bench beneath the window, and swung his leg over the sill.

The moon sailed in a sky the colour of sapphires; here at the back of the house no man stirred. Raoul jumped down lightly, and turned to help the Duke.

William was beside him in a moment, and lastly Galet. The jester put his finger to his lips, and led them to the wall that enclosed the house and its courtyard, and scrambled up, fitting his feet into the crevices in the rough side.

Over the wall they found themselves in the shade of great trees, outposts of the forest that crept up to the very walls of Valognes. A little way into the wood they came upon the tethered horses, William's own destrier, Malet, and the big horse Verceray. William vaulted into the saddle, and leaned over to stretch down his hand to the jester. "Thanks be to you, Galet the Fool," he said. "Lie close, good dog, and look for me at Falaise."

Galet mumbled his lips over the Duke's hand. "God keep you safe, brother. Away with you; you stay too long!" He disappeared into the shadows, and the horses moved forward, side by side.

The moon showed the rough road that led to the south. Malet bounded forward, snatching at the bit, and the sound of his flying hooves seemed to thunder in Raoul's ears. After him sped Verceray, and for a while they rode thus, one behind the other, galloping southwards.

Presently, drawing abreast of the Duke, Raoul stole a glance at him, trying to see his face. The light was too dim for him to distinguish more than the jut of the nose, and the tilt of the proud chin, but he thought he caught a gleam of the eyes under the black brows. The Duke sat straight in the saddle, as though he rode for his pleasure. Raoul, himself still tingling with excitement, wondered at his calm. As though he divined what thoughts were passing through his knight's mind, William turned his head, and said with the flicker of a smile: "This has happened to me before, many times, Raoul de Harcourt."

Raoul blurted out: "Are you never afraid, beau sire?"

"Afraid? No," said William indifferently.

They rode on shoulder to shoulder through the night. After a while William steadied the headlong pace, and again spoke. "Who opened the gate to let in my murderers?"

"Lord Grimbauld, with six others, lesser men."

The corners of the Duke's mouth twitched with a sudden gust of anger. "Ah, foul traitor! By the splendour of God, there shall be a reckoning between him and me!" The cold ferocity of his voice made Raoul shiver involuntarily. The Duke looked at him again, as though he measured his man. "This will be a hard ride. I must reach Falaise by morning. Will your beast hold up?"

"Yes, lord," said Raoul stoutly, "as long as yours." He glanced behind him, over the heath they had crossed. "I hear nothing yet, beau sire."

"They will follow me hard," William said. "My fair cousin dare not let me slip through his fingers now."

Raoul regarded him in awe. "Beau sire, did you know then, all the time?"

"That my cousin of Burgundy would be pleased to see himself on my throne? Do you think me a fool, Raoul?"

"Never that, lord, but you gave no sign, and when in my ignorance I sought to warn you, you seemed as though you did not care," Raoul said shyly.

"Nor do I care," William answered. "Heart of God, have I lived Duke of Normandy for eleven years to be affrighted now by a parcel of rebels? Hark ye, Raoul de Harcourt! the first thing in life of which I have remembrance is of my uncle Walter carrying me by stealth from my palace at Vaudreuil to a poor hut in the forest, there to lie hid from mine enemies. Often has he taken me thus, for from my eighth year my subjects have conspired against me greatly. They put to death my guardian, Thorkill, and they slew Count Gilbert, whom men called the Father of his Country. You have seen FitzOsbern, my Seneschal; his father, Osbern the son of Herfast, died in my service, slain at my door, and I a lad not yet in my teens. Spine of God, I have waded already through rivers of blood! I have learned to trust no man lightly, for those who should have defended me against the world have sought my death since the days of mine infancy." He broke off, and laughed sardonically. "Now it is Guy of the Soft Tongue who lifts up his head to strike a blow at the Bastard of Normandy! By my father's soul, there shall be a bloody reckoning." He urged his horse to a gallop; the night wind stirred the curls of his uncovered head, and carried an end of his mantle streaming behind him in a dark cloud. He turned his head, and Raoul saw his teeth gleam in the starlight. "Stay by me, Raoul the Watcher. By the living God, you shall see this Normandy under my heel!"

Side by side the two destriers pounded along the track. "Ah, lord," Raoul said eagerly, "it was for this that I joined your service. I am your man, to my death and after, my hands between yours, my sword at your call!"

"So be it!" William said, and he stretched out his square hand.

The horses drew close, till Raoul's knee brushed the Duke's. Their hands met, and grasped hard. "Beau sire, crush this serpent of unrest, and let us have peace in Normandy!"

"I will have war before I have peace," William said. "Splendour of God, it is time and more that this virgin sword of mine was fleshed! Hark ye, in a day, in a week, Normandy will be up and in arms against me. I can count upon this hand the men I know I may trust." His voice grated, and Raoul felt rather than saw his frown. "Falaise first, and then to France."

Raoul said aghast: "To France, lord?"

"Yea, to Henry my suzerain, to demand his aid."

Memories of old sores crossed Raoul's mind. "Seigneur, will you trust the French King?"

"He is my suzerain," William said curtly. "He dare not refuse me."

They rode on, slackening the pace again as they plunged into the murk of a forest.

"Who stands for you, lord?" Raoul asked.

"I shall see in a little space," William answered, with a kind of grim humour. "Of this western Normandy, perhaps none. Of Caux, and the Roumois, of Evrecin and Ouche, all the land east of the Dives, many." His horse stumbled over a tree-root, but was held together by a rigid hand. "I have had few friends in my life. My cousin of Eu stands faithful. They say he swore allegiance to me as I lay in my cradle. There is Roger de Beaumont, old Hugh de Gournay, De Montfort, whom you know. I have two uncles, half-brothers to my father: shall I trust them? Yea, while I can hold them in mine eye. In my childhood I had a friend in Edward the Saxon, he who is now King of England, but he could do no more than pray for me. Yet he loves me as I think few have. His brother Alfred dealt more in actions than in prayer, but he was a fool, and met his death at the hands of Earl Godwine. For the rest—I could name you more easily my foes. They are as numerous as the trees of this forest." He drew his mantle more closely about him. "Saw you one Ranulf de Briscassart at Bayeux, the Viscount of Bessin? He is a lean man and sour, and his eyes shift under mine. He stands for Guy. There is the Lord of

Thorigny, him they call Hamon-aux-Dents. A bandog, that one, who would do me a mischief if he could. These are powerful seigneurs, but there is a greater who I think stands with them." He paused. "So be it. If he lives he will one day serve me. He is that Néel de Saint-Sauveur, Viscount of Côtentin, who came not to Valognes. If he came it would have been as my true vassal. He came not. We shall meet in battle." He glanced up at the stars. "Press on: we must cross the Vire before dawn."

When they reached the border at last the horses were sweating and blown. Fortune favoured them with an ebbing tide, but the dawn was stealing upon them as they breasted the current. The water washed the riders' knees, and Raoul's teeth chattered with the cold. The horses scrambled up the bank on the further side, and stood with trembling legs, and heaving flanks. William was watching the grey light creep above the horizon. "We must leave Bayeux to the south of us," he said. "I dare not enter that town. On! there is no tarrying here."

At St. Clement they rested their horses for a while outside the little church. William, a religious man, went in to kneel a few minutes before the altar, with his strong hands clasped, and his gaze sternly devout. They mounted again almost at once, and now Raoul had difficulty in keeping up with the Duke, who forced the pace on ruthlessly. The last stars had disappeared as they skirted sleeping Bayeux, and the dawn-mist shrouded the town from their sight.

The sun was striking through the mist when they came to Rie, with its castle standing by the road. William would have passed it by, but the bridge was down, and a man was seen to stand on it, scenting the morning air. He had watched the labouring horses come along the road from afar, curious to know what men these were who rode foaming destriers so early in the day. As they drew abreast at a stumbling trot he recognized the bare-headed figure on the black horse, and gasped, and ran out to stop the Duke. "Seigneur! Seigneur! hold!" he shouted, and stood in the riders' path with his arms flung out.

The Duke reined in. The Sieur of Rie caught Malet's bridle, and cried: "What evil befalls, lord? How is it you travel thus, alone and in disorder?"

The Duke looked directly at him. "Hubert, dare I trust you?" he said.

"Yea, as God lives you may trust me, beau sire. Speak boldly! I am your man."

"Why then," William answered, "I am fleeing for my life. Do you seek to stay me?"

"For as long as shall suffice you to break your fast, lord, and mount a fresh horse," Hubert said promptly. "Enter and fear nothing! If your enemies come up with you I will hold my castle in their teeth."

They rode over the bridge into the bailey of the castle, and slid down from the saddles. Old Hubert de Rie was shouting lustily for his servants; he swept the two weary men into the hall of his castle, and in a little while the place teemed with hurrying bondmen, some bringing raiment for the Duke, some kneeling to bind the straps over the hose round his legs, one presenting a basin of water for him to lave his face, another holding a napkin, a third standing by to offer a horn filled to the brim with wine of France. While they dressed him William spoke over their heads to Hubert, briefly recounting what had befallen at Valognes. In the middle of this there came in three young men, solemn-eyed, lanky youths, who knelt before the Duke while their father proudly told over their names to his liege-lord.

"Behold your lord!" he admonished them. "You will be his escort. On your lives, leave him not till you have brought him safe to Falaise!'

"On our heads be it," the eldest of them said in a deep, serious voice, and put his hands between the Duke's.

So they rode at length to Falaise, leaving Hubert to lead the pursuers off the track. This he did so guilelessly that at the end of an hour's tricky riding, when he left the hungry band, they still believed him their well-wisher, and zealously followed up the road he had indicated.

At Falaise the Duke stayed only a night. The town was a loyal outpost in the middle of hostile territory, and news came in soon enough. All the land west of the Dives was in open revolt under Néel de Saint-Sauveur, and Ranulf, Viscount of Bessin, while in Bayeux Guy, the son of Count Raymond of Burgundy, was declared the true ruler of Normandy by right of his mother, Alicia, the daughter of Duke Richard II. His manifesto was made public, wherein he denounced William as base-born and unfit to govern. William showed his teeth when he heard of it, and rode at once to Rouen, escorted by a bodyguard of picked men.

The capital welcomed him with loyal alacrity. He was met with great pomp by his uncles, William, Count of Arques, and Mauger, the Archbishop of Rouen, riding in splendour at the head of the faithful vassals. Strangely in contrast to this cavalcade the young man in the plain tunic and flowing mantle reined in his horse hard upon its haunches, and stiffly returned the salute of half a hundred men. He lodged in the episcopal palace, and all that evening he sat in conference with his uncles: William, hostile, yet for the moment loyal; Mauger, sleek man, setting his finger-tips together, and regarding their whiteness in meditative silence. My lord Bishop kept great state, and housed his nephew royally. William lifted his brows at the wealth of gold plate and costly hangings, but said nothing. Raoul, wandering over the fine palace, caught a glimpse of an opulent lady, who wore silk and many jewels, but he also held his peace.

At the conference it was decided that the Duke should ride to the Court of King Henry, who lay at Poissy, and there petition his aid against the rebels.

The Count of Arques misliked the scheme, and spoke hotly of past wrongs. *"Allancz al roy?"* he repeated. "Go to the King? Heart of a man, are we to forget how Henry seized Tillières? I would not trust the French Fox, no, not I!"

But Mauger smiled, and said smoothly: "This is to bind him to us. He dare not refuse."

"So I think," the Duke said. His deep voice sounded oddly after Mauger's silken speech. "I will not nurse up old hostilities towards my suzerain."

He was gone again the next morning, riding at the head of an escort to the French border in his usual headlong way. He made his knights feel breathless, but they admired him. It was a tired but a proud company that at length reached Poissy, and reined in before the drawbridge of the castle. A herald cantered forward to the very edge of the bridge, and shouted his announcement in a voice like a clarion:—

"William, by the Grace of God Duke of Normandy, craves audience of his Most Puissant Majesty Henry, King of France!"

Poissy was startled; as the Duke's troop rode into the bailey men had already run to warn the King's attendants of his unexpected coming. Within an hour of his arrival William was ushered into the King's presence. He stalked in, attended by the Lords of Arques, Gournay and Montfort, and by three knights, of whom Raoul was one, and found the King seated on a dais in his chair of state, with his nobles round him.

William's hawk-gaze swept the hall. He advanced into the

middle of the floor, and knelt stiffly, looking into the King's face.

Henry rose from his chair, and came down from the dais with his hands held out, and a smile that was a little twisted on his thin lips. "Fair cousin, we cry you welcome." He raised the Duke, and embraced him. "You come in haste who send us no word to expect you," he said, watching the Duke under his eyelids.

"Sire, as my need is desperate so is my haste," William answered, coming more swiftly to the point than the Frenchman liked. "I am here to solicit aid from France in my Duchy."

Henry shot a quick look at Eudes his brother. Then his eyes were veiled again, and he said gently: "What dire need is this, cousin?"

Briefly William told his story, and at the end folded his arms across his chest, and stood awaiting the King's reply, never taking his eyes from that secret face.

The French nobles were whispering amongst themselves, covertly scrutinizing the straight figure before the King. William topped Henry by half a head and was built on lines that made the King look puny. He was dressed very simply in a tunic trimmed with gold, with his sword at his side, and his mantle hanging from his shoulders to his heels. Solid golden bracelets clasped his powerful forearms, and his cloak was fastened on his shoulder by a jewelled fibula. His head was bare, so that his strong, dark face could be seen by everyone in the hall. He stood squarely, and motionless, yet nothing about him argued repose.

Henry plucked at his gown for a moment, pinching the rich stuff between his fingers. "We must speak more particularly of this, cousin," he said at last. "After we have dined you shall give me your company."

At the end of the council that was held all the afternoon in the audience-chamber above the hall it was agreed that Henry should march into Normandy at the head of a French army, and upon a day appointed meet William with such ducal troops as he could raise. The Duke swept him along on the tide of his will; the French nobles caught the infection of his energy: the King found that his council was being swayed by his young vassal, himself driven relentlessly on whither he only half wanted to go.

Upon the following day the Duke was gone again, as abruptly as he had come. The King watched his departure from one of the windows, thoughtfully stroking his long

45

upper lip. At his side his brother Eudes said with a laugh: "By the Host, the Bastard seems to be a man, sire!"

"Yea," Henry said slowly. "He must be bound to me more closely yet."

"So we march to aid him against his rebels, brother. Is that how it runs?"

"Maybe, maybe," the King muttered. "I can use him, I think. Yes, I have work for the Bastard."

CHAPTER IV

The Duke's cavalcade rode into Rouen again to find it seething with armed men. The streets seemed to resound with the clash of steel, and the sun was bright on polished shields and the hauberks of the knights. The Duke's faithful vassals were pouring in in answer to his summons to war. From Caux and Brai they came, day after day; from the Evrecin and the Vexin, from Roumois and Lieuvin, while messengers rode in at all hours with promises from Perche and Ouche, Hiesmes and Auge, to join the Duke on his march westwards.

A large company met the Duke on his entry into the town. Raoul saw his overlord, Roger de Beaumont, and guessed that his father and perhaps one or both of his brothers were in his train. There were many others, and amongst them a tall man whom the Duke embraced very warmly. This was Count Robert of Eu. He was accompanied by his younger brother William, called Busac, and by a numerous train of followers.

Barons great and small thronged the palace. There was De Gournay, wise in war, with his boon comrade Walter Giffard, the arm-gaunt Lord of Longueville; young De Montfort; William FitzOsbern, the Duke's Seneschal; the Lords of Crevecoeur and Estouteville, of Briquebec, Mortemer, and Roumare, all with their meinies, all bristling in hardiment. Day after day they streamed into Rouen, hounds straining at the leash, a leash held taut between a young man's fingers.

"Not bad, not bad!" Hubert de Harcourt grunted, watching William de Warenne ride into the town at the head of his men. "But for every man of ours I'll be bound the Viscount of Côtentin has two." He shook his head, glooming. "Do you see the Lords of Moyon and Magneville? Do you see Drogon de Manceaux, or Gilbert Montfiquet? Where are the Lords of Cahagnes and Asnières? What word comes from Tournières? Where is Saint-Sever? Where is Walter de Lacy? We shall pit our might against theirs on the day appointed. You will not see them before, by my head!"

Feeling ran high against Grimbauld the traitor. The little loyal band of men who had followed the Duke to Valognes had rejoined him at Rouen, hot for revenge on the villain who had drugged them.

Beside William, Count Robert and Hugh de Gournay advised, but he outstripped them. A demon of energy seemed to possess him; they panted behind him in the spirit even as Raoul panted in the body. Boy followed boy now in right earnest. In a night, the night of a wild ride, a queer bond of amity had sprung up between the Duke and the youngest of his knights. Raoul rode behind William, slept at his door, attended him to his council, even carried his gonfanon when he galloped down the lines of his troops. Men lifted their brows; some sneered; some looked jealously, but he cared nothing for that while the Duke's imperative voice called a dozen times in a day: "Raoul!"

His father was puffed up with pride in the favour shown to his youngest-born, and could not at all understand how it was that Raoul himself showed no signs of a reasonable conceit. That Raoul had no ambition beyond his burning desire to serve the Duke was a matter of astonishment to him, and some misgiving. Respect for William he could comprehend now that he had seen the Duke at work, but that Raoul should lay his boy's heart with all its hoarded store of dreams at William's feet seemed to him a strange unwholesome business. He frowned over it, and growled: "Sacred Face! lads were made of sterner stuff in my day!"

The ducal army rode westwards to meet the French, passing Pont Audémer on the Risle, and crossing the Touque at Pont l'Evêque. Here and at other points along the march they were joined by reinforcements led by the barons from outlying districts. From day to day the Duke's scouts brought him word of the French King's advance. He had crossed the Frontier at Verneuil at the head of his levies, and marched to Hiesmes by way of Echaufour, and was on his way north through Auge to meet the Duke at Valmérie, a league to the south of Argences, and hard by the camp of the rebels on the plain of Val-es-dunes.

William crossed the Méance at the ford of Berengier, north of Val-es-dunes. Not a baron in his army but had his gonfanonier at his side. Gonfanons and knights' pennons stretched out in the breeze, a medley of proud colours led by the gold lions that waved over William's head. The poor folk crowded out of Argences to watch the host ride by. There were open mouths and round eyes, and men nudged one another, and whispered: "There he rides! That is the Duke, he on the black destrier. Jesu! but he looks older than his years!"

A girl's voice cried shrilly: "God aid, beau sire! Death to your grace's enemies!"

There was a cheer, a shout of "God aid! God aid!" The Duke rode by looking straight between Malet's ears.

The French had heard Mass at Valmérie at daybreak, and marched out to Val-es-dunes, where the rebel army was drawn up along the bank of the Méance. Over the high ground at Argences rode the ducal troops, and saw at their feet the plain of Val-es-dunes, without hill or valley or wood, sloping gently to the east in wind-swept bareness.

"A fine place for fighting," remarked Count Robert, riding abreast of William. "Néel has chosen his ground well, by the Host!"

Raoul looked at the silver gleam of the river, and thought: There will be blood on the water, and dead men floating down the stream. Who of us shall wake to-morrow?

It was plain no such misgiving crossed the Duke's mind. He spurred his horse to a gallop, as though eager to come upon the field of battle. Verceray leaped after, and the wind unfurled the gonfanon Raoul carried, and showed the lions golden on a blood-red ground.

The King of France rode out from his lines to meet the Duke. One of his nobles accompanied him; he wore a red mantle over his ringed tunic.

Everything is red to-day, Raoul thought. And shall be redder yet, God wot!

Verceray stamped restlessly, and champed at the bit; the wind shivered the silken gonfanon, and bent the grass underfoot in flitting shadows. Raoul looked towards the rebel army, drawn up in battle array at some distance. There too standards fluttered aloft, and the sun caught the tips of a wood of spears, so that they flashed dazzling points of light. The quiet plain stretched as far as the eye could see, and the Méance ran on untroubled, crooning its song. Suddenly Raoul found himself wishing that this tranquillity might remain unspoiled; in his mind he could see the ground torn up under the charging horses' hooves, and dead, bleeding men lying on the river banks; and hear, drowning the twitter of birds, the shouts and the groans and the clash of battle. He gave himself a shake, for these were womanish fancies, and men were born, after all, to fight. He fixed his eyes upon the Duke again, who was sitting with one hand on his hip, and his head bent towards the King.

Henry was pointing to a band of horsemen, nobly caparisoned, who held apart alike from the rebel troops and the ducal army. "Do you know who those men may be, cousin?" he asked. "They rode up a short space before yourself, and stand thus aloof. On whose side will they fight?"

William put up his hand to shade his eyes from the sun, and looked under it at the gonfanon fitfully displayed in the wind. "On my side, I think, sire," he answered. "That is the emblem of Raoul Tesson, the Lord of Turie-en-Cingueliz, and he has no quarrel or cause of anger with me."

There was a movement in the little troop, and a man was seen to come out, and ride at a canter towards the ducal army.

"Raoul Tesson comes himself," William said, still shading his eyes. He spurred Malet forward in front of the lines to meet the solitary rider, and sat watching under bent brows Tesson's approach.

The Lord of Cingueliz came up with a shout of "Turie!" that rang out fiercely across the plain. His mantle floated behind him, and he had a glove clenched in his right hand. He reined in his destrier with a jerk. "Hail, Duke of Normandy!" he said, and no man who heard him knew whether he mocked or no. His bright eyes looked full into William's.

"What do ye want of me, Raoul Tesson?" the Duke said calmly.

The Lord of Cingueliz rode up close. The Duke sat unmoved, but Raoul, anxiously watching, loosened his sword in the scabbard. "This!" said the Lord of Cingueliz, and his right hand came up, and he struck the Duke across the cheek with the glove he held. He laughed harshly. "It is done!" he said, and reined back.

There had come a growl of menace from the Duke's men behind him; spears were couched; there was a movement to press forward. The Duke flung up his hand to check the rush. His eyes did not waver from Tesson's face,

Tesson cast an unconcerned glance at the angry barons, and looked smiling back at William. "What I have sworn to do I have done," he said in a clear voice that carried far. "I have acquitted myself of my oath to strike a blow at you wherever I should find you. Henceforth, beau sire, I will do you no other wrong, nor ever raise my hand against you." He touched his helmet in a stiff salute, and wheeled his destrier to ride back to his waiting men.

The Duke laughed. "Thanks be to you, Raoul Tesson!" he called after him, and rode back to King Henry's side.

"That was well done, by my head!" Henry said, kindling. "They are fierce dogs, those men of Normandy."

"You shall soon judge of that, sire," the Duke promised.

Heralds from either side rode out, and back again. The Normans, led by William in person, the Counts of Arques and Eu, and the Sieur of Gournay, were on the right wing; the French, with their King and the Count of Saint-Pol at their head, formed the left wing. Facing them, the men of Bessin followed the gonfanon of Ranulf of Bayeux; and the wild Côtentin troops chafed behind Néel de Saint-Sauveur, he whom men called *Noble Chef de Faucon*. Raoul saw his standard, azure and argent, gleaming blue across the plain, and marked how he bestrode a restless destrier, and how his lance glittered as it caught the light.

He wound Verceray's bridle about his wrist, and took a firmer grip on the gonfanon he carried. He felt breathless, as though he had been running hard, and the blood drummed unpleasantly in his ears. His lips were dry; he licked them, and prayed that he might bear himself as became the Duke's knight, in this his first fight.

The sharp order to charge rang out, and he saw Malet bound forward, and followed close. Suddenly he was excited, not breathless any more, and not afraid.

The thunder of hooves was all about him; a great roan head drew abreast of him; he caught the swirl of a blue mantle, and the hard glitter of a shield, but his attention was fixed on the man who rode Malet so furiously into battle. Ahead of them the opposing troops were galloping towards them. Raoul wondered what would happen when the crash of meeting came. A shout of many voices dinned in his ears; he found that he too was yelling: "Dex Aie! Dex Aie!"

The noise of hooves grew louder as charge answered charge. Borne on the wind came the cry of the men of Bessin: "Saint-Sever! Sire Saint-Sever!" and the clarion call of Hamon-aux-Dents, roaring out: "Saint-Amant! Saint-Amant!"

The two armies came together with a crash that brought both sides to a jarring halt. Shield clashed against shield; in a tight pack men hacked and hewed, and the maddened destriers struck out with their plunging, steel-shod hooves. There was a man down, trampled under foot; Raoul heard him scream, and gritted his teeth. His grasp was sticky on the shaft of the gonfanon, his arm fast in the enarmes of his big kite-shaped shield. He forced Verceray on after the Duke, struggling through the press. Someone cried out that the King was down; there was a scuffle ahead; the Duke drove his lance home with all his great strength, and a horse fell. Raoul saw its red distended nostrils as it sank, and the terror in the dilating eyes. Then that faded, and he was warding off a spear-thrust with his shield. Verceray reared up before a man on foot who was desperately fighting with his lance among the slain. Raoul wrenched the big horse aside, and cut downwards with his sword. Blood spurted up over his leg; he swept on, over the dead, hacking his way to the Duke's side.

"Saint-Sever! Sire Saint-Sever!" With a howl the man who shouted slashed at the gonfanon Raoul guarded so jealously. Raoul's sword whirled aloft and hissed down through the air in a flash of deadly blue steel. The gonfanon was safe still, and a rebel went armless. Raoul shook the sweat out of his eyes, and shouted: "Death! Death! *Le bon temps viendra!*"

A man drove at him in a wild charge; he flung up his shield, and saw Grimbauld de Plessis' dark face, with a smear of blood across one cheek. Then Hubert de Harcourt's spear took Grimbauld unawares, and knocked him out of the saddle. Hubert was shouting: "Dex Aie!" and "Yield, yield, false knight!" Raoul saw his brother Eudes press forward; then he himself swept on, waving the gonfanon, close beside the Duke.

William was fighting with an energy that seemed untiring. Foam from Malet's mouth spattered his person; his helmet was dented from some glancing thrust, but under it his eyes were sparkling. He had thrown away his lance and fought now with his sword, hand to hand with Hardrez, the finest warrior of Bayeux. The veteran's sword clanged against his; he yelled out his lord's battle-cry of "Saint-Amant!" and as he shouted the Duke's blade beat his down, and the point was driven home to his unprotected throat. Blood gushed over his tunic; he fell with no more than a gurgle, and a riderless horse plunged desperately in the mêlée.

51

For how long the skirmish lasted Raoul did not know. He kept beside the Duke with a kind of bloodthirsty tenacity, snarling between his clenched teeth as he guarded the gonfanon from the many attacks made upon it. It was bloodstained and foam-flecked and the shaft was greasy in his hand, but it waved still over the Duke's head.

Absurd words thrummed in Raoul's brain: "Redder yet, God wot! Redder yet!" The shifting mass of riders passed like phantoms before his eyes. Sometimes one phantom would come close, and he struck it mechanically. Once he saw Guy of Burgundy's face in the thinning press; it was livid, and the eyes glared, but it vanished, and new faces swam before his vision, always changing, as faces change in uneasy dreams. Now and then the shrill scream of a wounded horse rose high above the uproar; sometimes one voice rang out in a rallying call.

The men of Cingueliz, holding off until the first jarring charge was over, had spurred forward at a well-chosen moment, and fallen upon the rebels' flank. They were mingled with the Duke's troops now, and ever and again that ferocious yell of "Turie!" sounded above the cries of "Dex Aie!" and the deep "Montjoie!" that came from the French lines.

Ranulf, the Viscount of Bessin, was the first to leave the field. As the heap of slain that littered the field grew, and the ducal troops pressed on, mowing down the rebels, he lost heart. William's dark face seemed to trouble his overwrought mind. He fought on doggedly, but when Hardrez, his beloved vassal, fell before the Duke, terror seemed to possess him. With a dreadful cry he cast his shield and lance from him, and rode away like a madman, bending low on his horse's neck, urging him faster, and faster still across the reeking plain.

Beside Raoul, withdrawn from the now desultory fighting, the Duke laughed suddenly. Raoul started: the sound of the Duke's laugh seemed to recall him to himself. He drew a shuddering sigh; the red glare went out of his eyes; he looked with a touch of horror at the man who could laugh in the middle of such carnage.

The Duke was pointing with his wet sword towards the flying figure of Ranulf. "God on the Cross!—like a goose with neck outstretched!" he said. He glanced at Raoul, amusement gleaming in his eyes.

Reaction all at once came to Raoul; he began to laugh in helpless gusts. He pulled himself together as the Duke's horse moved forward, and rode after, biting his lip. He found that he was shaking like a man in the grip of an ague. For the first time, now that he had done with fighting, he became aware of the smell of blood, and was seized by a fit of retching.

Guy of Burgundy followed Ranulf next, riding with the remnant of his men, and trying as he went to twist his scarf round his blood-boltered arm.

Néel de Saint-Sauveur alone of the rebel chiefs fought on with a kind of grim desperation. Hamon-aux-Dents lay dead on the field, spread-eagled where he had fallen. He it was who had killed his second horse under the King, but even as Henry sprang clear Hamon went down before the lance of a Norman knight.

"Splendour of God, I have a place about me for such a man as that!" the Duke cried, watching with kindling eyes the invincible figure that fought on under the azure gonfanon.

The Méance was already swollen with the corpses that drifted down its current. Man after man, casting spear and shield away, took to the river, some to struggle to the further bank, others to drown miserably in the tainted water. The Viscount of Côtentin was forced at last to own himself beaten. He drew off, rallying his men round his standard, and rode from the field, orderly even in retreat.

Some Norman and French chevaliers would have followed to cut him down. The Duke rose in his stirrups. "No!" he thundered. "By the living God, I charge you let that man go!"

God be thanked there are to be some still left alive! thought Raoul, trying not to look at the body that lay at his feet. It drew his gaze irresistibly. Once it had been a man, with a face for laughter or for tears. It had no face now: only a battered horror that had been crushed and torn by the hooves that had plunged over it.

The Duke saw Raoul staring, and glanced down to see what held his gaze. His brows twitched together, and that was all the sign he gave either of repulsion or of pity. "Come!" he said briefly, over his shoulder, and rode on to meet the King.

Henry was flushed and breathless. "By my faith, you are cool, cousin!" he exclaimed as the Duke saluted him. "Nobly done, Normandy. Yours is no virgin sword this hour!"

The Duke wiped it on a corner of his torn mantle. "Nay, I have blooded it," he said.

Henry took off his helmet, and passed his hand over his hot face. "I have work for you, Normandy!" he said.

"I am your grace's vassal," William replied formally.

"We will speak of this when we have rested," the King promised. "Sacred Face, my belly is parched!"

"By your leave, sire, I have no time now for resting," said the Duke.

The King stared at him. "Holy God, have you not had enough?"

"I have a fox to smoke out of his earth," William said "Guy of Burgundy has surely fled to his hold at Briosne. I like to finish my work, sire." He smiled at Count Robert of Eu, who had ridden up. "Do you follow me, Robert?"

"Yea, to hell's mouth," the Count said gaily. "Let us at all costs cut the Burgundian off from his supplies. It is well begun, but must be better ended." He beckoned Hubert de Harcourt forward. "Cousin, here is one who holds for you a prisoner you will be glad to shackle."

Hubert uncovered his head, and showed a red sweating face and bloodshot eyes. "Lord Duke, it is the contreytour Grimbauld," he said. Raoul grinned to hear the note of respect in his bluff voice.

"Ha! Is it so indeed?" William cried. "Let Hugh de Gournay carry him in chains to Rouen." He nodded at Hubert, and said jovially: "Your family serves me well. Be sure mine is no short memory." He turned again to the King, and raised his hand to his helmet. "Give me leave, sire. When I have finished my work, call on me for your need. I shall not be slow in answering. Raoul, follow me!" He wheeled about, and rode back to the body of his army.

Hubert stared after him, blowing out his cheeks; then with a "Haro!" and a slap on his destrier's steaming neck, he cantered after William, saying with a deep chuckle: "Ha, God! We are away again! Then haro, haro! follow this Fighting Duke!"

The Count of Eu, riding beside him, laughed, and said: "Is that your mind, old war-dog?"

"By God, it is!" said Hubert.

The King of France was left stroking his beard. "You are hot, you are hot," he muttered. "Yea, but your brain is cold, by the Face! I see my way. Be sure I shall call upon you, Normandy; be very sure of it." He became aware of Saint-Pol, blinking at him. "What, are you there, Count? How do you say? Shall I pit Normandy against Anjou?" He laughed soundlessly.

Saint-Pol turned it over in his slow mind. "That is to breed enmity between them," he said. "Geoffrey Martel is a vengeful man."

"Yea, why not?" the King said sharply. "Let the Norman wolf aid me against the Angevin fox. I perceive there is a cold devil in that man. Let the fox harry the wolf after. Thus the wolf grows not too great." He saw that Saint-Pol was plainly at a loss, and twitched the Count's mantle. "Look you, Count, I want no puissant wolf upon my Frontier," he said.

CHAPTER V

They smoked the Burgundian fox out of his earth at length, but the affair was not so quickly settled as might have been hoped. The donjon at Briosne was no hill fortress, but it was none the less a safe hold for that. A square squat hall, it stood upon an island in midstream, and kept watch over the Risle. The Duke came, frowned, bit his whip-lash with his strong white teeth, and gave out certain brisk orders. In a little space the besieged looked from the loop-holes at two wooden castles, one to the east, the other to the west. The Duke had sat down on either bank to starve his cousin into submission.

It was said that Guy of Burgundy let a great laugh, and counted himself saved already. The donjon could hold against a blockade until the winter; he may be pardoned for supposing that William's patience would wear out sooner. But he mistook his man. The Fighting Duke knew when to act in a fiery haste and when to hold his impetuous temper in on a tight rein. If Guy counted upon fresh disturbances in Normandy to lure William from his post he was disappointed. Néel de Saint-Sauveur had retired into Brittany, and was pronounced a wolf's-head, and his estates confiscated; Ranulf of Bayeux had fled no man knew whither; the Lord of Thorigny was dead at Val-es-dunes; and Grimbauld du Plessis rotting in a dungeon at Rouen, soon to die also, in his fetters. For the rest, Normandy wanted time to catch her breath. She began to know her Duke, and lay low for a while, licking her sores.

It is believed it was the Duke's relentless patience that prayed upon Guy's nerves. He began very early to be in a fret, and was often seen to chew his nails right down to the

quick. He was prepared for assault, confident he could withstand it; but his volatile temperament writhed under the
torment of slow waiting. There were anxious hearts at
Briosne these days, and men stared over the river at the
ducal camps, and each day courage ebbed, and hope died a
lingering death. When winter crept on, and bones pressed
through covering skins, despair stalked through the dark
castle, and men crouched apart in corners, hugging their
cloaks round them against the bitter cold. No one spoke any
longer of the raising of the siege. Only his friends besought
Guy on their knees to render up the keys of the castle. Guy
screamed at them in a wild fury that they wished him
dead.

"Nay, lord, nay; but here we die like rats in a hole."

Guy huddled on his bed, gripping his mantle round him
with twitching fingers. *"Gayter la mort, gayter la mort!"* he
muttered. His eyes, fever-bright, peered at the men about
him. He gave a cracked silly laugh. "Eh, do you mock me,
skeletons all?" He was taken by a fit of shivering. "Skeletons
from Val-es-dunes!" he said, panting. "I know you, by God's
death! What, do you fleer at me? Dead men! dead men!"
He hid his face, and broke into hard sobbing.

They succoured him as they could. He lay still on his bed,
staring up at the rafters, heeding none, but raving to
himself in a monotonous, dreadful voice that stretched the
nerves of those who heard him to snapping point.

Snow covered the ground and thin ice floated on the river
when the end came. They brought the keys of Briosne to
the Duke on the end of a lance, abasing themselves before
him. He said only: "Let Guy of Burgundy come before
me."

Guy came, carrying a saddle on his back in token of
submission. He walked with difficulty, staggering under a
load too heavy for his wasted limbs to support. At the
Duke's feet Galet brayed, and said: "Turn your ass out to
grass, brother: it is a galled beast."

He was kicked sprawling. "Hold your peace, fool!" the
Duke said with a rasp in his voice. He strode up to Guy
who knelt, awaiting judgment, and lifted the saddle from his
shoulders, and heaved it away with a crash. "Stand up,
cousin, and hear what I have to say to you!" he commanded, and set his hand under Guy's elbow, and raised him.

Guy's followers crept up to kiss the Duke's hand when he
had done speaking; the sentence was one of mercy: pardon
for the lesser men; no more than confiscation of his lands

for Guy, who was declared to be no longer a vassal of Normandy, but bidden, in a gentler voice, consider himself still the guest of his cousin.

Guy found it hard to speak; he moved his lips soundlessly; a tear rolled sluggishly down his cheek. The Duke summoned up FitzOsbern with a jerk of his head. "Take him away," he said. "Let him be housed with all honour." He clapped Guy lightly on the shoulder. "Go, cousin," he said. "You have nothing to fear from me, I promise you."

Later, when opportunity served, Raoul kissed his hand, kneeling.

William looked down at him with a smile lifting the corners of his mouth. "How now, Raoul?"

"Beau sire, I have seen your strength, and your justice, but now I see your mercy."

William pulled his hand away. "Pish! Am I a cat to worry a dead mouse?" he said disdainfully.

Guy of Burgundy stayed till spring in the Court at Rouen, but it was plain he wished himself otherwise. When the last snow melted on the hungry fields he craved leave to depart out of Normandy, and this being granted went away to his own land, a disappointed man.

With the spring came the promised call from King Henry. King Henry sent to summon his vassal to aid him in a war against Geoffrey Martel, Count of Anjou.

His need was urgent. A man labouring always under the conceit that his deserts were greater than his holdings, Martel had already caused some disturbance amongst his neighbours. The Counts of Chartres and Champagne could bear witness to this, and did so, with a great deal of noise. Maine, Normandy's neighbour, lay under his heel, for he was guardian to the young Count Hugh and exercised his right to the full. Having vanquished and imprisoned for a space the noble Counts of Chartres and Champagne, he took it into his head he might become greater yet, and set about the matter very drastically. In the spring of the year he renounced his homage to King Henry, and followed up this gesture of defiance by marching into Guienne and Poictiers. After several engagements he seized the persons of both Counts, and held them prisoners until such time as they should be forced to agree to his demands. These were extortionate, but there was no hope for the Counts but in surrender. It was thought a significant thing when the Count of Poitou died four days after his release. Guienne survived: maybe he drank from another cup. Martel asserted claims to Poictiers and married—by force, some said—a relative of the dead count. Thus matters stood when King Henry sent for the Wolf of Normandy.

At the head of his chivalry Duke William marched over the Frontier into France. Once more men who lived for little else put on their harness, and swore by the Mass that if that was the Duke's temper he was a ruler after their own hearts.

What King Henry made of it he kept carefully to himself, but it was surely now that he conceived his undying jealousy of his young vassal. If he had called on William only to fight under his direction he was soon to find who was the real leader of the expedition. It was William's word that carried the day; it was he who laid an unerring finger on weak places in the King's plans, and did not hesitate to condemn schemes that seemed a waste of time to his soldierly mind. King Henry might hide his chagrin under a silken smile; the French barons might glower their jealousy: William was left unmoved. They came to hate him, those proud Frenchmen, for his quick brain that outstripped theirs; for his clear foresight; for his reckless daring in the field, which cast the bravest of them in the shade; and most of all for the uncomfortable personality he had. All through his life men were to fear him and find it hard to meet the direct stare he bent upon them. Thus early the French were made aware of the ruthless strength of his will. The truth was he never swerved from his purpose, and would go to any lengths to achieve it. Own him master and he would be your good friend; oppose him and there could be only one outcome.

"Jesu, he is stark!" Roger de Beaumont said. "What shall come of it? I fear him, I promise you. Yea, I fear greatly. He is like no other man I have known. When is he weary? When does he ail? Bones of God, when will he fail of his purpose? Never, I believe! Eh, but he is hard!"

But they were proud of him, the men who fought under his gonfanon. Prowess in arms was the surest road to a Norman heart, and feats beyond their imaginings William showed them. His men boasted of him, and told how he was first through the breach at Meulan, slaying with his own hand no less than three stout warriors in his impetuous rush; how he lost his bodyguard in a wild chase through dim forests and how they found him after frenzied search, accompanied by four knights, and driving a score of prisoners before him. His fame spread. King Henry suggested with gentle concern that he risked his life too often. He spoke to deaf ears. A demon of recklessness possessed this Fighting Duke.

When the war was ended, and Martel had slunk snarling back to his kennel in Anjou, King Henry hid his jealousy beneath a smiling front, and very warmly thanked Normandy for his aid, speaking fair words, and embracing him right cousinly. Maybe he guessed that Martel was already planning vengeance on the stripling who had done so grievously by him, and so was able to smile with a good grace. They parted with expressions of friendship; the Frenchman went home to nurse his spite; and the Norman marched back to his Duchy to find it exultant over his victorious return and very ready to live at peace with him.

His fame had spread over Western Europe. From Guienne and Gascony, even from kings in far Spain came gifts of splendid destriers, and messages that were panegyrics on his skill and his courage. In one short trial of arms the Bastard of Normandy was become the hero of Europe.

For a space peace reigned in Normandy, but Martel was not the man to let injuries go unavenged. Suddenly, without declaration of war, he struck a shrewd blow at Normandy's pride. Marching up through Maine he seized the castle of Domfront, built by Duke Richard the Good, invested it, and swept on over the Frontier to the Norman border town of Alençon on the Sarthe. The town made no resistance, the Castle very little. Martel left a garrison there, laid waste the surrounding country, and returned home in triumph, carrying his plunder.

This time Duke William asked no aid of France. Leaving Alençon to the east of him he did what no one had expected, and appeared before Domfront a full week before they had thought to see him there. Such swift methods shocked the garrison: they contrived to send word to their Count, and looked down uneasily from their craggy height at the Duke's preparations for a siege.

There was no taking Domfront by assault. High on its rocky hill it stood, scowling over the valley of the Mayenne, impregnable and massive. The garrison took heart of grace, and talked of the day that should see Martel advancing to their relief.

Meanwhile the Duke established a blockade, and occupied his time between riding out to intercept supplies trying to reach the castle, and hunting in the forests near by. It was upon one of these expeditions that he was cut off by a party that had made a sortie from the castle for that purpose.

"Treachery, by God!" FitzOsbern cried.

"Very like," said William. "We will try our strength against these bold chevaliers."

Roger de Montgoméri blurted out: "Beau sire, they outnumber us five to one."

A challenging look was directed at him. "Ha, do you fear them?" asked the Duke. "Who follows me?"

"If you must go, beau sire, be sure we all follow you," growled De Gournay. "But, before God, it is madness!"

"If we do not scatter this rabble, trust me never!" said William, and led them over the wooded ground at the gallop.

Scatter the troop they did. They fell upon the Angevins almost before they were aware, and fought with such fury that the troop broke before their onslaught, and was chased back to the very foot of the castle hill.

"Was it madness, Hugh?" the Duke said, with a twinkle.

"Beau sire, I am very sure that a devil rides you," De Gournay answered frankly.

"I am very sure," murmured Raoul, "that the Count of Anjou thinks so, and fears it. Still he comes not!"

But the reason for Martel's delay was otherwise explained. At dusk one evening word was brought to the Duke's camp of a troop seen approaching at the gallop, led by one who waved an azure and argent gonfanon.

The Duke's eyes narrowed. "Néel de Saint-Sauveur," he said. "Well." He looked at FitzOsbern. "I shall see now whether I was mistaken in my man. If he comes in peace bring him in to me, William."

FitzOsbern went out, agog with curiosity. The Duke looked at Raoul. "I want this man," he said. "Now we shall see if I can win him to me or no."

There came the long winding of a horn, the trample of hooves, and presently the sound of voices, and of footsteps.

The tent-flap was swung back; the Viscount of Côtentin came in briskly with a swirl of his blue mantle, and dropped on his knee before the Duke, looking straight into his eyes.

For a moment the Duke returned the gaze, saying nothing. Then he spoke: "What now, Chef de Faucon?"

"Seigneur, I bring you two hundred horse out of Pen-thièvre," Néel answered. "I come from Anjou, hot-foot."

"What made you there, Néel the Rebel?"

"I'll work for Martel, seigneur," Néel said, with the flash of a smile.

"So!" said the Duke. There was a gleam at the back of his eyes; the corners of his mouth began to lift.

"Seigneur, a year back I did you grievous wrong. I have sought to repay."

"Is it your work that Martel holds off from me yet?" William asked.

"Mine, beau sire. I have done some small damage in Anjou, as I think, Now I come to you, my life in my hands."

The smile curled the Duke's mouth fully now. "I have a place about me for such a man as you, Néel," he said. "My thanks: I am well repaid." He looked towards the Seneschal. "FitzOsbern, let fitting quarters be given to the Viscount of Côtentin."

Néel rose up quickly. "Seigneur!" he said unsteadily.

"Take back your lands of me, Chef de Faucon," William said. He got up, and came round the corner of the table with his hand held out. "Let the past lie dead: I would rather have you for my friend than for my foe."

The Viscount bent and kissed his hand. "Seigneur, I am your man," he promised, low, and turned, and went out without another word.

The Duke lifted an eyebrow in Raoul's direction. "I can sometimes win men," he said, "even though they call me stark."

After this, news was soon brought of Martel's approach. Doubtless the Castle garrison soon got wind of it, and lifted up their hearts. As for William, he sent out his Seneschal and young Roger de Montgoméri with an escort to meet Anjou and learnt his business. These two heralds came back in a bristle of vanity, and told faithfully what had befallen.

It seemed they rode up, waving the herald's banner, and were taken straight before the Count himself. They found him swollen with arrogance, and reported him to be a man of full habit of body, with veins that rose up on his forehead when he was enraged. He greeted them with proud words, displeasing to them, and bade them tell their master he would meet him in battle upon such a day. Then, being enflamed by his own choler, and (said FitzOsbern) fretted by the maggot of vainglory that ate his brain, he burst out in a loud voice to tell them how the upstart of Normandy might know him upon the field of battle, by the red mantle he would wear, and the housings of his destrier.

This was to add fuel to a growing fire, as may be supposed. Without pausing to consider William FitzOsbern retaliated in kind. He said that in his turn the Duke would wear the purple of his high standing, and a circlet round his helm, and bestride a bay stallion sent to him by a King of Spain.

"Furthermore, seigneur," FitzOsbern told, "we said that if he were still in doubt he might know you by the golden lions that waved about your head, and by the stout warriors who gathered round you, very hot to avenge the insults sustained by you. I believe it to have been well said. I marked him to change colour."

"For my part," said young Roger, "I believe it was not the answer he looked for. He seemed much put out, and chewed his beard, and glanced about him this way and that."

Galet looked up from his seat in a corner of the tent, and said: "Why, the dog of Anjou is a great one for barking. Take a whip out and you will see him slink back to his kennel."

So it proved indeed. The Duke led out his army upon the term-day, but got no word of Anjou. It was heard later that he had withdrawn his troops in haste, and was marching homewards with a strong rearguard. He was the first of many to prefer an ignoble retreat to a meeting in arms with Duke William of Normandy.

What Domfront made of it no one knew. As for William he gave his sardonic laugh and returned to the business of reducing the Castle.

Martel having put himself out of court, as it were, the Duke leaped into one of his sudden swift actions. Leaving a small force at Domfront he led the remainder of his troops on a night ride to Alençon. He went by way of Menhendin and Pointel, and an arduous business he made of it. His chevaliers sweated behind him; some fell out on the road upon foundered horses, but the bulk kept on doggedly, setting their teeth in a determination not to be outdone by the tireless man who led them.

They appeared before Alençon in the morning light, grimed and sweat-stained; and stared through the lifting mist across the river at the town which lay beyond. The town itself was unfortified, but the Castle, with its straight road leading down to the gate-tower over the bridge of the Sarthe, governed all. Above its crenellated battlements floated the standard of Anjou.

"Wine of Christ, if I do not have that down!" the Duke swore.

Straightway he dismounted, and knelt at his prayers, for he was never one to forget what was due to God; and his men knelt with him. That being done, he rose up again and bathed his face in the river, and bent his heavy considering frown on the gatehouse that guarded the bridge. While he stayed thus, pondering, the people of Alençon had leisure to observe his force. Men gathered on the further bank of the river, and heads were seen to draw together in excited conference.

Those who kept the gate-tower marked the strength of the Duke's army, and seeing that he had brought no siege-engines with him, thought themselves safe in their strong-hold. Gaining arrogance with their feeling of security, they began to consider themselves already victors and some among them shouted out injurious words, and made signs betokening their derision.

The Duke noted these things with a gradually darkening brow. He gave curt orders, and his men formed up in battle array. The Duke was conferring apart with his captains, biting his whip-lash as he always did when he saw a difficult task before him, and carefully observing the disposition of the town. The men in the gate-tower, conceiving their jeerings to have gone wide of the mark, bethought them-selves of a good jest, and one likely to touch the Duke's pride nearly. There was a bustle, and a running to and fro; then a growl of fury ran through the Norman troop, and men clapped their hands to their swords.

Raoul found his brother Gilbert spluttering beside him. "Ha, God!" Gilbert stuttered. "See yonder! The lousy dogs!"

Raoul looked round and saw the defenders on the bridge hanging hides and furs over the battlements, and thwacking them with long sticks, and the flat of their swords. He flushed with quick anger, as the meaning was made plain to him. "Cross of Christ, what foul insolence is this?"

"Hail to the Tanner! Hail to the noble Tanner of Falaise!" shouted the men on the tower. "What, are you there, byblow of Normandy? How is the trade in furs with you these days?"

William's head was jerked up at that. He thrust his horse past Néel de Saint-Sauveur, who would have shut the sight from his eyes if he could, and came in full view of what was doing on the bridge. Men saw his knuckles grow white with the fierce gripping of his hand on his sword-hilt, and his mouth twitch with the rising tide of his rage. Rigid he sat, still as a stone upon his destrier; he was ice-cold, but with fire blazing under the frozen surface.

A hush had fallen on his troop. He spoke at last, molten words that crashed into the silence and made it shudder. "By the splendour of God, I will deal with those knaves as with a tree whose branches are lopped by the pollarding knife!" He swung his destrier round on its haunches; stratagem went by the wind; his rage consumed the men. Assault! Assault! The gate-tower was to be stormed and taken, burned to ashes, and the men in it dragged out to face his vengeance. Words of counsel were humbly spoken; he tossed them aside. By God's death he swore to raze the tower to the ground or never more to lead his barons into battle.

The greater part of his men were with him; only some older heads feared defeat, and murmured of strategy. He swept these aside; he drew his sword flashing in the sunlight, and thundered: "Who follows me? Speak!"

A full-throated roar answered him; he smiled, and Raoul saw his teeth gritted close.

Of that desperate skirmish on the bridge Raoul retained afterwards but the haziest memory. Missiles hailed about the besiegers; there was a sortie and some hard hand-to-hand fighting, when shield was locked to shield in the tight wedge, and men fell with despairing cries into the river below. From the tower they hurled javelins and rocks; Raoul had his helmet crushed in from a stone that hurtled upon him, and fell, half-stunned, still grasping his wet sword. Feet trampled over him; he struggled up with a great effort, warding off his own comrades, reaching his feet at last, bruised and shaken, but whole, swayed by the press about him.

They were up to the tower almost before he was aware, in a storm of missiles. Men came over the bridge with a battering-ram slung between them, a ram hastily made of a felled tree. Many hands bore it; there came the dull thud of its impact with the great door which closed the way under the arch of the tower into the town. For long the door held; those who drove the ram were dripping with sweat, and breathing in laboured gasps. Ever and again one of them fell from a javelin hurled from above; his place was taken at once, and the ram driven home again. The wood cracked at last, and split: the men of Normandy were in, under the arch, and battering down the smaller door that led into one side of the tower. It fell before the fury of their assault; they burst through the opening, and hacked their way up the twisting stair, up and up, over their own dead, till they drove the defenders from the stairhead, back into the guardroom above.

In all thirty men were dragged out, prisoners for the Duke's vengeance. He set fire to the tower, and the terrified inhabitants of the town fled to their homes, and those on the Castle-wall beheld the flames and the black smoke mounting higher and higher.

The Duke's baggage-train had reached Alençon by now, and men were busy setting up his tent, and preparing an encampment. The Duke stood at the bridge-head, terrible still in wrath, and watched the approach of his prisoners. Behind him his captains were gathered in angry support. His hands were blood-stained, gripping his red sword. He glanced down at it, and handed it to Raoul with a quick, impatient movement. Raoul wiped it carefully, and stood holding it, waiting to see what the Duke meant to do.

All that remained of the garrison were driven at the spear-point to face the Duke's wrath. FitzOsbern exclaimed: "Deal hardly, beau sire! Sacred Face, shall men who dare such insults be allowed to live?"

"They shall live," William said, "in a sort." Raoul paused in his task of wiping the blood-stained sword, and looked up sharply, frowning. "As a tree whose branches are lopped," William repeated with deadly emphasis. "They shall go footless and handless, living tokens of my vengeance for all men to see, and fear, by Death!"

A murmur of assent sounded from the barons; one of the prisoners gave a shriek of horror, and fell grovelling in the mud before the Duke. Raoul touched William's arm. "Beau sire, you cannot do that!" he said in a low voice. "Another man might, but no—not you! Not hands and feet both; you cannot maim them thus hideously!"

"You shall see," William replied.

"Rarely said, beau sire!" FitzOsbern declared. "In this way men shall know you, and dread your anger."

Raoul's fingers twisted round the heavy sword-hilt. He looked at the prisoners and saw some with defiant faces

65

turned to the Duke, some kneeling at his feet, some silent, some blubbering for mercy. He turned again towards William. "Your justice . . ." he said. "Your mercy . . . What of these?"

"Tush, you fool!" growled Gilbert in his ear.

"Grant us only death! Ah, dread lord, give us death!" wailed one of the prisoners, stretching his hands to William.

Raoul struck Gilbert's hand from his shoulder. "Give them justice!" he said. "This cruelty is not for such an one as you, seigneur!"

"God's Son, the Watcher turns pigeon-hearted at the thought of a little blood-letting!" someone exclaimed scornfully.

Raoul swung round. "I will let yours with a high heart, I promise you, Ralph de Toeni!"

"Hold your peace, Raoul!" the Duke said angrily. "What I have sworn to do I will do, by the living God! Not you nor any man can turn me." He made a sign to the men who guarded the prisoners. There was a cry of despair, a broken prayer for mercy. A block of wood was dragged forward, and a bucket full of pitch. A writhing man was flung down by the block, and his wrists wrenched over it. The axe swung aloft, and descended with a sickening thud. A high scream of anguish rose throbbing on the air, and behind Raoul Gilbert gave a grunt of satisfaction.

Raoul broke through the knot of onlookers behind the Duke, unable to bear the sight of the mutilation. A man stood in his way, trying to peep over the shoulders of his betters at the gruesome work on hand. Raoul struck him aside with a force that sent him sprawling, and thrust his way on through the crowd to the Duke's tent.

He found that he was still grasping William's sword. He looked at it for a moment with a white set face, and suddenly flung it from him so that it fell with a clatter in a corner of the tent. A second tortured scream from outside made his gorge rise until he thought he must be sick. He sank down on to a stool, and buried his face in his hands.

The screams and groans rang through and through his head; before his shut eyes gibbered the forms of maimed men, and the gloating faces of those who watched the execution.

After a long time the hideous sounds ceased. There was a murmur of voices, and the tread of footsteps all round the tent.

Galet crept in, and to Raoul's knee. "Brother, brother!" he whispered, and touched Raoul's sleeve.

Raoul looked up: "Fool, have you seen?"

"Yea, it is a red vengeance," the fool answered. "But will you break your heart for a parcel of Angevin swine?"

"Do you think I care for them?" Raoul said bitterly. "If I break my heart it is for William's shame." He fumbled at his sword-hilt and drew the blade from its sheath. His finger traced the runes graven upon it *Le bon temps viendra!* Ah, heart of Christ!"

Troubled, the fool said: "Yea, but what shall this signify?"

Raoul looked at him. "O fool, when shall this day's work be forgotten? It is in my mind that down the years when men speak of William our Duke they will remember this vengeance and call him Tyrant. I tell you, there is a stain upon his shield now no deed of justice, no feat of arms can ever wipe away."

"He is a stark man in his anger, brother, but you have seen him merciful," Galet said, uncomprehending.

"I have seen the devil let loose," Raoul said with a short laugh.

"Yea, he hath a devil like all of his house, but he keeps it throttled six days out of the seven."

Raoul rose, and sheathed his sword again. "But the seventh is the day that shall live in men's memories," he said, and went out, leaving the fool to scratch his puzzled head.

He did not come near the Duke until some hours had passed. Appalled at what they had seen, the Castle garrison sent to offer terms of surrender. They were granted freedom, and safety of life and limb. The last blood had been shed at Alençon, and without a blow the Castle capitulated. There was no plundering, no rape of women. The Duke's passion was throttled again, and once more men saw his justice.

A squire came to Raoul at dusk with a message from William, commanding his attendance. He went slowly to the big tent, and entered to find the Duke alone, seated by the table. A lamp hung from the roof of the tent, and lit the small space. William pointed to where his sword still lay. "Pick up my sword," he said, with a straight look under his brows.

Raoul gave it to him without a word. The Duke held it across his knee, and said: "I ride back to Domfront tomorrow." He paused. "Do you know young Roger de Bigod—a youngling with a face of wood?" he asked unexpectedly.

Raoul blinked, and answered: "If he is a vassal of the Count of Mortain I know him, lord."

"In his folly he spills news of a plot. The Warling Count is busy planning my ruin, and my good Uncle of Arques"—he smiled unpleasantly—"withdrew from the siege of Domfront a short hour after myself."

"God's death!" Raoul said, startled. "Arques? What will you do, seigneur?"

"A guard set about him at Arques should keep my uncle in check. I am sending to Mortain to bring the Warling Count before me. Him I will banish, for while I live the peace of Normandy shall never, by God's grace, be disturbed again by such revolts as we crushed at Val-es-dunes." He paused, and looked at Raoul, unsmiling. "Shall I send you to Mortain, or do you ride with me back to Domfront?" he asked.

Raoul returned his look gravely. "Why must you ask me that, my liege?"

"If I am too stark a lord for you, leave me!" the Duke said. "Think well: I shall not change for any plea of yours."

"I am your man," Raoul answered. "Now and always, as I swore that night when we fled from Valognes. I ride with you to Domfront."

There was no more said. On the following day they rode back to Domfront, leaving a garrison at Alençon. The news of the happenings there was before them. Terrified, despairing of Martel's return, Domfront surrendered, got easy terms, and thought herself fortunate. Although it stood in the county of Maine the donjon was garrisoned by Normans. The Duke marched on to Ambrières, built a stronghold there, and retired again into Normandy. He had thrust his Frontier out a little way into Maine, and that was all Anjou got by his rashness.

Away in France King Henry heard the news, and turned a very sickly colour. His hand played with his beard, and those near him saw that he plucked three hairs from it, all unaware.

PART II
(1051—1053)

THE ROUGH WOOING

"He must be a man of great courage and high daring who could venture to come and beat me in my own father's palace."
Saying of Matilda of Flanders.

CHAPTER I

As the long ship heaved on the waves one of the hostages
gave a whimper, and curled his body closer, with his knees
drawn up. Raoul was standnng by the bulwarks, looking out
over the sea. A pale moonlight turned the water coldly
silver, shimmering under a night-blue sky; now and again
flecks of foam glistened as though a star had dropped into
the sea. From the masthead lanterns hung as beacons to
show the other vessels where the Duke's ship rode. A small
cabin built in the stern had a leathern curtain across the
opening, and where this fell away from the door-post a
crack of yellow light shone. Amidships an awning sheltered
the hostages. A lantern was secured to one of the supports;
its glow illumined the faces of the three who crouched there
on fur skins. Overhead a fitful wind bellied the sails, and
from time to time the canvas slapped in the breeze, and the
ropes creaked and whined.

Again the youngest of the hostages whimpered, and
buried his face in the mantle of the man who held him.
Raoul looked over his shoulder with a faint smile. The boy
was so young and so unhappy. As he looked, the man
holding the child raised his head, and his eyes, which were
of a cold northern blue, encountered Raoul's. After a moment of grave regard he lowered them again to the fair
head upon his knee.

Raoul hesitated for a while, but presently picked his way
over the men who lay sleeping in their cloaks, and came into

the light of the lantern under the awning. The blue-eyed man looked up at him, but his expression did not change.

Raoul, who had been charged with the comfort of the hostages, tried in a few halting Saxon words to speak to him. The hostage interrupted with a slight smile, and said in Norman: "I can speak your tongue. My mother was a Norman out of Caux. What is it that you want of me?"

"I am glad," Raoul said. "I have wished to be able to speak to you, but you see how ill I am learned in your Saxon tongue." He looked down at the youngest hostage. "The boy is sick, isn't he? Shall I bring some wine for him? Would he drink it?"

"It would be kind," Edgar replied, with an aloof courtesy that was rather chilling. He bent over the boy, and spoke to him in Saxon. The child—Hakon, son of Swegn, grandson of Godwine—only moaned, and lifted a pallid woebegone face.

"My lord has not before been upon the sea," Edgar said in stiff explanation of Hakon's tears.

The third hostage, Godwine's youngest-born, Wlnoth, a boy hardly older than Hakon, woke from an uneasy sleep, and sat up, rubbing his eyes. Edgar said something to him; he looked curiously at Raoul, and smiled with a semi-royal graciousness.

When Raoul came back with the wine Hakon seemed to be exhausted from yet another spasm of sickness. When the drinking-horn was put to his lips he sipped a little between sobs, and raised a pair of tear-drowned eyes to Raoul's face. Raoul smiled at him, but he drew further back into Edgar's hold, as though he were shy, or perhaps hostile. But he seemed better after the wine, and inclined to sleep. Edgar drew the furs more closely round him, and said curtly: "My thanks, Norman."

"My name is Raoul de Harcourt," Raoul said, determined to persevere in his friendly advances. He glanced down at Hakon. "The boy is over-young to leave his home. He will be happier in a day or two."

Edgar made no reply to this. His silence was rather a natural taciturnity than a studied rudeness, but there seemed to be no luring him from it. After a moment Raoul rose up from his knee. "Maybe he will sleep now. Call on me for your needs."

Edgar slightly inclined his head. As Raoul moved away Wlnoth said: "Who is he, Edgar? What did he say?"

"He is the man we marked to ride beside Duke William,"

Edgar replied. "He says that he is called Raoul de Harcourt."

"I liked him," said Wlnoth decidedly. "He spoke kindly to Hakon. Hakon is a little fool to cry because he is sick."

"He cries because he does not want to go to Normandy," Edgar said rather grimly.

"He is a nithing." Wlnoth gave a small sniff. "I am very well pleased to go. Duke William has promised me a noble destrier and honourable entertainment. I shall ride in the lists, and shoot deer in the forest of Quévilly, and Duke William will dub me a knight." Then, as Edgar made no response, he said tauntingly: "I think you like it as ill as Hakon does. Perhaps you would rather have been outlawed with my brother?"

Edgar looked out across the silvered water as though he would pierce the darkness that shrouded the receding coast of England, but he still said nothing. With a hunch of his shoulders Wlnoth turned away from him, and disposed himself to sleep again.

Edgar stayed awake, nursing Hakon's head on his knee. Wlnoth's last words had bitten near the bone of the matter. He would far rather be in Ireland now with Earl Harold, than handed over like so much lumber to Duke William of Normandy. When King Edward had told him with his benign smile that he was to go to Normandy he had known all at once that he hated the silly King. He would have been at Harold's side then only that his father had forbidden it. He thought now, bitterly, that a short exile with the Earl would have been preferable to his father than this far longer exile which might last for God knew how many dreary years.

The Duke had journeyed to England a few weeks ago, and his arrival had followed hard upon a commotion set up by yet another foreigner. This was no Norman, but Count Eustace of Boulogne, who had created a disturbance at Dover. He had also come to visit King Edward, and upon his departure some men of his had fallen foul of the inhabitants of Dover. This had resulted in a skirmish, and some blood-letting; Count Eustace had journeyed secretly back to London with a complaint for the King's ear.

A scowl darkened Edgar's brow as he thought of this. King Edward's subjects, and especially those of Earl Godwine's south country, had hoped that he would send the obnoxious Count away with a flea in his ear. Edgar supposed that they should have known their ruler better than to

71

expect him to take sides against the foreigners he loved so dearly. But it still made him clench his hand when he considered how King Edward had promised Eustace redress.

It had made others clench their hands too, notably that strong man Godwine, and his sons, Harold the Earl of Wessex, and Tostig, his noisy third-born.

Now of all men King Edward most hated Earl Godwine. It was Godwine who, when Harold the Harefoot, base-born son of great Cnut, sat the throne, had cozened and then slain Edward's brother, Alfred, upon his ill-starred expedition to England. When Edward at last ascended the throne he found Godwine all-powerful, and had thought himself bound to overlook that dark deed. When Godwine broached the matter to him he had even felt himself obliged to marry the Earl's daughter Eadgytha, which had been an arrangement not at all to his taste. The marriage had gone forward, but the lady got little good by it. It was asserted that she had never entered the King's chaste bed, and not all her learning nor her piety could at all console her for the barrenness that was no fault of hers.

Upon the affair of Count Eustace at Dover Godwine had taken up arms in support of the injured citizens, and matters had for a while looked very ugly. The King in a hurry convened his nobles at Gloucester, but when Godwine and his sons appeared in force a few miles from the town and refused to attend the Convention without an army at their backs, Edward grew more than ever uneasy, and summoned a fresh Convention in London. London had a comfortable habit of loyalty. Thither came the nobles of the land, headed by Siward, the great Earl of Northumbria, and Leofric of Mercia, with his calm son Alfgar. These men looked on the power of Godwine's brood with jealous eyes. With them in support King Edward pronounced sentence of banishment over the heads of Godwine and his two sons, Harold and Tostig. His eldest son, Swegn, had been banished some time before for various turbulent dealings that culminated in his abduction of no less a sacred person than an abbess. He was not felt to be a loss.

At the same time as he triumphantly outlawed Godwine and his sons, Edward bethought himself that here was at last a good opportunity for putting away his Queen. He shut her in the nunnery of Wherwell, possessed himself of her treasure, and was able to feel himself more nearly a monk than he had done for many years. The lady made no complaint; possibly she knew her kindred well enough to be sure that though they fled now, they would very soon return. Earl Godwine set sail with Tostig for Flanders; but Harold, a man of independent habit, departed into Ireland with a few followers.

Having succeeded in outlawing the two men who most troubled him, King Edward thought himself now secure. In a mood of uplifted complacency he cured a poor woman of an ulcerous sore by laying his hands upon her, and was more than ever convinced of his own miraculous powers.

It was in such a mood of mild triumph that William found him. When the Duke of Normandy had been ushered with great ceremony into the King of England's presence Edward had come down from the High Settle and clasped the Norman in his arms, and embraced him many times. With tears in his eyes he tried to trace a resemblance in this stern, handsome man to the impetuous boy he had parted from ten years before. He wandered into a reminiscent vein, as old men will do, and recalled many incidents of William's childhood, from his birth onwards. The Duke smiled, gave him at least half of his attention, and kept the other half busy observing all that went on around him.

At a convenient opportunity Edward related his news, not forgetting the healing of the ulcer. He was pathetically gleeful at what he conceived to have been his strong handling of the situation, and he looked with simple pride in himself at one who at the age of twenty-three had also a reputation for handling situations strongly.

Approbation was clearly expected; William gave it, but a smile hovered round his mouth. In contradiction to this there was a look in his eyes that might almost have been a frown. He said slowly: "So I am not to meet Harold Godwineson."

Edward seemed to think this a matter for congratulation.

Being somewhat deep in William's confidence Raoul had very well understood the meaning of that shadow of a frown. William wanted to see Earl Harold, a warrior as famous in England as himself was famous through Europe. Knowing of that old promise made to William by Edward that if he died childless the Duke should be heir to his throne, Raoul suspected William of a desire to measure the man who might in the future play no small part in his life. The reason of William's visit to England he could guess, and all these imaginings he thought fairly confirmed when he learned that they were to carry back to Normandy with them two close relatives of Harold, and one thegn of importance who held lands under him. Obviously then Harold nursed pretensions to the Crown of England, and Wlnoth, Hakon, and Edgar were hostages for his good behaviour.

A rather cold feeling stole over Raoul. He peered into the future and could see only clouds veiling William's destiny. They were thunderous, he thought, shot with swift lightning, like everything else in his life. He wished suddenly that Edward would beget an heir of his own body, for William belonged to Normandy. England was alien and unfriendly, a land of golden-haired dogged men who looked with sullen eyes upon all foreigners, and wore flowing locks and long beards like barbarians; who drank themselves to sleep at night; had little learning; lived in rude houses; and built mean towns. Raoul had heard that they were loose-living. A Norman at the Court of King Edward had told him several scandalous stories. It was said that when a noble got one of his bondwomen with child he would very often sell her into slavery to far Eastern merchants. Raoul only half-believed that, but he had not liked the Saxons, and he had been glad to see the white cliffs of Dover fading in the distance.

He was roused by a hand on his shoulder. Looking round he found that the Duke had come silently out of the cabin. "You are wakeful too, beau sire," he said.

The Duke nodded. He pulled his mantle close about him to ward off the cold breeze. "Very," he answered. His arm lay along the bulwarks, clasped by thick bracelets which shone gold in the moonlight. "I am for Flanders," he said abruptly.

Raoul smiled at that. Two years ago, after the fall of Domfront, they had journeyed into Flanders, to the Court of Count Baldwin the Wise at Brussels, and there had set eyes on the Lady Matilda, my lord Count's daughter. A strange thing had happened then. As the lady sat beside her father, her pointed face framed in the braids of her pale hair, and her hands clasped like white petals on her gown, she had raised her eyes to the Duke's face, and observed him in a kind of aloof thoughtfulness. Her eyes were pools of light, hazel green. The Duke had stared back; Raoul, behind him, had seen how he stiffened, and had watched the slow closing of his hand. In one deep interchange of glances William had made up his mind. Later, in his chamber, he said: "I will make that lady Duchess of Normandy."

FitzOsbern blurted out: "Beau sire, she is already wedded to one Gherbod, a Fleming."

The Duke had thrown him a look of impatience, as at an irrelevancy. "She is the woman for me," he said crudely.

FitzOsbern, disturbed to see the lion bent on staking another beast's prey, tried to interest him in the lady's sister Judith, who was considered the more beautiful of the two. He dwelt upon the limpid blue of her eyes, and the richer curves of her body until he saw that the Duke was not listening to him. Matilda, a white slim lady, remote and inscrutable, had captured a heart no woman had touched before. The image of her face with its secret eyes and slow-curving smile glimmered day and night before the Duke's hot vision.

It was found upon inquiry that the lady was widowed, and had no mind to a second marriage. There was much dark work done, hints let fall, and evasive answers returned. The Duke swept back to Normandy, and announced to his Council his intention of taking a wife to himself. At this there was satisfaction to be seen on all but one face. The one belonged to Archbishop Mauger, who had his own reasons for wishing his nephew to die a bachelor. The Duke followed up his announcement by naming his intended bride. She was felt to be a sage man's choice; her father was a haut prince, and powerful: to clasp hands of alliance with Flanders would be a politic thing for Normandy.

Affairs began to move, but tentatively, in a manner unusual in the Duke's dealings. Secret embassies journeyed to and fro between Rouen and Brussels and achieved small success. Count Baldwin returned answers that drove his neighbour into a fume of impatience. Not only was the lady too lately widowed to think of espousals, but there was also some question of affinity likely to be displeasing to the Church.

Archbishop Mauger fell upon this with zeal. From him came the first check, on the grounds of Papal objections. In his opinion there could be no dispensation for such a marriage. No doubt he saw the way clear, knowing his nephew. The Duke rendered deep respect to the Church, and the tenacity of his nature might well lead him to remain a bachelor rather than wed any but the lady of his first love. A subtle man, Mauger, but he underrated the tenacity he thought he gauged so well.

The lion began to show his teeth. The Churchmen, all unconscious of gathering storm-clouds, met to discuss the problem, tossed in their minds between Mauger upon the one hand, and upon the other by that energetic half-brother of William, Odo, now Bishop of Bayeux. Lost in ecclesiastical argument the priests were blind to the signs of a rising anger in their Duke. When the wisest man in Europe, Lanfranc, Prior of the Abbey of Herluin at Bec, declared that the marriage was barred by the question of affinity, the storm-clouds burst with a clap of well-known thunder.

If the Duke's new-born love had been thought to soften him the message he sent to Bec dispersed that illusion. The messenger arrived with his horse in a foam, and bade Lanfranc, in the Duke's name, remove from Normandy within three days.

This was very black, and with any man but Lanfranc might have led to grave trouble. But Lanfranc knew his Duke. He heard the order in calm silence, and seemed to meditate within himself. His deep-set eyes travelled from one man to another of the messenger's escort and presently lighted on the face he expected to see. He turned, and went back into the Abbey, and the man he had recognized slipped away from his comrades and followed the Prior to his cell by a back way. When he had knelt and kissed Lanfranc's hand he stood up and looked the Prior full between the eyes. "You know our master, Father," was all he said.

"Yea, well do I know him," Lanfranc said. "He is swift to anger, treading a troubled path."

"But his anger is swiftly over."

Lanfranc smoothed his cassock with one thin hand. His smile grew. "Do you bring me counsel, Raoul de Harcourt?"

"Nay, who would be presumptuous enough to counsel Lanfranc? I say only that we take the eastern road tomorrow before dusk."

They looked at one another. "Go with God, my son," Lanfranc said gently.

Upon the next day, in the afternoon, the Prior set forth on his journey into exile, very poorly attended, and mounted upon a galled jade. He took a road that seemed strange to the monks who accompanied him, but when they pointed a more direct path to him he replied in enigmatic words, and kept on his chosen way.

After about an hour of leisurely riding a cavalcade was seen approaching at a pace that set up a cloud of dust. Lanfranc's chaplain, greatly alarmed, whispered in his ear that ill-fortune had brought the Duke out upon this road. He was anxious to draw aside into the shade of a wood, but

Lanfranc said meekly: "We will follow our road, and all shall be as God wills."

The cavalcade drew nearer, led by a figure there was no mistaking. Lanfranc held to the middle of the road, but reined in his sorry steed as the Duke came abreast of him. The big destrier stopped with a plunge and a snort. Monks and knights stood still behind their respective leaders. William was scowling. "Ha, Sacred Face!" he said. "Are you not gone yet, proud priest?"

"Beau sire," said Lanfranc, "I shall be gone the quicker if you find me a better horse."

The scowl did not lift yet, but a twinkle began to peep in the Duke's eyes. "Lanfranc," he said, "you have gone too far, by God!"

"Your horse for mine, beau sire, and I shall be further by nightfall."

"God's feet, I am not to be baulked!" William leaned forward in his saddle, and grasped the Prior's bridle. "Turn, Lanfranc: you shall ride apart with me."

"Your way is none of mine, seigneur," Lanfranc answered, looking at him very steadily.

"It shall be yet, I promise you. Are you against me Prior?"

"By no means," Lanfranc said. "You are too hasty, my son."

"School me then, Father. Show me an honourable way to my desires and I will own myself a rogue to be in a heat with you."

"That is very easily done," said Lanfranc, and rode ahead with him on the way back to Bec.

The upshot of all this was the departure of Lanfranc to Rome on ducal business. He took leave of William on very excellent terms, and the Duke knelt to receive his blessing, and promised a penance for his fiery temper. Ostensibly Lanfranc travelled to Rome to take part in a great argument on Transubstantiation with one Bérengier. It was unfortunate for Bérengier to be pitted against the greatest scholar of his age, but he argued with spirit, and interminably. It was not a trivial matter to be lightly decided. It took five years to refute Bérengier, which was done at last at a Council of Tours. But that is to look ahead. At the start of this discussion Lanfranc had other and more pressing business to attend to. Bérengier with his false doctrines served as a cloak to hide secret matters.

Thus affairs dragged on, and no definite answer came from Rome or from Flanders. The Duke went to England upon a visit to the Confessor, and since he spoke no word of it men thought that he had put by his thought of marriage. But on the heaving ship, with England lying behind him in the darkness he said to Raoul, abruptly: "I am for Flanders."

Raoul answered, smiling: "We believe you to have given up that business, beau sire."

"Ha, do you think so, Raoul?"

"No, not I. But you have other ambitions beside that have lately grown large," Raoul said significantly.

William glanced towards the hostages. "You heard a promise confirmed to me by King Edward. I am to have England."

"I heard," Raoul said slowly. "But is there no other word than his to that?"

"Yea, by the Christ! Mine!" said William.

"Beau sire, there is the Atheling Edward, and his son after him, who have nearer claims. There is Harold Godwineson, whom the Saxons love."

"England will go to the strongest hand," said William. "Trust me: I look ahead."

"And I," Raoul said a little sadly. "There will be bloody work done over this. What of our Normandy?"

For a moment William made him no answer. Raoul saw him frowning out to sea, his eyes fixed hawk-like upon some far-off goal. Still looking into the distance he said: "While I live I can hold at bay France and Anjou, both hungry for my lands. After me, soon or late, France will swallow all, and my race will perish, drowned in the tide of Frenchmen. I tell you I will carve for Normandy a fresh holding, a kingdom for my ancestor Rollo's dukedom; a land guarded by the sea and no fickle border fortresses; a land where my race and my name shall endure."

"England not France would then swallow Normandy," Raoul said.

"Maybe. But by God's death there will be Normans still!"

Silence fell between them. At last Raoul said: "And there is Harold, the son of Godwine, a great leader of men, so they say; himself a man of large desires." He jerked his head towards the sleeping hostages. "Do you think to hold him on that slender rein, beau sire?"

"Holy Face, not I!" William said, with a laugh. "Cousin Edward would have me take them. No harm."

"I wish we had seen Earl Harold," Raoul said reflectively. "By all accounts he is a man."

"A false brood," William answered. "One I have caged." He nodded to where they could see Wlnoth's fair head lying on a reindeer-skin. "Be sure I shall hold fast. But five remain: Swegn, Harold, Tostig, Gyrth and Leofwine. Two are boys yet, but Godwine's blood runs hot in their veins. One, Swegn, is an incontinent dog, a wolf's head, a violator of holy abbesses; let be for him: he will spin his own winding sheet. Another, Tostig, runs wasting like a boar with foam on his tushes: if he runs not on his own doom, and that a bloody one, trust me never. The last is Harold, whom we did not see. God will judge between us when the time comes. Edward fears him; Edward is hard-driven." His mouth curled. "King of England!" he said contemptuously. "King of England, holy saints!"

A voice spoke out of the shadows. "With leave, only one holy saint, brother. 'King, King, here is a strong force marching against you,' saith the Confessor's councillors. 'Softly, good friends,' mumbles the Saint. 'Here is more urgent matter.' And straight he lays his hands upon a serf's filthy sores, and falls at his prayers. Thus your King, brother." Galet came into the light, and postured, and smirked.

"Jest not at holiness," William said sternly. "God knows Edward performs great miracles."

"Yea, but not the greatest miracle of getting his good wife with child to rule after him," grinned Galet. "Will you fill your time at home with healing lepers, brother?"

"I have not the power, fool."

"Alack that you have so little saintliness!" said Galet. "It is a great thing to be a saint. Cousin Edward spends his days in prayer and his nights in dreaming holy vision. Pity the poor Queen! 'Will you get you a fine son to be King after you, sweetheart?'—'Fie, fie!' cries Cousin Edward, 'I am too chaste for such snug dealings.' So he tells his beads over, and prays God and His Mother to bless his continence, and leaves his England like a bone betwixt two hounds. There will be a merry dog-fight before all is done."

A gleam of white teeth showed in the moonlight. The Duke was smiling, but he said only: "You know too much, friend Galet. Pay heed lest I cut off your ears."

"Well, well!" said the fool, "I must then journey a second time into England and have the Confessor lay his hands on me. A noble pair of ass's ears would spring under them, I promise you."

"Enough of that!" the Duke said curtly. He swung an end of his mantle over one shoulder, and moved away across

79

the deck. "I am for bed," he said with a yawn. "Come with me, Raoul."

The fool's laughter followed him. "Yea, go sleep on your pallet at his side, Raoul," he said. "Soon comes a day when there will be no place for you in William's chamber. 'I am for bed, wife,' will say William; and anon: 'Kennel, Raoul, kennel for you.'"

They both laughed at that, but the Duke's laughter changed quickly to a frown. In his cabin he flung himself down on the bed, and stared up at the swinging lantern with his hands crossed behind his head. "That last arrow was not aimed so ill," he said.

Raoul drew the leather curtain over the doorway. "I will go to kennel with a light heart," he promised.

"Yea, but when?" William's gaze flickered to his face, and back again to the lantern. "I am growing out of patience. Spine of God, I have been patient too long! I will have either yea or nay. We go to Flanders."

"As you will, seigneur, but you have not learned yet to take nay for an answer," grinned Raoul.

"I have not before had traffic with women," William retorted. "What do I know? What is the mind of that lovely sleek dame? What mean women when they smile sidelong yet speak fair cold words? Subtle work! Deep, secret! She is a citadel so fortified I lay siege in vain. Shall I wait on while the citadel is strengthened against me? I am too good a general." He started up from the bed, and began to pace up and down in a fret. "She is a still flame, remote, guarded, and desirable, Holy Sepulchre!"

"A still flame," repeated Raoul. He looked up. "And you, that other flame? Not still, I think."

"Nay, I burn. White witch! Willow-witch, so slender I might break her between my hands! It will come to that yet."

"Jesu!" Raoul was half-startled, half-amused. "Is that how you will use your love?"

"Love!" William caught at the word, dwelled on it, spurned it. "She is my love and my hate," he said sombrely. "I tell you I do not know if I love her. All I know is that she is mine. Mine, by the Rood, to hold in my arms if I will, locking my mouth to hers, or to break—yea, to hurt, to crush if that should be my will. She lures me, rebuffs me, daring my manhood. God on the Cross, but my bed has been cold to me these many days!"

80

Raoul watched his restless striding to and fro. "What news from Lanfranc, seigneur?"

"None! He writes to me of patience, and then patience. Heart of a man, I will have her in despite of them all!"

"Beau sire, I think the Archbishop will never yield. You may send Lanfranc to Rome, but whom has Mauger sent to whisper in the Pope's other ear?"

"Let Mauger look to himself!" the Duke said angrily. "I think I should do well to rid myself of that lecherous fox! Does he want my throne for his brother of Arques, or for Michael, his own by-blow?"

"Who knows? Beware him, beau sire! I have heard already a murmur of excommunication. How then would you stand?"

"By the Christ, as I stand now!" the Duke said, his anger flaring higher. "If Mauger thinks to find my hand gentle on him for the sake of our kinship he will learn to know me better yet. God knows I will be gentle while I may, but if he will have me for an enemy, why, so be it!" He unclasped his mantle, and cast it swirling from him. "My trust is in Lanfranc for that part of the business." The furious look was dispersed by a sudden smile that showed the boy still in him. "For the rest, my Raoul, I will trust in myself, and go to Flanders."

"Well said," Raoul agreed: "I will have a little wager with FitzOsbern on the outcome."

The Duke lay down on the bed again, propping his head on his hand. "You will certainly win, Raoul," he said with a laugh.

"As to that, beau sire, are you so sure which side I take?" Raoul murmured.

The Duke sat up with a jerk. "Now by my father's head, if you are to doubt me——!" he began, but broke off as he saw Raoul laughing at him. He flung himself down again on the skins. "Wager as you will: he who lays against me loses," he said, and shut his eyes for sleep. There was just enough defiance in his voice to tell one who knew him well that for once he was not certain of success.

CHAPTER II

Of the three hostages Edgar was the most bewildered by all he saw in Rouen, and gave the least sign of it. Wlnoth, with characteristic easiness, exclaimed at every novelty and quickly accustomed himself to the new life; Hakon blinked at a strange world but was too young to speculate upon it. Only Edgar remained an exile, lonely in the midst of a shifting mass of foreigners.

For long afterwards he was to remember how Rouen had first appeared to him, a lovely city against whose grey walls the Norman Court shone in splendour. In the Duke's Castle, no homely building of wood, but a vast stone palace, were high vaulted halls, and many arches ornamented with chevrons carved in relief. Edgar's home in Wessex was built all of wood; inside the walls were covered with crude paintings and curtains to hide the rough surface, so that the house seemed friendly and warm when one stepped into it. In the Duke's palace were also hangings of woven stuff, but they were different from the Saxon *wahrift*. They were made of stiff tapestry, cunningly embroidered, but though they might be rich with gold thread, or glowing with red and purple silks, they were never bright with a medley of sharp colours such as a Saxon loved. They were used to cover archways or to line bed-chambers, but where the master-masons had worked mouldings on the walls no hangings hid these from sight. Edgar would walk down long echoing galleries, and think he felt the chill of the stone in his flesh.

At table it was long before he ceased to look for the boiled meats his palate craved. He could not stay his stomach with the dishes Normans liked. He wanted to see haunches of English oxen roasted on the spits, and instead the servers displayed cranes farced with queer pungent spices; porpoises dressed with frumenty; rose-mortrews, an unsatisfying mess of powdered chicken and rose-leaves; jellies dyed with columbine flowers; unwholesome subtleties such as dolphins in foyle, marchpane garnished with figures of angels, and white leaches embellished with hawthorn leaves and red brambleberries. Even the boar's head, which was borne in with trumpeters going before, was spiced till he could barely recognize its true flavour. He ate of peacock, a royal dish, and esteemed it less than the stubble-goose; he watched the Duke's carvers lift swans, sauce capons, unlace conies, dismember herons, and wished that instead of serving such rare food as this they were breaking good venison, or slicing plain boiled sheep's flesh.

The meats were served on silver dishes; the salt-cellars were gilt within and without, standing sometimes a foot high, their covers encrusted with jewels; fine surnappes of linen out of Ypres covered the tables; wine was not poured into horns, but into gold cups, or glass vessels tinted amber and blue and red, with spidery threads laid on, or gouts blown in their smooth sides. Pages of the Diaper scurried hither and yon; seneschals, stewards, ushers, chamberlains saw to the comfort of the Court. There were chairs to sit upon, elaborately carved with griffins' and eagles' heads; foot-stools embroidered with lions or flowers; beds with straw mattresses, soft reindeer-skins for chalons, and curtains on rings that slid along rods. Even the palace windows were glazed with crystal or beryl. Edgar knew that in King Edward's palace at Westminster there were such windows, and in great Earls' houses too, but at Marwell shutters kept out too strong a wind, or panels of horn set in wooden calmes.

In Normandy men wore long tunics of rich cloth; each one had his squire and his pages to attend him, so that the palace teemed with all these people, and servants quarrelled and fought, and fell over one another in their numbers. Splendour, wealth: Edgar's heart cried out for the ruder life in his English home. These Normans lavished money on the ornamenting of their houses and their persons and their monasteries, but in England men set little store by stately buildings or costly plate so long as platters were piled high and drinking-horns brimmed over. From scorn at their extravagance he passed to wonder at their curious austerity. They were at once more violent and more temperate than the Saxons. A Saxon thought no ill of eating to satiation and drinking to stupor; a Norman who showed himself glutton or drunkard was regarded with contempt by his fellows. In England men were slow to anger, but in Normandy swords flashed out at a word, and enmity flared high upon small provocation. Where their hatreds and their ambitions were concerned the Normans were barbarous in their ruthlessness as no Saxon would have stooped to be, but whereas in England it was becoming less and less the fashion to love learning and give honour to the Church, in Normandy men were strict in all religious observances, and a mere knowledge of reading and writing was no longer considered sufficient for any man of degree.

It was all strange to Edgar, and desolatingly alien. Unlike Wlnoth, who in one week had his hair cut short and his tunic made longer in imitation of his hosts, Edgar obstinately preserved his flowing curls and his golden beard, and continued to walk abroad in a tunic that barely reached his knees. He was prepared to dislike every Norman he saw, and had no difficulty in finding many worthy of his scorn. There were those like Archbishop Mauger, licentious men, smooth-tongued, lapped in luxury; there were cruel intemperate men like the young Lord of Moulines-la-Marche, who tortured pages for his sport. But there were also men of De Gournay's kidney, shrewd and roughly faithful, who commanded respect; there were eager impetuous men like FitzOsbern; wise politic men such as Lanfranc; friendly men like Raoul de Harcourt and Gilbert d'Aufay, whom it was hard to withstand. Like bees about a hive they swarmed before Edgar's wondering eyes; great names echoed through the lofty palace: Tesson of Cingueliz; Saint-Sauveur; Giffard of Longueville; Robert, the Count of Mortain, half-brother to the Duke; Odo, his brother, who came now and again from Bayeux in espiscopal splendour; Robert, the Count of Eu, whose gay laugh contrasted oddly with his brother Busac's scowls; William Malet, part Norman, part Saxon; D'Albini, the sleek cup-bearer; Grantmesnil, Ferrières, Montgoméri, Montfort, Estouteville: on and on rolled the sum of names, bewildering, grandiloquent, all haut seigneurs, some with ambitions that made them dangerous, some with swords fretful in their scabbards, some arrogant, some quarrelsome, all splendid restless figures, plotting, grasping, shouldering their way through a world that seemed hardly large enough to contain them. Amid the blaze of magnificence they created the Duke stood out, a man of a hundred moods, wise as Lanfranc, or impetuous as FitzOsbern, but always sure of himself, seeing his path clear ahead of him. One could hate him, but it was not possible to despise him. Edgar, whose hands had lain between Earl Harold's, would never render to Duke William liking, but respect was forced from him against his will. This he must give, but while he gave he knew that William cared nothing for the applause or the condemnation of any man. There was cold steel in the Duke, he thought, and at once his mind winged to Harold, his dear lord, who carried a warm heart in his breast, and drew men to him whether they would or no. Maybe the greater man stood aloof, remote from the gentler human weaknesses: Edgar's love for Harold cried hotly *No* to that, but gradually as he came to know William a little chill fear stole into his loyalty. The Duke might have moods of gaiety, of unexpected kindness, but nothing would ever be allowed to stand between him and his purpose. Edgar suspected that he would go to any lengths to achieve his ends, sweeping aside all scruples, all mercy, while with a relentlessness that had in it something overwhelming, he bent or broke men to his own unbending and unbreakable will.

Yet he commanded devotion, devotion of such men as Raoul de Harcourt, who had coaxed Edgar into friendship. In a mood of sullen homesickness Edgar said: "You think he cares whether you give him allegiance. I am very sure they are nothing to him, either friendship or enmity."

Raoul laughed at him. "Oho, do you know him so well? I thought you were too proud to notice any Norman."

"You are pleased to mock at me, but you know that is not so," said Edgar, reddening.

"When you thrust your chin up under that fine beard of yours, of course I mock at you," Raoul answered. "I never knew there were such stiff-necked men in England."

Edgar grew redder still. "If I have lacked in courtesy, I crave pardon," he said.

"O Saxon barbarian, you grow more haughty still!"

Edgar's fist clenched. "You shall not call me that— Norman shaveling!"

"Shall I not? But you may call me shaveling with my good will."

Edgar sat down on a stool near the bench along which Raoul sprawled, and gave his head a rueful shake. "You seek me out to laugh at me, I believe," he said. "Or to make me lose my temper and behave like the barbarian you think me."

"Oh no, I have wagered with Gilbert d'Aufay that I will make you leave hating Normans, that is all," Raoul assured him.

"I don't hate Normans," Edgar said. "I told you that my mother was one. I don't understand them, and it is not very pleasant to be an exile in a strange land, but I am not such a fool that I would hate a man for not being a Saxon."

"Nobly said," Raoul applauded lazily. "Soon you will even like us."

Edgar looked down at him with a lurking smile. "When you will be serious I do like you, as you very well know," he said. "You, and Gilbert, and many others. You have shown me much kindness, for which I thank you."

Raoul saw Gilbert d'Aufay crossing the hall, and hailed him. "Gilbert, here is Edgar giving us thanks for our kindness. He is very proud to-day."

"He is always very proud," said d'Aufay, strolling towards them. "He told me I was an idle dog because I bade him go hawking with me this morning. They do not hawk in England, Raoul."

"Nay, I said no such thing!" protested Edgar. "We love sport as much as you do, and maybe more. But I was not in the humour for it."

Gilbert sat astride the end of Raoul's bench. "Well, there is to be a welcome end," he said. "We are leaving you for the while, from what I hear. Is it so, Raoul?"

Raoul nodded. "It is so. You are to be rid of us both, Edgar. The Duke is journeying into Flanders, and we go with him."

"I am sorry," Edgar said. "I shall miss you. Will it be for long?"

"Who knows?" Raoul said, with a shrug of his shoulders.

The slow smile crept into Edgar's eyes. "I suppose the Duke knows, and if any other does it is you," he said shrewdly.

"You see more than one would guess," chuckled Gilbert. "Of course he knows, but you will never prevail on him to tell."

"I don't know," said Raoul. "Do you think William our Duke tells his secrets to any man?" He glanced towards Edgar. "Perhaps we shall see Tostig, who, they say, is at Count Baldwin's Court."

Edgar gave a snort. "What is that to me?" he said. "I am no man of his."

"Oh?" Raoul's brows began to lift. "But you are Harold's man, are you not?"

"Harold is not Tostig," Edgar said curtly.

"I believe you dream of this Harold of yours," remarked Gilbert, with a sly look. "He is to you what his love is to another man." As Edgar made no reply to this, but only coloured up in the betraying way he had, Gilbert said innocently: "What is he like? Is he like Wlnoth?"

"Wlnoth!" Edgar exclaimed indignantly. "Harold is like no other man. If ever you see him you will know why it is folly to compare him with any one of his brothers." As though regretting his outburst he shut his lips on further speech, and only replied to Gilbert's teasing with a furious look under his brows. Raoul rose up from the bench in a minute or two, and moved away to the stairs, saying over his shoulder: "Come, Saxon, else you will be at poor Gilbert's throat."

Edgar followed him up the stairway into the gallery.

"You are too serious," Raoul said gently. "Gilbert means no harm."

"I know." Edgar leaned his big shoulders against one of the arches. His head was golden against the grey stone; his eyes very blue. "I am out of temper," he said. "I have seen Wlnoth habited like you Normans, and aping your manners, and it has made me angry, and sore—here." He touched his breast fleetingly.

"Why?" Raoul asked, looking down absently into the hall below them. "He is young, and he does not feel like you that we are his foes." He turned his head, and found Edgar's eyes steadily fixed on his face.

"Can you say that you are not our foes?" Edgar said in a low voice.

"Is that how you think of us?"

"Not you, no. Your Duke is my foe because I am Harold's man, and England's. I know why I am here, why Wlnoth is here, and Hakon. But you shall never hold Harold on such a rein as that."

Raoul did not reply. He was looking at Edgar in a rather startled way, wondering how much he knew, or guessed. Edgar had folded his arms across his massive chest; the hairs on them were pale gold, like his ringlets, and his crisp beard. "King Edward can will his throne away," he said, "but Duke William will only reach it across our dead."

His deep, rather rough voice echoed faintly round the stone gallery. A queer silence followed it, and over Raoul, like a sudden chill, stole a feeling of prescience. He saw Edgar at his feet, with his golden curls dabbled in blood, and his vigorous limbs sprawling and limp. He lifted his hand to his eyes, and covered them as though to shut out a dreadful vision.

"Why, what is it?" Edgar asked.

"Nothing." Raoul's hand fell. "I am not your foe, not England's. My desires lead not that way."

"No, but you will follow your master as I shall follow mine," said Edgar. "Perhaps you won't want what he wants, but I think that will make small difference. We have chosen, you and I, to follow two men from whom there can be no turning back." He seemed to shrug. "What are they, our little loves and hatreds? Do you call yourself my friend?

You will be swept from me to serve William's ends when the times comes."

"But friendship may endure," Raoul answered.

They walked slowly down the gallery, side by side. "I wish . . ." said Edgar, "I wish. . . ." He sighed, and gave his head a slight shake. "We don't know what roads we may have to tread before all is done," he said. "Come back soon from Flanders: I shall miss you."

At the end of the week the Duke left Rouen, and entered Flanders by way of Ponthieu. His brother, the Count of Mortain; Robert of Eu; and Roger de Montgoméri accompanied him. He made all speed to Lille, where the Flemish Court then lay, and was accorded a gracious welcome by my lord Count, and his lady. The Wise Count accepted the pretext advanced for this visit without so much as a quiver of the eyelids. He ordered his people to escort the Duke to a noble set of apartments, and left nothing undone that was due to so great a prince as Normandy. He sat for an hour with William, and talked smoothly of many matters that might be supposed to interest his guest. But no word of espousals crossed his lips. William tapped an impatient foot, but curbed his tongue. They parted with ceremony, and as soon as the door had shut behind the Count William struck his hands together to summon his valet. It was not his custom to pay much heed to the clothes he wore, so that his retinue looked sideways at each other when it was heard presently that three tunics had been rejected, and the barber cuffed for having grazed the Ducal chin. At the dinner-hour William went down to the hall in state, attended by his own household, and preceded by various punctilious Flemings. He had chosen to wear a long tunic of crimson cloth embroidered with gold. Round his black head he had a plain gold circlet, and the mantle of his high degree hung from his shoulders to his heels, and was secured across his chest by a large fibula of precious stones. Gold straps bound the loose hose to his legs, and where the short sleeves of his tunic ended he wore massive gold bracelets over the sturdy flesh. This magnificent style suited him very well. The Countess Adela, a Frenchwoman, looked on him with approval, and murmured in her daughter Judith's ear that Matilda would be a fool to pass over so splendid a prince.

The Court was gathered in idle groups in the hall, awaiting the noble guest's appearance. When he came round the bend of the stair, Count Baldwin went forward to meet him, taking his lady and his sons Robert and Baldwin with him.

As she held out her hand to the Duke the Countess observed with an inward smile how he shot a quick look round. He kissed her fingers, and asked leave to present the Counts of Mortain and Eu to her notice. The lively Countess made little of Mortain, an honest young man of few words, but she was pleased to allow the Count of Eu to lead her to the high table.

The Lady Judith came forward at her father's bidding, and made her reverence to the Duke. She sent William an inviting glance out of her large eyes, but met with no more response than an unsmiling bow. She had a habit of chuckling deep in her white throat whenever anything amused her, and she chuckled now. "Lord Duke, I am happy to see you here again," she said demurely.

The Duke thanked her, and having touched her hand with his lips, gave it back again, and turned to Count Baldwin, who was speaking to him.

Baldwin had beckoned to a lusty young man who was lolling against one of the chairs, and now made him known to the Duke. He was Tostig Godwineson, a man of William's own age. He came up with a swagger, and looked the Duke over with bold unabashed eyes. He had a florid complexion that flushed easily, and features that were handsome in despite of their irregularity. He looked to be something of a fire-eater, which indeed he was, and it was evident that he held himself in no small esteem. Count Baldwin informed William that he was lately become the betrothed of the Lady Judith.

William's eyes kindled. "Ha!" His hand shot out, and gripped Tostig's. "I wish you joy in your spousing, and pray mine own may not prove more laggard."

The Count stroked his beard at that, but said nothing. He led the Duke to an armed chair on his right hand, and looked down the hall to the curtained arch through which his other daughter had just come. The Duke's eyes followed the direction of his glance; those who watched him saw him stiffen like a hound at the leash, and lean forward in his chair as though he would leap up from it.

The Lady Matilda came slowly up the length of the hall, bearing the wine-cup of ceremony between her hands. Her gown was of green coster, with long hanging sleeves, and a train that brushed behind her over the rushes on the floor. Under a veil of green, bound on her brow by a jewelled fermaille, her hair gleamed palely gold, and hung in two braids almost to her knees. Her eyes were downcast to the cup she bore; her lips were red in the cream of her face, still and folded.

She came up to the high table, and to the Duke's side, and lifting the cup said in a voice that was like the ripple of a brook: "Be of health, lord Duke!" She raised her eyes and looked fleetingly at him. It was as though a green flame stabbed him. As she bent the knee, and put her lips to the cup, he rose quickly to his feet. A tremor shook her; she took a step backward from him, but recovering in a moment, held out the cup with only the faintest blush in her cheek to betray her sudden alarm. Her vision seemed to be obscured by a blaze of crimson and gold, and a dark face that drew her eyes against her will.

William took the cup from her. "Lady, I drink to you," he said in a voice that rang deeply in her ears. He turned the cup with a deliberate movement that was watched by many, and set his lips to the place where hers had sipped.

He drained the cup in the middle of a profound silence. All eyes were upon him, all but my lord Count's, who studied a salt-cellar on the table with an air of abstraction.

The Duke set down the cup, and held out his hand to the lady to lead her to the seat beside him. She laid her own in it, and as his powerful fingers closed over hers her eyelids fluttered. The silence broke. As though recalled to their manners those who had watched the little scene began to talk again, and looked towards the Duke no more than was seemly. For all the heed he paid to the others at his table he might have been sitting alone with Matilda in a desert. He was half-turned away from Count Baldwin, leaning his right arm along the carved wood of his chair, and trying to induce the Lady Matilda to talk to him.

She seemed strangely loth. She gave him yea or nay for the most part, and would by no means look at him.

Count Baldwin occupied himself between his dinner and Robert of Mortain, who sat opposite to him; Tostig leaned sprawling in his chair, and between courses fondled Judith's white hand. He drank deeply, and as time went on grew flushed and noisy. His boisterous laugh sounded above the hum of chatter more and more frequently; he began to call healths, and slopped some of the wine from his cup over his tunic.

"*Waes-hael*," he shouted, staggering to his feet. "*Drinkhael*, William of Normandy!"

William turned his head. A slightly contemptuous look

crossed his face when he saw how Tostig reeled, but he raised his cup in polite response, and drank the Saxon's health. Turning back to Matilda he said: "So Tostig has set the spousing-ring upon your sister's finger? Do you know why I have come again into Flanders?"

"My lord, I have small understanding of the affairs of state," Matilda said in a cool meek voice.

If she thought to turn him by such an answer she mistook her man. He smiled. "I have come rather upon an affair of the heart, lady," he said.

She could not resist the temptation of replying: "I had not supposed, my lord, that the Fighting Duke had interest in such matters."

"Before God," William said, "I think I have interest now in nothing else."

She bit her lip. Under cover of the table the Duke's hand closed suddenly over both of hers, crushing them in his hold. Her pulses leaped under his fingers; an angry colour mounted to her cheeks. The Duke's smile held a hint of satisfaction. "Ha, is there fire beneath your calm, my fair?" he said in a quick low voice. "Tell me, are you all ice, or does the blood run hot in your veins?"

She pulled her hands away. "If I burn it is for no man," she replied, looking at him disdainfully. His ardent gaze beat hers down; she turned her face away.

"By my head, you shall soon eat those words, lady!"

"Lord Duke," she said, "you speak to one who has lain already in the marriage-bed."

He cared nothing for that; she thought his laugh betrayed the base blood in him, and curled her lip at it. But he was to startle her yet. "Found you a man strong enough to break down your walls, O Guarded Heart?"

She looked up quickly, and her eyes seemed to search his face. With a shiver she folded her hands across her breast as though she made a barrier against him. "My walls stand firm, and shall stand so to the end, please God," she said.

"Do you fling down your gauntlet at my feet, lady? Are you a rebel proclaimed? What have you heard of me, you who call me the Fighting Duke?"

"I am no subject of yours, fair lord," she said. "If I am a walled citadel indeed, I lie beyond your borders."

"So, too, lay Domfront," William replied. "Domfront calls me master today." He paused; she found herself compelled to look at him. "As you shall do, Matilda," he said deliberately. "I pick up your gauntlet."

91

Her cheek flamed, but she judged it best to hold her peace. He might see that he had gone too far by the way she turned from him to bestow her attention on her brother Robert seated a few paces below her. If he did see it had now power to abash him. She felt his glance possessively upon her, and was glad when the banquet came to an end. She went upstairs to the bower with the Countess and her sister, and they saw how her eyes brooded, and how she stroked the thick rope of her hair in the way she had when she was put about. The Countess hesitated on the brink of speech, but in the end went away to her own chamber with no word said. The maids of honour sat down to their stitchery, but when one of them would have given her embroidery to Matilda she put it aside with an impatient gesture, and withdrew to the window, and began to draw patterns with her finger upon the horn-panels, wrapped in her crowding thoughts.

It was not long before Judith came to join her. She slipped her arm round Matilda's waist, saying with a comfortable laugh: "Fie, you are hot! What snug work made you at dinner, coney?"

"Bastard manners," Matilda said. The words dropped slowly, under her breath.

"Why, how nice you are become! It is a noble bastard, and will make you a handsome lover." Judith fondled her slender neck. "He looks at you as though he would devour you. A hound to pull down a white doe, Holy Sepulchre!"

Matilda stood still, suffering the caressing hand. "I am not for him."

"I think you will be glad of him ere many days," Judith prophesied.

"I have had my fill of lovers."

Judith chuckled and squeezed her. "You never had but one, child, and I misdoubt me he came not so near your heart." She paused. "For my part, I find Duke William hath more spice to him than ever had Gherbod. Nay, nay, he was cold, sweeting: there was no warming him; and you—Jesu, you are meat for a stronger stomach!"

Matilda did not answer, but stood looking at her sister, queerly intent.

"If the Pope will grant a dispensation," remarked Judith insinuatingly, "our father would be glad of the marriage, as I think. William is a haut prince."

"I give him thanks." Matilda lifted her head. "I am a daughter of Flanders, born in lawful wedlock," she said proudly.

"Eh, what is this?" Judith tapped her cheek. "Normandy is no meagre prize."

Matilda's eyes were narrow under the white lids. "The Bastard reaches too high, by my soul!" she said. "I have a King's daughter for my dam, no tanner's spawn!"

"He is Duke of Normandy," Judith said. "What matter?"

"What, is base blood to mingle with mine?" Matilda said. Her hand clenched on the silk of her gown. "I say no, and no!"

Judith looked strangely at her. "God give you courage, sister, for I think I have surprised the secret you nurse."

"Saints! I have courage enough to withstand the Norman wolf!"

"But to withstand your own desires, child?" Judith harboured her in her arms. "O storm-tossed! O hungry heart! You shall find no comfort until William has his way and yours with you."

If Judith had plumbed a secret, Matilda did not know, but she had fear for a bed-fellow that night, and for the many that succeeded it. William haunted her; she woke trembling from uneasy dreams, and thought she could feel his will engulfing her. Certain, he meant to have her. He showed it in a dozen ways, cat and mouse work, disturbing to a lady of spirit. She would, and she would not: God knew what the end would be. She sat up on her bed in the moonlight, hugging her knees, resting her chin on them, like the white witch he called her. Her hair was a cloud of spun gold, veiling her; her eyes remained fixed and blank, but behind them her brain wove and twisted its ploys. Guarded Heart! Citadel Remote! Her lips lifted in a slow considering smile. She turned the words over, liking them, doubting them. She would have been glad to have the Fighting Duke in thrall, but he was made of dangerous stuff, holding a stark demon in leash. She caught a glimpse of it now and then: enough to warn her she played a perilous game with one unused to the subtleties of such an affair. Base blood! burgher manners! She lifted her arm and observed a bruise like a shadow on the flesh. Her fingers touched it. Jesu, the man knew not his own strength! She shook her head at it, frowned in an assumption of anger, but ended by thinking no worse of him for his rough handling. If she kindled him to a blaze and was herself scorched she would not blame him for that. His fingers had crushed her soft flesh so that she had to stifle a cry of pain. She knew herself at his mercy, and could not be sure that he dealt in so gentle a virtue. Yet she could be calm before his brute strength; what fear she nursed she kept for the intangible power he held over her. It crept up to set her shivering in the fastness of her chamber, and stalked beside her even when he was furthest away. If she was already both wife and widow she had still borne a virgin heart until Normandy strode up her father's audience-hall, and bent his hard stare upon her. She had seen the darkness of his eyes lit suddenly by an inward glow; he looked his fill; she felt herself stripped naked before him while anger fought exultation in her. Guarded Heart! Citadel Remote! Ah, Rood of Christ, if it were so indeed!

She shook her head. O frailty of poor women! Setting her teeth she built up her barriers, planning the besieger's down-fall. There was food there for consideration; her chin sank to its resting-place on her bent knees again; the moonlight showed an elf-woman weaving her spells, motionless and rapt.

Hatred burned in her. Wolf of Normandy!—desperate, marauding, marking his prey. Mary Mother of God, give aid to bring him fawning to her feet!

His strong face glimmered in her mind's eye; the blood coursed through her veins, and on her arm the bruise throbbed warningly. She pressed her hands to her side as though she would still her heart's beating. O dread Fighting Duke, leave that yet unassailed!

So she prayed, wordlessly, but slept to dream herself a bride again.

CHAPTER III

The cat and mouse work went on; the man grew bolder, the woman more incomprehensible to herself and him. What the Wise Count made of it few could guess. He preserved a bland mien, considered the Duke out of the corners of his eyes, and talked of everything in the world but marriage. As for the lady, she folded her hands in her lap and bore all with the secret smile that cloaked her mystery. The Duke might have been warned by the glimmer in her eyes, but what did he know of women? Nothing, he swore: it was too sure.

Sweeping his hand down from her neck over the swell of her breasts to her waist, he cried hotly: "What, is this to be denied? Fie, you mistake the matter, lady: you are for a man, by my head!" He flung out his arms; his smile held passion that swayed her against her will. She escaped from him, but left him sure of victory. Her barriers were crumbling under a more rigorous attack than she had expected. A lesser lady at this stage would have gone tumbling into his arms; Count Baldwin's daughter had more beside her heart to guide her. If the Duke made a breach in her walls this served to throw fuel on the fire of her pride. She was outraged: backed in the last corner she would fight the more dangerously.

Judith, wrinkling her brow, murmured: "This is a brand that may burn your fingers, coney."

"I will bring him low." There was no more to be got from Matilda. She would bring him low. What, he was presumptuous? He should learn what gulf lay between the noble and the base-born.

Of this the Duke had no notion. Others may have guessed; one who knew with what whip the lady lashed up her enmity was Raoul, and he was indebted for his knowledge to the Lady Judith, who dropped lazy words in his ear, and chuckled to see him change colour.

"Madame," he said earnestly, "the Lady Matilda would do very well to beware how she touches on that matter. I speak with good advice."

"Well! I suppose he cannot eat her," Judith said comfortably. She saw that he was troubled, and considered it time to inform her sister how the hint had been received.

Raoul's words savoured enough of warning to whet Matilda's appetite for more. She presently became aware of him, and at a morning's hawking contrived that her palfrey should amble alongside big Verceray. She was sufficiently adroit to lead the talk into her chosen channels; after very little preamble she said with a faint smile: "Surely his friends, messire, would do well to advise the Duke to abandon his new quarry."

"Lady, the Duke is not advised," Raoul told her bluntly.

She sent him an appraising look up under her lashes. "He is besotted." She paused. "If I wed again the groom must be of birth as noble as mine own. I speak plainly because I perceive you to be very much in the Duke's confidence," she added, between haughtiness and the impulse of a girl panting to come at her goal.

He shook his head. Meeting her eyes he read something of her mind in them. He felt pity for her all at once, suspecting that she was torn between two passions, both great in her. "Lady, here is counsel," he said. "With respect I would say, do not use that weapon against my master. Your woman-hood, your high estate would not protect you from his anger."

She did not leave smiling; one would have thought the warning had almost set her purring.

"He is my liege-lord, and dear to me," Raoul went on, "but I have come to know his temper. Lady, I must say God help you if you unleash the devil in Normandy."

He meant well, but blundered. Such talk made Matilda lick her lips. To unleash the devil in a man was an ambition ever likely to appeal to her. Had he a devil? Eh, what woman could resist the temptation to see for herself?

At the end of a week the Duke withdrew to his own Frontier. From Eu he dispatched an embassage to Lille with formal proposals for Matilda's hand. The question of affinity went by the wind; not anything his councillors could say had the power to make him delay further. He chose Raoul for his envoy and would not by any means heed his gentle dissuasions. In desperation, Raoul said: "Beau sire, you will have Nay for an answer, and that is what you have not yet learned to take."

"Yea or nay, an answer I will have," William answered. "Heart of God, this siege has lasted over-long already! Go demand the keys of that citadel in my name!"

The embassage set forth upon the following day, and came in due course to Lille, where no doubt it was expected. The noble escort was received with all courtesy, and the envoys led in due season to Count Baldwin's audience-chamber.

Montgoméri accompanied Raoul; both went richly dressed, and as solemn as befitted the occasion.

The audience-chamber was filled by the Flemish nobles and councillors. At one end of the room the Count sat enthroned on a dais, with his lady beside him, and Matilda upon a stool at his left hand.

Raoul and Montgoméri came up the hall attended by their squires. They were accorded a suave welcome, but the Lady Matilda raised her meek eyelids for a moment and sent a straight look at Raoul that boded little good.

He came to his business at once, and recited the Duke's proposals to the silent Court.

He ceased, and a murmur rose, and died again. The Count stroked the miniver that edged his mantle, and spoke conventional phrases. He was sensible of the honour done his daughter, he said, but this was a question not to be decided without deliberation and good advice.

"The Duke my master, lord Count, believes you to have been aware of his mind these many days," Raoul said with a disarming smile.

The Count glanced towards his daughter. It was plain he was not at ease. He touched again on the problem of affinity, and seemed as though he would be glad to shelter behind it. Acting on his instructions Raoul pushed that barrier down.

"The Duke my master has very reasonable hopes, lord Count, that this hindrance may be overcome. It must be known to your puissance that the Prior of Bec is even now in Rome, and sends us comfortable tidings."

Count Baldwin thereupon embarked upon a speech of some length. The gist of it was that he would be pleased to ally his house with Normandy, but that his daughter, no longer a maiden to be disposed of at will, might feel some repugnance towards a second marriage, and must be allowed to give her own answer.

Perhaps only Raoul had an inkling of what she would say. Certainly the Count had none, nor his Countess, obviously taken by surprise.

The Lady Matilda rose slowly to her feet, and made a reverence to her father. Speaking in a cool, very audible voice, and with her hands clasped demurely together, she said, picking her words: "My liege and father, I thank you for your care of me. If it be your will that I should wed again be sure that I know my duty towards you, and will show myself obedient to your commands as befits my honour and yours." She paused. Watching her close, Raoul saw the smile lift the corners of her mouth, and was prepared for the worst. Veiling her eyes she said: "Yet let me beseech, you, beau sire, that you will bestow my hand upon one whose birth can match with mine, and not, for the sake of our honour, permit the blood of a daughter of Flanders to mingle with that of one who is basely descended from a race of burghers." She ended as coolly as she had begun, and making a second reverence went back to her stool and sat down, looking at her hands.

A stricken silence hung heavily over the company. There were startled looks, and men wondered how the Norman envoys would stomach this insult.

Montgoméri flushed, and took a step forward. "Rood of God, is this to be our answer?" he demanded.

Raoul intervened, addressing himself to Count Baldwin. "Lord Count, I dare not take such an answer back to my master," he said gravely. Surveying the Count's shocked face he came to the conclusion that the discourteous reply had been prepared without his knowledge. Curbing Montgoméri with a frown, he said: "My lord, I await Flander's reply to my master's proposals."

Count Baldwin availed himself of the loophole gratefully. He rose to his feet, and made the best of a bad business. "Messires," he said, "Flanders is sensible of the honour done her, and if she is obliged to decline it, it is with regret, believe me. We should be glad indeed to bestow our daughter in marriage on the Duke of Normandy, were it not for the repugnance the Lady Matilda feels towards a second marriage." So he began, and went on at length, smoothing away the insult. The envoys withdrew, one thoughtful, the other smouldering with indignation. What Count Baldwin said to his daughter is not known, but it is certain he sent for Raoul de Harcourt late that evening and was closeted with him alone for a full hour.

"By the Mass, Messire Raoul, this is a very ill business," the Count said, greatly perturbed.

"Pray God it may not be worse mended," agreed Raoul dryly.

This seemed poor consolation to a harassed man. "I call you to witness, messire, those discomfortable words were none of mine."

"Count," said Raoul smiling, "for my part I judge it best to forget what women say."

The Count was relieved, but Raoul added significantly: "There were others present beside myself, lord."

"Spine of God!" said the Count irritably, "there was never trouble yet but a woman made it!"

His daughter would no doubt have been flattered. Coming away from the Count's room presently Raoul stumbled against Matilda in the gallery. He put out his hand quickly to steady himself and her, and felt the throb of her pulse beating against his fingers. In the lantern-light her face was no more than a pale blurred oval, but he could see the green flame of her eyes. He held her wrist still, and she suffered him. She spoke in a whisper, staring up at him. "Carry my message safe, messire, I charge you."

"God aid, I shall do my best to forget it," answered Raoul. He put his hand on her shoulder. "Were you mad, lady, to speak such words? Is this to deal nobly? Heart of a man, you have cut a weary road for yourself."

Low laughter broke from her, lacking mirth. "Let him know how I think of him. I am not for him."

Raoul let her go. He did not understand her, but it seemed to him that something more than hatred inspired her. "God send your laughter change not to tears," he said.

He would have passed on but she slipped in front of him. "Bear my message," she repeated.

"Lady, I wish you too well. What folly rides you? What do you look for?"

She clasped her hands round her neck. "Maybe I am too much a woman to know." Her hands fell away; she stretched them out to Raoul. "Tell him I am guarded yet!" There was a note of challenge in her voice; she looked anxiously into his face.

"Lady, are you so sure?"

The arrow was shot at random, but seemed to find a mark. She drew back, and he heard the hiss of her breath indrawn between her teeth. He went to his own quarters, wondering at her, and afraid of her.

In a cooler mood Montgoméri had sense enough to see that what they had heard was not by any means fit for the Duke's ears. He agreed to keep silence, but harped continually on the insult all the way back to Eu. The first face Raoul saw there was that of Mabille, Montgoméri's wife, and he could have sworn aloud from vexation. Young as she was, this lady, daughter and heiress of Talvas, the exiled Lord of Belesme, had already made a name for herself as a spinner of mischief. Raoul was very sure that she would get what news she wanted out of Montgoméri.

The Duke received his envoys with a certain formality. Raoul gave him Baldwin's smooth answer, and watching keenly he could detect no change in William's face. The Duke said nothing for a moment or two, but presently, raising his eyes, he asked: "What said the Lady Matilda?"

Roger de Montgoméri showed himself ill at ease, and began to fidget. Raoul answered serenely: "She bade me tell you, beau sire, that she was guarded yet."

William gave a brief laugh. "Ha, brave words!" he frowned down at his clenched hands. "So!" he said thoughtfully. "So!" He looked up, and dismissed the envoys with a few curt words. Raoul went off with Gilbert d'Aufay on his arm; Roger, still embarrassed, drifted out to see his lady.

It was impossible to discover what Mabille had to gain by the part she played. Those who hated her, and there were many, swore that a natural fiend possessed her. However this may have been, she certainly got all his news out of Montgoméri, and lost no time in turning it to wanton account.

She sat on one side of the Duke at supper. There was some light talk passed between them; as the meal drew to a close, and wine had mellowed the company, Mabille, looking at him with a sparkle in her eyes, complimented the Duke upon his good spirits.

"Why not, lady?" he retorted.

Mabille had a voice that was like honey, sweet and insinuating. She said softly, leaning towards him: "Beau sire, what is she like, this cruel fair who is so hard to please?"

William showed signs of a gathering frown, but answered pleasantly enough. Mabille's hand slid along the arm of his chair; her eyes lifted slowly to his face; she whispered: "Dear seigneur, you bear her insults right princely." Her fingers brushed his sleeve: her lips were tremulous, her vision clouded; you would have sworn the woman to be all melting tenderness. "Ah, but how dared she?" She reared up her head, as though in quick indignation, but then drooped it again. "Pardon, seigneur! it was my loyalty spoke."

Across the table Montgoméri passed his tongue between his dry lips. He cast a glance towards Raoul, but Raoul was out of earshot.

William set down his cup with a snap. "Death in life, madame, what is this?" he demanded.

She appeared confused. "Beau sire, pardon! I have said too much," she faltered. She looked in a frightened way towards her lord, who was by now in a stew of apprehension.

The Duke took account of that look, as indeed he was meant to. "By the Face, I think you have said too much or too little!" he said. His eyes flashed to Montgoméri's face. They held some menace, but he shut his lips on further speech, and presently turned to bestow his attention on the Count of Eu. He left the board presently, apparently in good spirits, but if Montgoméri hoped to hear no more of the matter from him he was soon disappointed. A page brought a summons to him to attend the Duke in his chamber; he went off with a backward glance of reproach at his lady. She was smiling and content, a devil with the face of an angel, he thought with a stab of bitterness.

He found William alone, pacing the floor of his chamber. William crooked a beckoning finger. "Enter, my honest messenger, enter! What do you tell your lady that you keep hid from me?"

Montgoméri floundered into speech, lost himself in a flood of words, and begged the Duke to ask Raoul de Harcourt for the truth.

The Duke crashed his fist down on the table. "Splendour of God, Montgoméri, I am asking you!"

Montgoméri said unhappily: "Beau sire, the Lady Matilda spoke unadvisedly, as women will. We had our answer from the Count's puissance, as was faithfully reported to your Grace."

"Montgoméri, speak!" The Duke's voice made Montoméri start nervously.

"Beau sire, with respect I say that I was no more than the companion of the Chevalier de Harcourt. From his lips you should learn what chanced at Lille." He encountered a look that made him goggle, and added hastily: "Seigneur, if we did ill to withhold the Lady Matilda's words from your ears it was out of love for Your Grace, and because it was not felt by us that those words were meant for you to hear."

"By God and His Mother, Montoméri, I think you did very ill when you told your lady what you dared not tell to me," said the Duke terribly.

With this the unhappy man felt himself to be in full accord. He stood straight, and said with what dignity he could muster: "I am at your mercy, beau sire."

The Duke replied: "Let me have the truth without more ado."

"Beau sire, the Lady Matilda said that she would obey her father in all things, but she prayed him, if he would bestow her hand in marriage, to choose for her a groom whose—who was—— Seigneur, the Lady Matilda used certain words concerning your Grace's birth which I dared not repeat."

"I think you had better repeat them, Montoméri," said the Duke in a still voice that was like the lull before a storm.

Looking at the ground, Montoméri said: "The Lady Matilda desired her father not to give her in marriage to one who was not born in wedlock, beau sire."

"Ha, God! Was there no more than this?"

His first indignation rose up again in Montoméri. "Yea, there was more," he said, forgetting caution. "The lady used very injurious terms towards you, lord, and dared to say her blood should not mingle with that of one who was basely descended from a race of burghers."

Raoul entered the room in time to hear these unwise words. Even as he shut the door he knew that it was too late to attempt to soothe or to palliate. Montoméri, in obedience to a signal from him, escaped thankfully, and made up his mind to stomach in silence his low-spoken: "Go, prating fool!"

Raoul set his back to the door, and listened with calm deference to the first outburst of William's rage. At at convenient moment he said: "Montgoméri told his tale ill. It is true she spoke those words, but she spoke them out of a woman's desire to wound what she maybe likes too well for her heart's peace. I believe you would do wisely to ignore her."

"Bowels of God, I will make her repent in tears of blood!" William swore. "Ah, proud widow! Ah, insolent dame!" He began his restless pacing again. "She will not have me for a lover. Then, by the Cross, she shall taste of my enmity!" He stopped short by the window, and stared out at the sailing moon. His fingers gripped the stone ledge; he laughed suddenly, and turning, said: "I am for Lille. If you ride with me, come! If you choose to stay, bid my page Errand saddle his horse."

"My thanks, beau sire. I think I will ride with you. But to what avail?"

"The Lady Matilda has misread me," the Duke said grimly. "She sent such a message as one might send to a nithing, a man of no weight. Well, I will school her."

More he would not say, nor could he be turned from his resolve to set out at once for Lille. Seriously alarmed, Raoul went off to bespeak the horses and to drop a word in the Count of Eu's ear. He hoped that half an hour's reflection might bring about some change in William, but was disappointed. When he saw him again the Duke seemed cool enough, but would listen to no entreaty, either from Raoul or from his cousin of Eu. Robert was between laughing and scowling, but knew his lord well enough to be sure no words spoken of man would turn him when he had that look in his face. He feared some foolhardy act of daring which the Duke had not yet outgrown, and exchanging a rueful glance with Raoul, he ventured to suggest that an armed escort should accompany William. This was refused with a scornful snap of the fingers. William flung himself into the saddle, and rode off at a gallop.

"Soul of a virgin, I fear him!" ejaculated Count Robert. "The devil is loose, Raoul!"

Raoul gathered up Verceray's bridle in his hand, and grinned. "Give us God-speed on this—love-quest!" he said, and vaulting into the saddle, galloped off in the Duke's wake.

There was no tarrying upon the journey. Ground that had taken the embassage two days to cover the Duke covered in a night. He stopped only once, at dawn, to change horses at a certain place on the road. He would rest nowhere; what food he ate was eaten standing, and in haste. He said little, but the nearer he got to Lille, the more impatient he grew. Raoul, aching with fatigue, was shaken by a fit of silent laughter. He was too tired to wonder any longer how the Duke meant to approach Count Baldwin's daughter, but he felt that William was in no state to present himself at the elegant court. Travel-stained, powdered with dust, he looked more like a hasty messenger than a ruling prince, but it was of no use to point this out to him. Raoul was not even surprised when he dashed headlong through the narrow streets of Lille to the palace gates, and through them without a check.

At the entrance to the great hall the Duke was recognized. A startled page gaped at him, and called to his fellows. Several people came hurrying up as William swung himself down from the saddle, and there was much bowing, and many tentative, apprehensive inquiries, and offers of escort to a bedchamber. The Duke thrust all these aside with no ceremony at all. He told Raoul to hold his horse. "What I have to do here will not keep me long," he said, and strode past the polite gentlemen into the palace.

There were some six or seven men in the hall awaiting the supper-hour. Tostig called out: "Bones of God, it is Normandy! What is your haste, Duke William?"

One of the Flemish nobles sprang up, and began to say that the Count and his sons were expected to return from a hawking at any moment. He broke off in the middle of this, for it was plain that the Duke was not listening. He clanked through the hall, and was gone up the narrow stair before anyone had time to do more than rub his eyes. It was seen that he wore his sword at his side, and carried a whip in his right hand.

In consternation the Flemings stared at one another. It seemed to them that the Norman Duke had gone moon-mad.

In the bower Matilda was seated on a cushion, working at a fine altar-cloth. The Lady Judith had the other end of it, and both fair heads were bent over the embroidery. Round them were gathered several maidens, all busy with some form of stitchery or another. There was a hum of talk which broke off suddenly as the door at the end of the room was flung open. Needles were stayed in mid-air; six startled faces were turned towards the door, and six pairs of eyes grew round with wonder.

William stood on the threshold, an incongruous figure in

the scented bower. Perceiving the look in his eyes, one of the maidens clasped her neighbour with a frightened whimper.

It seemed to Matilda that speech was impossible. Some leaping emotion choked her; it might have been fear, or it might have been triumph. She saw how the dust lay thick on the Duke's boots and mantle, how his face was pale and lined with the fatigue of hard riding, and the shadow of a small exultant smile touched her lips.

"Why, what is this?" said Judith. Amusement quivered in her voice. She got up, and moved forward a step, glancing from the Duke to her sister's still face.

The Duke stalked towards Matilda. She sat like a statue, watching him. He bent (she thought he swooped) and jerked her to her feet, holding her wrists in a grip that made her catch her breath. "Your message reached me safe," he said. "I am come to answer you."

"Eh, heart of Christ!" cried Judith, who guessed what was coming.

One of the maidens saw the lash of the Duke's whip shaken free, and began to cry. Matilda's lips moved stiffly: "You dare not!"

"Yea, madame, I dare," William said. For the first time she saw that smile he had which was like a snarl. "I have had men's limbs lopped off for the very insult you cast at me, proud widow." He pulled her into the middle of the chamber. "I will spare your limbs, madame, but by God, your sides shall smart!"

The maids were in a flutter, some staring as though they hardly understood, one sobbing for very horror, and all of them huddled together as far from this dreadful invader as was possible. The whip sang through the air; the girl who was sobbing hid her face, and winced every time she heard the wicked crack of the lash.

The Lady Judith had recovered her composure. When William raised his whip-hand she slid quickly to the door, and set her back to it with her hands flat on the dark wood, as though she would keep it shut. The eldest of the bower-maidens, aghast at seeing her mistress so brutally flogged, would have run out to summon help, but recoiled before Judith.

"Fool, do you want all the Court to know how the Lady Matilda was whipped?" Judith said scornfully. "Let be, let be! she will not thank you for screeching her hurts to the world."

Matilda was sobbing, but she had her underlip gripped

hard between her teeth, and would not allow more than a little moan to escape her. Her dress was torn, and her hair dishevelled; William's fingers were crushing her wrists till the bones ached. His merciless arm was stayed at last; her knees gave way under her as the last blow fell. He threw his whip aside, and caught her round the waist, holding her against him breast to breast. "Madame, you scorned me," he said, "but by God, you will never forget me!" His hold tightened; his left hand let go her wrists and forced up her drooping head. Before she knew what next was to come, he had kissed her full on her parted lips. She gave a little moan at that. He laughed suddenly and harshly, flung her from him, and swept round on his heel. She fell half-fainting to the ground, and lay there.

There was an urgent beating on the door; voices were heard in agitated conference outside. "Open!" William ordered.

Judith looked at him curiously. Her slow smile dawned; she bent the knee. "By my faith, William of Normandy, you are a brave man," she said, and moved from before the door, and pulled it wide.

An exclamation broke from the foremost of those on the threshold. Swords scraped in their scabbards; there arose a babel of indigation. The Duke showed his teeth, and stalked forward rather like a beast of prey about to make his spring. The gentleman fell back involuntarily before him. His eyes ran over them; he made no movement to come at his sword; he even set his hands carelessly on his hips. "Well, my masters?" he said sardonically. "Well?"

They were irresolute, but fidgeted with their daggers. They looked at one another, and lastly at Judith. Judith laughed, and said: "O want-wits! Stand aside: this is not for you."

"Holy God, lady . . . !" one began in a stutter.

"The Lady Matilda!" another gasped out.

A third started forward, hot words bubbling on his tongue. "Beau sire, you have done very ill, by the Blood! Not your Grace's high estate, not——"

"Foh!" said William. His hand fell on the indignant gentleman's shoulder, and twisted him out of the way. It was plain he held them all to be of no account. His look commanded; without quite knowing why they did so the gentlemen made room for him to pass, and out he went, very much the better man.

Raoul was waiting anxiously in the bailey. He drew a sigh of relief when he saw the Duke come through the door, but a second later caught a glimpse of angry faces behind William, and wondered whether it was to be a matter for swords after all. Apparently it was not. The Duke took the bridle in his hand, and leaped into the saddle. He became aware of the men who had followed him, and suddenly laughed.

This was not to be borne, not even from Normandy. A couple of men sprang forward to grasp at the Duke's rein; Raoul pulled his sword half out of the scabbard.

The Duke continued to be amused. "No, my friends, I think not!" he said, and drove in his spurs. His horse plunged forward, snorting; one man jumped clear, the other was knocked sprawling. The Duke was away before anyone could move; the clatter of hooves resounded on the paved ground, and grew fainter in the distance, till it became no more than an echo.

In the bower her ladies flew to succour Matilda, with little crooning noises, and fluttering hands. She was looking at the bruises on her wrists; they were alarmed to see her so rapt and still. Judith drove them out, slamming the door upon their protests. She came back to Matilda, and knelt by her. "Child, you would not be warned," she said.

Matilda's lips twisted into the semblance of a smile. "Do you pity me, Judith?"

"Not I, sweetheart. You have come by your deserts."

Matilda straightened her body with a grimace of pain. "What did they do to him?" she asked.

"Why, what should they do to such an one as he?"

"Nothing," said Matilda. "But they might have slain him. I wonder, did he think of that?" She lifted her hands and considered her bruises again. Her calm broke; she cast herself on Judith's breast, crying piteously: "Ah, ah, he has hurt me, Judith!"

CHAPTER IV

There was an air of expectancy about the Norman Court for many days after the Duke's flying visit to Lille. The tale of his doings there leaked out, and was whispered in various garbled versions from one man to another. But no man thought fit to mention it to the Duke himself. Some confidently prophesied that Count Baldwin's cartel of war would come, but these were proved to be wrong. No one knew what Count Baldwin said or thought when he returned from that fateful day's hawking and found his daughter bruised and prostrate, and his Court seething with impotent fury. Whatever his feelings he was not the man to allow these to thrust him unwarily into hostilities. He was a powerful prince, and no craven, but he quite definitely did not want to go to war with his Norman neighbour. "There is one man in the world," said Count Baldwin, "who has the art of war at his finger-ends, and that man is Duke William. I have said enough."

His nobles considered that he took Normandy's daring too meekly; the Lady Matilda nursed her sore sides, and spoke no word; Count Baldwin wrote careful letters to the Duke in Rouen, and digested his answers with a thoughtful eye. He judged it politic to tell his daughter she was a ruined woman. She propped her chin in her hands, and looked at him without apparent dismay.

"Matilda," said her father, "what prince will pick up that which Normandy has mauled? By the Saints, you were best in a nunnery, it seems to me."

Matilda said: "What prince would dare stretch a hand towards that which Normandy covets?"

"You mistake the matter, girl," said Count Baldwin. "Normandy has done with you."

"Nay, he will know no peace until I lie in his bed," answered Matilda.

"This is forward talk," frowned the Count, and left it at that.

In Rouen it was thought that the Duke must have abandoned all thought of marriage with the Flemish lady, but Lanfranc was not recalled from Rome. Archbishop Mauger, eating dulcets in his palace, spent a long hour of meditation upon this, and contrived to send word to his brother, the Count of Arques, who was, by reason of the ducal garrison about him, virtually a prisoner in his own wind-swept castle. Mauger was uncertain of the Duke's mind but he feared the tenacity of his nature.

Upon the ride back to Eu the Duke had said with a confident ring in his voice: "I shall have her yet, but by God's eyes she shall find no softness in me!"

"If that is the mind you are in," had answered Raoul tartly, "it seems to me you had best look for a bride you can love, and forget the Lady Matilda."

The Duke said: "I have sworn to have Matilda, and none other. Either for love or for hatred she is mine."

"A difficult conquest, William," was all Raoul would say. "Trust me, I shall conquer," the Duke replied.

That was the only mention he made of Matilda for many a day. He had other matters to occupy his thoughts, and upon his return to Rouen he plunged into an orgy of work, thrusting the marriage question to the back of his mind. Civil and ecclesiastical reforms held him busy for the rest of the year, drawing some groans from his hard-driven barons, and from Edgar, Thegn of Marwell, a grudging admiration. Edgar said slowly: "Yea, I see he is indeed a ruler. I thought him only a man of blood."

Gilbert d'Aufay, to whom this was addressed, laughed, and inquired what had provoked the tribute. They were seated by one of the upper windows of the palace at Rouen, which looked over the Seine to the Forest of Quévilly beyond. With his eyes on the far trees Edgar replied; "These new laws, the way he uses with men who are dangerous to his Duchy. He is very crafty; very politic."

"You have been watching him close, my Saxon," said Gilbert.

Edgar hunched his shoulder; a shadow flitted across his blue eyes. "What have I to do now but watch other men's deeds?" he said rather bitterly.

"I thought you were content enough," said Gilbert.

"Not content. Never that," Edgar answered. He saw that Gilbert looked a little hurt, and added: "Rest you, I do very well, and maybe I am no longer so grievously exiled since I have your friendship, and Raoul's."

"And others too from what I hear. But it is always Raoul with you." Gilbert cocked up a quizzical eyebrow. "You make a brother of him, do you not? Do you understand each other so well?"

"Yes," said Edgar uncommunicatively. He lifted a corner of his mantle, and drew it across his knees. "I never had a brother," he said. "I have just one sister Elfrida." He stifled a sigh. "She was a little maid when I left her, but I doubt she will have grown now."

"Maybe you will be free to return to England ere many months," Gilbert said, in an awkward attempt to console a homesickness he could plainly see.

"Maybe," replied Edgar, expressionless.

But gradually the desire for England was growing less in him. It was impossible to live for so long in Normandy without beginning to feel himself at home there. He had made friends; unwillingly he was interested in the affairs of the Duchy. A little sadly he thought that he was becoming like Wlnoth, a Normanized Englishman, and when Busac's rebellion broke upon Normandy he forgot he was a Saxon and a hostage; he only knew that he had stayed for so long in the Norman Court, and entered so often into talk that was all of the Duchy's weal that an attempt to overset the Duke's peace made him as indignant as his hosts. He saw the messenger arrive covered with dust, and an hour later met Raoul in one of the galleries of the great palace. Raoul said: "Have you heard what has chanced? William Busac has invested the Castle of Eu against the Duke."

"Who marches against him?" Edgar asked eagerly. "Will it be the Lord of Longueville, or the Duke himself? I would I might go too."

"Oh, the Duke himself," Raoul answered, carefully ignoring the last part of Edgar's speech.

They walked on down the gallery together, discussing the affair, wondering which barons were likely to join Busac, and which of them would be against him, until suddenly Edgar realized that he was talking as though he too were a Norman, and broke off, feeling himself neither Norman nor Saxon, but for the moment only a young man who wanted to ride to war with this other young man, his friend.

The Duke made short work of Busac, hotly assisted by the rebel's brothers: Robert, who had rashly entrusted the Castle of Eu to his care, and Hugh, Abbot of Luxeuil, who journeyed expressly to Rouen to urge the Duke to take strong measures. This was superfluous advice; the Duke had already departed for Eu, where, after the shortest of sieges, he took the Castle by storm, imposed penalties upon the quaking garrison, and sent Busac into banishment. It was soon heard that Busac had sought refuge in the King of France's Court, and had been received with kindness. That was significant enough; the King was beginning to show his hostility towards Duke William.

Busac's rebellion was one of many signs of unrest. With Val-es-dunes fading into a four-year-old memory Normandy began to lift up her head again. The Duchy was not wholly William's yet, and well he knew it. The greater part of his nobles might be with him, the serfs and burghers were his to a man, since he gave them rigid justice, but there were still those who preferred the old lawless way of life. In various districts brigandage was rife, private quarrels were settled by burning and death, and grasping barons seized what they could whenever they thought the Duke's back safely turned.

His hand was heavy on those who overset his peace, but throughout the second year of Edgar's exile tiny disturbances, like the scum bubbling in a simmering pot, occurred continually. It might be no more than the raiding of a neighbour's land; once it was a murder at a wedding-feast; once a band of brigands who made fifty miles of country unsafe for honest men to live in, but whether it was murder or brigandage it was always a sign of unrest, skilfully and secretly fomented by the man who lay so low at Arques.

Nearly a year after the happenings at Lille it was heard that Earl Godwine had joined forces with his son Harold. Next it was heard that King Edward had been pleased to inlaw Godwine and both his sons, and to bestow on Tostig, lately wedded to his Judith, the vacant Earldom of Northumbria. There came a new light into Edgar's eyes; even Normanized Wlnoth boasted that King Edward dared not oppose his kindred. Duke William appeared to bestow no more than a fleeting attention on the news, but in the seclusion of his chamber he struck his hand down on the table, and said in open exasperation: "God's death, was there ever so great a nithing as Edward?" He thrust his hand in Raoul's arm. "None, I am very sure, but you need not say that I said so."

Earl Godwine was not long to survive his reinstatement. In the spring of the New Year word came of his death, and a strange tale was brought by the merchants from England. It was said that the hand of God had struck Earl Godwine down at the King's board. He had called to his son Harold to bring him wine at the feast which was to mark his reconciliation with Edward. As he approached, bearing the drinking-cup, Harold almost fell, with a foot caught in some obstacle. Throwing out his right leg he recovered his balance, whereupon the Earl, in great spirits, quoted an old proverb: "One brother helps the other." King Edward, not so elated, said gloomily: "Ah, so would my brother Alfred have helped me had he lived, Earl Godwine."

The Earl had heard more than enough of Alfred's death. It was not his custom to pay any heed to the charge so often flung at his head, but upon this occasion he had drunk enough to make him resent the King's words. Breaking off a piece of wastel bread, he looked Edward angrily in the face, and said in a loud voice: "O King, if I had aught to do with Alfred's death, may this morsel of bread choke me!" With that he boldly thrust the bread into his mouth, was taken by a kind of seizure, very dreadful to behold, and fell down with foam on his lips and the bread stuck tight in his throat. An hour later he was a dead man, and King Edward was shaking his head in a way that showed he was not at all surprised.

But all this interesting news from England, even the growing power of Harold, could not keep the Duke's attention for long. He was busy with the breaking of his fierce colt Normandy.

Trouble drew him to the unquiet Côtentin; while he lay once more at Valognes a messenger reached him on an all but foundered horse, tumbled from the saddle, and delivered a sealed package into his hands.

The Duke was on the point of setting out with Saint-Sauveur upon a journey still further to the west. He was armed and cloaked; a straining squire held his horse; his knights were gathered around him. He slit the package with his dagger, and spread out the frail sheets of cotton paper.

FitzOsbern covered two pages with his account of disaster. No sooner had the Duke crossed the Vire than the prisoner at Arques struck at the safety of Normandy. He had won over the garrison set about him, and was now master of the Castle, and rapidly reducing the surrounding land of Tallou to a state of miserable slavery.

The Duke's face darkened; he let a great oath, and crumpled the letter in his hand. Néel de Saint-Sauveur asked anxiously what had befallen, and was told in a few words. The Duke tossed the crumpled letter to him; he spread out the sheets and read them, while the others gathered in the courtyard whispered together, and wondered what would come of it.

The Duke had taken Malet's bridle from the lad who held it, and before the Viscount of Côtentin had finished reading the Seneschal's message he was in the saddle, his horse sidling and dancing in a fret to be off. "Now I shall see which of you is ready!" quoth the Duke. "Now I shall see who will follow me! To Arques, messires!" He gave Malet his head, and the black horse sprang forward. Men jumped quickly out of reach of the plunging hooves; the Duke was away.

Upwards of fifty men streamed after him; six only were still with him at the end of that nightmare journey. They rode from Valognes to Bayeux, their numbers dwindling. At Bayeux the Duke had a brief interview with his young half-brother, the Bishop, and was off again in an hour. His knights followed him doggedly, knowing that his haste was not wanton. Reinforcements might even now have joined the Count of Arques, and if the jealous King of France were marching to his aid, as rumour whispered, the Duke's only hope of staving off a bloody campaign was to reach Arques before him.

They passed by Caen, and rode on towards Pont Audémar. There Gilbert d'Aufay dropped out upon a foundered horse.

"Eh, Gilbert, are you done?" Raoul called to him.

"A curse on this brute; he can no more," Gilbert answered. "Who rides still with William?"

"Néel is here, with two of his men; de Montfort holds close; the Viscount of Avranchin; myself, and some others yet: maybe a score. If I tarry I shall never catch William this side Seine."

"Go then. If I can come by a horse I will follow you." Gilbert waved him on, and began to rub his aching limbs.

At Caudebec Raoul's horse sank under him. The Duke rested his little troop by the river bank, and got news from a scout of a loyal band of three hundred men who had sallied forth to oppose the Count of Arques. Raoul was sent off to the capital with a message for FitzOsbern, and Saint-Sauveur rode beside him a little way at a walking pace. "Go with God," he said, smiling. "I will play the Watcher for once, ill though you may like it."

Raoul shook his head. "Nay, there is no more strength in me," he confessed. "I am done, and must have failed in another hour. Do not leave him, Chef de Faucon, for by this hand I tell you he will not pause though every man of you falls out upon the road."

"You have no need to fear me," the Viscount promised, and rode back to rejoin William.

Fording the river the Duke pushed on as hastily as he could to Baons-le-Comte, and from there towards Arques, crossing a ravaged countryside.

Within a league of Arques he came up with the force that had set out to guard his interests. Their leader was struck dumb at sight of his liege-lord, whom he thought to be in the Côtentin, and for a while could not find his tongue.

"Come, man!" the Duke said impatiently. "Do not stare at me as though you saw a wolf! What news of my uncle of Arques?"

Honest Herluin of Bondeville recovered his speech and his manners. "Lord, pardon! I had not thought to see you ere many days."

"That is very possible," replied the Duke, "but you see me now, and in some haste for your news, by the Face!"

Taking this broad hint, Herluin plunged into a recital of the disasters of Tallou. His scouts had found the Count so strongly supported that he thought it would be folly to attack him with no more than three hundred men. Many lords had joined Arques; their doings made scandalous telling. "Beau sire," said Herluin earnestly, "I pray you draw back upon Rouen till you may gather a sufficient force against these rebels. We are but a handful, and should be cut to pieces."

"Do you think so?" said the Duke. "With your leave, good Herluin, I will put myself at the head of your men, and try a fall with my rebels."

"Lord, lord, I dare not let you venture!" Herluin said in great alarm.

"Do you think you can stop me? I am very sure you were better advised not to try." The Duke smote him on the shoulder. "What, are you faint-hearted? I tell you, if once the rebels see me face to face they will never dare stand against me."

"Lord, we have had tidings of a great company out upon their affairs, and we held off from them since we are so few."

"Ha, this is good news!" the Duke declared. He swung himself down from his weary horse. "A horse, man!" His eye alighted on a bay mare that pleased him; he tapped her rider's knee with his whip. "Off with you, my friend!" he commanded pleasantly, and off the man got, wondering how he should fare afoot. The Duke did not concern himself with this. Mounting, he proceeded to make certain changes in the disposition of his small army. The six men who had kept up with him all the way from Valognes formed themselves about him in a bodyguard, and the troop moved forward at a brisk pace, and came soon on to the marshy flats that lay between the high ground of Arques and the sea.

These flats were commanded by a narrow spit of land near the junction of the Eaulne and the Varenne, upon which the Castle, like a bird's nest, was perched. To the left rose the chalk hills that guarded the coast; to the right, in the distance, a thick forest climbed the heights of Arques.

The Castle was mounted on a precipitous hill, and was further protected by a deep fosse dug at its foot. There was only one path up the slope, and this led to a second ditch dug round the Castle walls.

When the Duke came in sight of the place Count William's followers were on their way home from a day's plunder. Their meinie looked formidable, bristling with spears; Richard, the Viscount of Avranchin, who was related to the Duke through his marriage with William's half-sister, exchanged a rather rueful glance with Néel, and murmured something to the Duke that had to do with caution.

For answer William took his lance from the squire who carried it. "Brother Richard," said he, "I know very well what I am about. When these men see that I am here in person there will soon be an end to the affair." He gave the order to charge, and the troop hurled itself forwards over the flat ground to the foot of the Castle hill.

Count William's men were taken by surprise, and hampered by their plunder, but they managed to fling themselves into a hasty formation. Néel de Saint-Sauveur set up a shout of: "The Duke! the Duke!" which was taken up by a score of voices. In a full-throated roar Herluin's men fell upon the rebels.

The rebel leaders heard Néel's cry, and a moment later realized that the Duke was indeed at the head of the band. The word ran through their lines; men caught glimpses of a helmet ringed by a golden circlet, and panic seized them. If the Duke, who should have been at the other end of Normandy, had swept through the country to deal with Arques in person, the rebels had no stomach for battle. Their leaders could not rally them: they knew what manner of warrior William was. Before the shock of his charge they fell back, and in the space of a few minutes, discarding their plunder, they were flying to safety up the hill-path to the Castle.

The Duke stormed after them, right to the very gates of the donjon. A desperate skirmish was fought there, and it seemed for a little while as though William would force his way through. Reinforcements from within beat him back, and managed to draw up the bridge. Missiles were hurled from the walls; Néel de Saint-Sauveur grasped at the Duke's bridle, and dragged him out of range.

"Holy God, beau sire!" goggled Herluin, pop-eyed, "they fled like deer before the lerce-hounds!"

"Look you, my friend," said the Duke, "I am a general, which is a thing you appear to find marvellous."

"Beau sire, I do perceive it," said Herluin, and rode soberly back with him down the hill.

The Duke was joined soon after by an army led by Walter Giffard of Longueville, and those in the hold of Arques watched with uneasiness preparations for a blockade. The Count of Arques bit his lip, but when his captains quailed he

114

gave a short bark of laughter, and promised them relief from the French King.

This relief King Henry indeed tried to bring him, but he had planned to join forces with Count William before the arrival of the Duke. He marched over the Frontier, bearing in his train the Count's father-in-law, Hugh, Count of Ponthieu, and he seized the border castle of Moulins in Hiesmes, and gave it into the care of Count Guy-Geoffrey of Gascony. No man saying him nay, he pressed on towards Arques, and hearing what had already befallen there kept a weather-eye cocked for Duke William. Had he but known it his vassal was otherwise, holding in check those allies who would have been glad to join Count William. "Let Henry strike the first blow," the Duke said. "I have not renounced the simple-homage I owe him."

The King pushed on, gaining confidence as no sign came from William. He learned that Walter Giffard, and not the Duke, was in charge of the blockade at Arques, and rubbed his hands, and promised he would make a quick end. The end was quick indeed, but hardly in the manner King Henry planned. He unfortunately fell into an ambush laid for him at St. Aubin, and although he escaped with his life he lost there the greater part of his force, including the hapless Count of Ponthieu, who was slain before his eyes. He judged it time to retreat, and made the best of his way back to France what time Duke William, having had word brought him of the seizure of Moulins, returned to the siege. King Henry realized with annoyance that by his too hasty snatch at the Duke's property he had released his vassal from the feudal obligations William had hitherto held in such punctilious respect. So King Henry went home to plan Normandy's ruin, and the Count of Arques, knowing his nephew, offered terms of surrender.

Some of his followers demurred, maintaining that the Castle could withstand a siege of many months. The Count said in a kind of weary despair: "We allowed William to cut us off from France, and with the craven King's retreat died our hope. Do you not know William yet?" He struck his hands together, fuming at himself. "Heart of Christ, when he lay in his cradle, jesting I said to Robert, his father: 'We shall have to look to ourselves when he is grown.' True, O God! true! Would that I had strangled him in those early days, for by Death he has baulked me since at every turn! I am a ruined man." He drew his cloak over his face, and sat glooming.

"We may yet defeat him," one of his friends said stoutly. "Do you lose heart so easily, Count?"

The Count raised his head, and answered very bitterly: "O fool, I know when I have missed my mark. I thought to take William unawares, and failed. I am beaten, and do not need to be starved into miserable submission before I will own it. I struck a blow that glanced aside from William's shield. There is no striking twice at him." His voice shook with his grief. Controlling it, he said: "I must make terms with him. He is not a vengeful man." His head sank on to his hands. "Ah, bones of God!" he muttered in great anguish of spirit, "I was a fool to trust the French King! I might have succeeded else!"

He sent a herald to William bearing a message couched in meek terms, asking only safety of life and limb for himself and his men. It was a politic move, however his friends may have disliked it. He had weighed the Duke's character nicely: William would have used any means to force his uncle to surrender, but when he had achieved his end, and his foe owned himself beaten, all his pitiless enmity left him. Those who reviled him for a tyrant were much at fault; saving only when you roused the devil in Normandy he was never one to wreak vengeance on a beaten man. He granted the terms demanded at once, and when the gates of Arques were opened to him, rode in with his knights, and called his uncle privately to his presence.

Count William came unarmed and alone, a proud man wretchedly humbled. When he found the Duke unattended he knew that William meant to spare him an added humiliation, and he bit his lip, realizing his nephew's clemency, and hating him for it.

"William my uncle," said the Duke abruptly, looking him over, "you have done very ill by me, and it is time and more that an end was put to your affair."

The Count of Arques smiled. "Do you complain, nephew?" he asked. "You stand master in my Castle, and hold still the throne that might have been mine—*faux naistre!*"

"As to that," said the Duke frankly, "if I am bastard-born you at least dare not hurl that in my face. Have I no cause to complain of you, you who swore allegiance to me at my birth?"

The Count gave him back look for look. "By God, William, I would have ruined you if God had willed it so!" he said.

The Duke smiled. "This is to deal honestly at last. I know

116

it: you have been mine enemy these many days. What dealings had you with the old Count of Mortain whom I banished? Had you traffic with the Hammer of Anjou?"

"Men of straw both, like Henry of France," the Count said coolly. "I should have done better alone."

"Yea, you would have done better." He sent the Count a quick, appraising look, not unfriendly. "You have set many boulders in my path, my uncle, and I think this marks the end of our dealings."

The Count said with a flash of arrogance: "Not Guy of Burgundy, nor Martel, nor even France has been so dangerous a foe to you as I, William."

"Nay, for you are of my blood, and we are strong men, we who spring from Duke Rollo," William agreed. "But you will never succeed against me."

The Count moved away to the window, and stood looking out from the heights over grey miles of windswept country. A gull, wheeling in its flight, soared past the window, uttering a cry that sounded mournful in the stillness. There were clouds veiling the sun, and in the distance the trees bent before a strong wind. The Count's gaze rested on them without seeing them. "By the Host, I do not know how it is you stand here alive to-day," he said, half to William, half to himself. "You should have perished long since: you have had enemies enough." He looked over his shoulder, and saw the Duke smiling in the sardonic way he had. The smile spoke his belief in himself. The Count curbed a spasm of anger, and said evenly: "There was some talk of prophecies made at your birth, and of strange dreams visiting your mother. I never set much store by that; no, nor even thought to find myself—thus—before you." He made a gesture with his hand, and let it fall again to his side. "You were born under a fortunate star, William."

"I was trained in a stark school," the Duke replied. "Many have snatched at my heritage, you not the least of them, but no man shall take from me what I hold."

Silence descended upon them. With an oddly detached interest William of Arques looked across the room at his nephew, pondering him. "But of other men's holdings—eh, I wonder what you will snatch before the sands of life run out in you?" he said. His eyes dwelled long on the Duke's face. "Yea, I was a fool to venture," he said. "What now?"

"I take back Arques," William said.

The Count nodded. "Have you a cage prepared for me?" he inquired.

"No," said William. "You are free to go where you will."

The Count gave a cynical laugh. "Had I been the victor I would have shackled you fast, William."

"You would have been wise," answered the Duke grimly.

"Have you no fear that what I have failed to do now I may attempt again?" asked the Count.

"Nay; I have no fear," William answered.

"You strip me of my lands and bid me stay in Normandy. I thank you, William."

"I neither bid you stay or go. You are free to do as you will. I am Duke of Normandy, but you are still my uncle," William said in a gentler voice.

The Count heard him in silence, and in silence paced the room for a long time. A chill of defeat stole over him; he felt old suddenly and very tired. Glancing at the Duke's powerful frame he became aware of a dull resentment that ached in his breast. William was right: he would never wrest Normandy from him now. He was nearing the end of life, with his ambitions unfulfilled, and a curious lassitude taking their place: William had not yet reached his prime; life lay before him, ready to be conquered, as he would conquer it. A shiver ran through the Count; his jealousy surged up in him, jealousy of the other's youth and strength and mastery. He straightened his shoulders with an effort, and came close to the table beside which William stood patiently watching him. "I shall never live at peace with you, William," he said. "Give me leave to depart out of Normandy."

The Duke nodded. "I think you have chosen wisely," he said. "Normandy will not hold us both."

The Count gathered his mantle about him. "You are merciful," he said, "but I do not give you thanks." He went out with a heavy tread, and the sound of his footsteps died gradually away down the stone corridor.

CHAPTER V

News of all these happenings reached Flanders in due course, but for some time after the grim work at Lille no word was spoken at Count Baldwin's Court of the violent Duke of Normandy. Matilda saw her sister put into the marriage-bed, and later waved farewell to her when she set forth for England with her lord. "God's grace, I would not wed such an one as that!" she murmured, with her eyes on Tostig's florid countenance.

The Countess Adela said tartly: "Rest you, you will end your days a widow still, my girl."

Matilda folded her hands. "Madame, I shall be content to have it so."

"Do not take that tone with me, daughter," the Countess answered. "I am very well aware of your mind."

Matilda slid away from her, saying nothing, keeping her glance lowered. She guarded silence these days: poets hymned her frozen mystery; a quantity of bad verse extolled her witch's eyes. She listened to such effusions with just that faint smile on her lips that drove men wild to possess her. A minstrel of Franch spilled passionate songs at her feet, and turned pale for hopeless love of her; she let him kiss her hand, but she could not have said whether he had blue eyes or brown. She pitied the poor wretch, but while he sang to her she thought of her fierce lover William, and wondered, and turned in her mind this way and that. The poet went sadly away; after some days the Lady Matilda missed him, but when she was told that he had gone to the Court of Boulogne she said only: "Oh!" without surprise or regret.

A wandering chapman brought her the first news out of Normandy. Twice a year he made his journey from Rennes, through France and Normandy, over the border into Ponthieu, on to Boulogne, and then slowly north to Flanders. His long baggage-train of sumpters entered Brussels later in the year than was usual; he had fine cloths, and cunningly wrought jewels in golden settings; fancies from the East; trinkets out of Spain; enamel of Limoges, but he would not show his merchandise to the eager ladies of the town till the great ones at the Palace had picked them over. He spread embroideries before the Countess and her daughter; the bower-maidens cried out in admiration, but Matilda lifted a fold of the stiff cloth, and let it fall again. "Bah, I can do better with mine own needle!" she said.

The Countess chose some of his wares, and bade him seek out her Chamberlain for payment. She went away, and the chapman showed Matilda mirrors of silver with enamelled backs, cases of filigree to hold a lady's comb; two-pronged forks to use at meat; jars of precious perfume out of Araby. She turned them over with her white fingers while he told her what had taken this noble lady's fancy, or provoked that one's envy.

"What do the ladies buy in Normandy?" she asked.

He was voluble; his talk led him into snippets of scandal, slyly told; and from there to larger issues was no great step. "Normandy is unquiet, lady, and the roads not safe yet for an honest merchant. I lost two sumpters in Hiesmes, and had one of my rogues done to death by the robbers. But the Duke will amend all yet." He twitched a carpet from his pack and spread it out. "Lady, this I kept for you to see. Two I had when I set out from Rennes, but one the Duke's grace purchased. He would have taken the other, I believe, but I withheld it." He began to point out the worth of the carpet, but she interrupted him with a question: did Duke William set much store by such things?

Ah, but he was a very noble prince; he required always the best, and would pay for it without demur, unlike some others one might name, if discretion permitted. The Count of Boulogne now——! the sentence was ended by a shrug and a grimace. It was not thus with Duke William, harder to please, but no haggler over the just price. This year, alack, he had had poor fortune with him, for he was busy with his affairs. "They loom great, lady, I promise you."

Out tumbled the tale of Busac's revolt. She drank it in with parted lips; her bosom stirred with the leap of her heart. "He conquered?" she said faintly.

"Be sure, lady. He is too swift for his enemies. A great prince, a wise and terrible lord. Gracious lady, deign to look upon these turquoises, fine stones each one, fit for a queen to wear."

She made some purchases, dismissed him then and sat on into the dusk, her brain busy with his news. From the sound of it Duke William had put her from his mind while he grappled larger problems. She could fancy him in one of his storms of energy, intent only upon the affair of the moment, deliberately setting other matters aside. She cupped her chin in her hands. Would he remember her when his sterner work was done? The doubt teased her; she could find no answer to it, and stirred uncomfortably. He must remember it, remember even though he never saw her face again.

The months passed. Word came from Judith in bleak Northumbria, but no word came from Normandy. Under her outward calm Matilda was in a fret of impatience. She had hugged the conviction that William would assail her barriers again, and planned her defence and his undoing. He held off still: was it to make her yearn for him, or did he no longer desire her?

The chapman came again; she panted for his news, and

had cold comfort. The Duke had been in a jovial mood when the chapman saw him; he had bought jewels made for a woman's adornment. The chapman cocked a knowing eyebrow: bridals in the air, one might suppose. Closely questioned, he could tell little. It was thought in Normandy that the Duke meant to take a wife; some names were hazarded, but who could tell which fair lady would be the fortunate one?

Matilda showed a white hungry face. Her maidens found her in an unblinking stare, with her eyes wide as a cat's, and they were afraid, for when she looked just so she was most dangerous. But she paid no heed to them, and very soon recovered her calm. There was nothing to tell them of the turmoil raging in her breast. While she might still fancy William yearning for her she could rest content; talk of his marriage was like a whip-lash flicking the instinct of possession in her. She curled her fingers like claws; if she had him here now! if she could but come at the fair unknown! She was very sure she hated them both, and in a hidden fever waited with ears on the prick for fresh tidings out of Normandy.

The year passed. If the Duke kept silence to punish her, he was succeeding in his aim. Uncertainty kept her wakeful at nights; she was sharp with her maidens, impatient with those elegant courtiers who sang her praises. There was one, a noble Fleming, who laid his heart at her feet; she smiled upon him, and he fell on his knees to kiss the hem of her gown, calling her Frozen Princess. Exalted, Unattainable! She looked at him, and saw instead William's hawk-eyes, and thereafter was done with the poor man. Eh, this was no way of love, to grovel at a woman's feet, lost in a poet's ecstasy! A man should fight for what he desired; seize and not supplicate; hold fast, not stand in awed worship. The luckless suitor was dismissed; it is doubtful whether she thought of him again once he had left her presence.

The next news that came out of Normandy had nothing to do with marriage, but with warfare and conquest. Count Baldwin, hearing of the doings at Arques, of the French King's discomfiture, of Count Guy-Geoffrey's flight from Moulins before ever the Duke arrived there to recover his property, stroked his beard a long while, and said slowly: "Here is a man, the only one I have known, who can rule his destiny. My daughter, you did very ill for yourself when you spurned William of Normandy."

She made him no answer, but listened attentively to all the

talk of the Duke's achievement that was running round the Court. It was asserted by those who knew something of Normandy that the Count of Arques had been William's most dangerous enemy for some years back. Men demonstrated to one another what must have happened if the Duke had not reached Arques before King Henry, or if he had failed to send the Count's band flying back to their stronghold. Count Baldwin, hearing all these speculations, said dryly: "Messires, there are two men in Christendom today who deal not in that uncertain word *if*. One is Duke William; the other is myself."

Rebuked, his courtiers fell silent. Count Baldwin looked pensively out upon a vista of placid fields. "We shall hear more of Normandy," he remarked. He brought his gaze away from the window, and benevolently surveyed his Court. "Yea, much more," he said. "Val-es-dunes, Meulan, Alençon, Domfront and Arques: he will be growing puffed-up, I fear me. Here are no defeats, nay, not one." He shook his head sadly.

His son, Robert the Frisian, said with a significant smile: "Do you think that King Henry will be content with this encounter, lord?"

"I doubt it, I doubt it," Count Baldwin sighed.

"I shall own myself surprised if we do not soon see France sweep into Normandy to take a bloody vengeance."

"You are a man of foresight, my son," said the Count humbly.

From what they could hear in Flanders thereafter it seemed that the blow that had cleaved William of Arques from his allies had gone a fair way to settle the unrest in Normandy. Desultory news of politic measures—the strict enforcement of the Truce of God, the banishment of some malcontents, and the elevation of tried men—drifted to Brussels through various channels, and showed one anxious lady how detached from her Duke William had become. She saw him striding on to great deeds, leaving her behind him, swept always forward on the tide of his own energy. At once she stretched her hands to delay him, to have him catch her up and bear her with him into his tremendous future. She shook with her overpowering impulse to call him back to her; the Guarded Heart was quivering and defenceless, for Duke William had made her afraid at last, as one is afraid of the unknown.

Matters were coming to a fine pass with her. She strained her ears to catch the last rumour of his marriage. His silence conquered her; she had now little hope. Schooling herself to meet the expected tidings of his betrothal with decent composure, she was shaken like a leaf to learn of the arrival in Brussels of a Norman embassage.

She was sent for to her father's presence, and went with a deliberate step, and a face that told nothing of her inward tumult.

Count Baldwin said bluntly: "Look you, my daughter, Messire Raoul de Harcourt is here once more, with various haut seigneurs at his side, and proposals to put before me. I am advised he comes upon the business of two years back, which is a matter to astonish one, holy saints!" He eyed his daughter with uneasy severity. "I hold by my word, Mald," he said. "I will put no force upon you to thrust you to a second marriage, but as you value your skin and my honour let no discourteous words pass your lips this day!"

"What must I say?" she asked faintly.

"Nay, you should know your own heart," he pointed out.

"Before God, I do not," she answered.

Count Baldwin studied her awhile in silence. "You have had two years to learn it, my girl," he said dryly.

Her fingers picked at the braid of her hair. "Give me an hour yet, my lord," she said.

"My child," said the Count frankly, "you may have till the envoys come before me, and you shall then give them and me your answer, for, by the living God, I am not to be your mouthpiece a second time!"

She withdrew, but had not long to wait before she was sent for to Count Baldwin's audience-chamber.

Walking with a pounding heart but slow measured steps up the length of the hall, she was aware of strange faces turned towards her, watching her close. Her fingers gripped together in the folds of her silk *bliaut;* she sent a secret look up under her white lids and saw Raoul de Harcourt regarding her with an anxious frown. A knowledge of power swept over her; her lips trembled into a smile. This it was to be desired. She passed on to her place beside her father's throne, and sat down.

Count Baldwin addressed her without waste of words. As though the offer had never before been made and rudely rejected, he informed her that Duke William had sent to make proposals for her hand. She scarcely heard him; her mind was busy with its desperate problem. Snatches of what the Count was saying intruded into her thoughts. He spoke of a dispensation: she caught a glimpse of parchment scrolls; he

123

mentioned a form of penance: she understood she must build a monastery if she would wed Duke William, and looked at her father in an unseeing way that made him wonder what was in her mind.

His voice ceased. Matilda sat straight on her stool, holding her hands clasped tightly in her lap. The silence was so profound it seemed to hang over the hall like a doom. The Lady Matilda knew that they were waiting, all these people, for her answer, and she could think of nothing to say.

She passed the tip of her tongue between her lips. Staring down at her hands, she was fascinated by the faint tracing of blue veins just visible beneath the skin. A burgher's son, a tanner's by-blow! She saw that the silk of her gown was crumpled where her fingers had clenched it, and smoothed it absently. Yea, but if she denied herself a second time would she ever behold his face again? She could not be sure that she wanted to behold it; if she closed her eyes she could still see the heavy frown he had bent on her at their last stern meeting. A stark lover, a dread bridegroom! There was a fleck of white on one of her smooth nails; she considered it, absorbed in it. Guarded Heart! Citadel Remote! Colour crept up under her skin; she thought she could feel a two-year-old bruise throb on her arm. Let him go? She feared him, hated him; she was not for him.

Count Baldwin spoke. "My daughter, we await your answer."

She heard her own voice uttering amazing words. "Beau sire, it pleases me well," faltered the Lady Matilda.

She knew little of what happened after that. She saw Raoul later, alone, and he kissed her hand, and promised her a fair end. She looked blankly at him. Perceiving her bewilderment, he said: "Lady, be not dismayed. You will find great joy in this union."

There was a gentle look in his eyes that comforted her alarm. She said in a low voice: "Messire, I do not know why I said what I did. I am afraid."

"Madame, put such thoughts away from you. If you have seen the stern side of my master you shall soon see another very different mood in him. Have you no message to give me for him?"

"No," she said. "What message have I from him?"

"No words, lady, but this." Raoul opened his hand, and let her see the massive ring that lay in his palm. "This he bade me set upon your finger in his name, but I would not until I might see you alone, for it seemed to me you were put about, below in the hall, too hardly pressed, maybe." A smile lit his eyes. "Come, lady: it is his own."

She let him take her hand. She saw that the lions of Normandy were wrought on the ring; as it slid over her knuckle a shiver ran through her as though she felt some lingering retention of the Duke's power clinging to the golden circlet in the way a subtle perfume might cling to a discarded glove. She said, trembling: "It is too great for me, too heavy."

Raoul laughed. "Madame, I will tell Duke William that he sent you a ring that fits your finger very ill."

"Yea, tell him that, messire," she said.

She did not seen the envoys again. In the morning they were gone, and all that remained to tell of their visit was a man's ring that weighed heavy on a lady's shrinking finger.

In a very short space the bower-maidens were busy with bride-clothes. Tongues wagged over flying needles, and the Countess Adela tossed over piles of linen and sendal. As for Matilda, she felt that matters had slipped beyond her control. She sat apart, hedged by her reserve, twisting Duke William's ring.

She had thought he could come to Brussels in person, but he sent only the customary gifts and stilted letters writ in Latin, and signed *"Ego Willelmus cognomine Bastardus."* Scrutinizing the signature she flushed, wondering whether he inscribed himself thus to taunt her. She learned later that he used no other signature, and laughed involuntarily, thinking that it was like him to cast his birth in men's teeth so fearlessly. No other signs came from him; since he held himself coldly remote she must suppose his passion to have burned itself out. Her pride was whipped up by his attitude, and when at length the bridal party set forth for the Norman border, her litter carried a guarded lady, cool and perilous, holding herself in hand.

The Duke had sent an escort to fetch his bride to Eu, where the marriage was to take place. Peeping between the curtains of her litter, the Lady Matilda saw a blaze of mantles, a glitter of steel. Count Baldwin's cortège was cast in the shade by the splendour of the Norman cavalcade. The Lady Matilda blinked at the lavishness of her escort, almost purred at it. Cold he might wish to appear, but Duke William was displaying magnificence to his lady as a peacock might spread his feathers to impress his mate.

At Eu a great company met them. Matilda kept her face veiled and preserved a meek demeanour, but for all she did not seem to raise her eyes overmuch there was nothing escaped her. The Castle was alive with a multitude of noble lords with their ladies; with knights and stewards, pages, valets, ushers. Matilda's head swam; she was thankful when they led her to the apartments set aside for her.

There her own maidens, looking askance on the grand ladies appointed by the Duke to wait upon their mistress, bathed and dressed her in readiness for her first meeting with the groom. She suffered them to robe her as they chose. She looked out of the narrow windows upon a landscape grey in the dusk, and thought how bleak and grim was Normandy.

She was led down to supper by the Countess Adela, who had come to her chamber to be sure the tirewomen had done well by her daughter. The Countess conversed pleasantly with the Norman dames; her light voice sounded sinister to Matilda, sick with a leaping apprehension.

They walked along endless galleries from whose tapestried walls stitched faces looked down at Matilda. The Countess led her daughter by the hand; before and behind them went the ladies in procession, their trains rustling over the stone floor.

It seemed to Matilda that the vast banqueting hall was lit by a thousand candles. The little flames dazzled her; she could see only their yellow tongues as she passed up the hall to the dais set under the high windows, at the end. She mounted the dais; she heard her father's voice, and then a deeper than his which made her start under a stab of recognition. Her hand was given into a strong hold, which for all its strength was not quite steady; her blurred sight perceived vaguely the Duke's face as he bent to kiss her fingers. He spoke a formal phrase or two, and almost immediately let go her hand. She sat beside him at table, but it was FitzOsbern, upon her other side, who talked to her. The Duke seemed to be much occupied with Count Baldwin and his lady; when he addressed Matilda he spoke as he might speak to a stranger, yet he could not keep his eyes from her face.

Under this treatment she began to recover. Her sight cleared, she observed all that went on very intently, and was gracious to FitzOsbern, coolly self-possessed towards the Duke. She noticed that she was served off golden plate, and had rare dishes offered her. She partook of them sparingly, drank little, and soon retired with her mother and her train of attendants.

The Countess was delighted with Eu, and looked forward

126

to the visit to Rouen, with all its promised festivities, which was to follow the marriage. She approved the Duke's magnificence, and wished Matilda joy of a noble suitor.

Matilda lay lost in a great bed all hung about with stiff curtains, and said quietly: "I am well content, madame." She watched her mother go out, and wondered what the Duke's coldness betokened. It was long before she slept, and then her slumber was uneasy, and she woke many times in the night, troubled by frightful dreams.

Upon the following day she did not set eyes on the Duke until she was bound to him in wedlock in the cathedral church of Notre Dame of Eu. Her father escorted her in procession between ranks of staring people who had all flocked to Eu to witness the bridal. She was dressed in a long robe encrusted with jewels, with a train of many ells, carried by her bride-maidens. When she entered the church her eyes sought and found William, awaiting her by the altar steps, attended by his half-brother of Mortain, and other lords whom she did not know. He was dressed in purple and gold, armed, with his sword at his side, and a coronet round his helmet. His mantle streamed back from his shoulders and touched the ground behind him; it was lined with gold that shimmered whenever he moved.

Odo, the young Bishop of Bayeux, performed the ceremony, assisted by the Bishops of Coutances and Lisieux. In despite of the fact that she was a widow, and no maiden, four knights held a veil over Matilda's head.

After the marriage-vows were exchanged, and the blessing bestowed, and the wedded pair crowned with flowers, there was a banquet held at the Castle, with miming, and tumbling, and minstrels playing sweet music. A muzzled bear was led round on a chain with a monkey bestriding it; it walked on its hind-legs, and performed a shuffling dance to the sound of a tambour. Then a party of tumblers ran in, both men and women, and a minstrel sang a laudatory ode to the Duchess, accompanied by a harp and a cornicinus which set a flourish to the end of every line.

Since cock-crow the Count of Eu's servants had been busy slinging garlands of flowers from beam to beam; fresh rushes strewed the floor, subtleties which had taken the master-cooks three days to prepare were arranged on all the tables. They were not meant to be eaten, but to be admired. Some were dyed red with alkanet; others were covered with gilt leaves beneath sprays of silver. On the high table the bridal cake stood before the Duchess, crowned in allusion to the desired issue of the marriage with the figure of a woman in childbirth. A peacock in full plumage stood in the place of honour; no one looking at the ordered feathers could suppose that under them the bird was roasted and carved ready for serving.

A boar's head lying in a field and hedged round with roses was carried in shoulder-high to mark the beginning of the banquet; a scroll depended from its mouth, bearing a poem in praise of the pride. A Viand Royal followed it, venison in broth, and a subtlety that drew cries of appreciation from the Duke's guests. The cooks had fashioned the emblems of Flanders and Normandy in foyle, and linked them together with a seal which bore the inscription: "Be all joyous at this feast, and pray for the Duke and the Duchess and all theirs."

Pages were kept busy running to and fro with flagons of wine; men hailed the Duchess in a shout, and a hundred cups and more were raised to her. She sat on a throne beside the Duke, and smiled, and spoke mechanical words, and ever and again stole a sidelong look at the unyielding profile beside her. Once, feeling her gaze upon him, William turned his head, and looked down at her. There was a glitter in his eyes, the hint of a fierce, triumphant smile. "I have you now, wife," he said between his teeth.

She looked away, feeling the colour flood her cheeks. Had he married her with revenge in his heart? Was love dead in him? Mother of God, have pity if he looked like that!

She spurred up her fainting courage. Count Robert of Eu was speaking to her.

"Lady," he said, "how did it happen that you were brought to consent to a marriage with my cousin when he had so brutally used you?"

On her mettle, she replied lightly: "Why, Count, it seemed to me that he must be a man of great courage and high daring who could venture to come and beat me in my own father's palace, and therefore a fitting mate for me."

"Well said, cousin!" he applauded.

She glanced up to find the Duke looking at her. He had heard her answer to Count Robert, and there was a look in his eyes that might have been admiration. His hand moved as though to clasp her, but was checked, and gripped the arm of his chair instead. Her spirits rose; she believed she could read him at last. With a liveliness that made her new subjects like her at once, she went on talking to the Count of Eu, and to Robert of Mortain, who sat staring at her in undisguised appreciation.

The banquet lasted many hours, and the company grew merry. At last, with laughter and with jesting, the women surrounded Matilda and bore her off to the bridal chamber. She went smiling; the last sight she had of the hall was of many light-hearted gentlemen lifting their cups in a health to her, and of William standing by his chair, watching her under his black brows.

They undressed her, and laid aside the heavy bridal robes; they unbound the glory of her pale hair and combed it till it hung about her in a shining veil. She was put into the Duke's bed with whisperings and fondlings. Voices were heard outside, and the tread of footsteps. The ladies clustered to the door, and threw it wide to admit the bridegroom. He was escorted by a laughing company of his friends; at the door they left him; the ladies went out; and the door was shut behind the Duke.

The voices grew fainter; the footsteps retreated in the distance. The Duke stood for a moment, staring at his bride in pent silence. There was a blazing light at the back of his eyes; his mouth was set hard, as though he curbed himself. He came across the room to the bedside. "So, madame wife!" he said on a gloating note. "How stand your barriers now?"

Her eyes glimmered. All desire for revenge on him had left her. Smiling, she said: "My lord, have you taken me for love or for hatred? I would know."

He folded his arms across his chest, shutting himself in. "I have taken you because I swore to have you, madame, because I do not fail. I will break you to my hand until you learn to know me for your master, by God!"

She slipped from under the ermine skins that covered her, and stood before him, slim and white against the dark bedhangings. "I think you have no joy in this conquest, husband," she said, holding his eyes with her own. "My barriers are down, but can you reach my guarded heart?"

She was so close to him she thought she could almost feel the struggle that raged in him. He grasped her shoulders through the golden mesh of her hair. "God's death, Mald, I have sworn you shall find no softness in me!" he said unsteadily.

She said nothing; her smile lured his heart from his breast.

He snatched her up into his arms, holding her cruelly close, kissing her eyelids and her lips till she gasped for breath. She yielded to him, her ice melted, her body aflame. Half swooning on the tide of his passion, she heard him whisper: "Eh, I love you! Heart of Christ, there is no more than that, my dear desire!"

THE MIGHT OF FRANCE

"The French have braved our chivalry: let them deplore the venture."
Speech of the Norman Herald.

CHAPTER I

When Hubert de Harcourt saw his son enter the Castle of
Beaumont-le-Roger he had a sudden impression that Raoul
had grown in stature, yet when he looked more closely and
saw him stand beside his tall brothers he perceived that he
had been mistaken, and wondered how this could have happened.

Roger de Beaumont—he who had helped Raoul to the
Duke's service seven years before—greeted him with great
kindness today, and brought him into the hall with a hand on
his shoulder, so that Hubert feared Raoul would be growing
puffed up in his own conceit. But just then Raoul saw his
father, and he went towards him at once, and knelt to get his
blessing as meekly as you please, smiling up at him with that
unshadowed sweetness in his eyes which always made Hubert
think he saw his dead wife live again in her son. Hubert felt a
surge of tenderness rise up in him as he laid his hand on
Raoul's neat head, but he did not show this. He said something in a gruff voice about Raoul's scarlet mantle, calling it
a popinjay's cloak, but all the same, he was pleased to think
that his son wore even more splendid raiment than young
Richard de Bienfaite, who had been summoned from his
neighbouring lands to meet him. As Raoul rose up from his
knees Hubert shot a look past him, and observed with satisfaction that he had come to Beaumont-le-Roger with as
dignified an escort as befitted the Duke's envoy.

Everyone knew why Raoul had come into the Evrecin
bearing the Duke's mandate. For weeks past the crows had
been quarrelling in the tall trees round Harcourt, and even
without this omen of war all Normandy had known since the
siege of Arques that the French King was planning an inva-

sion to lay Duke William low. Chapmen and vagrants out of France brought news of great preparations afoot there, and although no one could be certain how strong a force the King was mustering, everyone had heard rumours that even princes in Gascony, and Auvergne had joined him. Far from being alarmed the barons were proud to know that Normandy's might had inspired her neighbours with such jealousy; they asked nothing better than to meet all these haut princes in battle, so that when, presently, Raoul made the Duke's plans known to them looks of dismay were exchanged, and expressions of frank disgust.

Raoul sat at the head of the long council-table with Roger de Beaumont beside him, and the other seigneurs of the Evrecin seated in two rows below them. He gave Roger the Duke's letter, but Roger was a poor scholar, having passed his youth in forays rather than in learning, and he suggested, to all the older men's relief, that Raoul should read the letter aloud to them, and be done with it. So Raoul opened the packet, and showed them the Duke's seal, at which they nodded wisely, and read slowly through from the opening address to the Duke's *"ames et foyables"* to the last greeting that ended the despatch.

Then he folded the sheets and laid them down on the table, and lifted a rueful eyebrow in Gilbert d'Aufay's direction.

Gilbert and Edgar the Saxon stood apart from the conference because they had accompanied Raoul only for friendship's sake, and had nothing to do in the delivering of the Duke's message. Gilbert whispered: "They don't like it, our good thick-heads. Raoul will break out laughing if you look at him, so keep your eyes this way."

"Well, I may be also a thick-head," said Edgar, "but if I were Duke of Normandy the French should not set so much as a foot inside the country unless they stepped across a field of slain."

"Of course you are a thick-head," said Gilbert cheerfully. "The French will outnumber us three to one, so Raoul thinks."

"You know very well you like the scheme as ill as anyone in Normandy," Edgar said. "I heard you say so."

Gilbert considered this for a moment. "That's true enough," he admitted. "Of course, if I were ordering this campaign I should meet King Henry on the border, because I've never heard of winning a war in any other way than that of fighting it out hand to hand. But I do believe in William.

You have never seen him in war. He has all manner of odd notions and plans, and they always seem to end just as he says they will, though everyone else thinks them folly. So even when you don't see that he is right, it is really much safer to follow him and do as he says."

"I call it a craven way of fighting," said Edgar scornfully. "Who has ever heard of retreating before the enemy without so much as a blow struck?"

Gilbert was secretly so much in accord with this point of view that he made no answer, but only nudged Edgar into silence so that they could hear what was going on at the council-table.

It was Hubert who found his tongue while his over-lord remained silent. "But what is all this?" he demanded. "The Duke cannot mean that we are to let the French come!"

"Why, it is counsel for nithings, not for men!" exclaimed Richard de Bienfaite. "Is the French King to be allowed to march into Normandy without so much as one serf to say him nay?"

Eudes, who was sitting beside his father, close to Raoul, leaned across Hubert to say with a hand shielding his mouth: "I'll wager you've misread the orders, you young fool, for all you are held to be such a fine scholar. Let someone else see the letter!"

Hubert said: "Hold your peace! What do you know of the matter?" because however badly he thought of the Duke's orders he was not going to permit Eudes to criticize either them or Raoul.

Raising his eyes from the board, Roger de Beaumont said slowly. "These are strange tidings to me, I don't deny. What do the Duke's councillors say?"

"At first, seigneur," said Raoul carefully, "they did not like it, but they saw presently that this war will be no Val-es-dunes, but a more serious affair, calling for greater cunning."

"Is it cunning to retreat?" inquired Baldwin de Courcelles, with elaborate sarcasm.

"You shall judge of that when the war is ended," answered Raoul politely.

"Let the King come into Normandy?" mused De Beaumont. "Well, this is a new way of war for old warriors to learn."

"It is rather lure the King into Normandy," corrected Raoul. "He comes in two divisions, the one to march under Prince Eudes, entering Normandy on the right bank of the

Seine with intent to overrun Caux and the Roumois; the other, with himself at its head, to come west of the Seine and march up through the Evrecin to join Prince Eudes in Rouen. With Eudes come the men of Rheims and Soissons, of Amiens, Meulan, and Brie, and all the host of Vermandois. I think Count Guy of Ponthieu will march under his banner, and perhaps Ralph de Montdidier and Renault de Clermont, the King's favourite."

"What, is Ponthieu to lift up her head again?" cried Henry de Ferrières. "Count Guy had best remember what befell his sire at St. Aubin last year!"

Richard de Bienfaite interrupted with a question. "Messire Raoul, you have told over a great host of men already, and do you say that is but half the force against us?"

"That is Prince Eudes' division. I cannot tell what other princes will march with him, but it is certain that the Hammer of Anjou stands against us, and that the Counts of Champagne and Poictiers and the Duke of Aquitaine will fight in one or other of the French divisions. The King is to lead the men of Bourges, and Berry, and Sens, all those from the lands of the Loire, and from Perche, and Montlhéry."

A rather shocked silence fell upon the company. After a moment or two Roger de Beaumont said: "If this is indeed the truth we shall need all the Duke's cunning to withstand such a force. But how do we know all these things? Is it what chance travellers say, or has the Duke sent spies into France?"

Raoul smoothed out a crease in the despatch. "Well. . . ." He paused, and looked up with a smile. "To be honest, messires, I have just come back from France myself."

Hubert sat up with a jerk. "You?" he said incredulously. "What should you be doing in France, boy?"

"Oh, I went to learn what I might," Raoul explained. "It was not very difficult."

Richard de Bienfaite looked at him curiously. "God's dignity, was it not?" he said. "I am sure I would not have ventured. How did you go, messire?"

"As a pedlar," Raoul answered. "But that is nothing. Only you may be certain that the King's forces are very much as I have described, and he means to crush Normandy as you might crack a nut." He drew his scarlet mantle closer about him, for a chill draught swept through the hall. "Now, messires, you see that we dare not oppose King Henry at the Frontier with reinforcements at his back. You have heard the Duke's will. Let the serfs drive the cattle into the woods; let all the fodder and the corn be moved out of Henry's line of march so that he may come upon no forage for his men. The same will be done on the east of the Seine: De Gournay has it in hand. When we have the two armies trapped in our midst the Duke will strike. If we fight on the Frontier we must fight as Henry chooses, in his good time. The Duke will rather choose his own time, and his own ground."

"But the French will lay waste all the south of the Evrecin!" objected De Courcelle, thinking of his own fat acres.

"Of course they will lay it waste," said Raoul with a touch of impatience, "but if we follow your plan of meeting them on the Frontier they will ravage the whole Duchy, and we shall be no more."

Someone midway down the table began to say: "All very well, but in the time of Richard Sans-Peur——"

"I cry your pardon, messire," said Raoul, "but this is not the time of Richard Sans-Peur."

Rebuked, the reminiscent seigneur fell silent. Roger de Beaumont said: "We shall obey the Duke in all his behests. We know him to be wise in war, and if De Gournay upholds him—why, that is enough for us!"

Raoul's eyes cautiously sought Gilbert's, and dropped again demurely. Gilbert said in Edgar's ear: "If old De Beaumont only knew what De Gournay said when he heard the orders!"

"Also, messires, the Count of Eu, and the Lord of Longueville," murmured Raoul.

These names carried weight. Gilbert whispered irrepressibly: "Of course Walter Giffard always says what the Duke wants, but they don't know that."

"At least the Count of Eu really does believe in the plan," Edgar pointed out. "He was the only one. What lies Raoul is telling!"

Raoul was speaking now of the Duke's Council, and it seemed from what he said that even FitzOsbern, who was accounted a hot-head, was at one with the Duke over the French campaign. From the smile that lurked in Roger de Beaumont's eyes Gilbert judged that this lord had a very good idea of the real state of affairs, but the others seemed to gain heart with Raoul's words, and after some more discussion the plans were finally accepted, if not quite approved. It was learned that the eastern division was to be commanded by the four chief seigneurs of the district: De Gournay would lead the men of Brai and the Vexin; Giffard of Longueville and William Crespin of Bec, those of Caux; and the Count Eu, all the men of Eu and Tallou. The Duke would command in person the western division confronting King Henry, and with him would march not only the men of Auge and Hiesmes, but all the forces of the Bessin under Tesson of Cingueliz, and the barons of the Côtentin headed by the gay Chef de Faucon. Hubert de Harcourt began to blow out his cheeks as the sum of names was told over, and the council ended presently with the company in a sanguine mood, expectant of victory.

Dinner followed the conference, and my lord's lady came down from the bower with her daughters, and with Gisela, Gilbert de Harcourt's dame, who was of kin to Roger de Beaumont, and had cajoled Gilbert into bringing her along with him this day. Gisela sat beside Raoul at the table. She was perhaps the only person present who did not want to talk about the coming war. While Gilbert de Harcourt argued pugnaciously with Edgar over the proper ordering of the campaign, and old Geoffrey de Bernay explained to his neighbours how Duke Richard Sans-Peur had managed his wars, she asked Raoul questions about my lord Robert, the infant heir to the Duchy. She had two sons herself, and was childing again in a few months, so that when Raoul admitted that my lord Robert had been troubled lately by coughs she was able at once to tell him of a remedy which the Duchess Matilda (being a foreigner) might not know.

"You must pluck a sprig of mistletow grown over a thorn-bush," she said earnestly. "This being soaked in the milk of a mare and given to my lord Robert to drink it, he will cough no more."

Raoul made a polite response. Gisela began to eat of a Lombardy leach, flourished and served with a sober-sauce, but she did not eat much of it because her quick eye had observed all manner of delicate dishes on the board, and she meant to taste of as many as she was able. She glanced round her, and wondered aloud whether the Lady Adeline would instruct her in the way to make appulmoy, and whether it were well to put a dash of cubebs in a blank desire. One of the scullions had just brought in a dish of curlews. Gisela finished up what was left on her platter in a hurry. The curlews were served with chaldron, and Gisela was occupied for some time in trying to make up her mind whether this was flavored with canelle, or powder-douce. Raoul could not help her, but she presently decided that there must be a dash of each in it, and perhaps a few grains of Paradise, as well. She became aware of Raoul's silence suddenly, and saw him staring down at the dregs of his hippocras in the abstracted

way that had always tantalized her. He seemed to be withdrawn, guarding his thoughts. Gisela looked wistfully at him,
and as though he were conscious of her regard he raised his
eyes and smiled at her. Gisela had married Gilbert, who was
a proper man with mighty thews and the strength of a bull,
but Raoul's smile tore at her heart. Ashamed of such
thoughts, she turned her face away, aware of his remoteness.
It gave her a tiny heartache, but she knew that she was really
very happy with Gilbert, and understood him far better than
she could ever understand Raoul. She stifled a sigh, and
began to talk to Eudes, who sucked his greasy fingers and
grunted occasionally in response.

Hubert leaned across the table to ask Raoul whether he
meant to rest the night at Harcourt. "And your friends?" he
added. Then, as Raoul nodded, he said: "I like that Saxon. I
wish you had his shoulders."

"I had rather have my own head," said Raoul with something of a grin. He glance down the table to where Edgar
and Gilbert de Harcourt were still arguing, with morsels of
bread and the lees of their wine to illustrate their theories of
war. "He and Gilbert are quite sure they could order this
campaign better than the Duke."

"To my mind," said Hubert, "they are talking plain sense.
Now you shall tell me, Raoul, since you are so clever, what
the Duke's orders mean? What is in his mind? What does he
think to do?"

"Oh, to drive the French out," said Raoul.

"A strange way to do that!"

"I don't know. William is no fool, father."

Edgar, hearing these words, set down his wine-cup, and
said loudly: "No, but if a man cares for his country's weal he
doesn't allow invaders to lay it waste."

"Edgar, you are three parts drunk," said Raoul. "If you
had your way we should blunder into the King's arms in one
desperate encounter, and the end would be that Henry would
lay the whole Duchy waste instead of one small corner of
it."

"I don't see that," said Edgar with the doggedness of the
slightly intoxicated. "William's plan may be crafty, but what
has a warrior to do with craft?"

A murmur of approbation greeted these words; under
cover of it Roger de Beaumont said softly across the table:
"Do you remember, Raoul, how at Meulan I said to you: 'I
fear him, our Duke'?"

"Yea, well do I remember. And King Henry feared him.

Didn't we see it? And he will fear him to the day of his death—with good reason."

Roger said dryly: "Hum! As I see it, my friend, the King is stronger than William to-day."

Raoul stretched out his hand towards a dish of petypanel, and began to nibble a piece of it reflectively. "William knows he will win," he said.

"A young man's faith," Roger replied. "But I am no longer in my grass-time. I tell you I mislike this business. Too many stand against us."

"Yes, but we have William," Raoul said. "Don't you see? All of us—yea, and King Henry too—think that the only way of winning is through might. But William thinks there is more to warfare than that. It is not to be our strength pitted against the French host, but William's skill against Henry's." He drank from his cup, and set it down again. "And Henry has no skill at all, from what I can see," he said cheerfully.

"What folly are you talking?" demanded Hubert, who had been listening with a puzzled frown on his face. "In warfare it is might that wins, I can tell you that."

Raoul shook his head obstinately. "No. Not this time. You will see. William's cunning will win the war, not the might of France, nor our chivalry."

"Well, we will hope you may be right, Raoul," said Roger. "But I should like to hear what Hugh de Gournay has to say to it all."

Raoul looked at him sideways. "He has declared for the Duke, seigneur," he said warily.

"Yea, yea, he would do so, as I do, and all true men must. Yet I wish we had an older head to direct us."

An hour later Raoul left Beaumont-le-Roger, riding with his father and his brothers north to Harcourt. Edgar trotted ahead with Hubert, and as Gilbert d'Aufay chose to amble along beside Dame Gisela's palfrey, Raoul was left to ride between his two brothers. They went in silence for some way, while Eudes thought of the dinner he had eaten, and Gilbert surreptitiously scrutinized Raoul's profile. Gilbert found it hard to remember that he had been used to scoff at Raoul. Of course Raoul still lacked the girth a fighting-man should have, and he still looked half the time as though he were quite detached from his surroundings, but he had somehow acquired a self-possession that impressed Gilbert, and there was no denying that in spite of his squeamish ways he did astonishing things, like going to France in the guise of a pedlar, or rebuking rich seigneurs as though he were one himself. More than ever he was a stranger to Gilbert. One could not guess what he was thinking about, and he had a queer disarming smile that made his eyes dance when no one else could see anything to smile at. Pondering it in his slow way Gilbert remembered that he had never known what went on behind Raoul's tranquillity. Only in the old days he had never considered it worth while to try to find out.

On the other side of Raoul Eudes spoke presently. Eudes did not wonder about Raoul; Eudes never wondered about anything. "You've got a fine new destrier there," he remarked. "But I don't know that I like a grey horse."

Raoul patted Blanchflower's neck. "Why not?" he inquired.

"Well, I don't know," Eudes said vaguely. "I would sooner bestride a bay like your old Verceray. You had better ride Verceray into battle—if there is a battle," he added with a gloomy look.

"God's pity, of course there must be a battle!" said Gilbert scornfully. "What notion have you taken into your head now?"

"All this talk of cunning and retreating," said Eudes. "I heard what they were saying while I was eating the fat-puddings. Young Raoul talked of winning the war by craft, and by the way they spoke of it you would think we were going to drive the French out without striking a blow." He gave a loud disparaging sniff. "Well, I am not like Raoul, addling my brains with bookwork and the like, and I didn't understand a word of it."

"You needn't be proud of that," said Raoul. "We are going to retreat first, and then strike. Now do you see?"

Eudes was unmoved. "It would be much better to strike first, and then we might not have to retreat," he said.

"There is something in that, you know," Gilbert pointed out.

"I thought you would see it," said Eudes, gratified.

Raoul did not say anything, and Gilbert thought: He's not listening, it's as though he doesn't think it worth the trouble to answer. He said testily: "Well, are you asleep, or have you grown too great to talk about such matters with us?"

"No, but I don't really understand it myself," said Raoul.

Mollified, Gilbert said: "You seemed to understand it very well, back at Beaumont."

"Oh, I had to explain it all there. I do understand William's plan, of course, but I don't see it all. I mean I shouldn't know how to lure the King on, or when was the time to fall upon him."

Gilbert grunted, and for a time they rode on without saying anything. Eudes broke the silence by asking suddenly: "Why does that Saxon wear a beard? Is it a vow, or a penance?"

"Neither. All Saxons wear beards," Raoul answered.

Eudes looked surprised. "Well, that's an odd thing," he remarked. "But he had much better shave it."

"I don't think you had better tell him so," said Raoul in some amusement. "He is very proud of it."

"I can't see anything to be proud of in a beard," Eudes said. "He looks like a barbarian."

"Well, take heed he does not hear you say so," advised Raoul.

Gilbert fell back to range alongside his lady, and as Eudes had nothing further to say either about the threatened invasion or about Edgar's beard, he and Raoul rode on in silence until they reached Harcourt.

At daybreak on the following morning Raoul and his escort started on their journey back to Rouen. Gisela gave Raoul a package of food to eat upon the way: Damascus cakes prepared by her own hands, and some slices of lard done up in a clean napkin. But when he gave her the farewell kiss she pressed a tiny object into his hand, whispering that he should wear it, and so be kept safe from all harm.

Raoul looked down at the gift, which seemed to be a little stitched bag on a silken cord. "All thanks, sister," he said. "What is it?"

"It is good fortune, Raoul," she said shyly. Her eyes fluttered to his, and away again. "You must wear it about your neck. It is the head of a stag-beetle, and will keep you safe."

Raoul turned the bag over rather ginerly, but since Gisela was plainly anxious that he should wear it he put the cord round his neck, and tucked the bag away inside his tunic. He got to horse, and waved a last good-bye, and trotted off over the bridge in the wake of his friends.

They reached Rouen in good time, and clattered through the streets to the palace. Here they found signs of arrivals. The Viscount of Côtentin had ridden in the day before with the chief among his vassals; and the Count of Mortain had come in that very morning.

Raoul slid down from Blanchflower's back, and began to

scrape the mud from his soft boots. Gilbert and Edgar lounged away to their own quarters, calling back to Raoul that they would see him at supper. Raoul ran lightly up the outer stairway to the main door of the palace, and passed into the vaulted hall. He met Mortain there on his way out to the base-court, and pulled up short with his hand raised in greeting.

Mortain's heavy face brightened. "Holà, so here you are, Raoul! William was asking whether you had not returned. Have you heard what he means to do? He has won De Gournay over."

"I thought he would," said Raoul. "When did you come, Mortain?"

"Oh, but an hour or so gone. I've appointed my vassals to meet me at Evreux. Saint-Sauveur is here, and Montgoméri, and Grantmesnil rode in yesterday. William is as cool as you please." A slow smile made his eyes narrow. "The Duchess dreamed she saw William's new haggard seize her prey, and they say that's an omen of success." He gave his deep chuckle, and passed on. Raoul ran up the stairs to his own chamber, and calling for a page began to strip off his mud-spattered tunic and hose.

As soon as he had washed off the travel stains, and put on fresh raiment he made his way to one of the audience-chambers above-stairs, where he was told he would find the Duke. Curtains of tapestry hung over the arched doorway; a page swung them back, and he went in to find William alone with his Duchess.

Raoul checked upon the threshold, and made as if to draw back. William glanced up under his frowning brows, but when he saw who it was who had entered the frown cleared, and he called a welcome. "In a good hour, Raoul! What speed?"

"They don't like it, beau sire, but they will obey. Roger de Beaumont can be trusted to see all done according to your word." He bent the knee to Matilda as he spoke. One quick look at her had shown him her face brooding and stormy, but the cloud vanished as she held out her hand to him. "Madame, how does my lord Robert?" he asked tactfully.

"He is well," Matilda said. A small, triumphant smile curved her lips. "He is greater than Mortain's boy, who is the elder by a month or more," she said with satisfaction. Raoul could picture her measuring her firstborn beside Mortain's heir to the chagrin of Mortain's lady, and his eyes began to dance. "And to my mind," added Matilda, "he is more comely. Though my lord may not observe it, I am very sure that you will, Raoul."

William pushed some documents across the table towards Raoul. "These from Longueville. He does my will, misliking it," he said with a laugh. "So do they all, even Mald here. She would quarrel with me if I would aid her to it, would you not, my heart?"

The Duchess came to the table, holding up her long gown in her hands. The brooding look had come back. "I wish you would do what they want," she said, with a kind of suppressed passion. Her fingers clenched. "I want you to fight the King and beat him," she said through her teeth.

William was watching Raoul read Giffard's despatch. "Madame wife, govern your babe, and leave me to govern my Duchy," he said lightly.

"You are the Fighting Duke," she insisted. "I like a man to fight against odds."

"So I do, my fair," said William, still watching Raoul.

"Meet the King face to face," she urged. "Do not permit him to set foot in Normandy. Ah, if I were a man!"

He turned at that, and looked up at her in some amusement. She had something of the old hungry flame in her eyes. Seeing it he laughed and put up a hand to clasp her wrist. "Holy Virgin, you are fierce, my girl! Rest you, I will drive the King out."

She said in a low voice: "You do not mean to fight him, beau sire. You cannot hide that from me."

He began to swing her hand to and fro. He had that intent look in his eyes that seemed to probe the future. "I do not want to fight Henry," he said.

She searched his face for a meaning. "Is he to wrest your son's heritage from him, then?" she demanded. "I say you shall not give up so much as one tithe of land, one border fortress!"

"Nor will I."

"What then?" She leaned towards him till her dress brushed his arm.

"If I can scatter Prince Eudes' Belgic host," the Duke said slowly, "I may yet avoid coming to blows with Henry himself. I know Henry. Mark me if he does not make all speed back to France." His fingers tightened unconsciously on her wrist, but she did not seem to feel the crushing grip. He smiled suddenly. "Trust me to make a peace worthy of this Robert of ours," he said.

Disappointed, she shook her head. "I want you to crush the King. You can do it. I know you can. Why will you hold off from him?"

William let go her wrist, and turned back to his despatches. "Eh, Mald, he is my suzerain," he said impatiently. "That is what you will not understand."

A voice spoke from the doorway. "And Brother William is himself a suzerain. God save you, sister, and pity the fool." Galet slipped round the curtain, and squatted down among the rushes, and began to juggle with some sheep's bones, casting them before him, and peering at them with mutterings and grimaces.

"What are you doing?" Matilda asked, half curious, half disdainful.

"Reading the future, goody, to see what heritage shall be my lord Robert's." He bent over the bones, and suddenly swept them together. "Eh, it is too great for me to read, too great for him to hold!" he cried out, and jumped up, and began to twist his body into weird contortions, while William went on reading his despatches, and Matilda stared down at the bones in uneasiness and alarm.

CHAPTER II

To the sound of tuckets and of drums, under a medley of banners, argent and or, gules and azure, King Henry brake the Norman border. He came with the flower of his chivalry, haut princes at his side, in his ears the sound of trumpets, the jingle of horse-trappings, the creak and groan of his carts and wagons.

From every corner of his dominions his vassals flocked to his standard. Thibaut the great Count of Champagne was here; Aquitaine's young Duke; Nevers's prince; while here fluttered the emblem of Auvergne, and there the wind spread Angoulême's banner out against the pale spring sky. Horse and foot, lords, knights, esquires, and men-at-arms streamed over the border, wasting as they passed, with Rouen for their goal, and a Duke's abasement for their guerdon.

The sword was out against William from Vermandois to the Pyrenees. For seven years his fellow-vassals had watched Normandy weld his Duchy to one loyal whole, wrest from Martel towns in Maine, repulse his suzerain with loss, thrusting out his Frontiers little by little. Those like Geoffrey the Count of Gascony and William of Auvergne who had sent eulogies and gifts to Normandy four years ago, to-day sent armed men. Admiration had given place to fear of William's growing power and bitter jealousy of his success. If the Hammer of Anjou did not care to venture his person in the field there were others to fill his place: puissant Counts from far and wide, at the head of their levies, nobly mounted, splendidly beseen, flaunting their colours in Normandy's teeth.

"Ha, sire! where cowers the Bastard now?" cried Renault de Nevers. "Heu! heu! bay the Wolf!"

Henry's face was pinched and sallow under the shade of his helmet. "No sign of William yet?" he muttered, and began to pluck at his beard. "Strange, by our Lady, strange! Would he not meet me on the border? And he a proud man!"

"He has fallen back upon Rouen, sire," the Count of Saint-Pol said confidently. "How should he face our host? If Prince Eudes makes speed through Caux to Rouen we shall crush the Bastard there between our two forces."

But there was no Norman army at Rouen, had the King but known. East of the Seine old Hugh de Gournay hovered among the hills of Drimcourt watching the fires to the south that told of Prince Eudes' slow advance; and by the river Andelle Count Robert of Eu's spies brought him tidings day by day, while his men of Tallou chafed and swore at his waiting policy, and kept their swords ground to a fine edge. Prince Eudes pressed on by the fords of Epte, his army in high fettle, loaded with plunder, leaving in its wake a torn and bleeding trail.

West of the Seine, as it were pacing his army step by step, Duke William harried the King's advance. The French force was drunk already with easy success. What women they found they took, the men who had not fled from their homes were put to the sword, or worse. Small wonder that William's barons were straining to break free from the curb-rein he held so tightly. A serf was of little account until a foreign tyrant slew him; but when that happened Norman swords flashed out, and the seigneurs made ready to protect their own to the last drop of their blood. If they chose they might oppress their villeins, but no stranger had the right to lay a finger upon slave or freeman of Normandy. The French King had dared. They would have fallen upon him then and there; even the Viscount of Côtentin, who swore he would follow his Duke into hell's mouth, thought him mad to hold his force in check.

"Seigneur," he said desperately, "men will call you craven!"

"Will they so, Néel?" the Duke said grimly. "But they shall not call me Rash Fool, by Death!"

"We could scatter them, beau sire. They are hampered by plunder, their men unruly, their leaders careless already, so sure they are of victory!"

"Chef de Faucon, what men think you we should lose in that encounter?" asked William.

Néel gave him a blank look. *"Qi de ceo?* What's that to the purpose!" he said. "Men must needs fall in battle. What would any loss matter if we did but drive the King out?"

"Fine counsel!" William said roughly. "Look to the future, Viscount! What rede will you give me when the King comes with a fresh force to vanquish me, and half my strength lies buried on these plains?" Then, as Saint-Sauveur was ruefully silent, he said: "Trust me, Néel: I will drive out the King, but it is he who shall lose men in that encounter, not I."

They looked one another in the eyes. Néel raised his hand to his helmet. "Beau sire, whether you are right or wrong I am your man," he said.

Raoul Tesson of Cingueliz, riding in from an expedition to cut off French foraging parties, echoed these words later, but thought it time to strike. "Look you, seigneur, my men have tasted blood," he said, pulling off his gauntlet. "Can I hold them off the King's throat, think you?"

The Duke knew his man. "Are they too strong for you, Tesson?" he asked softly.

"By God's death they are not!" swore the Lord of Cingueliz.

"Nor are you too strong for me," said William. "I say you shall still hold off from Henry's throat."

The Lord of Cingueliz burst out into a laugh. "I am answered." He turned as Raoul came into the tent, and nodded to him. "Well, Messire Raoul, you see me back again. There are some three score men will not rejoin the King this night," he said with a swagger.

"So I heard," Raoul grinned. "Do not eat up all Henry's host before I get back to see you do it."

"Ha, are you for the east, my friend? Do you need an escort?"

Raoul shook his head. Tesson said: "Well, God keep you. See you bring us good tidings from Robert of Eu." He went out, and the tent flap fell into place behind him.

Raoul rode out of the camp at dusk, heading north and

east towards the Seine. It was not the first time he had ridden between the Duke and the commanders of the eastern division, but his father, who saw him go, wished that some other man had been chosen. There was no knowing what might befall a solitary rider crossing this ravaged territory, and he could not help feeling that Raoul was just the person to blunder into the hands of the enemy. He watched Raoul until he was quite out of sight, and turned slowly away at last to find Gilbert d'Aufay at his elbow. Hubert would not have liked it to be known that he was worried about his son, so he squared his shoulders, and said in a jovial way that he hoped Raoul would not fall a-dreaming before he reached the Count of Eu's camp.

Gilbert fell into step beside him, and said with a smile playing round his mouth: "What a queer creature Raoul is! He says he hates fighting, but when someone has to ride on an errand like this it is always he who wants to be the man to go. Nothing would do but that he must be the one who went to get news out of France, earlier in the year. Really, I did not think he would come safe out of that, and as for Edgar, who never can believe that anyone who lacks his own inches is good for anything, he was mourning him as dead from the day he set forth."

"Oh," said Hubert, strutting a little, "Raoul may have some foolish notions, but he has a head on his shoulders for all that, and I daresay he knows how to take care of himself when there's the need."

"None better," replied Gilbert. "Yet one never would think it, for to hear him talk you would imagine he had never had a sword in his hand, nor done anything out of the common way in all his life." He paused. "Perhaps that's why one likes him so much," he said. "He doesn't boast, like the rest of us, and for all he says he hates bloodshed he can fight as well as any other man if he has to. I've seen him slit a man's windpipe up as coolly as you please," he added, and gave a little laugh.

"Did he so?" said Hubert, pleased. "And when was that, Messire Gilbert?"

"Oh, at St. Aubin last year, when we routed the French. He and I were creeping up to see how the King's force lay, and stumbled on a sentry in the dark. Raoul knifed him before he could let so much as a gurgle."

Hubert was so much cheered by this tale that he went off quite happily to his own quarters, and was able to envisage

Raoul deftly cutting the throats of all those who might seek to oppose him on his present journey.

Meanwhile the French still made their way ponderously northwards. Grain their foraging parties could not find, and those who went after the cattle in the woods rarely came back again, but houses and monasteries and churches could yield a store of treasure, so that no fear of being cut off by the Norman soldiery could deter parties of Frenchmen from sallying out in search of such prizes.

The Norman army still kept a reasonable distance between itself and the invaders, but small detachments ranged the countryside, and harried the King rather after the manner of a swarm of gnats.

Henry's councillors thought that they had nothing to fear from the Duke, and were not much disturbed by his troublesome raids. They were sure that their approach was driving him back, and that they had only to trap him between themselves and Prince Eudes to force him at last into an engagement. But Henry, remembering the gleam in those hawk-eyes, was wary, keeping strict watch at nights, expecting each day to have to beat off one of the sudden attacks for which the Duke was famous.

From his brother at the head of the Belgic host he had but desultory news. More than one French scout set out from Eudes' camp never to be heard of again, and more than one French despatch found its way into Duke William's hands.

In the Norman camp there were three anxious hearts, but King Henry knew nothing of this, and would not have thought it a matter of much importance had he been told that one Norman knight had not been heard of for five days. But when Duke William opened his eyes to each fresh dawn the first thing he said to the men about him was always: "Is Raoul returned?" When they answered: "Not yet, beau sire," he made no sign, but folded his stern lips rather closer, and plunged into the day's business without apparently thinking any more about his favourite's plight.

But Raoul's father and Raoul's friend could not so easily conceal their anxiety. Hubert went about with a long face, and resentment in his breast, and Gilbert was rather silent, and lingered about the outposts of the camp at night. Once, when Hubert went to the Duke upon some business or other, William said as the old man was leaving the tent: "I have sent scouts to Drimcourt."

Hubert said: "What should that avail my son, seigneur?"

William did not seem to notice the surliness in Hubert's voice. "I want to know what has befallen," he replied.

Hubert grunted. His resentful eyes met William's across the tent; he thought he could read some shadow of anxiety behind the Duke's cold self-possession, and remembered that William was also Raoul's friend. He looked away, and cleared his throat, saying gruffly: "I daresay he is safe enough."

"God send it," said the Duke. "He is dear to me: I have not many friends."

"I am very sure he is safe, seigneur," said Hubert stoutly. "I shall not lose any sleep on Raoul's account, for the boy is probably lying snug enough in Count Robert's camp all the time we are thinking him slain."

But in spite of these brave words Hubert did lose quite a lot of sleep on Raoul's account. He would not join some of his friends that night, who meant to while away a few hours over the dice, but went away to his small tent, and lay down on the pallet with his mantle spread over him, listening to the sounds outside. They were ordinary enough: a wolf howled in the forest to the west; men sleeping under the stars moved with a cough or a grunt, or spoke one to another in low drowsy voices; the camp-fires crackled; and from time to time the horses tethered to stakes driven into the ground, stamped, and fidgeted with their headstalls. There were no other noises than these to attract Hubert's attention until suddenly he thought that he could hear the pounding of hooves galloping towards the camp. He raised himself on his elbow, listening; the sound became unmistakable, and he scrambled up from his pallet just as a challenge rang out sharply from one of the outposts.

Hubert flung his mantle round him inside out in his agitation, and set off at a jog-trot in the direction of the sounds he had heard. He was overtaken by Gilbert d'Aufay, and young Ralph de Toeni, who had been playing chess together by the light of a horn lantern. "Did you hear a challenge?" Gilbert asked. "Is it the French, or Raoul?"

William's big tent loomed up before them. Feeling rather foolish, Hubert said: "I daresay it is neither. There is no sense in running to question the sentries." He looked severely at Gilbert, and Gilbert said tactfully: "No, but we may as well wait here to see who it was."

The flap of William's tent swung back; the Duke stood in the opening. "Who was that rider?" he said sharply.

"I don't know, beau sire," Gilbert began, "but we thought——"

"Go bring me word who came in," the Duke said. He saw Hubert standing in the moonlight, and beckoned to him with an imperious crook of his finger. He noticed that his mantle was all inside out, and said kindly: "If it is Raoul he will come straight to my tent. Wait with me, and we shall soon know."

Hubert followed him into the tent, where the Count of Mortain was seated, and began to explain that he had not jumped up from his pallet to see if it were Raoul at all, but had chanced to be near the Duke's quarters when the challenge sounded. He did not get very far with this explanation, for in a few minutes footsteps were heard approaching, someone dragged the tent flap aside, and Raoul lurched in, clinging with one hand to the side of the tent, and blinking at the light of the lanterns that swung from the centre pole. His face was grey with fatigue, his eyes heavy and bloodshot, and his left arm, which hung limply at his side, was rudely bound round with a stained scarf.

"God be thanked!" The exclamation came from the Duke; he strode forward to Raoul's side, and thrust him into his own armed-chair by the table. "I have been thinking you dead these three days, my friend," he said. His hand pressed Raoul's shoulder slightly; he glanced impatiently towards his half-brother. "Wine, Robert!"

Mortain was already pouring wine into a horn from a costrel that stood upon the table. Hubert snatched it from him, and put it to Raoul's lips as though he thought Raoul had no strength to hold it.

Raoul took the horn with the shadow of a grin, and drank deep. Then he fetched a sigh, and looked in rather a dazed way from one to the other of the three faces bent so eagerly over him. Gilbert, who had followed him into the tent, saw the blood trickling from under the bandage round his arm, and said suddenly: "I'll go call the surgeon!" and hurried out.

"I don't want a surgeon," said Raoul in a voice thick with weariness. He sat up, and looked at the Duke. "I could not come before," he said.

"What tidings do you bring me, Raoul?" the Duke asked. "Where lies Prince Eudes?"

Raoul pushed the damp ringlets back from his brow. "Fled—all fled." He gave a faint shudder. "There are ten thousand dead at Mortemer. I stayed to bring the tidings." He fumbled in the wallet at his girdle, and pulled out a sealed packet. "These from Count Robert."

"God on the Cross!" Mortain cried. "Ten thousand dead?"

The Duke took the packet from Raoul and slit it open. While he read the despatch, and Mortain and Hubert plied Raoul with questions, Gilbert brought the surgeon into the tent, and this worthy laid bare an ugly gash on Raoul's forearm, and began to bathe and tend it.

Hubert said, inspecting the wound: "That's nothing. How did you come by it? Not at this fight at Mortemer?"

"This scratch? Oh no, I had nothing to do at Mortemer. I was set upon about five leagues from here, I think." He looked down at his arm, which the surgeon was holding over a bowl, and said: "Tie it up, man! I can't bleed like a pig all over the Duke's tent."

The Duke came back to the table, holding the despatch in his hands. "Don't be a fool, Raoul," he said. "Do you suppose I mind a little blood?" He sat down on one of the stools. "Well, Robert writes he has scattered the Belgic host, and holds Guy of Ponthieu captive. Now tell me how it went."

"It is all muddled in my head," Raoul complained. Again a faint shudder shook him. "I can't get the smell of blood out of my nose," he said with a look of disgust.

"Never mind about that," said Hubert. "Don't you see the Duke is waiting to hear your story?"

Raoul smiled across at William. "Oh . . . yes! Well, when I reached Count Robert he was encamped by the Andelle and had got news from Ralph de Mortemer that Prince Eudes had marched into Mortemer-en-Lions, and was housed there with all his force . . . If you don't give me something to eat I can't tell you anything. I have been fasting since yesterday."

"Mass! Are you not famished?" Mortain, appalled at such a privation, rose up hurriedly from his stool, and went to where the remains of the Duke's supper still stood against the side of the tent.

"Yes, but I could come by nothing because all the serfs are fled in terror of the French." Raoul took the bread and meat from Mortain, and fell to. Between mouthfuls he said: "I gave the Count your letters, beau sire. Then his spies came in with the news of Eudes being at Mortemer, and Robert, hearing how the French were busy sacking the place, and guessing that those who were not drunk that night would be lying with the bordel-women, gave orders for a swift march by night upon the town, and sent word to Drimcourt to advise De Gournay, and the Lord of Longueville." He drank deeply, and nodded at William. "All this as you would do it, beau sire."

"That was three days ago?" said the Duke, consulting the despatch.

"Yes, I think so. We fell in with De Gournay on the road, and came in sight of Mortemer before dawn, and surrounded it. Ralph de Mortemer was with us. He said the Castle held out still, but that made no odds. Eudes, and the other princes—Ponthieu and Montdidier, and Herbert of Vermandois, and the Count of Soissons—oh yes, and Clermont, of course—were housed snug enough. It was just as Robert thought: they were all either sleeping off their liquor, or wenching, and kept no watch. We came up without a soul being the wiser."

"Did Robert follow my counsel?" interrupted the Duke. "Drunk or not, they were fifteen thousand strong, as I judge."

Raoul winced as the surgeon pulled the bindings tight round his arm. "Rest you, seigneur, he wasted no lives. All was done as we planned here. Robert set fire to the outlying houses, and had brands dipped in pitch flung into the town by the balistas." He broke off, staring before him as though he saw again that flaming hell.

"That was well thought of!" Mortain cried. "I'll warrant the place burned merrily!"

Raoul gave a slight start, and glanced fleetingly towards him. "Yes." He drew a long breath. "It did burn quickly."

"But what then?" Hubert asked, nudging him. "Were they all roasted alive, or did they fight?"

"Some—those who were too drunk to move—were burned. Most escaped from the town. Robert's men guarded the streets, but the French fought like men possessed. But they had no time to rally to their leaders: we cut them down as they tried to break out. Waleran of Ponthieu was slain: I saw him go down; Count Guy himself was taken, and Montdidier. Eudes escaped; I think Renault de Clermont too: I'm not sure. Mortemer was only ashes by noon, with charred bodies, and the reek of burned flesh——" He got up suddenly. "Oh, I don't want to talk of it!" he cried angrily.

"Holy Face, one would think you didn't want the French to be slain," said Hubert, gaping at him.

"Of course I wanted it!" Raoul flung over his shoulder. "I would have fired the town with my own hands! But they did fight like heroes, and I suppose I need not enjoy hearing the screams of men roasted to death, need I?"

"Go to bed, Raoul," the Duke said. "We all know that you fight like a wood-fiend during the battle, and turn sick as soon as it is done."

"God's death, I am not sick!" Raoul said sharply. "We have scattered the French, and I don't care a stiver for aught else." On his way to the opening of the tent he paused, and said over his shoulder: "I slew two myself, very nastily. Those who dealt me this." He touched his wounded arm, and his rueful grin crept up into his eyes.

"Slit their windpipes?" inquired Hubert hopefully.

Raoul looked surprised. "No, ripped up the guts of one, and rode Blanchflower over the other. Gilbert, I'm so tired I can't stand without reeling like a drunk Frenchman. Give me your arm, lest I be shamed before the whole camp." He went out, leaning on Gilbert's shoulder, and not until they were in their own small tent, and he had stretched himself out on his pallet did he speak again. "It's a pity Edgar could not have been there," he remarked sleepily. "He would have liked it much better than I did."

"I expect you liked it well enough while it was doing," remarked Gilbert matter-of-factly.

Raoul's eyes had closed, but he opened them again, and looked up at Gilbert in a doubtful considering way. "Yes, I did—part of it. But some of it was horrible. Many of the Frenchmen had no time to put on their hauberks, and they had lost their weapons, so they were just hacked to pieces, and some thrust into the flames to perish. You wouldn't have liked that. You wouldn't have liked to hear the women screaming either. And there was one little child ran naked out of a house ... Oh well! It is war. But I wish the child had not been one of our people."

"If the French had conquered there would have been more than one Norman brat slain," Gilbert pointed out.

"Of course. I'm glad we have avenged ourselves. The French sacked and burned all they could lay their hands to on their march to Mortemer." His eyelids drooped wearily. "One hates them. Yet when you see them die like that you can't help being a little sorry." He opened his eyes again, and they were twinkling. "I expect my brothers were right, and I ought to be in a cloister after all," he remarked, and, turning on his side, was asleep almost at once.

He was the only man to sleep any more that night. As the dawn stole above the horizon the French were awakened in their camp by a horn winding eerily through the stillness. The guards grasped their gavelocs more tightly, listening and wondering. The horn sounded again, and a third time. It was close at hand, but the morning mists shrouded the trumpeter from view. Heads were raised; men scrambled up asking what was the matter, whether the Normans were upon them? and the Count of Nevers, disturbed by the sudden commotion, came out of his tent with a mantle thrown over his thin tunic.

"A horn, lord," one of the guards told him. "Someone is without our lines. Ah! ah! what is that?"

Fulk of Angoulême came up with his rolling gait, and his hose all unbound. "What's this?"he snapped, but was checked by Nevers's upflung hand.

Once more the sennet sounded, ending its call on a triumphant flourish.

"Whoever it is must be upon that hillock," muttered Nevers, peering to where they could perceive the shoulder of a slight hill rearing up through the mist.

Across the intervening space a shrill voice flung its message. "My name is Ralph de Toeni," it cried. "I bring ye tidings!"

A murmur rose amongst the Frenchmen; Nevers strode forward, straining his eyes to pierce the dim light. The wind was blowing the mist in wreaths across the hill, and through it they could just distinguish the figure of a mounted man silhouetted in the faint light. Clearly his voice floated to their ears. "Hasten with your carts and carriages to Mortemer, and carry off your dead!" he called. "The French have braved our chivalry; let them deplore the venture! Eudes the King's brother is fled; Guy of Ponthieu is captive; the rest are slain or prisoned or dispersed. It is the Duke of Normandy who tells this to the King of France!" A mocking laugh ended his speech; something fluttered on the end of his lance: it might have been a gonfanon. He wheeled his horse about, and disappeared into the mist, and the sound of the charger's hooves was quickly muffled in the fog.

Several of the French soldiers rushed forward in the vain hope of catching the herald; their figures became shadowy in the mist, and one among them cried out suddenly in a voice of alarm.

Nevers leaped after them. "What is it?" he shouted, dreading he scarcely knew what hidden peril.

The man who had cried out was pale with fright. "A hare jumped up almost under my feet, lord, and ran across the path. Ill-omen! ill-omen!" He crossed himself, shivering, and his companions drew close together in awed silence.

The sun was riding high when Raoul emerged from his tent, and there seemed to be a bustle of preparation on hand. He yawned, and went off to the Duke's tent to hear what fresh tidings had been brought. He found William with his chief barons, and from the dust on his clothes it was evident that one of them, Hugh de Montfort, had just come in with news.

"What now?" asked Raoul of Grantmesnil, who was standing near the entrance.

"The King is in retreat already," Grantmesnil whispered back. "Ralph de Toeni took the tidings to him, and De Montfort says the French have broken their camp, and are marching south."

"Brave King!" chuckled Raoul. He made his way through the group about William in time to hear Tesson of Cingueliz say eagerly: "Let us fall upon his rear, beau sire! We will make a speedy end, I promise you."

"Let him go; he has enough to trouble him," the Duke replied. Then, as disappointed faces were turned towards him, he said: "What, am I to set all Christendom against me by striking down my suzerain? We will attend him to the border, Tesson, and cut off his stragglers, but there shall be no blows exchanged between Henry and me." He saw Raoul, and picked up a packet from the table. "Raoul, are you well enough to ride for me once more?"

"Be sure, seigneur."

There was a laugh in the Duke's eyes. He looked significantly at Raoul, and said: "Then bear these to Rouen, and tell the Duchess Matilda that not one tithe of land, not one border-fortress have I let the King filch from Robert's heritage!"

CHAPTER III

Past Conches, the hold of Ralph de Toeni, hastened King Henry by forced marches, pressing south in dreadful dismay. When a sweat-stained scout had staggered into his presence with the confirmation of the Norman herald's tiding, he had fallen down in a kind of seizure, with a thin line of froth on his lips, but he recovered as his physician laboured over him, and in a voice that made the princes round him fear for his reason he whispered a terrible malediction on Eudes who had failed him, and on William who had triumphed over him. He lay silent then while the princes murmured amongst them-selves, and it was seen that his grey lips were drawn back from his teeth in a ghastly grin. Presently he rose up from the couch on which they had laid him, and though he shook as with a fever, he was able to direct what should be done. To those who would have sought an engagement with the Duke's forces he returned a bitter answer. He was for France again, and the word went out to break camp. Ignominiously the King hurried out of Normandy; it was as though he looked continually over his shoulder like a beast hard-driven, listen-ing for the baying of William's hounds. Past Conches he hastened, over the Iton, crossing the Frontier between his holds of Verneuil and Tillières.

Spurring in his wake the Norman Duke frowned upon those two castles, and bit his whip-lash, and said suddenly: "I will have a donjon raised to keep a check on Tillières until such time as I am master there again." Thus the Castle of Breteuil had birth, and in the year that followed, stone by stone its impregnable walls rose upon the bank of the Iton. "This shall be your charge, William," the Duke said gaily to FitzOsbern. "Hold it safe for me, and you shall be Count of Breteuil."

"By God, I will!" FitzOsbern swore.

A treaty was made and signed between King Henry and his vassal. The King was compelled to confirm William in all his conquests, to engage never again to assist his enemies against him, and at the chosen meeting-place the kiss of peace was exchanged between the two princes, one a shrivelled man with bowed shoulders and pouches under his eyes, the other a straight-backed warrior so charged with vigour that the King seemed old and frail indeed beside him. They kissed, one with hatred in his heart, one with indifference. King Henry retired planning his vengeance, and Raoul de Harcourt, glancing over the four articles that made up the treaty, said with a quick look up under his lashes: "Do you think he will abide by this, beau sire?"

William shrugged. "Maybe. If he breaks faith with me he stands a traitor confessed, and I see my way."

They had not done with fighting yet. Though the Hammer of Anjou had held off from Henry's side in the late campaign he had not been idle. He had marched up through Maine to join Geoffrey of Mayenne in battering down that castle at Ambrières which William had built after the fall of Domfront. William's cartel reached Anjou in his own Coun-ty; the Norman gauntlet was flung down with an arrogance that made Martel grow purple with rage. Normandy announced that he would appear before Ambrières upon the fortieth day. Turning to Mayenne, Martel let a great oath, swearing that if he allowed William to seize Ambrières nor Geoffrey nor any other should call him lord again. These were bold words, but uttered in heat. When the Norman chivalry appeared before Ambrières there was no sign of Martel to dispute their right.

The Duke went swiftly to work, and the Angevin garrison, knowing itself betrayed by its over-lord, surrendered at the first assault. The Duke built up the damaged keep, strengthened the walls, and after waiting some weeks for Martel to get the better of his fear and come to face him, withdrew into Normandy, and there disbanded his army, under orders to the men-at-arms to hold themselves in readiness to join him upon three days' notice, should need arise.

The need arose just as soon as the Duke had foreseen it would. When intelligence was brought him that Normandy had sheathed the sword at last, Martel plucked up his courage and entered into an alliance with his stepson, Duke Peter of Aquitaine, and with Odo, uncle to the young Count of Brittany. Aquitaine came fresh from the disasters of the previous year. He had seen a great King's army cut to pieces; if he had led his men into Normandy contemptuous of her bastard ruler he marshalled them in retreat with alarm and a new respect born in him. Dimly Duke Peter realized that in the despised Bastard of Normandy he had come face to face with the one man in Christendom who knew how to use strategy in warfare. But when Anjou called upon him William's force was disbanded. Duke Peter gathered his men under his rather draggled banner, and led them to join the man who long ago had earned for himself the name of the Hammer.

But the Count of Anjou's hammer-blows had been struck at enemies who could resist only enough to give him some right to be thought a conqueror; he walked over their humbled forms to encounter one who stood in his path with a drawn sword, and stern eyes watchful under his night-black brows. Anjou, after the first measuring of swords at Meulan, had retreated before this invincible young man, and he had never since then been able to rid himself of the fear that had crept under his armour of vainglory.

The three princes—Martel and Peter and Odo—marched boldly into Maine, never dreaming but that with William gone the garrison at Ambrières would surrender at the first blow. They tried to take the Castle by storm, and were thrown back with heavy loss. The lions of Normandy continued to wave above the squat keep, and from the ramparts the defenders taunted Martel with his failure to meet William upon the term-day.

The princes sat down to starve the garrison into submission. Duke Peter was in a restless, fidgeting mood, with ears on the prick, and eyes turned anxiously towards the Norman border. Martel said strongly: "Mark me if I do not speedily hammer down these walls!" After ten days of rigorous blockade the garrison sent out a present of fresh meat and wine to the besiegers, and those who were with Martel when he received this gift feared that he would die suddenly of an apoplexy. He could not comprehend the spirit that prompted this gay piece of insolence, but when Ambrières had capitulated meekly to Duke William she had been held by men who dared not trust their over-lord to bring them relief. She was held now by men who knew beyond all doubting that their Duke would not leave them to struggle alone.

Nor were they mistaken. To Martel came scouts with shocking tidings: Duke William was on the march.

The three princes held a council, then another, and a third, unable to decide what were best to do. Day by day the scouts rode in: Duke William was coming in force, and swiftly.

Aquitaine saw Martel as a pricked bladder, and discovered a pressing need to make all speed to his own dominions. Martel cried out loudly that he was betrayed; blustered a little, boasted a little, and drew off his troops when Duke William was within half a day's march of Ambrières. Odo went with him, willy-nilly, and Duke William arrived to find only smouldering camp-fires to tell of the enemy's late presence in the district.

This time he did not retire until he had accomplished two things very injurious to the Count of Anjou. He besieged and took captive Geoffrey of Mayenne, and he extended his Frontier from that outpost of Ambrières, westwards to a point south of Séez. Geoffrey was sent to Rouen to join that other illustrious prisoner, Guy, the Count of Ponthieu, until both should acknowledge William to be their suzerain, and Anjou, in impotent wrath, watched from afar the thrusting forward of the Norman border.

William caused his new castle to be built upon a height. When the plans were spread before him he looked at Raoul with a questioning lift to his brows, but Raoul shook his head. A faint smile passed between them: William turned to

Roger de Montgoméri, and said bluffly: "Will you hold fast for me, Roger?"

"Yea, lord, be very sure," Roger answered promptly.

Later, Gilbert de Harcourt burst out at Raoul as though he could not contain himself. "Is it true what FitzOsbern says, that the Duke offered this hold to you?"

"He offered it, yes."

"You young fool!" Gilbert cried. "You'd none of it?"

"Of course not. He did not want me to take it, you know," Raoul said calmly. "What should I do with a border-fortress? Is that work for me?"

"A proper man would ask no more," Gilbert replied.

Raoul laughed, and said with a gleam of mischief: "Content you, the Duke has a better use for me than to thrust me to a border-hold."

"Bowels of God, you set some store by yourself, Master Stiff-Neck!"

Linking his hands behind his head, Raoul tilted his chair back on its legs, and said lazily: "Well, men call me the Watcher."

This was perfectly true, but it annoyed Gilbert to hear Raoul say it, just as Raoul had known it would, and he stumped off muttering to himself at his brother's upstart ways.

Montgoméri called his new castle La Roche Mabille, for his wife's sake, and set about the ordering of it at once. Looking south to the hazy distance that hid the County of Anjou from view, the Duke said with his short laugh: "If that windbag comes when my back is turned, Roger, send me his head for a *Hanguvelle*—a New Year's gift."

But it seemed that Anjou had had his fill of marching to and fro. No sign came from him then or for many days.

As for the Duke, he retired once more into Normandy, and reached Rouen in time to hear the bells pealing for the birth of his daughter Adeliza.

There were feasts to mark the event, and the great court of the palace saw miming and jousting. William made Wlnoth Godwineson a knight because he acquitted himself well, and unhorsed his man. He would have knighted Edgar too, but Raoul shook his head. Edgar would joust with the Normans in the way they had taught him, his eyes fairly sparkled with his zest for the sport, but Raoul did not think he would accept knighthood at Norman hands.

When he came out of the lists, hot, and flushed and

victorious, Edgar impulsively: "I wish we had this way of fighting in England! To feel a good horse under you, and a lance in your grip—eh, that is a sport I have been glad to learn! I should like to ride into battle as you do."

Raoul watched him drain a bugle-horn to the dregs. "Do you never ride into battle?" he asked.

Edgar tossed the horn aside, and began to mop his hot face and neck. "No, we don't use destriers as you do. And we have our battle-axes, of course, instead of your lance." He paused, and his animation died down. "The battle-axe is the better weapon," he said.

"I don't believe that," Raoul answered, to provoke him.

"Of course it is better!" Edgar said. "Why, man, I could strike your Blanchflower's head from his neck at a single blow of my axe!"

"A rude barbarous weapon," murmured Raoul.

"You had best pray you may never have to meet it," said Edgar grimly.

At his words a shadow seemed to fall between them. Raoul was not looking at him, nor did he answer. Edgar thrust an arm through his, and began to walk with him towards the palace. "I don't know what made me say that. Perhaps it will never happen. My father writes that the King has sent for the Atheling to come into England, so maybe it is he who will have the crown, and neither your lord nor mine."

"The Atheling? God send Edward names him his heir!" said Raoul with a lightened brow. He pressed the Saxon's arm. "If that should come upon us: my lance to your axe——" He broke off.

"I know," Edgar said. "Did I not say it four years ago when first I came into Normandy? Well, maybe it will not come after all."

"No. Not if Edward chooses the Atheling. Is it four years, Edgar?"

"Four years," Edgar said. His mouth curled disdainfully. "I begin to think myself as much at home as Wlnoth and Hakon do."

Raoul stopped, as though a sudden thought had occurred to him. "Edgar, is that true?"

Edgar shrugged his big shoulders. "It sometimes seems to me that I am all Norman," he said. "I joust with you, and speak your tongue, live with you, make friends amongst you, chafe because I may not ride to war with you, rejoice because your Duke has driven out the French——"

"I didn't know you felt like that," Raoul interrupted. "I thought—— Edgar, the Duke would make you a knight, but I said you would not wish it. Shall I speak with him again?"

"My thanks to Duke William," Edgar replied at once, "but I will never take knighthood from his hands. I am Harold's man." He thought that this sounded ungracious, and added in a more docile voice: "It is not because I do not like Duke William, you know. I did not mean that."

"I know," Raoul answered. "Do you think I would not say the same? But for all that you do not like William, do you?"

It seemed at first as though Edgar were not going to answer, but after a moment he said: "No. That is—— No, I do not like him. I can't help admiring him, of course: no one could. But what has he to do with any man's liking? Loyalty he may command; obedience he will enforce; but love——? Oh, no, he does not look for that!"

"Perhaps you do not know him yet," Raoul said.

Edgar looked at him with the hint of a smile in his eyes. "Do you think any man knows him, Raoul?" Then, as Raoul was silent, he said: "Oh, he has great kindness for his friends, but never have I seen him try to win men to him as——" He stopped.

"As Harold does?" suggested Raoul.

"Yes," Edgar admitted. "I had Harold in mind. All men love Harold. But all men do not love William. They fear him, they respect him, but how many would count it happiness to die for him? FitzOsbern, maybe; Saint-Sauveur; Tesson; his cousin of Eu; yourself—those who are his friends. But I tell you the meanest serf would give his life for Harold."

They walked slowly on in the shadow of the curtain walls. Neither spoke again until they had rounded a corner of the chapel in the inner bailey and stood beneath the towering keep itself. Then Edgar, looking up at a narrow window set in the grey stone, said on a lighter note: "Well, I'll wager there at least lies one who feels no love for William."

Raoul glanced up. "The Count of Ponthieu? No, but he will have to bend to William's will whether he likes or whether he hates him, just as Geoffrey of Mayenne bent."

"What of the Archbishop?" inquired Edgar. "Is he to bend too?"

"Mauger!" Raoul said. "I think his course is run."

They began to mount the steps leading up to the great door. Edgar said, chuckling: "William FitzOsbern told me yesterday how he found Mauger when he went to wait on him last. Did you hear of it?"

"No, but maybe I can guess."

"It made even our sour-faced Albini laugh," said Edgar. "You know how FitzOsbern can tell a tale. He said they told him that the Archbishop was at his devotions, but in he would go, to await Mauger's leisure. Some fool of an usher, not understanding what was whispered to him by the steward, led William straightway to the Archbishop's closet, and called his name. In William marched, just in time to see fat Mauger scuffling his leman off his knee, and trying to look as though his fingers had been busy with his rosary instead of paddling in her neck."

"God's eyes, in his very closet?" demanded Raoul, half-scandalized, half-entertained.

"In his closet," nodded Edgar. "It was that red-haired wench, Papia, that used to drive the swine to market every Friday, the wench who ran from Moulines-la-Marche when he would have taken her. Don't you recall her? Well, she's housed in Mauger's palace now, decked out in silks and gold chains, as grand as the Duchess herself."

"A bondman's slut!" Raoul said disgustedly. "So that was what Galet meant by his jest last night! Well for Mauger if this does not reach the Duke's ears."

"Oh, the Duke is bound to hear it," Edgar declared cheerfully. "All the Court knows."

"Then we shall have a new Archbishop at last," said Raoul.

He was right, but the Duke did not choose to make his uncle's amours the reason for his deprivation. Although Lanfranc had obtained the dispensation for William's marriage with Matilda, although the master-masons were still labouring over the plans of the two monasteries that were the price of it, and two infants had already been born of the union, Archbishop Mauger had not abated one jot of his disapproval. His ambitions, which had been frustrated by the fall of his brother of Arques, had gradually resolved themselves into a malevolent desire to see his two-powerful nephew laid low. Some said that letters passed between him and the French King; be that as it might, when the news of the King's flight reached Rouen the Archbishop changed colour, and those who stood near him saw that his pouched eyes held an expression of sickly hatred. He had been accounted a subtle man in his prime, but he was old now, and disappointment had blunted his wits. He chose this inauspicious moment to denounce the two-year-old marriage as though there had been no sanction obtained for it in Rome, and to excommunicate Duke William from the Church.

It was the pretext for which the Duke had been waiting. His heavy hand fell on the Archbishop at last: Mauger was deprived of his see, and bidden depart out of Normandy in twenty-eight days. He was succeeded by one Maurilius, monk of Fecamp, a man of many virtues, and as famous for his abstinence as Mauger had been famous for his incontinence.

On the day that Mauger set sail for the Island of Guernsey Galet twitched Walter of Falaise's stool from under him as he was about to seat himself at the Duke's board, and stout Walter sat down with a thud among the rushes. "God's belly, if I do not break your skull for this, fool!" Walter rumbled, aiming a blow at him.

Galet skipped out of reach, crying shrilly: "Eh, there is another of Brother William's uncles down!"

The Duke's lips twitched; the Court broke into open merriment, and Walter picked himself up from the floor with a good-humoured grin, and a shake of his honest head.

CHAPTER IV

"A hart of twelve, lord!" cried one of the huntsmen above the sound of the mort. He bent over the still breathing animal, and drew out his hunting-knife. FitzOsbern said disgustedly: "I'll be bound that's the brute I could not bring down yesterday. All the good fortune is with you, beau sire."

But William was looking at his bow as though he saw it for the first time.

"I wish I could shoot as he does," Edgar told Raoul. "I have rarely seen him miss."

Raoul answered rather absently. He was watching the Duke, wondering what thought had occurred to him to make him suddenly so abstracted.

The Duke had an arrow in his hand; he balanced it on his finger, looking thoughtfully down at it. FitzOsbern noticed this odd conduct, and inquired if there were anything amiss. The Duke did not seem to hear him. For a moment or two he went on turning the arrow between his fingers; then he jerked up his head, and said briefly: "I have done. Raoul, will you ride back with me?"

"Well, here is a short day's sport!" exclaimed FitzOsbern. "Have you had your fill of it already, seigneur? Albini, do you go too? Edgar, you have had no fortune yet: do you stay?"

"I want only Raoul," the Duke said over his shoulder.

They rode side by side down the forest-track. The Duke had the lash of his whip between his teeth, and he was frowning in a way that showed his thoughts concentrated. After a while Raoul said: "Well, seigneur? What now?"

William turned his head. "Raoul, have you ever thought that one might use arrows in warfare?"

"Arrows?" Raoul looked rather surprised. "Could that be done?"

"Why not?" The Duke spurred on at a brisker pace. "Men-at-arms could be trained to use bows. They might carry them as well as their gisarmes." He stared ahead, still frowning. "No. A man fighting with sword or spear must hold a shield beside. There must be some other way."

"If a beast can be slain by arrows a man can too, of course," said Raoul slowly. "But how might an archer contrive to take aim in the press of battle? He must surely be cut down at once, for he could not guard himself."

"If he were in the press," the Duke agreed. "But my archers could shoot from an hundred paces, and so have no need to guard themselves." His eyes lit; he said in his impetuous way: "By the Face, I think I have solved a riddle that has plagued me these many days! I believe bowmen might wreak great havoc amongst the enemy."

"So can spearmen," said Raoul, misliking it.

"But while we fight hand to hand it must be the stronger side that wins," William insisted. "If the King were to bring a host across the border again, think you I could drive him out? Yea, if I can lead him to a snare once more. But if I must pit my strength against his in a battle such as we fought at Val-es-dunes? What then?" He paused. "But if I had bowmen, shooting from a place of safety? Bones of God, there would be room then for my strategy!"

"Yea, but if you hold off these bowmen, seigneur, they must perforce loose their shafts into the backs of your own knights," Raoul objected.

The Duke thought for a moment. "True. And if I so placed them that they could aim along the enemy lines they would still find marks in my own men, struggling in the mêlée." He turned to look at Raoul; there was animation in his face, and the corners of his mouth had begun to lift. "Raoul, I tell you I will change the whole way of war!"

Startled, Raoul said: "Beau sire, surely you will not seek to send us, your knights, into battle with bows instead of swords!"

"Nay, but do you not see that there might be more to my battles than my knights' swords? What if my bowmen were to strike the first blow shooting at sixty, an hundred paces?"

"Why, they must kill or wound many, I suppose," Raoul admitted. "Would you send them in advance, then? Where stand your knights?"

"Drawn up behind in support," the Duke said promptly.

Raoul nodded. "The enemy charges: it seems to me your bowmen must bear the first shock, and so farewell bowmen!"

"Not so. I will have them fall back behind my chivalry. That could be ordered. What do you think? Don't frown: I am not wood-wild yet."

"It is in my mind," said Raoul, "that the barons will take it amiss. Will you put bows into the hands of serfs? Your Council will say it is a thing unknown."

"So said they when I retreated before the French," the Duke retorted, and set his horse at a gallop towards the bridge across the river.

His bowmen became known soon enough as his new foible. Some of the barons were opposed to such an innovation; some regarded it with indulgent smiles; many were captious, yet interested. The Duke cared nothing either for scorn or approval, but set on foot the training of his bowmen, and was forever riding out to mark their progress or planning campaigns in his private closet. He drew strange diagrams with quill and ink, and his captains scratched their heads over these, and yielded at last a reluctant interest. That a man should fight battles with pawns from a chessboard was something so new that it had to be regarded with suspicion. Warfare as the barons understood it was a matter of chivalry charging to sound of tucket and of drum; strategy was of the roughest order: one chose one's ground, one laid ambushes, or made surprise attacks, but while the battle raged there could be nothing more to it than hand-to-hand fighting in a tight pack. But the Duke bent over his miniature battlefields, and moved his pawns this way and that, slowly evolving a more intricate way of war than his captains could understand.

That he was preparing to withstand a fresh attack from his suzerain everyone knew, for although King Henry had signed the treaty of '54, no one supposed that he would abide by its articles. Men's eyes looked towards France, and hands were not far from sword-hilts during the three years of peace which followed the taking of Ambrières.

Two years after Mortemer the Atheling Edward died in London, leaving two daughters and an infant son, Edgar, to the King's protection; and in Rouen Guy, the Count of Ponthieu, at last submitted to Duke William's terms for his release. Guy had been housed as befitted his rank, and no indignity had been put upon him, but he soon saw that though William might treat him with courtesy he would never release him until the price was paid.

Ransom was offered and refused. "You shall pay me homage, Count, no gold," William said.

"By God I will never bend the knee to Normandy!" the Count swore very earnestly.

"Then by God, Count, you will not again see Ponthieu," William replied without heat.

"I have offered you a King's ranson!" Guy said.

"I will take your oath of fealty," answered William.

"Duke William, you have mistaken your man!" the Count cried with spirit.

William smiled. "Be sure, Count, that between us two it is not I who mistake my man," he said, and on those words went out.

The Count glared after him, but ended by burying his head in his arms. In after-years he was heard to say: "If I had been so sure of myself as that man I believe I might have conquered the world."

He was prepared to endure shackles, a dungeon, perhaps torture, but it was no part of William's policy to arouse hatred in one whom he meant to make his vassal. The Count was honourably entreated, and might have whatsoever he desired, save only freedom. Walking upon the battlements he would look always towards the east. Beyond the plains, beyond the river that wound through them like a silver thread, over the far hills, eastwards and northwards still lay Ponthieu, awaiting her lord's return. His eyes grew dim with looking; he thought he could hear the waves breaking upon his foam-drenched shores, and see the grey towers of his capital. Over his head a standard slapped in the wind; he looked up and saw the golden lions of Normandy waving above him.

For a year he clung to the hope that he would wear out the Duke's patience. He saw his fellow-captive, the Count of Mayenne, render homage to William, and go riding homeward. He stood firm still, but he knew now that William would never relent. The second year dragged wearily past; the Count grew sick of despair, and no longer looked towards Ponthieu.

William, visiting him in his apartments, said: "They tell me you are ailing, Count, but I think no physician of mine can cure your malady."

"That is true," Guy answered bitterly.

The Duke walked to the window, and beckoned. "Come, Guy of Ponthieu," he said.

Guy looked at him for a moment, then walked forward to stand at his side. The Duke pointed through the opening. "There runs the road to Ponthieu," he said, "by Arques and Eu; a day's ride, Count."

Guy would have turned away at that, but the Duke's hand descended upon his shoulder. "Your lands are masterless," he said. "Soon comes a day when another man will rule in your stead. Get you back before it is too late."

Guy broke from under his hold, and began to walk about the room. The Duke stood still by the window, watching him impassively.

"Though you hold me captive till my death you shall not wring liege-homage from me!" Guy flung at him.

"I have not asked for it. But simple-homage you shall pay me, as Brittany pays."

The Count paced on in silence, turning it in his mind for the hundredth time. Liege-homage, which he had dreaded, would have meant that he must become a vassal such as any baron of Normandy, who received investiture in his lands on his knees, stripped of his sword and his spurs, his head uncovered and his hands between the Duke's, and took oath to become William's man thenceforward, serving him with life and limb and worldly honour. But simple-homage, which Normandy paid to France, was unaccompanied by such feudal obligations. There would be no humiliating livery of seisin, when the suzerain in person put his vassal in possession of his lands, nor would he be bound to serve William with troops in time of war, or to go into captivity as hostage for him if ever that need arose. An oath of fealty was all that was required of him. He turned suddenly, and said as though the words were forced out of him: "Simple-homage for my freedom: so be it!"

William nodded, and said in a matter-of-fact way: "To-morrow we will set a seal to this business. There will be nothing then to keep you longer."

Not many weeks after Guy's release the Duchess was brought to bed of her third child. Lost in the coverings of her great bed Matilda nursed her cheek in her hand, and would scarcely look at this second daughter who bade fair to be so like her. She had wanted to bear another son, just such an one as my lord Robert: dark, sturdy, and so high-spirited that he would beat his governors with his little fists· if they dared to gainsay him. She glanced resentfully at the fair mite, and presently said. "I would dedicate her to Holy Church."

"A good thought," William replied. He was shown the child wrapped in her bearing-cloth; his eyes rested on her indifferently enough, but all at once gleamed. He said with a laugh: "Rood of Grace; here is your very image, Mald!"

"Robert was the stouter babe," she answered.

But a year later a second boy was born to Normandy, and there were public feastings, and the Court kept night-rule for nearly a week, while Matilda lay crooning over her babe, and dreaming of the future that should be his. He was not a robust child; he cried fretfully for hours together, and not even the chaplet of mistletoe he wore could preserve him from the convulsions that from time to time attacked him. The physicians were never far from my lord Richard's side, and it seemed as though Matilda's ears were always on the prick for the faint echo of his wail. My lord Richard absorbed her attention for many months; she had little to spare for the Duke's archers; little even for the news of King Henry's secret activity. Her husband had no interest outside these two pressing matters.

It was known that Henry and the Hammer of Anjou had once more joined hands in an alliance against Normandy. Once more a great host was assembling; once more plans were laid for the plundering of William's Duchy; once more William called his knights together, and made ready to defend his own.

The French and the Angevin forces were expected to cross the border in the springtide of '58, this being a season always suitable for warfare; but King Henry, aware of his vassal's preparations, used a cunning of his own, and held off for several months.

"He will delay until I have disbanded my force," William said after three months of waiting. "So be it!" To the dismay of his councillors he disbanded his army then and there, keeping only a small force round his person.

Men who had grumbled at the cost of keeping a large army idle now shook their heads at such reckless tactics.

"The King will sweep into Normandy, and what hope have we with half our strength lost?" De Gournay demanded.

The Duke spread his plans out upon the table, and it was seen that he had had rough maps drawn of his Duchy. De Gournay grunted: "What shall this avail us?"

"Friend Hugh," said William, "is it known to us that the King means to march up through Hiesmes with the whole of his force, striking northwards to Bayeux—here?" He laid his finger on the map.

"Yea, it is known." De Gournay gave a chuckle. "He will never again venture in two divisions against us. If that Frenchman we seized spoke truth Henry means to turn east from Bayeux to ravage Auge. What then?"

The Duke made him look at the map. "Here I may catch him, or here, or even here."

"What, are we to play the same trick again?" inquired Count Robert of Eu. "Is he to march up unopposed? The corn is standing, William: he will do great injury."

Mortain gave a great yawn. "Oh, we beat him before! Where shall you lie, William?"

"Here, in mine own town."

They bent over the map, and saw his finger upon Falaise, his birth-place. De Gournay rubbed his nose. "Well ... But he will pass you to the west if he make Bayeux."

"But I shall lie between him and Auge."

"If he means to reach Auge he must cross the Orne and the Dives," said De Gournay. "The Orne at Caen, certainly; no hope of an ambush there. The Dives——" He broke off, and looked sharply at William. "Ha, do you plan to take him at the ford of Varaville, seigneur?"

"Where else can he cross the Dives?" William said. "Not at Bavent, nor at Cabourg. At Varaville, where the tide runs in faster maybe than he knows, we may hope to catch King Henry and that Angevin dog, Martel."

"Normans and French have fought before at Varaville," said Walter Giffard. "But why must we wait for him to reach thus far, lord? There are other places where we might catch him."

"A score," the Duke agreed, "but none so sure. If he heads for Varaville, as I think he will do, I have him at my mercy." He rose up from the table, and clapped the Lord of

Longueville upon the shoulder. "Bear with me, Walter," he said, smiling. "I have not yet led you to defeat."

"God's light, that thought was not in my mind, beau sire!" Walter said in a hurry. He coughed and exchanged a look with De Gournay. "What part in this will your bowmen play, seigneur?"

William laughed. "Trust me, they shall win the day for us, old war-dog," he said, and saw his councillors go off shaking their heads at what they deemed his folly.

In August, when the corn was on the ground, King Henry broke the Norman border again after a truce of four years, and plunged into Hiesmes with Bayeux for his goal. At his side, swollen with the self-esteem no reverse could abate, rode the Count of Anjou, a gorbellied man with a choleric complexion. With him were joined his two sons; Geoffrey, his namesake, called Als Barbe, and Fulk le Rechin, crabbed and surly, picking quarrels with friend and foe alike. King Henry had something to do in keeping the peace between this belli- cose trio and his own barons. France might join hands with Anjou in a common cause, but no Frenchman had any love for an Angevin. Squabbling broke out very early in the allied camp, and upon more than one occasion daggers were drawn between the rival men-at-arms, and ill-feeling flared high between their leaders.

Anjou was for battering down the donjons they passed upon their route. King Henry, observing fosses newly cleaned, and walls impregnably repaired, would waste no time in fruitless sieges. If he could sack Bayeux and Caen and ravage the rich land of Auge he would then be in a position to dictate terms to Duke William. This he told Martel, but the Count, who had become bull-headed with increasing years, was too easily diverted from his goal by the sight of a fortress held by some enemy. He was for turning aside to wrench from Montgoméri's hold that castle of La Roche Mabille which had galled his pride for three years. Curbing his exasperation King Henry weaned him from this project only to see him blunder along a fresh trail. He had an old grudge against one Walter de Lacy, and since de Lacy's hold lay upon their road, or very near to it, Martel could see little sense in leaving it unmolested. He devised a plan for splitting their force in twain, with himself at the head of one half to lay siege to such castles as housed men towards whom he nursed a personal spite, and King Henry at the head of the other half to march on to Bayeux.

It was not likely that the King, with the disaster of Mortemer in his memory, would agree to such a plan. Martel was dragged off his quarry again, and lured northwards with promises of plunder for his reward.

The French followed their usual custom of war upon this march to Bayeux, trusting to get absolution for the atrocities they committed. Unfortified towns, hamlets, bondmen's dwellings were spoiled and burned; any man found lurking in hiding was slain in such a way as to make good sport for the soldiery; the women were seized and shared amongst the men-at-arms. No religious qualms hindered the King from sacking the abbeys and monasteries he found, but for the most part the monks, forewarned by their vigilant Duke, had carried their treasures to places of safety. Martel, incensed at such miserly ways, flew into a passion, and seized the person of an abbot, threatening to see whether torture would induce the good man to reveal the hiding-place of his treasure. Scandalized Frenchmen intervened: this was going too far. It needed all King Henry's eloquence to convince the Count that such dealings could end only in his excommunication.

In such wise the invading force made its way north through Hiesmes to the Bessin, but however his men might plunder and burn, however careless Martel might grow, King Henry saw to it that whenever he lay in a town the guards were vigilant all night. King Henry had no mind to be burned in his bed as had been the unfortunates at Mortemer.

Hearing from his scouts of the strict watch kept by the enemy, Duke William laughed, and said mockingly: "What, does the King think I have only the one ruse in my head? Come, come, you must be schooled, O timid King!"

The French force reached Bayeux loaded with plunder, but the King was soon convinced that the town was too strongly fortified to yield under an assault. It was commanded by Duke William's warlike half-brother Odo, who was not deterred by his holy calling from ordering the defence in person, a mace in his hand instead of a crozier, and his dalmatic tucked up to allow him to bestride a horse. Directed by their fiery young Bishop the inhabitants of Bayeux repulsed the attacking party with a storm of javelins, darts, boulders, and pitch; and when the French fell back in disorder some bold chevaliers made a sudden sortie and did much deadly work before they were finally chased back into the town.

King Henry abandoned his plan of sacking Bayeux, and drew off towards Caen, laying waste the whole countryside. Bishop Odo laid aside his mace, and took up a quill to write the news of Bayeux' triumph to his brother.

170

Reading Odo's Latin phrases in Falaise William said with a curling lip: "God's dignity, could Henry do no better than that? By the Rood, I could think of a score of ways to take Bayeux!"

Day and night his scouts galloped into Falaise with tidings of the King's progress; day and night barons such as impetuous Tesson of Turie-en-Cingueliz and gay Hugh de Montfort led their skirmishing parties to harry the enemy's flanks. Step by step William was watching the King's advance, like a hawk hovering before his stoop.

King Henry was by no means careless of his vassal's might, but he knew that William had disbanded the greater part of his army and was far too wise a warrior to hurl his little force at the invading host. He feared surprise-attacks by night, or ambushes laid for him upon the road, but from open battle he thought himself safe. While he lay at Caen his guards were doubled, and the penalty for drunkenness amongst his men was death. But no sign came from William, and King Henry began at last to lend ear to those who said that the Norman dared not attack him. He pushed on eastward, and it was seen that he was in better spirits than he had been for many months.

But while he approached nearer and nearer to the ford of Varaville the man whom he believed to be afraid of him called in his skirmishing parties, and summoned all the franklins and bondmen of the district to arms.

The King's scouts crept as near to Falaise as they dared, but could learn nothing. They reported that the Duke still lay in the town, and had made no movement to march out. Emboldened, the King led his host on. Once across the Dives he would feel himself safe; only at the crossing over the narrow causeway that led through the marshes did he fear a mischance. He kept a strict watch for the Duke, expecting to hear of a sortie from Falaise. Within a day's march of Varaville he had certain tidings that William had not stirred from his post. He gave a cackle of laughter, and said to Martel with unwonted good-humour: "The Wolf's cunning has failed him at last! I thought to hear of him marching to lay an ambush for me at Varaville, and I tell you had I heard of a sortie from Falaise I would have turned south to Argences rather than have risked an engagement at that treacherous ford." He rubbed his dry hands together. "Ha, William, do you sleep?" he said with something approaching glee.

Martel called boisterously for wine. While he drank success

with Henry, and cracked jests over the Normans cowering in safety, there was not a knight nor a man-at-arms left in Falaise. The Duke had moved at last, when all fear of such a happening was banished from King Henry's mind, and was marching north with a speed the laden French force could never hope to emulate.

The army he led had a strange appearance. A body of his chivalry rode in the van with polished hauberks gleaming in the hot sunlight, and gonfanons waving on the ends of lances. Behind came a motley gathering of spearmen and serfs, some wearing breastplates and carrying their proper shields and gavelocs; some clad in leather tunics, with bows in their hands some holding scythes and hatchets for weapons, and mounted on whatever horses they could come by.

"Holy Face!" exploded Hugh de Gournay, "what rabble is this we lead?"

The French reached Varaville when the tide was at its lowest. A causeway led through long marshes to the ford; beyond, upon the eastern bank, a different country held out its promise to the invaders. There were no boggy flats ahead of them, but gentle hills rising immediately beyond the river bank.

Slowly the van led by the King and Martel in person forded the river, and began to climb the heights upon the further side. Upon the causeway the unwieldy rear-guard made ready to follow: horse, foot, sumpters, and laden wagons. The tide was rising as the last of the van made their way across the ford. King Henry, surveying all from the hills beyond the river, began to fear that the water would soon be too high to allow men to pass, and sent out the word to make all speed. Martel caught his arm unceremoniously, and pointed with a shaking finger across the river. He tried to speak, and made only a gobbling noise in his throat. The King looked up quickly, and saw armed men to the west, galloping down the causeway. He shouted an order, but as the words left his tongue his favourite, Renault de Clermont, cried out: "The marshes, the marshes! God on the Cross, look yonder where the swamps are alive with men!"

The King started forward, glaring where Renault pointed. Amongst the rushes and rank shrubs of the swamp men were running along the hidden paths only they knew, leaping from foothold to foothold, winding in and out of the bushes, to close in on the causeway.

The King sent a messenger galloping down to the ford with orders for the men on the causeway. "A few spearmen and a horde of serfs," he said, with his gaze still on the marshes. "Do you lose heart so easily, Renault? You shall soon see that rabble beaten off, I promise you." He looked towards the horsemen, halted at some distance, and said: "Ha, the Wolf tarries yet awhile. He mislikes the look of my meinie, messires." His voice changed. He said sharply: "God's grace, what is that?" His hand gripped de Clermont's shoulder; his eyes were fixed on the men scattered over the marsh. "Bowmen!" he whispered. "Arrows . . . !"

Martel found this so ridiculous that his spirits revived. "Ho ho! does the Bastard think himself at the chase?" he demanded. "A good jest!"

"Jest!" the King cried. "God's pity, where is your jest?" He swung his horse about, calling to Saint-Pol with new orders.

Across the river William's bowmen had already loosed their first volley of shafts. Some fell short, some soared over the Frenchmen's heads, but many found their marks. The men on the causeway were thrown into disorder, frightened by the rain of arrows; those who had formed hastily to oppose the advancing chivalry were seized by panic, and huddled together on the narrow road, unable to retaliate, and appalled by a form of attack they had never before encountered. Some spearmen tried to struggle through the marsh to come to grips with the archers, but they did not know the paths, and the ooze sucked them under.

The King was livid, and his hand shook on the bridle. His first thought was to wheel the van back across the ford, but while he sent out commands for a new formation his captains urged him to see how impossible a return across the river had become.

The tide was running in fast, and even while Henry swung his men about the archers and the spearmen on the marsh were spreading along the river bank to hold the ford.

"Sire, sire, our foot can no longer wade across!" Saint-Pol cried.

"My Chivalry can make it still!" the King flung back at him.

Montdidier interposed. "Madness, sire, madness! We cannot do it; we should fall before those accursed arrows as we struggled across. There is nothing we can do!" He put up his hand to shade his eyes from the sun. "Ha, Du Lac has them in hand again! See, beau sire, they stand fast!"

"The Bastard is moving forward," Saint-Pol said, watching the horsemen far down the causeway. "He is there in person;

I can see the golden lions of his gonfanon. Now God send our men throw him back! Ah, heart of Christ, can no one reach to those bowmen?"

A renewed storm of arrows was whistling over the causeway; it was plain to the watchers upon the eastern bank that the terror of this death from afar was throwing the French rear-guard into blind confusion. The Norman spearmen had reached the causeway over the marsh and fallen upon the French flank; the horse, charging down the causeway itself, threw the front lines into chaos. The French were bewildered, not knowing which way to turn. Arrows sang through the air; the Norman foot was all amongst them, fighting hand to hand; and the weight of the chivalry was forcing them back and back to fall victims to the archers and men-at-arms who held the ford behind them.

In impotent anguish King Henry watched half his army cut to pieces. He tried to throw his chivalry across the treacherous river, but the water was rising fast, and a hail of arrows drove him back. He sat huddled upon his destrier, unable to take his eyes from the skirmish on the western bank, and saw his men fighting desperately, not to beat back the Normans, but to escape from the death that seemed to be all amongst and around them.

Montdidier found his tongue, while the rest stood in agonized silence. He stuttered: "Bones of the saints, what way of fighting is this? Ah, cravens, beat them back! they are but a handful! God's death, have we not one leader below there?" He turned away, unable to look any longer at the dishevelled rabble on the causeway.

They dragged the King from the ground at last; he sat bowed upon his horse, and suffered them to do as they would. Of his rear-guard not a man escaped from that day's battle. The fight raged all amongst the wagons and the gear of the army; those who were not slain in hand-to-hand combat, or pierced by the deadly arrows, tried to flee across the marsh. Some perished with dreadful cries in the swamp, slowly sucked under the mud and the green water; others were followed by the Norman peasants and either slain or taken prisoners. A few flung themselves into the river in a desperate attempt to swim across to the eastern bank, but their hauberks weighed them down, and they could make no headway against the current. The water was churned up, with tossing limbs and dead bodies floating on the tide; the causeway was littered with overturned carts, their loads of forage

174

and plunder spilled about them. Here the carcase of a horse blocked the way; there a mound of dead men heaved with the last feeble struggles of some wounded soul pinned under the heap of slain.

Hugh de Gournay wrenched out an arrow that was stuck fast in the thick leather of his tunic. "My thanks, beau sire," he said with grim humour.

William's charger was standing amongst a heap of scattered treasure. A battered chalice glinted in the dust; a length of sendal shimmering with gold thread was trodden and twisted under the restless hooves; vessels of silver, jewelled chains, a gleaming fibula, lay spoiled upon the road, dabbled in the blood of a disembowelled horse that sprawled incongruously beside them.

The Duke was watching the retreat of the French vanguard across the river, but he turned his head when de Gournay spoke, and saw the arrow. "Are you hurt?" he asked. "I am sorry, Hugh: that was not as I meant it."

"A scratch, no more. It was almost spent when it reached me. But must your bowmen find marks amongst your own men, beau sire?"

The Duke laughed. "Nay, that shall not happen again. Yet will you say my bowmen did not win the day for us?"

"If they were ordered aright," said de Gournay, cautiously feeling his shoulder, "they might do well enough."

"What, do you uphold the archers at last, Hugh?" inquired Count Robert of Eu, who had come up, picking his way across the dead. He removed his helmet, and threw it to his squire. "If the dolts had but held their hands when they saw us engage the French we should have lost scarce a dozen men, I believe. How say you, Walter?"

The Lord of Longueville grunted. "Well, I saw some of our men struck, but that was because redeless serfs loosed the shafts. Now if there were a body of skilled archers, schooled under new captains . . ." He pursed his lips, planning the formation of such a body.

Robert stole an expressive look at the Duke. There was a smile hovering about William's mouth. "Shall my archers be kept then, Walter?" he asked innocently.

The Lord of Longueville, interrupted in his meditations, said: "Kept? Oh—ah! kept! Why, all Christendom will use archers after this day's lesson! Would you use them no more because they are as yet unskilled, beau sire? Nay, nay, we must devise how best to order them." He nodded kindly at his young master. "You must have patience, seigneur, and you shall soon see a very different body of bowmen at work."

The Duke bowed. "My thanks, Walter," he said gravely. He picked his way over the debris on the road, and murmured in Robert's ear as he passed: "Give Walter and old Hugh de Gournay but seven days and they will be sure my arrows had birth in their own brains!" He rode on to see what prisoners had been taken; the Count of Eu lingered long enough to hear the start of a dispute between these two boon comrades, Giffard and de Gournay, over the best way to dispose a troop of archers, and then unobtrusively drew off.

The remainder of the King's army was in full retreat. All the plunder, the forage, and the accoutrements of war were lost to Henry, and it seemed as though the disaster had affected his brain. When he spoke at last it was to urge a speedier flight. High words passed between him and the Count of Anjou. Martel said blusteringly: "At least it was not I ordered this craven retreat. No, by the body and bones of God! Had I the command I would have faced the Bastard in battle."

At that the King fell into a fit of dreadful laughter, and reminded Martel of his old retreats from Domfront, and from Ambrières. In such melancholy fashion did these two allies at length part company. The crippled host reached the border, and passed into France and safety. King Henry had pitted his might against Normandy for the last time.

It was soon seen that the ruin of his hopes had seriously affected his health. He seemed to have aged ten years in a day, and displayed a listlessness that shocked his nobles. He was forced to sue for peace with Duke William, and while his councillors laboured to mitigate the humiliating terms demanded he sat apart, huddling his mantle round him, and staring into space. The terms were read to him; he nodded his head as though here were no great matter. Only when the article was reached that gave back Tillières to Normandy did he show any signs of chagrin. Then his mouth twitched, and his faded eyes blazed suddenly with some of his old passion. But the brief fit passed; he assented to all, and bade his councillors see that the peace was soon sealed.

In Rouen the Duchess lay again in William's arms. She was crushed against the rings of his hauberk, but seemed not to heed the steel bruising her flesh. She said eagerly: "You have won back Tillières, lord?"

"I have won back Tillières, according to my word," he replied.

She was in a glow: eyes, cheek, and heart. Her mouth invited his caresses. "Ah, William, you are worthy to be the father of my sons!" she crooned.

He held her from him, gripping her arms unmercifully. "Is it burgher-blood that is mingled with yours, wife?" he said.

There was a harsh note in his voice, but if she remembered the seven-year-old insult it was but fleetingly. She hardly heard what he said; she was brooding over his triumph. "O Fighting Duke, if I were but a maid again!" she said. "You might take me then, a conqueror's guerdon!"

She could enflame him still, driving everything but his love for her from his head. He caught her close to him, saying softly: "Shall I not take you though you are maid no longer, my guarded heart?"

"I am all yours," she said, laying her hands on his breast.

Hardly a year later Normandy was rid for ever of her two great enemies. King Henry, who had fallen into a sickness after the signing of the peace, lingered through the winter and the spring, but died at last, worn out with grief. His death was followed in a few months by that of Martel. It was as though Duke William had sapped their life-blood.

Martel left his county divided between his two sons. "Nothing to fear there," said William.

Philip, King Henry's son, inherited the Crown of France, but since he was still a child King Henry's will named Baldwin, the Count of Flanders, Regent during his minority. In death King Henry had sought to redeem the follies of his life. No abler man could have been found to hold the reins of government, none more honest, none further-sighted. But vassals in Auvergne and Vermandois, Aquitaine and Gascony, Burgundy and Angoulême, heard of the King's choice with dismay.

If Baldwin was to govern France, Normandy was freed from her last puissant enemy. For thirteen years Duke William had stood upon the defensive, his peace threatened first by his own rebel barons, and then by France and Anjou, hedging him round with spears. Now, at the age of thirty-two, he stood secure. East of him Ponthieu rendered homage; west, Anjou was cleft in twain by Martel's will; south, France was governed by a wise Count who was Duke William's father-in-law.

It was with misgiving that the vassals journeyed to swear their oaths of fealty to King Philip at his coronation. Last of them all came Normandy, and men who had never seen the Fighting Duke out of battle-harness now saw him surrounded by a retinue the Court Chamberlains were hard put to it to house, and magnificent in a way that cast the noblest of the vassals in the shade.

"Well, wife, well," said Count Baldwin, using no ceremony, "it seems to me that our daughter chose wisely when she chose Normandy for spouse."

"He is grown too arrogant for me," the Countess, a French-woman, replied: "Where shall all this end, my lord?"

Count Baldwin stroked his beard. "It is in my mind," he said slowly, "that it is not yet begun."

"Why, how should that be?" she asked.

Looking at her thoughtfully, the Count said: "We have seen him beat back all who would have snatched from him his heritage. How stands he now, think you?"

"Safe, God wot!" she answered.

"Yea, yea," he nodded. "And shall that content him? I fear it may not, wife."

THE OATH

"Harold, ye cannot deny that ye swore an oath to William upon
holy relics."
Speech of Gyrth Godwineson.

CHAPTER I

"Now tell me it all, right from the start," Edgar said. "Holy
Thorn, but you are burned as brown as a nut! You took no
hurt?"

"Not so much as a scratch." Raoul thrust a hand through
his arm. "And you? What has chanced since I saw you?"

"Oh, nothing!" Edgar said. "Rouen has been like a tomb
since you all rode away to Maine." They walked on slowly
through the palace gardens. The ground was hard with frost,
and a fringe of snow lay on the edge of the grass. "I had
news out of England a month ago," Edgar said. "My father
writes of Harold's victories. While you have been conquering
Maine he has conquered the Welsh." His cheeks showed a
faint flush of pride. "Harold carried Griffyd's head and the
beak of his ship back to London," he said. "Think you that
was well done?"

"Very well done," Raoul agreed. "He must be a mighty
warrior. What other tidings?"

"Little enough. Wlnoth has taken a leman. Tell your tale.
Is it true that the Duke entered Le Mans without a blow?"

Raoul nodded. "He kept that for the last. You know his
way. We wanted no more bloodshed than had need be. But
who holds Le Mans holds Maine."

"Was Walter of Mantes in command there?"

"No, it was held for him by the chief among his friends.
Geoffrey of Mayenne was one. I knew that dog would never
keep faith."

"Well, let me hear how it went!" Edgar said impatiently. "I
have been wishing myself beside you all these weary
months."

Three years before, after the death of Martel, Heribert,

179

the youthful Count of Maine, had become Duke William's man. Freed from the Angevin tyrant he yet did not feel himself strong enough to stand against Martel's two successors. He approached William, for whom he cherished a deep respect, and entered into an engagement with him to hold Maine as Normandy's fief in accordance with the charter granted to Duke Rollo in ancient times. A treaty was drawn up between the two princes; Count Heribert's sister Margaret was formally betrothed to Lord Robert, the heir of Normandy, and Heribert pledged himself to wed Adeliza, the Duke's eldest daughter, as soon as she should be of marriageable age. Duke William was found to be an over-lord of a very different kidney from Martel, so that Heribert, a man of feeble health, thought he could do no better for Maine than to make a will bequeathing it to the Duke, should he himself die without lawful issue. In two years this possibility had come to pass. Count Heribert, on his death-bed, warned his nobles against such tyrants as Walter of Mantes, the spouse of his aunt Biota; and Geoffrey, the hungry Lord of Mayenne; and with his last breath commanded them to submit themselves to Duke William.

It was not to be expected that the Manceaux could be united in desiring a foreigner to be their Count. A strong party gathered about the standard of Walter of Mantes, who claimed the throne in the right of his wife. They entered and fortified the town of Le Mans, and declared Walter and Biota to be their new rulers.

Thus, in the year '63, Duke William had put on his battle-harness again and marched out at the head of his forces, not this time to defend, but to conquer. As ever, Edgar had yearned to ride with the army; he had even petitioned William to let him go, but the Duke had said: "And if you should fall in battle, Thegn of Marwell? I have pledged my knightly word no harm shall befall you. What would you have me say to King Edward who entrusted you to my care?"

Edgar had gone disconsolately away, and watched, later, the army ride out from Rouen without him. Now the campaign was ended, and once more the palace teemed with the lords and knights of William's court. Edgar had dragged Raoul apart at the first opportunity, and taken him out into the frosty gardens to learn what had befallen. "Tell me it all, right from the start!" he said.

"Oh, at first there was little enough!" Raoul answered. "We harried the country to affright the people, since we desired no bloodshed. That was easily done: they hold William in such dread they will fly for their lives if they but catch a glimpse of his spears. We burned a few dwellings, seized some forage for our men, and pressed on, taking what towns lay in our way. And so came to Le Mans. To tell the truth, we wondered how we should capture that citadel, for it is built high on a hill and well fortified."

"But there was no siege?" Edgar interrupted. "FitzOsbern said——"

"No seige, no assault," Raoul answered, laughing. "They called it the Joyeuse Entrée. I warrant you the burghers had had their fill of Walter's captains by the time we reached Le Mans. They sent to welcome us, and when we were assured we were close in support chased out Mayenne and the other lords gathered there. William rode in over the flowers that were strewn under his charger's hooves."

"They welcomed you?" Edgar said incredulously. "Strangers? Invaders?"

"Be sure they desired us to come. You have not seen Walter of Mantes or his men. Maine was groaning under their yoke when we came to claim our right. And all men know that William is a just prince."

Edgar shook his head. "Yea, but—— Well, after your Joyeuse Entrée?"

"We marched from Le Mans to Mayenne, and finding it so situated it would yield to no assault we took the place by fire."

"What, as was done at Mortemer?"

"Yes, but this was a harder task. Everyone said there was no taking Mayenne, it was so strongly guarded. We took it in half a day."

A shrill cry of Haro! made him break off. There was a scuffle in some bushes near at hand, and young Roger FitzWilliam, FitzOsbern's eldest-born, broke through, hotly pursued by the sturdy boy who was heir to Normandy.

Roger stopped when he saw the two men walking across the grass, and drew back, but Robert came on full-tilt, shouting: "Holà, Messire Raoul! Do you know my father has brought my betrothed home with him? Her name is Margaret. But of course you know, do you not? She is going to be my bride." He planted himself in Raoul's path, lifting his handsome head to smile in a friendly way at the two men.

"I wish you joy in your spousing, my lord," Raoul said. "Have you seen the Lady Margaret?"

"Oh yes!" Robert answered, straddling his legs. "She is older than I am, but such a little pale creature you would scarcely credit it. My mother says she will be reared with my sisters, but Adeliza does not like it because Margaret will be of more consequence than herself, besides which she is jealous because Count Heribert died, and she is no longer betrothed. As for Margaret, I tell Adeliza of course she must be of more consequence, because she is to be my bride, and when my father dies I shall be Duke of Normandy." He began to dance along beside Raoul. "And when I am Duke I will make every day a holiday, and Roger there shall be my Seneschal, and we shall have jousting and hunting all day long."

"In the meantime," Edgar interrupted, "I think you have escaped from your governor, little lording, and will soon be under the rod."

Roger, who was hovering in the background, grinned sheepishly, but Robert only tossed his head and said: "That is as may be. Now that my father is home again I know I shall have but poor sport. I wish he would ride away to fight another war."

Raoul said only: "That is foolish talk. How do your brothers? They will be grown since I saw them, even as you are."

"Oh, they are well enough," Robert answered. "William is a silly babe still, and as for Richard he should be with us now, only that he is so slow he can never keep up with Roger and me."

"It was not very well done of you to run away from him," remarked Edgar.

"I think I can hear him coming, messire," Roger ventured. "We did not mean to leave him, but you see we were playing at chase."

"For my part," said Robert frankly, "I would be glad to lose Richard. Just hark at him! He is more of a babe than Red William."

My lord Richard's voice was heard lamenting beyond the bushes. He came into sight, a thin child with his mother's fair locks and pale colouring. When he saw his brother he began at once to scold him. "I hate you, Robert! You hid from me! I shall tell my father of you, and you will be beaten."

"So will you if you tell the Duke we ran away from our books," retorted Robert. He began his restless prancing again, catching at Raoul's mantle. "Ohé, I wish there was no

182

such thing as Latin! I would like to learn only my knightly exercises, and be upon my horse all day long."

"Ho, you will never ride as well as I can, because your legs are too short!" cried Richard. "Messire Raoul, the Duke saith that Robert should be called Curthose because he has such short——" He got no further. With a furious cry of "Swineshead!" Robert plunged at him, and they rolled over together on the grass fighting like two wild cats.

Edgar hauled Robert off with one hand and held him fast while he raged and struggled. Over his head he said: "True sons of a Fighting Duke, I warrant you, Raoul. . . . Have done, lordling! You will bring your masters out upon you with all this uproar."

This fate came to pass. Watching the three boys marched off under escort to the palace, Edgar said: "The Duke has bred an heir who will plague him sorely, I think. Already Robert falls foul of him."

The words were spoken half in jest, but held more truth than Edgar knew. Of all his children, Robert, his first-born, in whom his hopes might have been supposed to lie, was furthest from the Duke's heart and understanding. Robert was impetuous and could brook no opposition; it was unfortunate for him to have an autocrat for sire. There was enough of his mother in him to make him hard to manage, and he was apt to run against discipline from a natural perversity. His mother adored him, and sheltered him from Duke William's wrath whenever she might. He began very early in life to look on the Duke as a tyrant; he was afraid of him, but since he was Matilda's son he hid his fear under an intractable front, and so came under William's displeasure a dozen times in a week.

As for the other children, it was not to be supposed that issue born of so stormy a union could live at peace for long at a time. The ducal nurseries echoed to the sound of quarrelling; Robert fought Richard; Adeliza defied her governesses with an intrepidity that braved even the rod; the little nun Cecilia betrayed an arrogance hardly in keeping with her saintly calling; while even three-year-old William demonstrated to the world that he had a temper to match his fiery head.

Watching his son from afar the Duke said impatiently: "Eh, Raoul, shall I have no worthier successor than Curthose? Bones of God, I had more judgment when I was no older than he is now than he will have when he reaches my present years!"

"Patience, beau sire: you were bred in a harsher school," Raoul answered.

The Duke saw Robert go off with his arm flung round the shoulders of Montgoméri's son, and said contemptuously: "He is too easy; he must always make himself beloved. When have I cared for such things as that? I tell you Robert has heart for my head."

Raoul was silent for a moment, but presently he said: "Seigneur, you are a stark prince, but is it so ill to have a warmer heart than yours?"

"My friend, I stand supreme to-day because my heart has never ruled my head," the Duke said. "If Robert learns not that lesson in time, all that I hold now he will lose when I am with my fathers."

As time went on the Duke could see little in Robert to make him unsay those words. Throughout the winter life at the palace was often disturbed by my lord Robert's pranks and his father's speedy vengeance. Lord Robert cared nothing for his governor's beatings, but complained between laughter and scowls that Duke William's hand was too heavy.

The spring came, and Robert was kept busy with the knightly exercises he loved. Peace reigned for a while between him and his father, nor were there any troubles in the Duchy to break a monotony unusual in Normandy. Gilbert d'Aufay said with a yawn: "Heigh-ho! I could wish another Count of Arques would arise to give us work to do."

"Watch Brittany," Edgar advised him. "I have heard some chance talk."

"Edgar, you always hear these things!" said Gilbert. "Who told you? Was it Raoul? Is Conan of Brittany denying us fealty?"

"That I do not know," Edgar said carefully. "It was not Raoul. FitzOsbern let fall something that made me wonder, that is all."

"Well, God send we have something soon to liven us," Gilbert said, with yet another yawn.

His prayer was answered sooner than he could have expected, and in a way no man had foreseen. The Count sat at dinner one day in late spring when a sudden stir arose outside the great doors, and angry voices were heard expostulating. The Duke sat at the high table on the dais, facing down the hall to the entrance. The meal was over, and the company was in merry mood, with the wine and the dulcets still on the tables.

When the disturbance rose in the base-court the Duke looked frowningly towards the door, and FitzOsbern went hurrying off to inquire into the meaning of so unseemly a noise. He was no more than half-way down the hall when there was a scuffle at the entrance, and a voice was heard to cry desperately in broken Norman: "Audience! I crave audience of the Duke of Normandy!" A moment later a protesting usher was thrust so rudely backwards that he fell sprawling on the rushes, and a tattered mud-stained stranger forced his way into the hall, dragging in his wake two men who had snatched at his mantle to detain him. He wore a short tunic, rent in several places, and splashed with mud; his helm was lost, and his long blond ringlets were tossed into disorder and damp with the sweat on his brow. He stopped midway up the hall, staring about him at the surprised faces all turned towards him. His gaze swept them by and found the Duke, seated still and watchful in the middle of the high table. He flung out his hands, dropping on to his knee. "Aid, aid, lord Duke!" he cried. "Give me a hearing, and justice!"

Edgar started round on his stool, breaking off his talk with William Malet in mid-air, and seemed to peer at the stranger in doubt and incredulity.

The Duke lifted his finger, and the men who still held the stranger let him go. "No man asks justice of me in vain," he said. "Speak! What is your need?"

A stool rasped on the stone floor; Edgar sprang to his feet.

"Alfric! God's soul, do I dream?" With a bound he was off the dais and at the stranger's side, clasping him in his arms. Some quick Saxon speech passed between them; their hands were fast-locked. In obedience to a signal from the Duke one of the stewards filled a cup with mead and carried it to the stranger.

"How came you here?" Edgar demanded. "I hardly knew you, so many years it is! Eh, my friend, my friend!" He pressed Alfric's arm and raised him, unable to find words. "Here, they have brought you wine! Drink! you are nigh spent!"

Alfric took the cup in a shaking hand, and drained it. "Harold!" he jerked out. "In desperate plight! Speak to the Duke for me, Edgar! Will he hear me?"

Edgar grasped his wrist. "Where lies Earl Harold? Not dead, man, not dead?"

"Nay, not dead, but in dire peril. Will Normandy aid? I cannot well talk in this tongue: be my spokesman!"

The Court sat in expectant silence, watching the two Saxons; the Duke turned his head and crooked a finger toward William Malet, who had Saxon blood in his veins. William went to him, and said softly: "He is saying that Earl Harold lies in desperate plight." He looked towards young Hakon. "Do you know who he may be, Hakon?"

Hakon shook his head. "Nay, but Edgar knows him. He craves aid of Normandy. He says will the Duke see justice done?"

"Be very sure." William leaned forward in his chair. "Bring the stranger before me, Thegn of Marwell. Why does a Saxon call on me for aid?"

"Seigneur, it is for Earl Harold!" Edgar said. Raoul had never seen him in such agitation of spirit. He turned back to Alfric, and asked him something. Alfric began to tell his story, speaking in a weary, disjointed manner, and prompted by many sharp questions. The Duke leaned back in his chair, and waited.

At last Alfric's voice ceased. Edgar swung round to face the Duke. "Lord, Earl Harold lies prisoned in Ponthieu, in peril of his life.... Where is the place, Alfric? ... At Beaurain, lord, held by Count Guy. I cannot make out: Alfric is not sure, but he says it is some law they have in Ponthieu regarding shipwrecks. Alfric says they were upon a voyage for their pleasure, but meeting contrary winds were driven on the rocks off the coast of Ponthieu, their ship foundering, and themselves struggling to land. But there some fishermen seized them—Alfric says a man shipwrecked is legal prey in Ponthieu. I don't understand that. He says a man washed ashore may be prisoned and tortured for promise of enormous ransom." He stopped, and looked inquiringly at the Duke.

"That is the custom in Ponthieu," William answered. "Go on. How came Count Guy to seize the person of Harold Godwineson?"

Edgar turned again to Alfric, translating the question. "Seigneur, he says that some among the fishermen, discovering who Harold was, set off to advise the Count, betraying our Earl for gold!" His hands clenched. "The Count came in person to seize Harold, and those with him, loading them with chains.... Who was with Harold, Alfric?"

The answer drove the colour from his cheeks. He passed his tongue between his lips, and put up a hand to his tunic, as though he would loosen it about his neck. He swallowed twice before he would trust himself to speak again, and then his voice was a little unsteady. "Lord, there were with Earl Harold some thegns known to me, and his sister, Dame Gundred, and—and Elfrida, mine own sister, seigneur, waiting upon Gundred! Alfric only escaped, and has come here hot-foot to implore your aid." Suddenly he bent his stiff knees, and knelt. "As I do, lord Duke. You are Ponthieu's suzerain: give aid for Harold and those with him!"

The Duke's eyes lifted; in them was an expression hard to read, but Raoul saw them gleam. "Be at ease," he said. "Aid you shall have, and that speedily." He summoned up his High Steward. "Let the Saxon Alfric be housed according to his honour and mine. FitzOsbern, attend me to my chamber. We will send envoys to Ponthieu this day." He came down from the dais, and paused for a moment before the two Saxons. Alfric, seeing Edgar upon his knees, knelt also. The Duke said briskly: "Up, man! We shall ride to meet Earl Harold tomorrow."

Catching at his meaning Alfric kissed the Duke's hand. Edgar rose up from his knees, and stood with folded arms, ashamed of his own show of emotion. The Duke smiled rather curiously at Alfric's broken words of gratitude, and went out, attended by FitzOsbern.

Edgar bent quickly, and raised Alfric, and pushed him on to a stool at one of the tables.

"He will indeed rescue Earl Harold?" Alfric asked anxiously.

"Oh yes!" Edgar replied. "His word is given. Yet I wonder . . ." He stopped, and sat down beside Alfric. "Tell me, tell me, how does my sister? my father? If you but knew how I am hungry for tidings out of England!"

Perceiving how weary Alfric looked, and how much in need of food and wine, Raoul came down from the dais, and laid his hand lightly on Edgar's shoulder. "Let your friend eat, Edgar. Ho, there! Bring meat and wine for the Duke's guest!"

Edgar took his hand and Alfric's, and brought them together. "Raoul, this is my near neighbour, Alfric Edricson. Alfric, this is Raoul de Harcourt, my good friend." He looked up, and his grasp on Raoul's wrist tightened. "The Duke will rescue Harold from Ponthieu," he said, as though the words were forced out of him. "But tell me—assure me—Harold is not a second time betrayed?"

Raoul met his look gravely. "What ill thought is this?"

"Nothing." Edgar brushed the back of his hand across his brow. "There is misgiving in my heart. In the Duke's eyes methought I saw—triumph. No: heed naught. I speak like a fool."

Scarlet and yellow flashed before them; the bells on the jester's cap tinkled. Galet stood cuddling his bauble. "Nay, it was well spoken," he said with a queer chuckle. He slipped past Edgar, who was frowning at him in suspicion, and tweaked the hem of Raoul's tunic. His lips moved; the words he spoke reached Raoul's ears alone. "When the lion snatched the fox's prey from his very maw, was that a rescue, think you?"

Raoul turned on him with an angry exclamation, and a hand raised to strike, but the fool dodged away, and went scuttling from the hall, laughing as he ran. His laughter echoed oddly round the rafters; it sounded elfin, like the laughter of a mocking sprite.

CHAPTER II

Far into the night, long after the *couvre-feu* bell had been rung, the two Saxons talked together in the tower-chamber that was Edgar's. Edgar's page brought wine and cakes and spread them on the table, while Alfric sat looking about him in wondering silence at tapestry hangings, costly furs, and silver candle-sconces. When the page had withdrawn he took one of the wine-cups in his hand, and began to trace with his finger the design raised upon it. He said: "You are nobly housed, I see."

"Well enough," Edgar said, too used by now to silver and gold and rich hangings to think them worth remark. "Tell me of England! Were you with the Earl in Wales?"

Alfric began at once to talk about the Welsh campaign. Edgar sat with his chin in his hands, but very soon a puzzled frown appeared between his brows, and he interrupted Alfric with questions that made him stare.

"Stay, who is this Edric you speak of?" Edgar demanded. "And Morkere? Is that one of the sons of Ethelwulf who lives by Pevensey?"

"Ethelwulf!" Alfric exclaimed. "No indeed! Why, Morkere is Earl Alfgar's son! Surely you must know that!"

Edgar reddened, and said humbly: "You forget that I have been an exile for thirteen years. So Alfgar has a son of age? I hardly realized—— But go on: does Alfgar live at peace with our Earl? I remember him to be so prudent a man he would never stand——"

"Alfgar has been dead these two years," Alfric told him. "He left two sons of age, Edwine and Morkere. But neither has his wisdom. Morkere must needs be quarrelling already with Earl Tostig—you know that he has Northumbria, I suppose?"

"Of course," said Edgar. "His dame is sister to the Duchess Matilda, so that I have heard tidings often enough of him—more than I liked. Does he agree with Harold, or is it between them as it was ever?"

"The same. He does so ill in his earldom Harold would be glad to get him outlawed, and to that end is working. Tostig is our foe. He hates the Earl, and when the King dies—"

"Oh, the King, the King! I would he might live till all of us lie buried!" Edgar said quickly.

"I never thought you had so much love for the Saint," said Alfric, staring at him. "In England, all of us who are Harold's men are but waiting for Edward's death to proclaim Harold King." He leaned forward across the table that separated them. "Edgar, you must know: what passed between Duke William and the Confessor when you were given as a hostage?"

Edgar said reluctantly: "I do not know. That is—I have no certainty. There was an old tale spread that the King meant to name Duke William his heir. They believe it here. But when Edward sent for the Atheling out of Hungary I thought there must lie the end of all scheming, for the Atheling was Edmund Ironside's true son, and the only heir to England."

"Yea, but he died. He was no man for the Saxons. Why, he was as foreign to us as the Saint himself! But of course men wavered to him for the sake of the blood. God be praised, he died, and as for the son, the little Atheling Edgar, he is a child and may be passed over. As I see it, Harold is safe. He is all-powerful, Edgar: you do not know. I suppose he must suspect this Norman Duke, but England stands behind him. He has been at work for years to render himself secure. If he can be rid of Tostig the thing is done. Gyrth and Leofwine are leal men both, and hold all the south country." He broke off. "Why do you look like that? Are you not Harold's man?"

Edgar rose up quickly. "What, must you ask me that?"

Alfric poured more wine into his cup. "I cry your pardon. You are so much changed I could not but wonder."

Edgar looked at him in a startled way. "Changed? How am I changed?"

"Well. . . ." Alfric drank off his wine, and sat turning the cup in his hand. "To say sooth—you have become so like a Norman," he said bluntly.

Edgar stood still as a stone. "A Norman? A—Norman? I?"

"You have lived here so many years I suppose it must have happened," Alfric said excusingly.

Edgar flung out his hands. "Holy Face, look on my beard, on my short tunic at which they laugh here! Can you say I seem to you a Norman?"

Alfric regarded him from under puckered brows for a moment. "It is not in your looks, nor in your Saxon habit," he said slowly. "But when you speak, using Norman oaths; when you greet your friends here; clap your hands to summon pages habited in royal colours; and think gold cups and spiced meats no matter for remark, then do I see the Norman in you."

Edgar came to the table and laid his hand on Alfric's, gripping it hard. "You are wrong. Body and soul I am Saxon—*tout diz, tout diz!*"

Alfric smiled a little. "Yea? And what words were those—Saxon?" Then as Edgar looked bewildered, he said: "You do not know when you speak the Norman tongue, so used you are become."

Flushing, Edgar answered in a constrained voice: "If my tongue slipped that signifies naught. The words mean—always."

Alfric laughed. "Loose me, then. Must my bones be crushed because you are Saxon still?"

Edgar let him go, but Alfric's words seemed to rankle. "When you see Wlnoth Godwineson you will not think that it is I who have grown like a Norman," he said.

"I saw Hakon below there. Where was Wlnoth?"

"Not here. The Duke has given him an establishment at Roumare. He abides there with his Norman meinie, and his leman. It is a *lieslode*, I think." He caught himself up on the word, and corrected it. "An estate for life, I would say."

"For life! Well, no harm. Harold wants no more of his brothers in England. Let Normandy hold Wlnoth; he is of small account." Alfric got up, and stretched himself. "I do not like these Normans. A black-avised race, much given to display. Who was that loud-speaking man who went out with the Duke, and came back later swaggering as though he were alderfirst in the land? He who poked a finger in your ribs, making jest of some matter passing my knowledge?"

"Why, the Seneschal, FitzOsbern," Edgar replied. "Did I not make you known to him?"

"Nay, and I had no wish to clasp hands with him," said Alfric, yawning. "He is the very spit of some of the Saint's Norman favourites. He wore red to make one blink, jewels to dazzle, and strutted like any peacock."

Edgar opened his mouth to retort, and shut it again, compressing his lips. Not noticing his friend's ominous silence Alfric said: "I hate a man to wear silks like a courtesan."

"You judge too hastily," Edgar said. "FitzOsbern hath a noble soul." He saw Alfric smile sceptically, and added: "He is my friend."

"I cry pardon then. It seems you have many friends here in Rouen."

"And that none of them have the good fortune to please you," said Edgar.

Alfric looked sharply up at him, and found that his eyes had a stony expression in them. "I did not mean to offend you Maybe you have grown used to a strange people and do not see the faults I see."

"I know their faults," Edgar replied. "When I first came among them I felt as you do. But I have had great kindness from them which I shall not easily forget." He glanced at the candles on the table. "The candles burn low; it must be late. If we are to ride to Eu to-morrow we had best get to bed." He picked up one of the heavy candlesticks and slipped a hand in Alfric's arm. "I'll light you to your chamber," he said, trying to banish the constraint from his voice. "It will seem like our boyhood's days when we ride side by side to-morrow. Do you remember how we took bows and shot a hart of ten upon Edric Digera's land, and were soundly trounced for it?"

"Yea, that do I!" Alfric answered, smiling at the recollection. "It was an ill hap that brought Edric across our path that day. How long ago it is! Edric was slain in the Welsh wars, God rest his soul. His brother's son sits in his room to-day."

With his hand on the door-latch Edgar said, surprised: "How is that? He had at least one son when I left Marwell, and I heard that Dame Elgifu was childing again."

"Oh, he had a pack of brats, but they were lepers every

191

one," Alfric replied. He stepped out of the room on to the turn of the stair. "I lose myself in this great palace," he complained. "Am I lodged near to you?"

"Not far," Edgar said. He held up the candle so that its feeble light showed the way. "This tower is new built. It was finished only three years ago. They let me have my lodgings in it so that I might be close to my friend Raoul. He is the man with the smiling eyes whom you saw in the hall. He has been my friend these thirteen years. You must like him for my sake."

"With goodwill. But I think I shall not long be in Normandy. The Earl will hardly wish to tarry. No one knows how long the King may last, and if Harold were to be absent when he dies all might yet miscarry.... What a huge, chill place this is! How can you be at home here? It is as big as King Edward's palace at Thorney, and as lofty as the great Abbey he is building there."

Edgar led the way along one of the galleries, and up another stair. "My father wrote me of the King's Abbey. It is long a-building." He opened a door, and stood back to let his friend pass in. The room was lit by a single rush-light, but a sleepy page jumped up from a pallet at the foot of the carved bed, and put a taper to the candles on the table. "Have you all that you desire?" Edgar asked. "If there is aught else tell me, and I will speak to the boy for you."

"Nay, there is aught," Alfric replied. "Sleep is all my need." He looked round him. "The Duke uses me with great pomp. This is a lodging for a prince."

Edgar wrinkled his brow. "Well, if I remember rightly, a prince did sleep here once. It was Robert the Frisian, Count Baldwin's first-born, when he was here with the rest of the Flemish Court for the Duke's nuptial rejoicings." He grinned suddenly. "He was a wild lad in those days, I can tell you. I sometimes think my lord Robert, his nephew, favours him. Gilbert d'Aufay and I had something to do in getting him to bed and keeping him there after one of the feasts. He was so drunk nothing would do, but he must try to pick a quarrel with Moulines-la-Marche, with intent, so he swore, to slit his gizzard. A good riddance had he done it, but of course it might not be. Gilbert and I strove with him." He saw that Alfric's smile was perfunctory, and realized that a memory he did not share could hardly be supposed to amuse him. He picked up his candle again, and said rather flatly: "I'll leave you; you will be glad of a night's rest." He hesitated. "You do not know what it means to me to see you again after all these years," he said awkwardly.

"And to me," Alfric answered at once. "Why, it is so long we meet almost as strangers! Earl Harold must prevail upon the Duke to let you return with us to England, and we will teach you to forget all your Norman ways." Aware of the gulf that lay between them he tried to bridge it. "I have missed you often: indeed you must come back with us."

"I would I might." Edgar's voice sounded rather desolate. He moved towards the door. "I have been an exile too long," he said sadly.

He went back along the gallery to the stair that wound up past Raoul's door to his own above it. Outside Raoul's chamber he paused, and after a moment's indecision lifted the latch and went in.

The candle-flame held near his face woke Raoul. He blinked, and started up on his elbow, groping instinctively for his sword.

"You are not in the field now," said Edgar, laughing. "And your sword, happily for me, is in that far corner. Wake up: it is only Edgar."

Raoul rubbed his eyes and sat up. "Oh!" He looked at Edgar, puzzled. "But what are you doing?" he said.

"Nothing. I have just taken Alfric to his chambers."

"Oh, bearded barbarian, have you wakened me to tell me that?" demanded Raoul indignantly.

Edgar sat down on the edge of the bed. "I don't know why I came in," he confessed. "Shall you ride to Eu with us to-morrow?"

Raoul lay down again, and regarded Edgar with a sleepy twinkle. "All Saxons drink deep," he murmured, "and I suppose when friends meet after long absence——"

"If you mean that I am in my cups, shaveling, you are at fault," Edgar interrupted. "Do you ride with us tomorrow? I wish you would."

Raoul seemed to be drowsing, but he opened his eyes at that, and they were wakeful all at once. "Yea, I ride. But I hardly thought that you would want me. You must have much to say to Alfric."

"Yes," said Edgar in his most expressionless voice. "But I want you to be there to greet my sister, and—and to see Earl Harold." The words sounded lame even to himself. Something ached in his breast; he supposed it must be his heart. He wanted to tell Raoul of its load of disappointment, yet could not. He thought Raoul would surely understand how bitter it was to find a gulf lying now between himself and the friend he had been so overjoyed to see. Alfric and he had been as strangers. Alfric had talked of an England which seemed more remote than the England of Edgar's dreams. Names remembered by him were forgotten there; new men whom he did not know had risen in place of the old; he wondered whether he too were forgotten. For thirteen years he had dreamed of his own country and the comrades of his youth, believing that he would find his lost happiness again when his hands lay in theirs, and his feet stood firmly on English soil. It had never entered his head that constraint could lie between himself and such an one as Alfric. He remembered with a pang that he had had no closer friend, thirteen years ago. Yet reunion, long looked for, long desired, had brought only a deeper sense of exile. Alfric belonged to a dead past. Here, quizzically regarding him, lay the only friend who counted, the friend who shared his memories and could read his heart. He turned his head and looked down at Raoul with a queer little smile. "Do you remember," he said, "when the Flemish Court was here how the Frisian tried to knife William of Moulines?"

Raoul laughed. "What, when you emptied a pitcher of water over the noble guest to sober him? Yes, I remember. Why?"

"No reason," Edgar said after a slight pause. "And as for the pitcher of water, that is one of Gilbert's lies. It was knocked over by ill chance, and if the Frisian was drenched it was more his fault than mine. And so he owned, upon the next day."

"Have it as you will," said Raoul sleepily. "I wish you would go to bed. First you tell me you have taken Alfric to his chamber; then you ask me if I ride with you tomorrow; and now you must needs know whether I remember a jest over ten years old. Was it for this that you woke me?"

"Nay, but I did not wish to sleep," Edgar said, "so——"

"So I must not either. All thanks, Saxon."

Edgar got up. "Alfric hopes Duke William may be prevailed upon to release me," he said inconsequently. "Do you think . . . ?"

"No," said Raoul, "because I shall beg him to hold you fast." He raised himself on his elbow again. "Edgar, you cannot leave us yet! Has Alfric thrust us all from your heart?—FitzOsbern, Gilbert, Néel, myself?"

Edgar did not answer for a moment. His eyes looked straight into Raoul's; he said at last in a low voice: "I think it is you alone whom I have for friends now. You need not have asked that."

All that he could not say lay behind the words; a friend would understand, he thought, and probe no deeper.

There was a short silence; then Raoul said lightly: "And if you keep me awake any longer you will have one friend the less, Edgar als Barbe. That in your teeth!"

The shadow seemed to retreat; the friend had not misunderstood. Edgar chuckled, and went out, oddly comforted, with a retort flung over his shoulder. But Raoul lay awake for some time after he had gone, frowning at the shaft of moonlight that lay across the foot of his bed. "O William my seigneur," he said softly, "I wish you had not taken Edgar, for I think you have spoiled his life."

In the morning the night's misgivings seemed absurd. Edgar rose with a feeling that he had been unjust to Alfric. In a day or two, he thought, their old relationship would return; meanwhile his sister and his Earl lay hardly more than a day's ride distant from him, so that there was room for nothing in his breast but a strange, leaping excitement such as he had not known since his boyhood's days. He began to be in a fidgeting mood as soon as he learned that the Duke would not set forward upon the journey until after the dinner-hour, and could hardly be brought to realize that no good purpose could be served by hastening to Eu any sooner.

"Even as it is you will arrive in advance of the Earl," FitzOsbern assured him. "Consider, Edgar! If our envoys reached Count Guy this morn, as I think likely, the Count must send to Beaurain to release Harold, and I shall own myself surprised if you see him before tomorrow noontide."

Edgar detained him. "Stay, William! What if Count Guy will not release Harold?"

FitzOsbern burst out laughing. "Why then, we shall carry our arms into Ponthieu! Rest you, he is not so great a fool."

"What message sent the Duke?" Edgar asked anxiously.

"A brief one," FitzOsbern replied. "He bade Guy render up your Earl *sur peine de cors et d'avoir.*"

Edgar was frowning. "A brief one. . . . Arms into Ponthieu. Why should he care so much what befalls Harold?"

He drew back from FitzOsbern. "There is something I do not see, some danger threatening. William, as you love me, does the Duke mean any harm towards Earl Harold?"

"None in the world," FitzOsbern answered promptly. "Now do not be in a fret for nothing, Edgar. No harm comes to Harold of which I know aught, and I am Seneschal here, and not quite ignorant, I believe."

Just before the dinner-hour Wlnoth Godwineson rode in with several gentlemen of his household. From a window in the gallery Alfric saw him enter the base-court, and called to Edgar: "Here is a fine creature ridden in! Did ever you see such a pretty youth? Who is it? How can you admire these Normans?"

Edgar looked over his shoulder. In the court Wlnoth had dismounted, and was shaking imaginary dust from his long cloak of vermeil. "That is no Norman," said Edgar with grim satisfaction. "That is none other than Wlnoth Godwineson, my friend. Best come down and give him greeting."

"Wlnoth! that popinjay!" Alfric gasped. He followed Edgar down to the hall, unable to find words to express his disgust.

Wlnoth entered by the great doors as they rounded the last bend of the stairs. Alfric saw that the cloak of vermeil was lined vert, and clasped on one shoulder by an ouch of emeralds set in gold. He wore a close-girt tunic of sendal reaching almost to his ankles, and purfled with a design of cinquefoil, vert on white. His boots were made of soft cheveril; a scent of musk hung about him; and he wore a great many rings and bracelets. He greeted Edgar with a white hand uplifted. "I am come hot-foot," he said in the Norman tongue. "So Harold lies shackled on these coasts! *Sire fires gart!*"

"Has Alfric Edricson a place in your memory, Wlnoth?" Edgar asked unemotionally, and pushed Alfric forward.

Wlnoth gave his hand to Alfric, and said a few graceful words. He spoke Saxon like a foreigner, and it was plain that he had little interest in his countrymen. He soon made an excuse to leave them, and passed on up the stairs to the gallery, negligently playing with the light whip he carried and humming a snatch of song under his breath.

He and Hakon were both of the party that set out for Eu that afternoon. Hakon rode alongside Edgar and Alfric, but Wlnoth cantered ahead with his Norman friends. To Edgar's annoyance they rested the night at Arques, but in spite of this they reached Eu next day in good time.

Count Robert, warned of their arrival, was awaiting them with new of Ponthieu's approach.

"We will ride to meet him," said the Duke. "Does he bring all his captives with him, as I bade?"

"So I understand," Count Robert answered. "A squire came in an hour back with a message from Guy promising obedience. He escorts the Earl in person. I am told they ride very friendly together, their tercelets upon their wrists, as at a day's hawking."

This was found to be true. Less than an hour's ride out of Eu the Ponthevin party was sighted, led by two men who rode side by side, apparently on terms of complete amity. The cavalcades drew nearer; beside Raoul Edgar was leaning forward in his saddle to look more closely. Raoul heard him say: "He is the same: not changed, not changed one jot!"

The Duke's small meinie was halted on the road, all but himself dismounted. Count Guy and his companion spurred their horses on in advance of their escort, and rode up in a cloud of dust. Through it Raoul saw Earl Harold, a giant of a man sitting his horse as though he were part of it. His mantle streamed out behind him, blue as his fearless eyes; his fair hair was tossed by the wind; he wore a crisp golden beard, neatly trimmed; but what drew men's notice towards him was the muscular strength of him, and the quick smile that never seemed to be far from his lips.

He reined in his horse before the Duke, and bowed low over its wither. "Hail, Normandy!" he said. His voice was clear and pleasant; he spoke Norman with only a faint accent.

The Duke was sitting easily, a hand on his hip. His straight gaze seemed to absorb Harold. He pricked forward until his horse almost brushed the Saxon's. "Greeting to you, Harold Godwineson," he said. His hand left his hip; he stretched it out to Harold.

Harold took it in a firm clasp. For a space the grip held. Those watching saw the ribbed muscles on each powerful arm, the gold bracelets both men wore glinting in the sunlight. Blue eyes looked full into grey. Gilbert d'Aufay whispered suddenly in Raoul's ear: "Thus two great ones meet at last. How fair he is! how dark our Duke!"

"Harold's thanks to Normandy for his aid" the Saxon said. He turned to the Count of Ponthieu, who stood a little part, and said with the flash of a smile: "Count Guy makes me full amends for what has passed. I would recommend him to your kindness, lord Duke."

"Your Earl is generous, Edgar," Gilbert murmured. "I would rather have recommended him to the Duke's justice."

"That is not Earl Harold's way," Edgar said proudly.

William was looking at Count Guy. The Count rode up close. "Seigneur, I have obeyed," he said, with a certain dignity.

William smiled a little. "Ask what ransom you will of me, Count: it shall be paid," he replied.

Guy flushed in quick surprise, and stammered a few words of gratitude.

"And that," whispered Gilbert triumphantly, "is Duke William's way, my Saxon."

"Ride to Eu with us, Count: we will make terms, you and I," William said. "Earl Harold, I have here three men of yours you will be glad to meet again." He crooked a finger towards the Saxons in his train, and Harold swung himself down from the saddle.

"Wlnoth!" he cried, and strode forward a pace, opening his arms to the brother so many years his junior. He caught the elegant Wlnoth by the shoulders, and held him away from him, looking into his face with eyes alight with laughter. "Out, you are grown from a babe to a man!" he said. "What, Hakon? My little nephew, you are became a very maypole, dwarfing me, I swear!" He embraced them, and saw Edgar upon his knee beyond them. Wlnoth and Hakon were put aside; Harold went to Edgar and pulled him to his feet. There came that warm look into his eyes, that unsuspected gentle note into his voice that made men love him. "Now here is one who has changed little," he said. "Edgar, my friend, God be thanked I find you still the same!"

"And you, lord," Edgar said, the words choking in his throat.

Harold did not let go his hands. "I have your sister in my train. I have been an ill friend to you to lead her into danger. But she has taken no hurt, and is a brave maid, worthy of you." He released one of Edgar's hands, and clasped Alfric's. "My thanks, Alfric: you have done well by me."

The Count of Ponthieu's escort had come up; strange knights were all amongst the Normans. Harold led Duke William to a litter slung between horses, and presented Dame Gundred to him.

"What think you?" Gilbert inquired of Raoul.

"Of the Earl? I see why Edgar loves him so well."

"So do I," nodded Gilbert. "Someone told me he is older than William. I should not have thought that. Where is Edgar? Oh, gone to meet his sister, I suppose!"

But in a few moments Edgar was at Raoul's side again, an eager hand on his arm. "Raoul, I want you to come to my sister. She is a woman grown, and I left her a little maid! I had not realized—— But come! I have told her of you, and she is wishful to know you, my friend."

Raoul beckoned to his squire to take his horse's bridle. "With all my heart," he said, and followed Edgar towards the second litter.

"Elfrida, I bring you Raoul de Harcourt," Edgar said. He held back the curtains of the litter, and looked proudly at Raoul.

"Lady——" Raoul began easily, and broke off, staring. The words of welcome died on his lips; manners went by the wind: Raoul de Harcourt was looking into the sweetest face he had ever seen.

"Elfrida speaks your tongue as well as I do," Edgar said, supposing a lack of Saxon to be the reason for Raoul's stricken silence.

A pair of big eyes smiled trustfully into Raoul's; he thought he had never seen eyes so blue. A hand came out of the covering rugs; a shy soft voice said: "My brother's friend commands my friendship too, messire."

Raoul held out his hand to take hers. Edgar was surprised to see his lean brown fingers so unsteady. They closed reverently over Elfrida's. "Lady, you are right welcome," Raoul stammered like a tongue-tied boy.

CHAPTER III

In Rouen Matilda received both the Saxon ladies with courtesy, but eyed Gundred, a haughty managing dame, a little askance. She was quick to sum up her own sex, and almost immediately assumed towards Gundred a gracious condescension that was designed to show that proud lady the gulf that lay between Earl Harold's sister and Normandy's Duchess.

Not to be outdone Gundred at once made play with the name of her sister Eadgytha, the Queen. Matilda raised her delicate brows, and said softly: "Alas, poor soul, that she has brought her lord no heirs!"

Gundred was pardonably annoyed. "Maybe that might rather be the King's fault, madame," she said bluntly.

Holding her own last-born, a babe still in its swaddling-bands, upon her knee, Matilda smiled. The smile might have betokened polite interest, or it might have betokened a mild scepticism. Gundred thought it best to turn the conversation into safer channels.

Towards Elfrida the Duchess used none of this edged politeness. Elfrida had gone plump down upon her knees as soon as she set eyes upon my lord William, that red-headed four-year-old, and held out her warm arms to him. There was no surer road to Matilda's heart; she could even forgive Elfrida for having long golden braids that made her own locks fade to flaxen. "You have a kindness for children, damsel?" she said.

"Oh indeed and indeed, madame!" Elfrida answered, looking shyly up at her.

"I see that we shall do very well together," Matilda promised.

Being a lady of discernment it did not take her many days to see how matters shaped between Elfrida and Raoul de Harcourt. The Duchess had more than once laid deep schemes for Raoul's espousals, but he had evaded these so often that for some years she had ceased to look about her for a bride worthy of him. Her quick eye now observed certain tell-tale signs to pass between him and the Saxon maid, and she did not know whether to be pleased or sorry. She contrived to find out from Dame Gundred what the girl's dowry would be: it was respectable, but to Matilda's provident mind not great enough to warrant her marriage to a Duke's favourite. She mentioned the matter to the Duke; he opened his eyes at it; he had noticed nothing. When assured that the Watcher was beginning at last to look beyond his lord he laughed, and seemed to think he would derive amusement from observing Raoul in a damsel's toils. The question of dowry left him unmoved. Matilda said: "Her marriage is in Earl Harold's gift. Would he see her wedded to a Norman?"

"Her marriage will be in my gift before all is done," he replied. "If Raoul is hot for her I promise you I will dower her nobly, my thrifty Mald."

When next he saw Elfrida he gave her more than his usual cursory glance. She found a direct stare bent upon her, and looked gravely back at him in a way that pleased him. He remarked to his Duchess that the damsel had a brave eye, and made a point of accosting her when opportunity served. When he chose he could be quite unalarming; Elfrida, who had hitherto thought him an awesome prince, found him unexpectedly jovial, and afterwards confided to her brother that she thought no two people could be kinder than the Duke and Duchess of Normandy.

Edgar was surprised, and a little perturbed. He hoped secretly that Elfrida would wed Raoul, because he loved them both, and had soon seen how Raoul regarded his sister, but when she showed a tendency to admire Duke William he was shocked, for to his mind no one who owed Earl Harold allegiance could cherish affection for William.

As for Earl Harold, he was moving through the Norman Court with the ease that was natural to him. He was fond of hawking and of hunting at force, and since he had a gay humour and a wonderful mastery over horse and hound, the barons at once liked him. He had a proud look; it was plain that he was accustomed to command; but he was never above his company, so that he made friends wherever he went. All through his life he was first a man whom men liked, but he had also a name for being a great lover. It was said that he had many lemans; Alfric had spoken the name of one lady so beautiful that she was called the Swan-neck as being Harold's mie. No doubt she was languishing in England now, awaiting the return of her splendid lover, while he rested in Rouen inflaming by no more than a chance look, a sudden smile, the hearts of many susceptible Norman ladies. He drew women as though they were moths and he the bright light round which they fluttered. There were a score of hearts in Rouen he might have plucked had he chosen, but he held off, steering an easy course through all this heady adulation, and gave only one lady cause to think she had him in thrall. And this was no less a personage than the Duchess herself.

Watching his liege-lady, Raoul began to wonder, and to know misgiving. She was sparing no pains to attract the Earl; she might be older, but she still had the mysterious lure that had caught and held Duke William. Now she turned her witch's eyes upon Harold, weaving new spells. Raoul saw it, and his brow wrinkled in a puzzled frown. He knew her too well to suppose she had room in her heart for any but her lord, and her fine sons. He watched closer; there was no love in her eyes, but they were dangerous as he had not seen them since she planned Duke William's downfall.

One evening before the supper hour he stood in the gallery

looking down at the hall where the Court was gathered into little groups. Earl Harold was beside the Duchess's chair, and it seemed as though some light traffic was passing between them. Raoul stood still, frowning and wondering. He heard a step behind him, and turned his head as the Duke came up.

William stood beside him, and looked down at the hall. He spoke without taking his eyes from the group about Matilda's chair. "What think you, Raoul? What manner of man is Harold?"

"One who does not show his whole mind to the world," said Raoul instantly. "A man of high courage, and large desires."

"I think I have his measure," William said. "He is more subtle than he would wish to appear; a leader certainly, a ruler—perhaps. He has not yet met his match." He watched Matilda smile up into the Earl's face; he was of a disposition that brooked no rival; what he owned no other man might touch; but he seemed unperturbed at the sight of his dame's behaviour.

Raoul saw satisfaction in his eyes, and all his wondering was done. "When does the Earl set sail for England, beau sire?" he asked. There was a hint of severity in his voice.

William's lips curled. "Do you think I am very likely to let Harold slip through my fingers?" he said. "I have him at last; save at a price I shall not let him go."

"He threw himself on your mercy!" Raoul said hotly. "Trusting to your chivalry!"

"My friend, one who nurses such ambitions as Harold carries in his breast dare place his trust in no man," said William.

Raoul looked at him in a startled way, and with a gradually darkening brow. "Beau sire, when you sent to deliver Harold from Ponthieu Edgar begged me to assure him the Earl was not a second time betrayed. Now by God's light you give me cause to wonder whether he had not reason when he asked that question!" He saw a smile flicker across the Duke's mouth, and his hand descended on William's wrist and gripped it almost unconsciously. "William, my seigneur, I have been your man these many years, following you blindfold, knowing that your way never led to dishonour yet. But now I see you changing, made ruthless by your too large ambition, forgetful of all but a crown. Dread lord, if you mean harm to Harold who trusted in your knighthood, take my sword and break it across your knee, for you are no more a master for me, or for any man bound by his vows of chivalry."

The Duke turned his head and regarded Raoul with a faint gleam of amusement. He said: "O Watcher, you are my man to the day of your death or mine. Not Harold, nor even the fair Elfrida can wean you from me."

Raoul jumped at that, but answered steadily: "You only can drive me off from you."

"I shall not do it." He flicked Raoul's hand with one finger. "Loose this grip. Is every passer-by to see me thus rudely used? I will be as careful of Harold's ease as of mine own, but he shall not leave Normandy." He took Raoul's arm in a friendly hold, and walked slowly along the gallery with him. "Have faith in me yet. I will put no constraint upon him; he shall dwell in my palace as my most honoured guest—yet, and be entertained by my Duchess, as you have seen."

"If you constrain him not," Raoul said practically, "he may ride to the coast as soon as he lists."

"He is too wise. I have placed trusted men about him to serve his needs; he cannot escape their vigilance. He knows that though I beg him to stay with us a while yet I have it in my power to enforce that—request. Do you think him a fool? I am sure he is not. He will not risk putting his suspicions to the test: none but a madman would provoke the Wolf in his lair. And so I hold Harold upon a chain forged of his own suspicions."

Raoul could not forbear a grin. "William, am I to be cozened by such smooth words as these? Do you think I do not know you? If Harold were to throw all upon the chance of flight you would have him seized before a man could cry Harol!"

"I might do so," the Duke said calmly. "But it would suit my purpose very ill to put an open restraint upon the Saxon. There will not be the need."

They had reached the door leading into the Duke's solar, and passed into the room. It was small, and rather stuffy, with a slit window set in the deep stone wall. Tapestries hung all round it, depicting the lives of certain saints; there was a table in the middle of the floor, and a couple of chairs stood beside it. The Duke sat down in one of these, and leaned his arms upon the table.

"William, it is unworthy," Raoul said. "He came, thinking no ill, and is betrayed."

"He came with his eyes open, knowing me for his foe, trusting in nothing but the certainty that I would deliver him from a more pressing danger."

"If he knows you to be his foe how should he place himself in your power? You might, for all he guesses, slip poison into his wine, or arrange some seeming accident at the chase."

"My thanks to you, Raoul. Yet I think I have not earned the name for ridding myself of mine enemies by such means as that. Consider again: were Harold to die in Normandy all Christendom would point at me, his murderer. Would Holy Church support my claim to England then? Would any man? Nay, Harold must know himself safe from poison or chance arrows. But he cannot escape me, and that also he knows."

"To what end? Will you hold him for ever? That way, too, you must have every honest man against you."

"Nay, I shall not hold him for ever," the Duke answered. "He shall bind himself by oath to uphold my claim to England. That oath sworn I will speed him on his way hence."

Raoul wandered to the window and stood there, leaning his shoulders against the cold stone. Across the room his eyes frowned into William's. "He will not do it."

"He will do it."

"Torture would not wring that oath from such an one as he."

"Not torture, nor fear of death. But the King is stricken in years, and might die—who knows?—today, tomorrow, a year hence. If Harold were to be absent from England when Edward is coffined, think you there are no others ready to snatch at opportunity, and a crown? There is that wasting boar Tostig; there are those who desire to set up the child Atheling; there are Edwine and Morkere, the sons of Alfric, of Leofric's blood. Let Harold but get news that the King is in failing health and he dare not tarry longer outremer. He will take the oath without any threat of mine to urge him."

"And be forsworn, saying that you forced it from him. How are you served?"

"Very well. If he breaks his covenant he will stand forth for all the world to see and scorn: a perjured man. The Church will stand for me then, and I will not move unless I receive the Holy Father's sanction. Let him declare for me and I may leave Normandy assured that no man will break my borders while I am away."

Raoul said nothing. Turning his head he stood gazing out of the window at the sky and the chasing clouds. He saw a tomorrow that made him afraid. Glory it might hold; for Normandy perhaps a future splendid beyond his dreams; but before these could be attained dark crafty policy must go before and a sea of blood be crossed.

Two clouds drifting past the narrow window merged gradually into one and sailed on towards the setting sun. He watched them with unseeing eyes, while his hand, lying on the deep embrasure, slowly closed and tightened. Beyond the tortuous policy, beyond sorrow and bitter strife a crown lay waiting for the strongest hand to seize it. The Duke would dare that high emprise, and no Norman looking to Normandy's future could deny his wisdom. Long ago William had seen the perils that would always beset Normandy, hedged as she was by jealous neighbours, and guarded by fickle borderholds; he had seen a goal ahead, a kingdom for his ancestor's dukedom, and had determined to win for his posterity that glorious heritage. Dubious statecraft might be needful to his end; bloodshed, and death, and the misery of a whole nation; perhaps years of unending strife, but these would not daunt him.

But Raoul was not made of this stern stuff. More to him than ultimate achievement was present suffering, the severing of friendship, and the unscrupulous scheming that, while it might raise William the ruler high above other rulers, must make William the man lose chivalry in ambition.

He swung around suddenly. "I cannot like it!" he said. "All that you would urge I too can see, yea, and desire for Normandy's sake and your fame. But I have a friend out of England whom I have loved for long years. Must I turn my sword-point to his breast? I have seen warfare; I have seen how invaders laid waste this Duchy; I have seen men tortured, and women raped, and babes spitted upon gisarmes; I have seen whole towns given to the flames, and heard the wail of a people sore oppressed. Can you win England without bloodshed? If you will reach a throne it must be across the Saxon dead. Thus Edgar said once, and he spoke only the truth."

"But I shall reach that throne," the Duke said. "You think of your friend, of little lives and deaths, but I am thinking of Normandy, and the years that will come when I am with my fathers." He looked across at Raoul; his voice cleaved a deep silence. "I must die, but I shall leave behind me a name that will endure, and a people made safe through mine endeavour."

Raoul sighed, and came towards the table again. "It is a

high goal, splendid and terrible," he said. "Yet I would give it all for peace, and a happiness you will not find."

The Duke laughed. "You shall have your happiness, Raoul, if you deem that to lie in a woman's arms; but peace I cannot promise you. I may lead you to glory, or I may lead to death, but though peace is the end to which I am striving I think we shall not see it in our days." He rose, and laid his hands on Raoul's shoulders. "Look you, my friend, whatever ill befall us, however grim the work we may have to do, we shall yet leave behind us for our sons the foundations of a noble heritage." His hands fell again; his voice changed; he said lightly: "Touching this happiness of yours, O Watcher, if I win a crown you may win a wife."

"Seigneur, this is not the first time you have spoken to me in these strange terms," said Raoul. "I think the Duchess's grace hath been interesting herself on my behalf." He cast a shrewd glance at the Duke, and was satisfied he had guessed correctly.

"I have had some speech with the maid Elfrida," the Duke said. "She seems to me an honest damsel, and one worthy of you. I shall lead you to your bridal-bed yet."

Raoul smiled a little, but shook his head. "How may that be, if you plan to snatch England by the strong hand? If you prevail I must come to her as a blood-stained conqueror, a hated foe."

"Raoul," said the Duke, "once I asked you to read me the mind of women; now it is I who will tell you that women are not as men, and in my experience they do not hate their conquerors. Tenderness is not so much their need as strength. You may use them ruthlessly, in such a way as must provoke in any man a bitter hatred and a desire for vengeance, and they will think no worse of you. Never waste gentleness to capture a woman's heart: she will deem you a weakling, and be done with you." A twinkle lurked at the back of his eyes. "I have given you wise rede, my friend. Guard it: it will stand you in good stead."

Raoul laughed at him. "Brutal rede, William, and from the mouth of one whom I know to be the best of husbands."

"Yea, but from the start I have been master, and to the end I shall remain so," the Duke said.

Raoul tried to picture himself using Elfrida as the Duke had once used Matilda (and, for all he knew, might still use her upon occasion), but he could not imagine such a scene at all. The Duke loved a fierce lady fiercely; Raoul did not think that Elfrida was fierce. She was gentle, and very sweet, and the sight of her filled him with a desire to protect her against the whole world. He had seen William grasp his Duchess in a hardy embrace that took no heed of the bruising of her flesh; Raoul thought that if ever he were permitted to take Elfrida in his arms he would not use her so.

The Duke moved towards the door. As he opened it for him an idea occurred to Raoul, and he said suddenly: "Seigneur, does Earl Harold know what you require of him?"

"He may guess," the Duke answered. "I make no open demand upon him till I see him urgent to be gone from Normandy. I know with what manner of man I have to deal. If I were to broach this matter now he would give me a plain No for answer, and once that word has passed his lips no fear of death or worse, no consideration of policy would avail to make him unsay it. Change No to Yes, owning me his master?" He laughed. "He would rather die an hundred deaths."

"Beau sire, do you like him?" Raoul asked curiously.

"Yes," replied the Duke, without hesitation.

Raoul blinked. "And yet you will use him thus!" He shook his head. "I do not understand that way of liking."

"He is the first of all mine enemies for whom I have felt respect," said the Duke. "I am a greater man than he is, because I think he has the heart you say I lack, but he is a man, which France was not, and Anjou was not, and certainly Guy of Burgundy was not. Yet for all his strength, and for all his craft, you will see that Harold will not prevail against me, for when his heart is moved he will follow its impulse, sweeping aside the colder counsel of his brain. That I shall never do. Like me the less if you will, but grant me this: I do not fail."

"No, you do not fail," Raoul said. He smiled. "I will not like you less, William my lord. But Harold, has he not asked you why you hold him captive?"

"No, and will not. I do not hold him captive; I entreat his company a while longer, and my Duchess beguiles the time pleasantly for him."

"Yes, but he must surely guess that something you want of him!"

"But as little as I desire to tell it does he desire to ask it of me. Too hasty speech today might ruin all his plans and mine. He waits, hoping for guidance, or some lucky chance; and I wait, biding my time."

He had fairly plumbed Earl Harold's mind. When he threw

himself upon the Duke's protection the Earl knew very well that he was walking into a snare from which he would not easily escape. The Duke's courtesy did not deceive him, and when William said: "Let me not hear you talk of leaving us soon, Earl Harold," he knew just how he stood, and wasted no dignity upon further argument. No restriction was put upon him, he was the Duke's honoured guest, but about his person were placed Norman servants who, he did not doubt, had strict orders not to let him from their sight. He lifted a thoughtful eyebrow at these gentlemen and made full use of them. Earl Harold's Norman servants were kept hard at work to fulfil all his behests; they groaned in the spirit, and had an uneasy suspicion that the Earl was amusing himself at their expense.

It seemed he had a way of amusing himself, however hazardous his position. No shadow of anxiety wrinkled his brow, no trace of resentment marred his easy address. One day he would ride out with the Duke with his tercelet on his wrist, flying at the brook for mallard; another day he would accompany Robert of Mortain to hunt deer at force, with a fine horse between his legs, and fleet greyhounds coursing to bring down the wounded bucks; a third day he would be absent till sundown with FitzOsbern, or Hugh de Grantmesnil, boar hunting in the depths of the forest of Quévilly. He took part in jousts, and showed how a Saxon wielded his great battle-axe; he was present at feasts, laughed like a man without a care in the world at Galet's quips, gave a purse filled with saluz d'or to Taillefer, the Duke's favourite minstrel, and was on the best of terms with his hosts. But escaping once from a company of his new associates he went away to his own apartments with his arm flung across Edgar's shoulders, and when the door was shut and he knew himself unwatched the smile was wiped from his face, and he said abruptly: "I am a prisoner." He moved silently to the curtain that shut off his bed-chamber and pulled it back. No one was there. After a swift glance round the room he came back into the solar and sat down on a chair covered with marten-skins. He brushed the soft pelts contemptuously with his hand. "Lodged nobly, and nobly served, but as much a prisoner as though chains still fettered my ankles as they did at Beaurain." He laughed, and looked lazily up at Edgar. "What, so long a face? Laugh, man, it is a good jest."

"Lord, FitzOsbern, whom I would trust, swore to me no harm was purposed towards you!" Edgar said, disregarding this behest.

"Why, not the least in the world!" Harold agreed. "Was ever man so courteously used as I? Servants at my commands—stand away from the door: one may be listening there—horses, hounds, and hawks for my pleasure; sports devised to while away the time for me; feasts in mine honour; a Duchess to lure my thoughts from England: what more princely entreatment could I desire? But if I ride abroad a spy rides behind me."

Edgar gave a little shiver, and said in a low voice: "If that is so, lord, then touch no food or drink the taster has not first assayed!"

A gleam of amusement shone in Harold's eyes. "You think I stand in danger of being poisoned? I am sure I do not."

"If William is holding you captive, lord, you can trust in nothing here in Normandy!" Edgar said, with a kind of suppressed violence. "Poison has not hitherto been his way, no, nor lack of chivalry, but he has set his will upon the getting of a crown, and I tell you nothing, nothing will be let stand between him and his purpose! I have not believed it, but it is true that when certain among his foes died suddenly, disloyal men whispered——"

"Oh yes, yes!" Harold said impatiently. "I have no doubt men whispered that the Duke had sent his foes a subtle poison. So have men whispered about me, with as little truth. Leave poison to lesser men: neither William nor I deal in such base tools. Not my life is threatened, but my freedom, which is more precious."

Edgar went to him, and dropped on his knee beside his chair, grasping his hand. "Dear my lord, if I might but give my life for yours, or stay a prisoner for ever that you might be freed!" he said. He raised Harold's hand to his lips. "Ah, what accursed hap cast you on these shores!"

"Why, Edgar, what is this?" the Earl said gently. "Your life for mine? We shall go hence together presently, and laugh at this day's boding."

Edgar rose up from his knee, and began to pace about the room. "What does Duke William want of you?" he threw over his shoulder.

Harold was playing with a long chain he wore about his neck. "He has not told me," he said, watching the swing of the golden links. "Nor have I asked him." He began to smile a little. "And I do not think I shall ask him."

Edgar stopped short to stare at him. "Is it not England?"

"Well, of course it is England," Harold answered. "But he

has not said so. And that is what I do not understand." He paused, and added thoughtfully: "Nor dare I ask."

"Dare!" Edgar exclaimed. "What words are these on Harold's tongue?"

"Wise ones, I promise you. I must wait. Some chance word may yet show me the Duke's intent. Is it to hold me until Edward is dead, and himself crowned King of England? I do not think it. Never a Saxon would bow his neck for William's yoke while Harold was known to live. No, William is not the man to make so great a blunder." He bit one of the links of his chain reflectively, his eyes narrow as though they tried to probe the future. "Something to bind me," he said at last. "I have never needed to walk more warily. Maybe Ponthieu was after all the less dangerous foe. But William is more generous."

"If you will own him master," Edgar said dryly.

"You have him wrong. He knows I should never do that." He let fall his chain, and turned his head to look at Edgar. "For many years I have desired to meet William of Normandy, and I will stake my honour he has also desired to meet me. Well, we have met, and measured each one the other, and behold! we are agreed we like each other very well, and will fight to the death." He laughed, but was grave again very soon. "This I swear to you: while there is life in me William shall never wrest England from Saxon hold. When you see him crowned King of England I shall have taken the swan's path." He saw the frown in Edgar's eyes, and said: "So little faith in Harold?"

Edgar started. "Liege-lord!"

"You frown."

"Not from want of faith in you, lord. But you lie in William's power, and I am afraid because I know him. Maybe you will say, as Alfric says, that I am become like a Norman, holding their Duke in too great respect, but——"

"Alfric is a fool," interrupted Harold. "I see little of the Norman in you, though you use their tongue unwitting, and have made friends amongst them."

"Alfric does not like that," Edgar said, glad to be able to unburden his sore heart. "He finds me changed, grown apart from him, and he will not see that my Norman friends are not—— But it is of no moment."

"Alfric can never see a Norman without wanting to come at his *seax*," said the Earl. "Let him be; he will soon leave grieving over you to shake his thick head at me for liking in their own land a people I would drive from England at the

210

sword-edge. As for William, I say you cannot hold him in too great respect. But hold me also in respect, and do not fear for me at his hands."

"There is something else," Edgar said, hesitating. "Something my sister has told me that I misliked. She spoke of a strange awesome prophecy. Lord, what dire fate is predicted for England?"

Harold lifted his brows. "Do you set store by such things? If you had lived at Edward's side all the years I have known him you would pay little heed to dreams and prophecies. The King feeds upon them. When last I saw him he had had a vision of the Seven Sleepers turning upon their left sides after two hundred years upon the right." His eyes were brimful of merriment. "This, he assured me, is an omen dreadful to mankind, presaging earthquakes, and pestilence, and famine, changes in kingdoms, victories of the Christians over the pagans, and nation rising against nation. All this for seventy-four years, if my memory serves me, at the end of which time the Sleepers will turn back upon their right sides, and I suppose we may expect a little peace."

"The prophecy I have heard is stranger than that, lord," Edgar said seriously. "My sister said it hath been known since the time of Vortigern, who was King over the Britons. It tells of a vision Vortigern was made to see in a pond, foreboding the coming of the Saxons to England—and other things."

"What, do men remember that old prophecy again?" Harold said. "Yea, I know it, but I had not heard it was talked of in these days. It was made by one Merlin, a Churchman, but it contained nothing but wild words. Vortigern saw a red and a white dragon in a pond which fought together, the red triumphing over the white, and driving it to the edge of the water. There was something beside, concerning two vases, and two rolls of linen, but what they did in the pond I cannot tell you. The red dragon is said to have been our Saxon emblem, and the white the Britons that held England before us. I forget what else there was. It was writ down, I think, but it was of less moment even than Edward's dreams."

"Lord, my sister tells me there has been seen a stranger flitting through the south country whom some thought to be mad, and others were sure was no human form, but a wood-fiend. And he has appeared to man, and repeated the old prophecy, saying that a people shall shortly come in ships and in tunics of iron, taking vengeance on perversity." He paused, trying to recall the words Elfrida had repeated.

211

" 'There shall come two dragons,' " he said slowly, ". . . two dragons——"

"What, more dragons?" Harold murmured. "This is worse than the devils Edward predicts will wander through the land."

" 'And one,' " Edgar went on, unheeding, " 'shall be slain by the arrows of envy, and the other shall perish under the shadow of a name. Then shall appear a lion of justice at whose roar the insular dragons shall tremble. . . .' What may that portend, lord?"

"God knows; I do not." The Earl rose to his feet, and Edgar saw that he was frowning. "I do not like this prophecy," he said, "and less do I like the man who spreads it abroad."

"Lord, what bodes it?" Edgar asked in a hushed voice.

"Nothing. But when men lend ear to such ravings then are suspicion and alarm bred. I would I were at home." For the first time he showed his inward fret. "Holy Cross, was ever so great a mischance as my ship's foundering off Ponthieu? You tell me tales of a man or fiend who should be seized and heard of no more were I in England. And who knows what silly work the Saint will busy himself with while I lie caged in Normandy? Gyrth and Leofwine are too young to take my place at his side; Tostig would do me a mischief if he could; and if the King were to die on a sudden——" He stopped. "This is to no purpose. Edgar, a warning in your ear! Let no word concerning the future escape you. All Christendom knows that I stand beside a crown, but I have not said it, and I want no man of mine to prate that Harold will be King when Edward dies. It is understood?"

"Yea, lord, it is understood. Yet I do not see . . "

"The Witan will choose me for King because I am the people's hero. I have no other claim. If it were known that I aspired openly to Edward's crown there would be an outcry raised against me by every other claimant, even perhaps by Holy Church. Guard silence, I charge you."

Edgar nodded. "On my life. But if the Duke will not let you go, lord? What then?"

An indomitable look came into Harold's face. "I shall go," he said. "I know not how, or when; I only know that I shall be in England again before the King dies, because all hangs on that, and I must not fail." There was a ring of certainty in his voice. He said strongly: "No matter what the cost, no matter by what means, I shall escape from Duke William's net."

CHAPTER IV

Raoul was not the only man in Rouen who had lost his heart to Elfrida. She very soon had a court gathered round her of ardent gentlemen who swore to the chagrin of the Norman maids that blue and gold were the only colours for a damsel. She had not been used to court life, and at first she regarded her worshippers doubtfully, and was shy of their wooing. They found her modesty irresistible, and redoubled their efforts to please. She had posies of eglantine and sweet-briar laid at her door; verses were left where she would be sure to find them; trinkets offered to her upon the bended knee. Once Taillefer of the golden voice sang a song in her praise at the dinner hour, and was pretty well covered by the gifts tossed to him by the lady's suitors. But Elfrida blushed red as her little shoes, and would not raise her eyes from her lap. One or two damsels, slighted for her, were as spiteful as they dared to be, but discovered that meek as she was she could still hold her own if her anger were roused.

It was not many weeks before she had grown accustomed to be hailed Star of Beauty, White Doe, Golden Desire, and she soon learned to listen undismayed to catalogues of her charms recited without regard for her blushes by gentlemen of a poetic turn of mind. When Baldwin de Meules first made his rhymes to her she turned a startled reproving pair of eyes upon him, for he informed her that her limbs were bathed in moonshine, and her bosom whiter than the swan's. But she soon found that he meant no harm at all, and she schooled herself not to draw back in the way that made the Norman ladies sneer at her. At the end of two months men might drown in the sea of her eyes, or be made faint by the perfume of her hair, or be slain by her vestal glance without awaking anything more than a mischievous crow of laughter in her. This was thought to be her only fault—if she had a fault at all, which some denied. She had a disconcerting and apparently unquenchable habit of letting a giggle escape her when a man was most in earnest. What heightened the fault in her was that it was well-nigh impossible to refrain from joining in her mirth, so infectious was it. Some drew off in a huff: she laughed the more, naughty little chuckles that made one's lips quiver in spite of one's annoyance; some reproached her: her eyes showed a hundred dancing lights.

Her laughter had to be endured, even shared, but she could never get her court to see wherein lay the real jest. For her this lay nearly all in the reflection that she, who had always considered herself a very simple maid, was being wooed as a peerless beauty by a dozen gentlemen who should have known better.

Edgar, who had started to play the watch-dog over her, abandoned the task at the end of the first month, and devoted himself to the service of Earl Harold. He had very little opinion of the knights and vavassours and damoiseaux who flocked round his sister. They were mostly young men whom he remembered as lads hardly out of women's care, and he said scornfully that they were untried, full of tricks and silly fancies. Elfrida, who stood in some awe of her large brother, said demurely that though her admirers might not be of such consequence as Edgar's haut friends, yet she could not suppose that such cronies of his as bluff FitzOsbern, or William Malet would feel the smallest interest in a maid so young and unimportant as herself. Edgar, who had very soon seen what effect her beauty had had on men of all ages, said nothing more, not wishing her to grow puffed up in her own conceit.

Her court grew, but there was one who did not join it. Surrounded by her subjects, Elfrida cast wistful glances towards Raoul de Harcourt, who held apart. She had had little speech with him; he had never offered posies to her, nor extolled her loveliness, nor striven for a place at her side. She met him sometimes if she sought her brother's company; often when she knew him to be with Edgar she would make an excuse to join them, but though he smiled, and kissed her hand, he nearly always retired to let her be private with Edgar. Such conduct naturally determined her to know more of him. Had he tried to find a way to catch her interest (which he had not) he could not have found a surer snare. She had liked him at first sight: she had had no very pleasant time in Ponthieu, and his had been one of the first faces she had seen after her release which held kindness and welcome. Since he was Edgar's friend he had a claim on her regard; she was ready to be on easy terms with him. It seemed he would not: she did not know how to read his aloof conduct, and the more she watched him, the more she wondered about him, the greater grew her desire to know him better. She thought that perhaps he did not like women, and since he was unmarried, and, according to the notions of one-and-twenty, no longer young, this seemed a probable answer to the riddle. But very often she would see him looking at her from afar, and she soon noticed that when he entered a room where she sat his eyes would search for her as though by instinct. She began to be afraid that he was too exalted a personage to seek her company. He seemed to be of great consequence, for he always sat at the Duke's table, and not only did her young suitors speak to him with deference, but he was obviously held in affection by both the Duke and the Duchess. No one under the rank of the Duke's kind—and not by any means all of these—was permitted to go in and out of the ducal apartments at will as Raoul did. Elfrida had admirers with grandiloquent titles, who displayed great magnificence, but she was shrewd enough to see that the quiet Chevalier de Harcourt was of more account than these. Very high seigneurs called him friend, and stiff-necked barons such as de Gournay and Tesson of Cingueliz, who used the most brief of addresses towards any whom they thought below their degree, would hail Raoul without a trace of this haughtiness. He was always arm-in-arm with some puissant baron, thought Elfrida. Edgar had said that none stood closer to the Duke, save it be his brother of Mortain, or his Seneschal FitzOsbern. She supposed that she must not expect so remote a man to be interested in her. But although, being a sensible maid, she made up her mind she must not wish Raoul to approach her, she went on wishing it, secretly, because there was no other man in all this teeming Court whom she liked so well.

His very quiet seemed to her only to add to his dignity. Other men might swagger through the halls, trailing mantles rich with orfrey, loudly asserting their importance, dazzling a poor stranger-maid with their splendour, but she did not think they appeared to advantage beside the straight, calm-eyed knight who made no stir, wore nearly always a soldier's mantle of plain vermeil, and was hardly ever heard to raise his voice above its ordinary low pitch.

She made a hero of him, chiding herself for her folly: imagined him to be far above her, courteous always, but kind rather than friendly, and all the time the man was deep in love with her, and could not keep his eyes from her face if she were in the same room with him.

He saw her surrounded by younger men than himself, apparently happy in their company, and it did not seem to him that she regarded him as anything more than her brother's friend. Ruefully he reflected that in all likelihood she considered him a greybeard. There was little enough arrogance in him, but he could not bring himself to swell a court composed of untried youths, or to sue for favours with a score of others.

Matters might have continued in this way for ever had it not been for the rude conduct of William, Lord of Moulines-la-Marche, the Duke's cousin upon the distaff-side.

Between Raoul and this seigneur there had never been much love lost. The Lord of Moulines was of an intemperate disposition that accorded ill with Raoul's, and he had a natural ferocity which he was at no pains to bridle. His pages were often seen to blubber out their hearts in some secluded corner, and it was no unusual thing for his horse to be led back to its stable with bleeding flanks torn by his merciless spurs. He was married, but his lady enjoyed little of his company, for at one or other of his houses there could always be found some light woman whom he had taken to mistress. None of them remained for long, since he tired of them quickly, and was ever on the look-out for a fresh charmer.

He came on a visit to the Court when Elfrida had been there some eight weeks or more, and his attention was immediately caught by her unusual beauty. It was not to be supposed that he would consider her in the light of a possible leman, but he could not be placed near such fresh loveliness without attempting to trifle with it. He had a handsome cruel face, and a manner pleasant enough when he chose. He began to pay his addresses to Elfrida, and as soon as he saw that she was a little afraid of him the beast of prey, which his foes swore lay in him, purred gently, and stretched lazy claws.

Elfrida had been warned of him. One of Matilda's ladies had told her dreadful stories of his vengeance, so that however much she was teased by his love-making she dared not breathe a word of it to Edgar lest he should intervene and draw down the Lord of Moulines' wrath upon his head. She contrived for some time to hold the man at arm's length, but she was unfortunate enough to walk straight into his arms one day in one of the long galleries of the palace.

He was lounging on a bench when she rounded the bend of the stair that led down from Dame Gundred's chamber to the gallery. There was no one else in the gallery; she had a suspicion that he had planted himself there to waylay her, and because she feared him she would have drawn back.

But he had seen her, and he sprang to his feet. "The fair Elfrida!" he said, and advanced towards her.

"So please you, lord," she answered in rather a small voice. He was standing before her, blocking the way. She said: "I must not tarry: I am stayed for."

"Why yes, pretty elf-maiden," he smiled, "I stay for you. Will you leave me disconsolate?" He tried to take her hand. "Fie, you are a chill maid!" he said. "See, does this trinket like you?" He dangled a chain studded with garnets before her.

She replied with dignity: "I thank you, I must not take so precious a gift."

"Eh, take it, my dear," he said, "it is nothing worth." For a brief cynical moment he tried to remember for which of his lemans he had first bought it. "I would give you better things than this poor bauble."

"You are kind, lord, but I would have you know that I have no liking for such toys," Elfrida said firmly. "Pray you, let me pass. Indeed I am stayed for."

He had succeeded in getting hold of her hand; he drew her towards the bench, and his right arm slid round her waist insinuatingly. "Nay, you would not be so cruel," he said. "Am I never to see you alone? You have a rabble of silly boys for ever gathered round you, or else you are mewed up amongst the bower-maidens. And so am I driven to a madness of desire." He had her fast round the waist now; his fingers gripped her side; he put his free hand up to her cheek, and pinched it playfully. The colour leaped up under his fingers. He laughed, enjoying her confusion, and let his hand wander downwards over her neck.

She made an effort to break out of his prisoning arms. "Loose me, lord!" she said, trying to keep her voice steady. "This work ill-befits your honour, or mine. I pray you let me go! The Duchess stays for me!"

"Quoy, mistress, you are my captive," he said, teasing her. "What ransom will you offer? I shall demand a large one for so peerless a prisoner."

"Lord, this jesting is unmannerly. Must I call for aid?"

He took her throat in his clasp; his face was bent close; she thought she had never seen so greedy a mouth, and gave a frightened sob. "Your cries shall be stopped with kisses, willow-maid. Nay, hold not off, I will do you no hurt, but only maybe wake the sleeping passion in you." He let go her throat, and wrapped both his arms round her, holding her breast to breast. "What, am I the first to sip your sweetness, little virgin?"

It was at this timely moment that Raoul came up the stair

217

at the other end of the gallery, and walked towards the door of one of the solars. He glanced casually along the gallery, and what he saw made him pause with his hand already raising the latch. He stood still, looking towards Elfrida with an alert questioning lift to his brows.

Moulines had let her go when he heard the step on the stairs, but he still barred her passage. She was seriously alarmed; tears were starting in her blue eyes; she turned an imploring gaze on Raoul.

His hand left the latch; he came down the gallery, not hurrying, but deliberately.

"Well, Messire Watcher?" snapped Moulines. There was a growing note in his voice. "What make you here? If you want aught of me let me hear it, and so be done!"

"My thanks to you," Raoul answered imperturbably. "I want nothing but your room, Moulines, and that as soon as may be."

The Lord of Moulines' temper flared up. "Spine of God, this to my face, upstart? You grow large in your own reckoning! Get you gone: I promise you you stand in some danger."

"Keep that tone for your own underlings, Moulines-la-Marche," Raoul said, unmoved. "Lady, let me lead you to the Duchess's bower."

She moved towards him gratefully, but Moulines pushed her back. "Stay you there, maiden: myself will be your escort." He turned a snarling face upon Raoul, and his hand fumbled at the dudgeon of his knife. "So, Chevalier! The Duke my cousin shall hear of this insolence."

Elfrida saw the gleam of a smile in Raoul's grey eyes. "You will find him in his chamber," he said. "Go tell him you are enraged with me. I give you God-speed on that errand." Amusement lurked in his voice, but he was watching Moulines' hand, and his own hand slid to his belt.

Moulines, knowing that a complaint against Raoul would be more likely to bring down the Duke's wrath on his own head than on the favourite's, lost the last rags of his temper, and sprang at Raoul with his dagger out.

Elfrida cried:" 'Ware! oh 'ware!" but it seemed that Raoul was prepared for the savage onslaught. His hand flew up; steel clashed against steel; Moulines' knife fell with a clatter to the stone floor, and Elfrida saw blood spurt from a gash across his wrist.

Raoul stamped his foot down hard upon the fallen knife. The steel broke with a snap. "Get you hence!" he said, more

218

sternly than Elfrida had ever heard him speak. "More of this, and it is I who will approach the Duke's grace."

The Lord of Moulines, sobered by a little blood-letting, was already rather ashamed of his treacherous assault. He said angrily: "You provoked me to it. Carry what tale you will to the Duke: I am not done with you yet." He gripped his wrist between his fingers to stay the bleeding, rolled a hot eye in Elfrida's direction, and went off towards the stairs.

Elfrida ran to Raoul's side, quite overcome by such bloody happenings, and clasped his arm with both her trembling hands. "Oh, alack, alack, what will he do?" she asked, raising her scared eyes to his face.

His hand covered hers. "Why, nothing, lady!" he said. "You must not be afraid of him. I will see to it he comes not near you again."

"But it is for you I am afraid!" she said. Her lips quivered. "He is so stark a man, and it is I who have brought it all upon you, and I know—I have been told how dreadful is his vengeance."

Raoul looked first surprised, and then amused. "William of Moulines' vengeance! Why, lady, you have no need to fear for my safety. I have known that hothead these many years, and this is not the first time there has been steel drawn between us." He saw that she was still pale and frightened, and drew her towards the bench. "I have a mind to let some more of his blood for alarming you so," he said. "Will you not rest here awhile? I will stay beside you, and keep off the ogre."

The Lady Elfrida, who was stayed for by the Duchess, sat down upon the bench without demur, and smiled rather wanly at her preserver.

Raoul knelt, still holding her hands in his. "There, he is gone, child," he said. "You are quite safe. Presently, when you leave trembling, I will take you to the Duchess, and you will forget this unmannerly brawl."

She looked shyly at him. In his eyes was a light that set her heart fluttering. She looked away. "Messire, you are so very kind," she murmured. "I thank you for your protection. Indeed, I—I have no words to tell you . . ." Her voice faded away; she hoped he would not think her very silly, but was afraid he must.

There was a tiny silence. Raoul broke it, saying in a low voice: "You have no need to thank me. I would ask no more of fortune than to be allowed to serve you."

Her hand jumped under his; she raised her eyes to stare at

219

him. "Serve me?" she echoes. "Me? I— thought you did not like me, messire!" The words were out before she could stop them. She blushed rosily, and hung her head.

"Like you, Elfrida!" Raoul gave an odd laugh. He bent his head, and kissed her slight fingers. "I think I worship you," he said.

A tremor shook her; he could not read her face, but she did not draw her hand away. "If I were to journey into England, to seek out your father," he said, watching her, "could you find it in you to wed a Norman?"

This was swift work, too swift for Elfrida. She said faintly: "Indeed, messire, indeed—I think I must go to the Duchess, who stays for me."

He rose at once, fearing that he had alarmed her. They walked slowly down the gallery. Elfrida's hand lay on his arm. She stole a glance at him, wondering whether he would say any more, dreading lest he should, afraid that he would not. She searched in her mind for a phrase that should give him hope yet not dishonour her maidenly decorum. She could think of nothing, and they had almost reached the Duchess' apartments. In desperation she said: "My father has granted me this boon, that I shall not be wed until my brother returns to England. It is a vow I made to Our Lady long years ago, messire."

Raoul stopped, and faced her. "But when he does return, Elfrida?"

"I do not know—I do not think that my father would wish to see me wed out of England," she said shyly.

She looked so sweet he had hard work to keep himself from kissing her there and then. She pulled her hand free of his hold on it, and drew back to the door of the bower. When her fingers clasped the latch she ventured to peep at Raoul again. She stood hesitating; the dearest little smile trembled on her lips; she said, breathless at her own daring: "I do not—dislike Normans—myself, messire."

He started forward, but she was gone before he could reach her, and the door had shut with a clang behind her.

He sought Edgar in his chamber that night as the bell for *couvre-feu* was ringing through the streets. Edgar was seated by the table inspecting his hunting-spear by the light of a cluster of candles. He looked up as Raoul came in, and smiled.

"Holà, Raoul!" He pushed a stool forward with one foot. "Sit! I have seen nothing of you all day." He saw Raoul look significantly towards the page, who was collecting an armful

220

of weapons for the chase, and stretched out a hand to grasp the boy's shoulder. "Off with you, Herluin," he said. "Take that gear with you, and see there is no speck upon my spear when next I go hunting."

Herluin said: "No, lord," in a meek voice, and sped forth.

Edgar looked inquiringly at his friend. "Something of moment, Raoul?"

"Yes," Raoul answered. He did not sit down, but wandered over to the platform under the window, as though irresolute.

Edgar watched him with a twinkle in his eyes. "What dire happening are you going to tell me? You rode my horse Barbary out to Lillebonne this day: have you lamed him? Or is it that your good father will not send the greyhound from Harcourt that he promised me?"

Raoul smiled. "Neither." He turned, and came back into the inside of the room. "Edgar—could you see your sister wedded to a Norman?"

At that Edgar jumped up and caught him by the shoulders. "What, man, is that how it is with you? Yea, with goodwill, so you be that Norman."

"My thanks. And your father?"

Edgar's hands fell again to his sides. "Maybe, if I spoke for you. I do not know." He sounded troubled all at once, and there was a frown in his eyes.

"I have little to offer," Raoul said awkwardly, "because I have not cared to hold lands and a title. I have only my knight's fee, but I think the Duke would advance me if I desired it. There was some talk of it, but I chose rather to stay at his side, and saw no good in the possessions he would have given me. But if I took a wife ..." He paused, and looked gravely at Edgar. "What do you say?"

For a moment Edgar did not say anything at all. He seemed to find it hard to discover words to express his thought. When he at last spoke it was hesitatingly. "It is not that. No man in Normandy has more power than you to become great in wealth and in puissance. Well do I know that the Duke would advance you if you but winked an eyelid. I have no fear that you might not find means to pay the morgen-gift." He grinned suddenly, but the grin faded. "It is not that," he repeated. "Because we have been friends long years, and because I know no man more worthy to take Elfrida's hand in wedlock I would desire it—nay, I have desired it, above all things." He lifted a fold of the heavy curtain that hung round his bed, and began to pleat it between his fingers. "But these are dreams, Raoul: foolish, idle dreams."

Raoul stayed silent, waiting for him to go on. Edgar looked up from his pleats. "So deep a gulf lies between!" he said, as though beseeching Raoul's understanding of all that he would prefer not to say.

"Yet you have often told me how your father took a bride out of Normandy," Raoul said.

"Yes. But it was different then." Edgar closed his lips firmly, unable to explain further.

"Do you then forbid me to approach your sister?" Raoul asked directly.

Edgar shook his head. "I would like too well to call you brother," he replied. "My word is for you, but I fear what the future may hold. Nor"—he smiled faintly—"are betrothals thus arranged. You and she are not franklins to fall in love and wed at will, my friend."

Raoul felt suddenly impatient. "Heart of a man, if the Lady Elfrida will trust herself to me I will have her in despite of every customary usage!"

"There spoke the Norman," Edgar said softly. "Marauding, grasping, marking his prey!"

Anger rose in Raoul, but he curbed it, saying in a calmer voice. "That was not deserved. Though I speak wildly you know full well I will do nothing out of the honourable way."

"I do not doubt you," Edgar said. "But I see a weary road ahead."

Spring was in Raoul's blood, making doubts and forebodings so alien to his mood that again he was conscious of that stab of irritation. "God's death, Edgar, can you not forget? What shall it signify to us little men if our leaders nurse ambitions? I will not think in this boding vein, I tell you!"

Edgar regarded him with the flicker of a smile. "Go your ways then," he said. "You know what it shall signify, Raoul. I have no more to say."

Having wrung permission from Edgar to address Elfrida, Raoul wasted no more time. He found the lady shy, but she did not rebuff him. When he walked across a room towards her she always had a smile for him, and if his horse ranged alongside her palfrey at a morning's hawking she would contrive to ride a little apart with him. It was not long before he spoke of love to her again: this time she did not run away. She knew that she ought not to listen to a man who had not her father's sanction; she knew just what a modest maid would say and do, and yet she swayed ever so slightly towards him. After that who could blame him for catching her in his arms?

Thus they plighted their troth. Holding her hands in his, Raoul said: "I might send letters into England, to your father, yet I like that way very ill. A cold answer should I have, think you?"

"I fear it," she answered. "It is true my mother was a Norman, but my father does not in general like Normans since the King has favoured those in England so much. If Edgar would speak for us perhaps he might look more kindly on you."

"Edgar will stand my friend. I will come into England as soon as may be after your return." A sudden fear seized him. "Elfrida, there is no pledge binding you?"

She shook her head, flushing, but began at once to explain how this had come about; for to be over twenty, unwed, uncloistered, and not even betrothed, was a circumstance so unusual that it cast a slur upon a maid. She looked into Raoul's smiling eyes, and said with quaint dignity: "Indeed, it is no fault of mine, messire."

The smile grew; he kissed each of her fingers separately till she reproved him, saying that at any moment someone might come along the gallery and observe them. At that he let go her hand, and put his arm round her waist instead. She did not say anything at all to that; maybe since they sat upon a bench she found the support of an arm welcome.

"Tell me how it was not your fault, my heart," Raoul said in her ear.

Seriously, with awe in her blue eyes, she told him how she had been betrothed when still a child to Oswine the son of Hundbert the Strong, master of eighty hides of land in the Earldom of Wessex.

"Did you like him?" Raoul interrupted.

She had hardly known him. She had never seen him alone, she said, for in England it was not customary to be private with a man until one was bound to him in wedlock. He had been a proper youth but he had died in a dreadful manner, just as she became of marriageable age. He had a quarrel with one Eric Jarlessen, a strange fierce man who came from Danelagh to live in Wessex. Elfrida did not know why they quarrelled, but she thought Oswine had done the Dane some injury. Then, one Shrove-tide, Oswine was smitten with a wasting fever, which some said was jaundice, since his skin took on a yellow hue; but though he swallowed nine lice fasting for nine days, and though a live frog caught on St. John's Eve was placed on his wrist to draw out the fever, it was all of no avail. The fever did not abate; the man wasted away day by day until at length he died, stricken in the very prime of life.

"Then," Elfrida went on, slipping her hand unconsciously into Raoul's, "certain men made accusations against Eric, among them being Hundbert, who was Oswine's father. It was said that Eric had been outlawed from the Danelagh because he had practised abominations there, and was thought to deal in witchcraft." She made the sign of the Cross quickly, shivering. "These men declared that they knew him to have used *stacung* against Oswine—you do not know that word? It is when a man makes an image of his enemy, and sticks a thorn into it, praying for his death."

"Black magic!" Raoul said. "Faugh! What was done then to Eric?"

"At the shire-gemot he was hailed before the shire-reeve, and denying the charge, demanded trial. So a holy priest held in his hand two billets of wood, one with the Sacred Cross drawn on it, and the other quite plain; and Eric, having prayed God to declare thus the truth, boldly drew forth one billet." She shrank closer to Raoul. "And upon the piece of wood which he pulled from the priest's hold was nothing, so that all men knew that God had declared him to be a perjured man, and that he had slain Oswine by *stacung*, which is witchcraft."

"And then?" Raoul said.

"Some said that he should pay were-geld—that is the blood-wite that is placed on a man's head if he be slain. Oswine was a King's thegn, as my father is, so that the price of his slaying was as much as twelve hundred shillings, which perhaps Eric could not have paid. But the shire-reeve judged that the crime was too black to be wiped out with silver, and he ordered that Eric should be put to death by stoning. And this was done at Hocktide. I did not see it, but I was told. And that is why I am still unbetrothed."

Both her hands were folded on Raoul's breast; his cheek brushed hers. "Are you sorry now, little bird?" he asked.

"No," she confessed. "Not now."

CHAPTER V

The weeks slid into months, and still Earl Harold was
honourably entertained at Rouen. Every sort of diversion was
offered for his amusement, and no one spoke of his departure. Nor did he attempt to escape, though some among his
followers thought he had opportunities enough. Alfric, when
the Earl rode out to visit Wlnoth at Roumare, devised a plan
for slipping away unseen from Wlnoth's lodge, and riding for
the Frontier. Harold, aware that his every movement was
watched, and being reasonably sure that all the ports and
Frontier posts had been warned long since, would lend no ear
to the project. He learned through Edgar, who had received
letters out of England, that King Edward was in good health,
and the country quiet. He could afford to wait, and if his
polite captivity irked him he was not the man to show it. So
good was the mask he wore that even Alfric believed him to
have grown careless, and wrung his hands over it in great
bitterness. But the Earl was not careless. He told Edgar that
if it had done no more for him this stay in Normandy had
taught him to know Duke William and his subjects as he had
never hoped to know them. By the end of six months there
were few men of standing whom Earl Harold had not met.
He saw such war-like barons as the Viscounts of Côtentin
and Avranches, and said: "Good fighters, these, but no
more." He made it his business to be on friendly terms with
the Duke's advisers, FitzOsbern, Giffard, the Lord of Beaumont, and others such. "Leal men, those," he said, "but
o'erruled in all things by their master." He observed the
lesser barons, men like the standard-bearer, Ralph de Toeni,
and the Lords of Cahagnes, Montfiquet, and L'Aigle. "Turbulent men, needing a strong hand over them." So he dismissed
them. But when the Prior of Herluin at Bec, who was one
Lanfranc, came on a visit to Rouen, Earl Harold spoke of
him in very different terms. "That man is more dangerous
than all," he said softly.

Edgar was surprised. "I had thought you would like the
Prior, lord," he said.

Then the Earl said something that seemed incomprehensible to his thegn. "I would he were my councillor," he said.

Edgar frowned. "He is very wise, I know. Men say it was

225

he arranged the Duke's marriage. I think he does sometimes advise William."

The Earl looked at him, half-smiling. "Amongst all the nobles of this Duchy I have sought in vain for the one who stands behind the Duke, dropping subtle counsel into his ear. Now I know where this one may be found, and I promise you I fear him."

"A councillor! Does the Duke need one?" Edgar said.

"Not for government, perhaps, nor for warfare, but for deep crafty work—yea, he needs one," Harold answered.

"What of Anselm?" Edgar asked. "He too has a name for great wisdom."

Harold shook his head. "A very holy man, that one, too holy to give the counsel Lanfranc's subtle brain could devise."

He said no more, but his words remained long in Edgar's head. Edgar said once to Gilbert d'Aufay that he supposed Lanfranc to be much in the Duke's confidence, and knew by Gilbert's laugh how right Earl Harold had been. Foreboding stole over him; he saw his lord surrounded by foes using hidden weapons, and his helplessness to aid Harold made him short-tempered, and as resentful towards his hosts as he had been thirteen years before. Since each one knew his own master's mind, and might not speak of it, an imperceptible estrangement began to grow up between himself and Raoul. Beneath all their friendly talk a knowledge of secrets lay. Edgar, trying not to let the policies of their leaders part them, thought bitterly that Raoul cared for no one now but Elfrida; Raoul, understanding what sore resentment lay in Edgar's heart, tried to reach a hand to him across the gulf, and thought that Edgar's devotion to his lord was turning friendship into enmity.

Once, gripping Edgar's shoulders, he said: "Whatever is done, whatever path I may have to tread, you know that I did not choose that path, Edgar."

Edgar shook him off, saying in a sullen voice: "You are a Norman, and William's friend. Of course you must want the thing he wants."

Raoul looked at him for a moment, then turned away. He left Edgar staring out of the window under lowering brows, and could only guess that beneath the scowl and the anger, the heart's ties strove with pride of race and fealty. Later they met upon the stair, and Edgar turned and went back beside Raoul, saying awkwardly: "Forgive me: I have been out of temper these many days."

Their hands clasped. "I know," Raoul said. "But whate'er betide, before God and the Blessed Virgin and the Pheasant, I swear I am your friend, both now and always."

Autumn merged into winter, and light snow covered the house-tops. Edgar rode out to Harcourt with Raoul to present compliments and gifts to old Hubert upon his seventieth birthday, and Alfric said disgustedly to Sigwulf: "Edgar cares for no one but his Norman friends, and I believe he would sooner be among them than with us, his countrymen. He scorns Wlnoth for aping Norman manners, but though he himself may still wear his beard and his short tunic, he is for ever leaving us because he has promised to ride out with FitzOsbern, or must keep tryst with that loud-prating baron whose men shout Turie! when you meet them upon the road."

In the New Year a fresh interest came to occupy the minds of Normans and Saxons alike. In Brittany the young Count Conan, who had thrown off his governors a year before, had already given signs betokening an intractable disposition. One of his first acts had been to cast his uncle Odo into prison, loaded with shackles. News had come to Normandy of this and certain other proceedings. He bade fair to be a tyrant as his father and grandfather had been before him, and it was whispered that he meant to renounce his fealty to Normandy as soon as might be. In the early spring of '65 he sent his cartel to Duke William, announcing in the language of a young and boastful man, that he was no longer a vassal of Normandy, and would meet the Duke at the Frontier upon a certain date. It was thought that the Norman border-hold of St. Jaques was the main object of his hostility, and messengers soon brought tidings that he was marching against the Mount of Dol, which held out for the Duke.

William received the Count's cartel without the least sign either of surprise or anger. "All alike, these Breton princes," he said. "I have been waiting for this."

By the time supper was laid in the hall below stairs the word had gone round that Normandy was for war again. Duke William took his seat at the board, and as the assay of the first dish was made, he turned to Harold, and said: "How say you, Earl Harold? Have you a stomach for battle at my side?"

This was so unexpected that every Saxon head was jerked up in surprise. The Earl waited before he answered till he had served himself from the dish one of the stewards presented on his knee. Watching him, Raoul wondered what lightning calculations chased one another through his mind. The eyes told nothing; the firm lips still faintly smiled. The Earl wiped his fingers on a napkin. "Why, with good will," he said calmly. "Have you a place for me, Duke William?"

"I will give you a detachment of my troops to command," the Duke promised.

Edgar, who knew the customs of chivalry, was not so much surprised by the Duke's request as his fellow-Saxons. As soon as supper was at an end he followed the Earl upstairs, and begged him to intercede for him with the Duke, so that he too might be allowed to ride to war. He could barely contain his soul in patience until he knew William's answer, and when he saw Harold again the question fairly jumped from his anxious eyes.

Harold nodded. "You are to come," he said. "At first the Duke seemed little likely to grant it, but your friend Raoul added his word to mine, offering to stand as pledge for you should you be slain, and FitzOsbern too, and Hugh de Montfort. So between jesting and earnest the affair was settled. Wlnoth and Hakon must remain here. Hakon would be glad to go, but Wlnoth——" He broke off, shrugging. "He is the only one amongst us six who seems to have no drop of Godwine's blood in his veins," he said. "Let be for that: he is of small account." He glanced over his shoulder to be sure no one was within earshot. "Did you expect to hear Duke William make that request of me?"

"No," Edgar said, considering it. "Yet it is often done. What was in his mind, lord?"

"If I knew what William had in mind I should have no need to fear him," replied Harold flippantly.

Edgar frowned at that. "You do not fear him, lord," he said.

"Do I not?" The Earl laughed under his breath. "Well, maybe you are right. I suppose he wants to see me in the field, to observe what manner of commander I am." He lifted a quizzical eyebrow. "And since I also desire to see what manner of commander he is, I said that I would fight this war with him. So are we both served."

"You do not think"—Edgar stumbled over the words— "you do not suspect that he may hope for your death in battle?"

"No." Harold weighed it in his mind. "No, I think not." His sudden smile flashed out. "If he does, he will be disappointed, my Edgar. I do not mean to fall in this war."

As soon as Elfrida learned of the coming expedition she was very much alarmed, and when Edgar made a mock of her fear, she sought comfort of Raoul, and was sure she would never set eyes on either of them again.

"But, my heart, I have been in a-many wars and come safe through them," he pointed out. "This will be no more than a brief campaign, and you will see us back again before you have learned to miss us."

This she could not by any means allow. Hiding her face in his mantle, she informed him in a muffled voice that she missed him the instant he left her presence. There could only be one answer to this, and he made it. But she was not done with fears yet. Fixing big eyes on his face, she begged him to take more than ordinary care of himself, for he was going to fight a terrible people, she said, who were bred to war alone.

This made him laugh; he wanted to know who had put that notion into her head, and she at once repeated all the fables told of the Bretons by old wives and other such credulous persons. She said that everyone knew that Brittany was full of fierce warriors, who behaved like barbarians, each man taking as many as ten wives at a time, and begetting upwards of fifty children, and living for nothing but rapine and blood-shed. When Raoul burst out laughing she went away very cross, with her little chin in the air, but she forgave him later, and would even admit that the tales she had heard might not be all of them true.

To reach Brittany the Norman army marched south to Avranches through a country rich with orchards and pasture-land, and crossed the treacherous sands under Mont St. Michel to a place where the river Coesnon poured its flood into the bay. Here the passage was full of hidden perils; a man-at-arms, weighed down by his breast-plate and heavy shield, took a false step and disappeared half from view, sucked under by the greedy quicksands. His comrades tried to pull him out, but the sands were stronger than they, and the luckless spearman sank still further until only his shoulders and his thrashing arms remained above ground. He belonged to Earl Harold's division, and the Earl was riding close behind, picking a careful way across the passage. He saw the disaster, and the unavailing attempts to save the victim, and flung himself quickly down from the saddle. The spearman's comrades found themselves thrust roughly aside; the Earl planted his feet wide on the edge of the firm sand, and leaned over to reach the terrified man. Desperate hands clutched at his; men saw the Earl's arm stiffen till one of the bracelets he wore snapped under the strain. The muscles stood out ribbed and hard down his powerful loins; the sands gave forth a sucking sound, as though loth to relinquish their prey; the Earl threw his whole weight back, and the spearman was wrenched clear, and dragged to firm ground.

The fellow grovelled at Earl Harold's feet, kissing them with tears running down his cheeks; a great cheer rose from the ranks. Raoul, who had seen it all from the further bank, knew now why men loved Earl Harold enough to die for him.

The Earl paid not the slightest heed to the cheering. He pulled off the broken bracelet, and tossed it aside, and catching his horse's bridle, sprang into the saddle again.

When his horse climbed the further bank he found that the Duke was waiting for him there. "Splendour of God, Earl Harold, that was nobly done!" William said. "I have seen mine own strength surpassed for the first time." He laughed and looked the Saxon over with approval. "Yet I beg you will not again risk your life for a spearman, my friend," he said.

"No risk," the Earl answered lightly. "I could not see the fellow drown, poor wretch."

There was little talked of among the men-at-arms that day but the Saxon Earl's huge strength. The feat made a deep impression on the minds of all who saw it. Duke William said to his brother Mortain: "Had I stood in his shoes and done that it would have been from policy, that those who followed me might be enflamed with respect for my prowess. Earl Harold had no such thought in mind, but the outcome is the same." He jerked his thumb towards the Earl's detachment. "He has them with him now, which he had not before. You shall see how well they will do presently."

Mortain grunted. "Silly work to take such risks for one spearman."

Raoul, riding on the other side of William, interrupted to ask curiously: "The feats you performed at Meulan, then— deeds that made men call you hero: were those done from policy?"

The Duke laughed. "That was in my rash grass-time. Yea, policy for the most part."

He spoke no more than the truth when he said that the troops he had given Harold were now with him. If they had been discontented before at being placed under a foreign leader, they now forgot that grievance and swore he was a man to follow. Such good feeling was there in the division, that when the army crossed the border into Brittany, and marched on Dol, the Duke had no hesitation in deputing Earl Harold to relieve the town.

He watched that skirmish from his camp upon a neighbouring hill-side, and made several observations. He said: "A leader of men, as I thought, and keeps a cool head while the fight is on." Scrutinizing Harold's tactics, he nodded, and said: "Yea, thus did I before I learned a surer way." Later he watched Harold swing his right flank into action and smiled. "He is unused to the ordering of a body of horse, and I think my archers irk him a little. Sacred Face, that axe is a weapon to beware!"

The Saxons had gone into battle with their axes slung at the saddle. The Earl wielded a bi-pennis with both hands, to the astonishment of the Normans, and Raoul saw Edgar's old boast made good. At one blow Harold severed a horse's head from its neck.

The skirmish did not last long, for Count Conan was inexperienced in war and overweighted by force of numbers. He drew off in retreat after a taste of Harold's quality, and fled to his capital at Rennes.

That night in camp Edgar sat in Raoul's tent, polishing his axe with loving care. It was plain he had enjoyed the fight, and would be glad of another.

"Well, you will have that," Raoul said lazily. "We shall follow Conan, you may be sure. I wish you would let a squire clean that axe."

"I had rather do it myself," Edgar replied. He held it up, twisting it so that it caught the light. "Is it not a man's weapon? Eh, old friend, I am glad to feel you in my grip again!"

Raoul lay on his pallet with his hands linked behind his head. He regarded Edgar with a grin. "If I wanted to slay an ox I might be glad of it," he said provocatively.

"An ox!" Edgar said indignantly. He stroked the thick handle. "Do you hear that, O Drinker of Men's Blood?"

Raoul pulled a grimace. "Silence, barbarian! If you are going to talk to that hideous weapon, get you gone! I do not like blood, nor warfare either."

"Raoul, you should not talk in that way," Edgar told him. "If any heard you who did not know you——"

"They would no doubt think that I meant it?" Raoul put in.

"Yea, how should they not?"

"I do mean it," said Raoul sweetly, and shut his eyes for sleep.

Edgar was seriously disturbed by such an admission, and did his best to make Raoul see the folly of his squeamishness. It did not seem to him that his words impressed Raoul, for after twenty minutes the grey eyes opened sleepily, and Raoul said with a yawn: "Holà, are you still there, Edgar?"

Whereupon Edgar rose up with dignity and stalked back to his own quarters.

However, his faith in Raoul was restored soon enough, for the Duke marched on Dinan and took the town by fire and assault, and Edgar, himself plugging into the thick of the fighting, found that Raoul was always in the forefront of the battle, apparently unmoved by the carnage. They fought side by side through the breach in the walls. Raoul slipped on the loose stones and fell; Edgar's axe whirled above him; he roared: "Out, out!" in the Saxon tongue, and a Breton fell across Raoul and splashed his hauberk red with blood. Raoul heaved the still writhing body aside and scrambled up.

"Hurt?" Edgar shouted above the noise all round them.

Raoul shook his head. Not until the fight was over, and the Norman troops lay in the town did the incident occur to either again. They lost each other in the battle and met again hours later in the market-place. Raoul was in charge of a body of men-at-arms who had been set to work to quench the fire in the town; it was dusk when Edgar came upon him, and he was standing in the glow of a blazing house, grimed and sweat-stained but unhurt.

Edgar waited until Raoul had shouted an order to one of his men, and then laid a hand on his arm. "I have been searching high and low for you," he said. He added with a characteristic lack of emotion: "I began to think you must have been slain."

"Néel could have told you where I was," said Raoul. "Ho, there! stand from under that wall!"

A little boy in a scorched tunic ran barefoot across the cobbles shrieking for his mother. Raoul caught him and tossed him into Edgar's arms. "Hold this babe!" he commanded, "or he will run on his death. That house is doomed."

Edgar tucked the terrified child under one arm, inquiring mildly what he was to do with the brat. But Raoul had moved away to direct the saving of a house which the flames

232

were barely licking on the further side of the market-place, and he did not hear the question. Edgar stayed where he was and endeavoured to stay the child's wailing. To his relief the shrill cries brought a woman up hot-foot. She tore the boy out of Edgar's hold, and clasping him to her breast spat forth a torrent of words. As she spoke the Breton tongue Edgar did not understand what she said, but the ferocity in her face and voice left him in no doubt of her meaning. He tried to explain that he had not harmed the child, but she understood him as little as he understood her, and took a menacing step towards him with her fingers curled as though she would claw out his eyes. He retired in haste behind a heap of charred litter, and she darted away with a final malediction just as Raoul returned to join him.

Raoul was shaken with laughter. "O dauntless hero! O brave Saxon! Come forth, the foe is in retreat."

Edgar came out from behind the débris with a shame-faced grin. "Well, what could I do? The woman was a very she-devil. A murrain light on you, shaveling: it was your fault for thrusting the brat into my arms."

Raoul began to wipe the sweat and the dirt from his face and neck. His chuckles died away; he watched his men running up with full buckets of water. "Hell's work, this. And you like it!" He brought his gaze back to Edgar, and said suddenly: "I think you saved my life, back there on the walls."

"When?" said Edgar, wrinkling his brow.

"When I stumbled, want-wit."

"Oh, then!" Edgar considered the matter. "Yes, I suppose I did," he admitted. His eye brightened. "It was a rare stroke, straight down at the join of the neck to the shoulder. I have not lost all my skill in these years of my exile."

"Well, my thanks to you," Raoul said. "Praise the saints, this day's work will end the war! Conan surrendered the town in person."

"Yes," said Edgar. He sounded slightly regretful. "I'm for my supper," he announced. "Do you come with me?"

"When I have seen the last spark quenched. Where is the Duke?"

"Up at the Castle with the Earl and de Gournay. Conan is putting as good a face to the matter as may be, and sups at the Duke's table this night, so FitzOsbern told me. If I were William I would put him in shackles." He began to walk away, but paused when he had taken no more than three paces, and said over his shoulder: "The Duke knights Earl Harold." He did not wait to hear Raoul's answer, but walked on with long strides across the market-place.

Raoul looked after him. "And you wish that Earl Harold had refused it," he said softly, and turned back to his work.

The ceremony of knighthood took place the next morning. The Earl stood unarmed before William, who girded a sword that hung from a jewelled belt about his loins, placed a helmet on his head, and a lance in his hold, and laid his hand on Harold's right arm, speaking the accustomed words.

Conan having been forced to renew his allegiance to Normandy the Duke set his face towards Rouen again, and withdrew across the border into Avranches. He and Earl Harold rode side by side, apparently the best of friends, sharing one tent and one table, and passing long hours together in close converse.

At St. Jaques upon the border they rested for a day and a night, and as was usual when the Duke was known to be in the neighbourhood, the people from all around came flocking to his camp, some with grievances to lay before him, some desiring to see him from curiosity, and many in the hope of largesse from the rich lords who accompanied him. Most of the beggars were cripples or lepers, and the tinkle of the lepers' bells was heard all day round the outskirts of the camp. Such persons were rarely permitted to approach William, but at St. Jaques FitzOsbern came hurrying up when the Duke sat at meat with Earl Harold outside his tent, and exclaimed unceremoniously: "Beau sire, I would you might set eyes on the spectacle I have this moment seen! Never have I known so strange a prodigy!"

"What prodigy is this, William?" the Duke asked indulgently, too well-used to FitzOsbern's enthusiasms to be easily stirred by them.

"It is a woman with every part twofold to the navel," FitzOsbern told him. "Seigneur, you smile, but as I live she hath two corses, two heads, two necks, and four arms. And these being joined at the navel the two parts are supported on a single pair of legs and feet. Raoul, you were on the outposts an hour ago: did you not see it?"

"Yes," admitted Raoul with a look of distaste. "It is a great wonder, but very horrible."

The Duke turned his head to look up at the favourite, standing behind his chair. "Is it in truth a wonder, my Watcher, or is this one of William's tales?"

Raoul smiled. "Nay, it is wonderful enough, but it would turn your stomach to look upon it."

"My stomach is not easily turned," William replied. "How do you say, Earl Harold? Shall we see this prodigy?"

"I would give much to see it," said the Earl. "A woman with two heads! Can both mouths speak? Can one speak and the other be silent?"

Galet the fool sat curled up by the Duke's chair; William pushed him with his foot. "Up, Galet! Go bring this prodigy before me."

FitzOsbern was answering the Earl's question. "Nay, but they could once. The creature's father, a villein from nearby, told me one half was wont to eat while the other spoke, or to sleep while the other lay awake. But a year ago one half died, leaving the other alive, which is a thing I deem more marvelous than all."

"One half dead and the other half still living! Can such a thing be?" said Harold incredulously. "I have a great desire to see this strange awesome woman."

Raoul said in his quiet way: "I pray you may not turn sick at the sight and the stench of it, my lord."

Harold looked up at him inquiringly. Raoul said only: "You will see: it is no pleasant sight to my mind."

The Duke laid down a capon-bone which he had been chewing. "Lend no ear to Raoul, Earl Harold. Some call him the Watcher, but others know him as the Squeamish, and the Friend of the Friendless. Do I say truly, Raoul?"

"So I believe. But I did not know that had come to your ears, beau sire."

The Duke smiled. "Yet you know me as well as any," he remarked cryptically. He saw the fool approaching, and beckoned to him. "Well, do you bring me the Seneschal's prodigy, friend?"

"Yea brother, she comes." Galet pointed to where a queer veiled figure was walking towards them with slow, dragging steps, led by a serf who had hold of one of her hands.

The Duke pushed his platter aside, and leaned his arms on the table. "Come, my man, bring me your daughter that I may see with mine own eyes how God has fashioned her," he said pleasantly.

From out her muffling draperies the woman spoke in a thin toneless voice. "Lord, the devil made me, not God in his mercy."

The Duke frowned. "What blasphemous words are these on your lips, wench?" He made a sign. "Come closer, and strip off these coverings. You have shown yourself to my men-at-arms for gain: now show yourself to me."

She came up close to the table; a nauseating aroma of decay hung round her, the reek of putrefying flesh. Earl Harold raised his napkin to his nose suddenly, and held it there.

"Now you shall see whether I spoke truth or not, seigneur!" FitzOsbern said.

The woman's father, after much louting to the Duke, began to unwind the coarse falding that wrapped the mis-shapen form about. He stood back when it was done, saying proudly: "Thus was she at birth, gracious lord."

"And the only joyful part of her was her belly, which cried: 'Praise God, here have I two mouths to feed my hunger!' said Galet. He poked his bauble at Earl Harold. "What, cousin, are you sick?"

Harold got up quickly, fumbling at his belt for the purse that hung there. He had changed colour when he saw the woman stand naked before him, and the sight of the dead half of her hanging from her side and weighing her down, made his gorge rise. The flesh was crumbling with decay; the shrivelled arms hung down to the ground, and swayed with every movement the woman made; the head jolted and nodded, and the flesh looked worm-eaten, rotting away from the bones.

The Earl flung his napkin aside as though impatient with himself for needing it, and went close up to the figure, laying his hand on the sad living head. "God pity you, poor soul, as I do," he said gently. He put his purse into her hand, closing her slack fingers over it, and strode off without a backward glance.

The Duke watched him go. "It turned him sick, yet he could touch it, mastering his loathing," he murmured. His eyes met Raoul's for a brief moment. "Yea, he hath great-ness." He turned back to FitzOsbern. "See to it the wench has a purse from me, William." He looked the woman over critically. "My girl, I think your Purgatory is served here on earth. Go your ways." He saw the couple draw off, and said briskly: "Bah! a vile stench! Give me that rose, William. What fond wretch threw it to you?"

FitzOsbern laughed, and pulled out the flower from the fibula that held his mantle together, and gave it to the Duke.

William sat holding it close to his nose. "You were right, Raoul: a horrible sight," he said.

Galet, who had been silent for some time, drawing figures in the dust, lifted his head and fixed his eyes on William. They glowed with an unearthly light; sweat stood on his brow; he said in a voice unlike his own: "Brother, you have seen a riddle you have not the wit to read."

"Read it for me then, fool," the Duke said, still breathing the clean scent of the rose.

"You have seen England and Normandy, brother, two countries, yet joined under one ruler; both hale once upon a day, but one now dead, rotted and stinking, hanging on the other, which still by its wealth and vigour supports it."

"Folly!" said FitzOsbern scornfully.

The Duke did not raise his eyes from the rose he held. "Go on, friend Galet. Which of these two by your reading is Normandy?"

The fool pointed a bony finger, and they saw that it was shaking. "Do you not know, Brother William? Eh, but you know full well, you of the hawk's eyes! Normandy is that carrion flesh that saps the life-blood from England. For England shall take out of Normandy all that she can give, and leave her languishing to die, as you have seen today—yea, and as your sons' sons shall see in the years to come, to their bitter cost!"

FitzOsbern stood staring with dropped jaw; Raoul was watching the Duke, who had glanced quickly at the jester under his brows.

There was a moment's silence. The Duke's hard gaze left Galet's face. "So be it," he said deliberately, and bent his head to sniff at the rose again.

CHAPTER VI

They rode northward to St. Lo, upon the Vire, in the wild Côtentin country. Here messengers met them from Rouen, with letters for the Duke. He read them quickly and only dwelled long upon one, which brought him tidings out of England. He handed the sheet presently to Earl Harold, saying: "These concern you, I think." While the Earl read the letter he went on slitting open his various despatches, and never once raised his eyes to see how the Earl received the news contained in the brief account he held.

But Harold's face betrayed nothing. He read unhurriedly, his eyes thoughtful. The letter told of the King's failing health: he hunted less often than of yore; spent much time in prayer and meditation, and was fretful with the masons at work upon the Abbey that was slowly building to the glory of St. Peter on the Isle of Thorney, outside London. This was to be his last resting-place, and he had taken a notion into his head that the masons would not have reached the end of their labours before his body was ready for its sepulchre.

The despatch went on to tell of trouble in the north, where Tostig ruled. Earl Harold folded it carefully, and gave it back to William. The Duke had taken quill and ink, and was writing an answer to Rouen. His pen moved boldly, with thick downward strokes characteristic of the man.

Not lifting his gaze from the cotton-paper under his hand, he said: "I find I have little patience to waste on such turbulent men as that brother of yours, my friend."

"I have none," the Earl replied rather grimly.

William went on writing for a while in silence. He came to the end of the sheet and sprinkled fine sand over it and shook this off presently on to the floor. He laid the sheet aside and dipped his quill into the ink-horn again. "I think," he said, with a deliberation the Earl found maddening, "I think that it is time you set sail for England, Earl Harold."

The Earl felt an itching desire to get up and move about the small room. He curbed it and sat still, his eyes on William's face. "It is time, and more," he said, as though he picked his words. He watched the Duke's pen travel across the sheet, once, twice, a third time. He found that his fingers were drumming against the carven arm of his chair, and closed them on the hard wood to stay their fidgeting. He wanted the Duke to speak, but William went on writing. The Earl's brain weighed and rejected phrase after phrase. He said at last, abruptly: "Be plain with me, Duke William: what is it you require of me?"

The Duke raised his eyes at that, and laid aside his quill. Pushing the papers from him he linked his hands together on the table, and said: "Earl Harold, many years ago when I was an untried boy still in the care of my guardians King Edward dwelled in my Court and was my friend. In those days he made me a promise that if ever he became King of England, and begat no children of his own body, myself should be his heir." He paused, but the Earl made no remark. He was leaning back in his chair, his head resting against the dark wood. His face showed nothing but a calm interest. The Duke looked him over with a certain measure of approval. "Fourteen years ago," he went on, "I journeyed into England upon a visit to the King, when he renewed his promises to me, giving me as hostages, Wlnoth, Hakon, and Edgar, the son of Eadwulf. This I think must be known to you?"

"I have heard it," Harold answered, expressionless.

"The King is stricken in years," William said, "and I am not the only one who looks towards his throne."

The Earl's eyelids flickered, but he said nothing.

"There is Edgar, the child-Atheling," William continued after an infinitesimal pause. "I have little doubt there are many will seek to set him up."

"It is very like," Harold said. He moved his hand so that a ring of balas-rubies which he wore caught the sunlight; he studied it through half-closed eyes.

"I need a man to hold for me in England," the Duke said, "guarding my interest until the time comes when Edward is called to his fathers—and after."

"Myself?" There was a hint of steel in the Earl's voice.

"Yourself," William agreed, "bound by oath to uphold my claim."

The Earl smiled. He looked up from his ring, and found William's gaze upon him. He met it full, and while a man might count fifty the long interchange of glances held, in a silence unbroken by any other sound than the high sweet song of a lark lost somewhere in the blue haze outside. "So that is why you are holding me," the Earl said at last, without surprise or heat.

"That is why," William answered. "To be honest with you, Earl Harold, had you been other than you are I would not have spent these pains on the matter. I tell you in all frankness you are the only man I have met in all the years of my life for whom I have felt—respect."

"I am honoured," Harold said ironically.

"You may well be," the Duke replied with a gleam of humour. He watched the last grains of sand trickle through the hour-glass upon the table, and turned it.

"What bribe do you offer me, my lord Duke?" Harold asked.

The Duke's lips curled. "Earl Harold, many things you may call me, but I beg you will not call me Fool. I keep bribes for lesser men."

Harold inclined his head slightly. "My thanks. I will word it thus: what reward will you bestow upon a son of God-wine?"

The Duke considered him for a moment. "Harold, if you choose you may stand second to me in England," he said. "I

239

will give you my daughter Adela in marriage, and engage to confirm you in the possessions you hold today."

If the Earl saw anything ludicrous in the offer of espousal with an infant years younger than the offspring of his own first marriage, he gave no sign of it. "Why, this is noble!" he murmured. Again he studied his ring. "And if I refuse?"

The Duke, knowing his man, replied: "Using no half-words, son of Godwine, if you refuse I shall not let you depart out of Normandy."

"I see," said Harold. He might have added that he had seen for many months, and long since weighed the chances of escape, and considered what must be his answer to the Duke's demands. There was no smile in his eyes now; his lips had taken on a stern look. He drew in a deep breath, as though he had come to the end of a struggle that cost him dear, but his voice, pleasant as always, perfectly under his control, betrayed nothing of this. "It seems that I have no choice, Duke William. I will take the oath," he said.

He told Edgar that night what he had done. Edgar lighted him to his chamber, and when he would have left the Earl at his door Harold said curtly: "Wait: I have something to tell you." He dismissed the sleepy page who was holding a taper to the candles on the table, and flung himself down on a chair that stood against the wall, out of the circle of light. "Shut that door, Edgar. I leave for England in a week, or maybe a little more, taking you and Hakon with me. Wlnoth remains."

Edgar stayed still by the door. "Leave for England?" he echoed stupidly. "Do you tell me the Duke has relented?" He sounded incredulous, but as a thought occurred to him he added with some eagerness: "Is this because you did so well by him in Brittany, lord? I know that he loves courage, but I never dreamed——" He stopped, for the Earl had given a scornful laugh under his breath. Edgar took a quick step forward, trying to see his lord's face. "What is the price of freedom?" he demanded. His hand closed on the edge of the table and gripped it.

"I have promised to swear an oath to him, engaging to uphold his claim to England," Harold said. "To deliver up to him when the King dies, Dover Castle, and to wed his daughter Adela as soon as she is of marriageable age."

"Soul of God, are you jesting?" Edgar snatched up the heavy candlestick from the table and held it high above his head so that the light fell on the Earl's face. "Are you mad, my lord?" he said harshly. "Jesu, are you mad?"

The Earl put up a hand to shade his eyes. "No, I am not mad," he answered. "I take the only road that leads to freedom."

"Swearing away a crown, a life's ambition!" The candlestick shook in Edgar's hold. "What of us, the men who have trusted in you, followed you, died for you? God on the Cross, is it Godwine's son who speaks?"

The Earl moved restlessly. "Fool, do you not know that if I refuse to take the oath William will never let me go? What of you then, you who trust in me? Should I not fail you? Answer!"

Edgar set down the candlestick with a crash. "Lord, you leave me without words, without understanding. Be plain with me, I beg of you!"

"I have told you: it is the only way left to me. If I refuse I must remain a prisoner, and lose what I have striven for all my life." He paused, and added meaningly: "Have you forgot how I swore to you a year agone that I would escape his net, not matter by what means, or at what cost?"

"What shall it profit you, this shackled freedom?" Edgar said. He realized suddenly what the Earl's words implied, and sank down on to a stool by the table, resting his head in his hands. "Oh, heart of God!" he said. His fingers writhed in the strands of his hair. "I am dull-witted indeed," he said bitterly, "to think that Harold Godwineson would be torn asunder before he broke faith. Forgive me! I have fed on dreams."

The Earl rose, and stood before his thegn, leaning his hands upon the table that separated them. "Tell me, with whom shall I break faith: with William or with England?" he asked sternly. "Speak! With one or other it must be. Shall I shrink from staining mine honour, and betray our England to this Norman tyrant? Is that what you would have me do? Is that work for Harold Godwineson? Torch of the Gospel, if that is the image you nurse of me, banish it and know me for myself, no puppet of your fancy! I stand for England, and England I will hold till the breath leaves my body. Think me what you will: though I break faith with all others, to England I will still be true. What shall I care though my soul be damned in hell, if it must be said of me that what I did I did that England might be safe?" His voice filled the room; he ceased, and a deep silence fell. The candle-flame burned steadily, unshaken by any draught; beyond the window a star shone in the darkness.

The hoot of an owl broke the quiet. Edgar started, and raised his head from his hands. "Forgive me!" he said again, in a changed voice. His face darkened. "What devil's cunning to put this upon you! Ha God, there shall be a reckoning! Yet might he not guess, lord? Might he not suspect that such an oath would not bind you?"

"Guess! He knows," Harold answered. He began to move about the room; a short laugh escaped him. "Lanfranc!" he said. He unclasped the belt that girt his tunic round his waist, and threw it on the table. "What, do you not see it all yet? Think, when England's crown is set upon my head what an outcry will be raised by William against Harold, a breaker of his oath!"

"It is black, lord," Edgar said in a low voice. "An offence against God and chivalry, a stain upon your shield." He rose suddenly and pushed back his stool. "I thought he had a kindness for you! All these weeks while you have slept, ate, fought together—ah, he bears two faces, the Wolf!"

Harold paused in his striding up and down; he looked curiously at Edgar. "You are wrong. You think he has counterfeited liking for me. He does like me, and if I would bend to his will I might be sure of his friendship. Why, he offered me—— Well, no matter for that. I have chosen the path I must tread." He came close to Edgar, and gripped his arms. "Your heart misgives you: do you think mine is not heavy at this hour? Stand by me; trust in me yet, though I lay perjury upon my soul. I need your trust as never before."

He let him go. Edgar dropped on his knees and put up his hands, palm to palm. "God knows I trust in you, my lord, and you know too. Come what may I will follow you to the end."

The Earl laid his hands lightly on either side of Edgar's. "Yea, I know." He raised his thegn. "It grows late, and there is no more to say. Leave me now, and pray that William may not require so solemn an oath of me as must put me, in the breaking of it, beyond the Church's forgiveness."

They took the road again next day. Edgar rode close behind the Earl, holding aloof from his Norman friends. FitzOsbern rallied him on his coldness, but stopped soon enough, warned by Raoul's frown. He cantered alongside Raoul, and said: "What ails him? I have not seen him so glum these many years."

"Let him be, FitzOsbern!" Raoul said wearily. "Cannot you guess how he must hate us?"

"Hate us!" ejaculated FitzOsbern. "What, because of this oath to be sworn at Bayeux? No, no, what is that to him?"

Raoul heaved a sigh of exasperation. "What would it be to us if William stood in Harold's shoes today? Oh, I do not doubt that Edgar loves his friends still, but in his heart is bitter hatred of our race. Leave him: you can do nothing."

"But I see no reason," FitzOsbern persisted. "No force has been put upon the Earl; it is settled between him and William as between two who understand each other well. Now why out of hell do you laugh?"

"No force?" Raoul repeated. "God's eyes, FitzOsbern, is torture the only force you know? I would we were done with this business."

They came to Bayeux in due course, and were received there by the Bishop. If the Earl's eyes searched for the Prior of Herluin in the assembly they found him not. Earl Harold was as gay as ever, talking easily to the Duke, and to Odo, often laughing at some jest as though no care weighed on him. Only his followers, Edgar, and Alfric, Sigwulf, Edmund, Oswine, and Earnulph, wore grave faces, and watched him with trouble in their eyes. Each one was in his confidence, each one had sworn to keep silence, but though they said stoutly that no oath extracted thus could bind him, foreboding crept over them, and a vague alarm possessed their minds.

Nothing was done upon the first evening of their stay in Bayeux, but upon the following morning the ceremony of binding by oath took place in the council-hall of the Castle.

The Duke sat upon a throne of state, wearing his coronet and holding a drawn sword in his hand, the point upwards. Behind him were gathered his knights and nobles; before him, in the middle of the hall, a large tub stood, covered by a cloth of gold that entirely concealed it. Near this Odo the Bishop was waiting, attended by his chaplain and several priests.

It was a very bright morning, and long beams of sunlight, slanting down through the windows, showed dust-motes dancing, and barred the hall with gold. Warmth stole into the vast grey hall, and, through the unglazed windows, the hum of the busy town.

The Earl came in last of all with his own followers behind him. He wore his byrnie, but his head was uncovered. A blue mantle hung from his shoulders, and there were golden bracelets on his arms. Raoul had an odd fancy that he had brought the sunlight with him.

He paused for a second on the threshold, looking quickly

round. The Duke, remote on his throne, FitzOsbern beside him, Mortain, Grantmesnil, Tesson, Saint-Sauveur, De Gournay, De Montfort, Giffard—he saw them all in that one swift glance. They stood still, their hands on their swords, watching him, grimly, he thought.

He walked forward unhurriedly; he was pale, but perfectly calm. A faint frown lay between his eyes, and his mouth was set in grim lines. Behind him his Saxons formed a semi-circle.

The curtains over one of the archways parted, and a priest came into the hall bearing two reliquaries which he set reverently down upon the draped tub before Odo. Harold looked at them without any change of expression, and fixed his eyes upon the Duke again.

A sigh of relief came from Edgar: the reliquaries held less significance than he had feared.

The Duke moved, leaning forward a little on his throne; the edge of his sword caught the sunlight and the heavy mantle he wore fell away from one arm and showed a lining of ermine. His deep compelling voice was pitched so that no word he spoke was missed by anyone in the hall. "Earl Harold," he said, "you are come here for what purpose you know. I require you, before this noble assembly, to confirm by oath the promises you have made to me: To act as my vicar at the Court of England so long as Edward the King shall live; to do what lies in your power to secure the Sceptre to me after his death; to render up to me the Castle of Dover, and other such castles as I may deem needful to be garrisoned by Norman troops. These things you have promised."

"These I have promised," the Earl said mechanically.

The Bishop moved forward a pace; Earl Harold scarcely heeded him. He was looking across the hall at William, and at William's Court, trying to read the dark faces that confronted him. He noticed that Raoul de Harcourt never once raised his eyes from the sword-hilt under his two hands; he saw that FitzOsbern was frowning as though in discomfort, and that a gleam of eagerness shone in Mortain's eyes. He looked quickly back at William, but could learn nothing from that strong impassive countenance.

He suspected all at once that something lay behind the silence and the intent watchfulness that surrounded him. He glanced down at the reliquaries. They were ordinary enough: the trap was not there. Some warning instinct whispered in his brain; again he looked round the hall, again was conscious of an atmosphere of tension, of pent anxiety that signified more than he could see. Almost he drew back, but recovering himself stepped deliberately up to the reliquaries, glinting on the cloth of gold.

He stretched out his hand over them and thought that a faint sigh ran round the hall. It was too late to refuse the oath now. He drew a long breath and began to repeat the terms he had agreed to.

No tremor shook the steadiness of his hand; his voice was clear and unfaltering.

". . . to do what lies in my power to secure the Sceptre of England to you; to render up to you my Castle of Dover, and others such as you shall hereafter deem needful." He paused; his voice gathered strength. "So may God help me, and the Holy Gospels!" he said. The words rang sternly, and the echoes caught them and carried them among the rafters.

Swords were raised; the barons cried: "God aid him!"

Their voices seemed to thunder in the Earl's ears. His hand fell to his side again; men saw that he had grown deadly pale, and was breathing short and fast.

He heard the sigh again, unmistakably, and saw upon faces that had before been anxious covert smiles of satisfaction.

The Duke made a sign to his brother. The Bishop beckoned two of his attendants forward, and they removed the reliquaries from the golden cloth, and raised it. A musty scent reached Earl Harold: the tub which the cloth had hidden was filled with human bones, and it did not need Odo's soft explanation to tell the Earl that these were the bones of holy saints.

He shuddered, and started back, covering his face with his hands. A sword rasped behind him; Edgar's voice cried out: "Tricked! tricked! Out, Norman dogs!"

The Earl pulled himself together quickly and grasped Edgar's wrist in a grip of steel. "Back! The oath is taken." He turned to face the Duke again. "What more remains to do?" he said harshly.

"No more," the Duke replied. "Upon the bones of Saints you have sworn. It is done."

For a moment they looked at one another across the space that separated them; then the Earl swept round on his heel and went quickly out.

Again steel rasped in the hall. Mortain jumped round to see Raoul slam his sword home in the scabbard. "For God's sake, let me pass!" Raoul said. His voice shook with a kind of rage. "I have had my fill of this work!" he thrust past the astonished Count, strode to the narrow stair, and disappeared round the bend of it.

Grantmesnil shrugged, and whispered in Mortain's ear: "The Watcher will go too far one of these days. Will the Duke stomach this rude leave-taking?"

The Duke gave no sign of having noticed Raoul's departure. Handing his sword to the Chancellor, he dismissed the Court, and went out with his brothers and FitzOsbern.

Upstairs Raoul ran on Edgar in the narrow passage. Both stopped short, and for a moment neither spoke. Edgar folded his arms on his chest; his eyes smouldered still; he said in a fierce low voice: "Thus your Duke! Thus this Norman Wolf! False knavish trickster!"

Raoul pressed his lips together; his brows were drawn close; he said no word.

"A ruse to cheat Earl Harold! And you knew! Yea, you knew, all of you, and stood by in silence while that devil's work was done!"

"Enough of that! As I do not condemn your master, who swore an oath with perjury in his heart, so keep your tongue from mine!"

Edgar said swiftly: "What do you mean? Who says that Harold had perjury in mind?"

"Why leaped he back from the relics in dismay?" Raoul flung at him. "Oh, rest you, my lips are sealed! But who lies deepest in shame: my master who conceived this plot, or yours who swore a solemn oath, scheming as he swore how best to break it? Let us be done with this, I beg of you! Our words lead nowhither, save to bitter quarrelling."

He would have passed on, but Edgar stayed him. "Do you uphold Duke William? You?"

"Till death!" Raoul said violently. "Now let me go!"

Some of Edgar's wrath seemed to die in him. "You do not. Nay, I can read you, my friend. Eh Raoul, what an end to all our hope, what an end to friendship, when we are torn apart by such dealing!" He put his hand to lay it on Raoul's arm, but let it fall again. "A drawn sword lies between us. I am glad we fought together in Brittany." He stared at the ground, but raising his head again in a little while, said: "Bound, both of us, yet when I think of all that is held by the past—friendship and what small happiness I have known—I can hear some voice in my heart that cries, heedless of fealty: 'Would to God I had no lord!' "

"Ah Christ, and in my heart also!" Raoul said. His smile

went awry. He held out his hand. "Across the sword . . ." he said.

Edgar clasped it, and did not at once let go. He seemed to find it hard to speak. He said at last: "You would have come with us to England. Do not, Raoul. I thought to light you to your marriage-bed, but what has passed this day ends that dream with all else that we two held dear."

"I know it," Raoul said. "But let me still cherish hope! Edgar——" He broke off, and pressed Edgar's hand. "I cannot say it. I shall see her again. When do you set sail? As soon as may be?" He gave an uncertain laugh. "God's pity, it will be strange in Rouen with you gone!"

They left Bayeux the next morning. The Earl rode beside William as he had done each day for many weeks. Neither spoke of the oath, but when they came to Rouen and lay again in the palace the question of the Earl's betrothal was broached. He was solemnly affianced to the Lady Adela. She did not stand as high as his elbow, and was torn between pride in her future lord and exceeding great awe of him. He had an easy way with children, and lifted her in his arms and set a kiss upon her cheek. The memory of his smile was to remain with her all her short life.

There was no more to do but to take leave of the Norman Court. The day after his betrothal Earl Harold rode away to the coast, and amongst his escort was Raoul de Harcourt, ranging close beside Elfrida's litter.

Their farewells had been said. She had lain sobbing in his arms like a tired child, while he stroked her hair and whispered to her of courage and hope. "I shall come to claim you," he said. "As God lives and reigns, I shall come to you." He held her closer still. "Wait for me: trust me! It will not be long. And in whatever guise I come—remember that I love you, yea, and would give my life to spare you pain! Remember that always, O my little love!"

She promised, wonderingly, searching his face for his meaning.

He said: "I can tell you no more. Only remember! and though the future hold grief and bitter anguish, think this: as Edgar is bound, so too am I, by ties I cannot break."

"I am afraid! I am afraid!" she said. "What grief but this parting? What anguish? Raoul, Raoul!"

"Please God, none!" he said. "But know this, my heart: if it should chance that I may reach to you only by the sword's path, then, by Death, I will take that path!"

PART V
(1066)

THE CROWN

"There is no road for retreat."
Speech of William the Conqueror.

CHAPTER I

It was not long after Harold's return that another visitor came to Normandy from England. This one was Tostig, Earl of Northumbria, who arrived with his wife and children in a mood of sullen anger, and presented himself at Duke William's Court with an involved tale of treachery, hatred, and unbrotherly dealing on his lips. It was impossible to unravel his story, but one fact emerged clearly: Earl Tostig had culminated his reign in Northumbria by behaviour of such violence that his subjects rose against him as one man, and declared for Morkere, the son of Alfgar. They were supported by Earl Harold. It was at this point that the tale grew incoherent.

Duke William, looking his guest over with a sardonic eye, wasted no more time upon it. Judith, closeted with her sister, was somewhat more explicit.

Judith had grown stout, and white streaked the brown of her hair. She had acquired a comfortable habit of placidity, and spent the greater part of her day in eating sugar-plums. Her lord's vagaries left her as unmoved as everything else in her world. She observed Matilda lazily, and remarked: "Eh my dear, I see you are slender still! Well-a-day, and is it seven or eight children you have borne your lord?"

"Eight, and three of them sons," said Matilda proudly.

"They are all very like him," Judith said. "How many years is it since the Fighting Duke stalked into our bower at Lille, and flogged you?"

Matilda was unperturbed by this old memory. "As many years since I put you into Earl Tostig's bed."

Judith ate another sugar-plum, and carefully licked her fingers. "Well, that is like to have been an ill night's work. He was then a fool, and is now a wolf'shead." She yawned. "This is no way to combat Harold, to get himself outlawed. That sleek cat Eadgytha was to blame."

"The Queen?" Matilda paused in her stitchery to look up.

"She and Tostig hatched the plot to slay Gospatrick last year. The King had nothing to say to it then, but your lord let Harold go and I warrant you he had the matter at his finger-end soon enough. It was farewell to Tostig within a month of Harold's return." She seemed to meditate within herself. "Tostig plans largely. They have great desires, all the sons of Godwine. But I doubt my spouse is not the man to carry these to a successful issue. More I do not say."

The Duchess thought of her own very different lord, and smiled secretly. Judith lay back at her ease, watching her out of her sleepy eyes. "Yea, coney," she said. "You think that you chose more wisely at last than I. I do not gainsay it. A proper man is Duke William. I remember he would have nothing to say to me when he came a-wooing you."

Earl Tostig remained at the Court some weeks, airing his grievances, but departed to spend Christmas in Flanders. The sisters embraced lovingly enough, but the old intimacy was lacking. Each nursed secrets; neither was sorry to see the last of the other.

Christmas passed quietly. Raoul rode south to see his father, and remembered how Edgar had gone with him on so many other visits to Harcourt. He urged his horse to a brisker pace, trying to cast off the memory, but beside him rode some phantom of Edgar, and he thought that he could hear an echo of the old song of Brunanburgh which Edgar used to sing. At Harcourt Hubert inquired for him, and seemed surprised to hear that he had gone home to England. Hubert's memory was failing, but he did not like to be reminded of this. He said: "Had he not a sister?" He was pleased to think he could remember that, and with an effort sought in his mind for her name. "Elfrida!" he pronounced at last, triumphantly.

Her name, spoken after so many months, made Raoul start. He thought it lived only in his dreams. A flush stole into his lean cheeks; he said: "Yes. He has a sister."

"I never saw her," Hubert said. "But Edgar I knew well, yea, and liked. What ailed him that he must needs to go to England?"

"He is a Saxon, father," Raoul said gently.

"Well, I know that," Hubert replied rather testily. "But he lived among us long years—enough to make Normandy his home. Is he coming back?"

Raoul shook his head. He turned away, and stirred the wood-fire to a blaze, bending over it so that Hubert could not read his face.

"A pity," Hubert remarked. He relapsed into one of the sudden forgetful silences of old age, and sat staring into the fire as though he saw pictures of the past there. He smiled and nodded, and presently dropped off into an easy doze. When he woke again he had forgotten Edgar and wanted only his supper.

In Rouen the Duke kept Christmas with good cheer, and prayer, and hunting. My lord Robert set a trap of a sack of flour on a half-open door for his corpulent great-uncle Walter, and counted the day well spent when the jester was blamed for it.

A sharp frost set in after Christmas; water froze in the gutters of the palace, and snow covered the leaden roof. Men went abroad in fur-lined mantles, and the Duke's sons made a slide in the bailey which was even better sport than they had expected, since no less than three noble gentlemen stepped on it unawares.

The cold weather, though it made other men long only for fires, seemed to increase the Duke's energy. He spent whole days at the chase, and the woods echoed continually to the sound of his huntsman's horn winding a mort. The hardiest of his court accompanied him on these expeditions, but it was observed that his most devoted friend had in part deserted him. The Chevalier de Harcourt pulled his scarlet cloak close round him and shivered at the sharp wind, and prayed the Duke to hold him excused.

"Raoul," said Grantmesnil slyly, "is mumpish because he has lost his fair lady."

A look cold as the ice on the river was directed towards him. The truth of Grantmesnil's gibe did not make it more palatable to the Chevalier.

If there was any truth in his plea that he hated the bitter wind he was not alone in his complaining. One day in the New Year, the Duke took boat across the Seine to the forest of Quévilly to hunt the deer there, and he was the only man of the party who did not grumble at the cold. The gaunt tree branches bore thin crusts of snow; the ground was hard and cracked with frost, and the men's breath made little clouds of steam in the clear air. They had to stamp their feet to keep the blood flowing, and Grantmesnil, blowing upon his chilled fingers, grunted: "No weather for hunting, this."

The Duke had brought down a hart of twelve. He did not seem to feel the cold; his cheeks were flushed, and he had thrown off his mantle to give his arms greater play. The huntsmen were driving up more beasts; Ralph de Toeni began to fit an arrow to his bow, but complained with a laugh that his fingers were all benumbed. William de Warenne shot and missed; the Duke drew his arrow to the head.

The bow was bent when an interruption occurred. A messenger from Rouen had come up at a stumbling jog-trot, and now ran towards William and dropped on his knee before him without pausing to allow the Duke to loose his arrow. His leather tunic and his boots were stained with salt water; he seemed to have come far, and in haste. "Lord," he said, panting, "they told me to seek you here!"

The Duke lowered his bow with an impatient oath. He turned and looked frowningly down at the messenger. An angry reproof hovered on his tongue but was checked. He gave his bow abruptly to his forester and signed to those about him to draw back out of earshot. "Speak, then! What tidings do you bring me, you out of England?" he said.

"Lord, Edward the King is dead, and was coffined upon the day of Epiphany, and the wake-plays are done. Harold Godwineson is crowned King in his room."

"Crowned!" The Duke turned rather pale. "Is this truth indeed?"

"Yea, lord, it is truth. Stigand the Archbishop anointed Harold, himself being under interdict. Harold reigns in England this day." He paused, and seemed at a loss to know how to continue.

"Well?" the Duke said sharply. "What more?"

"Lord, Harold has taken to wife Aldgytha, Griffyd's widow and Earl Alfgar's daughter," muttered the messenger.

He saw the Duke's hand clench suddenly, and cringed, but William did not strike. Turning, he went back to the huntsmen, who were watching him in surprise and alarm. He paid no heed to them, but took his mantle roughly from the page who held it and flung it round his shoulders. In a silence that was felt to be more terrible than any outburst of anger he strode quickly away down the track that led to the river.

His sudden wordless departure was so strange that no one knew what to make of it. Hugh de Grantmesnil looked blankly at De Toeni; William de Warenne said in a puzzled undertone: "What has chanced? I have never seen him behave thus before. We had best go with him, but say nothing."

The three barons gave their bows to their squires, and followed the Duke in wondering silence to the river. They saw how heavy was the frown on his brow, and how he continually tied and untied the strings of his mantle, and not one of them dared to address him. His boat was awaiting him at the landing-stage; he stepped into it with so little care that it rocked perilously for a moment. He sat down in the stern, still without speaking or glancing towards his escort. His eyes stared across the water; his fingers went on fidgeting with the strings of his mantle. Grantmesnil, who was watching him covertly, saw the twitch at the corners of his mouth, and nudged De Toeni warningly. Thus had the Duke's mouth twitched when he had banished these two some years ago in a fit of black rage. De Toeni gave a little shiver and laid his finger on his lips. Blameless they might both be today, but they knew and dreaded that sign of a rising anger in their lord.

When the boat's keel grated on the shingle of the further bank De Warenne jumped ashore to offer the support of his arm to the Duke. William sprang to land without apparently perceiving the outstretched hand, and made his way at a brisk pace towards the palace.

Behind him his attendants followed in as deep a silence as his own. For all the heed he paid to them they might not have been there.

He stalked into the hall of the palace. An usher who had hurried forward to take his cloak and his gloves of marten-fur fell back in startled dismay before the look on his face. The Duke brushed past him to a bench by one of the stone pillars, and cast himself down on it, and drew his mantle across his face.

There were several gentlemen in the hall, and it was plain that they knew the cause of the Duke's conduct. One of them began to whisper in De Warenne's ear; De Toeni caught the words: "Harold is crowned King of England," and gave a little grunt of understanding.

Grantmesnil jerked his thumb towards the ambry, and the ushers who still lingered uncertainly in the middle of the hall went out on tiptoe.

A sparrow, flying in at one of the high unglazed windows, made the barons start. De Warenne whispered: "Should we speak to him? Should we withdraw?"

Before Grantmesnil could answer the uneasy silence was broken by an oddly incongruous sound. Someone was coming down the stairs humming a gay tune to himself.

Involuntarily De Toeni glanced towards the Duke, but William had not moved. Round the bend of the stair came FitzOsbern with Raoul behind him. The Seneschal had one hand on the rope; a ring of amethyst glinted on his finger; a bracelet upon his forearm was studded with the same jewels. His jovial eye took in the group of men by the door and twinkled. His voice rose on the lilt of his little tune.

De Warenne made a sign to him to be quiet and pointed towards the Duke. Both FitzOsbern and Raoul looked round; the song was broken off; the Seneschal went across the floor to the Duke's side and laid a fearless hand on his shoulder. "Up, seigneur, up!" he said cheerfully. "What do you here? Of no avail to keep silence now: the tidings were spread before ever you came back from the forest."

The Duke let his mantle fall; the scowl had left his brow, but he looked to be in no very pleasant mood. "William, Harold Godwineson is forsworn, and reigns King in England this day."

"I know it," FitzOsbern answered. "What, did you place faith in him, beau sire?"

"Too much," William said. He got up and began to pace about the hall. His eye fell upon the gentlemen by the door; he said impatiently: "Splendour of God, what make you here?"

"Beau sire, give us leave to withdraw," Grantmesnil said hastily.

The Duke gave a short laugh, and continued to pace to and fro. The gentlemen went out; FitzOsbern tucked his hands in his jewelled belt, and said: "Seigneur, you are too greatly put about. By conquest shall you take England. What do you say, Raoul?"

Raoul was standing by one of the long trestle tables with his arms folded on his chest. He answered: "Nothing. The Duke knows my mind, and has known it these many days."

William said over his shoulder: "Rest you, my friend, you shall have Elfrida for your warison."

It was not thus he had planned to take her, yet what else remained? "Oh, if life were the easy concern we thought it in our grass-time!" Raoul said wearily. He went slowly to the fire and stood staring down at the smouldering logs.

Behind him he heard the quick give-and-take of words

254

between the Duke and FitzOsbern. The Seneschal was for putting matters in warlike train at once; in his imagination England's crown was already on William's head. He spoke of ships, of arms, and as he listened Raoul knew that one half of him strode ahead of FitzOsbern on that bloody campaign, striving to reach to the heart's desire down a path lined with swords. What other way? None, he thought. Yet when he heard FitzOsbern urging the Duke to send his cartel of war to Harold that other half of him grew angry, and he turned, saying sharply: "O rash want-wit! When did William our Duke need urging into battle? Give gentler rede, or hold your peace. Spine of God, can you too see no more than victory?"

FitzOsbern stared. "Why, do you doubt we shall have victory?" he demanded. "Is there in Christendom a greater warrior than Normandy?"

"All thanks, William!" said the Duke, with a laugh over his shoulder. "Is there, Raoul?"

"None," Raoul said. "And when this work is ended there shall be none more blood-stained."

"I know, I know," the Duke said. "But we have talked this over many times, Raoul. You cannot turn me now."

He looked at FitzOsbern. "I will send envoys into England," he said. "No cartel—yet."

"To what purpose?" objected FitzOsbern. "What more do you look for, beau sire? He has broken a sacred oath, and spurned the Lady Adela, your daughter. What more, a' God's name?"

The Duke paid no need to him. "I have need of Lanfranc," he said. "William, let one be ready to bear a packet to Bec within the hour." He found that he was still holding his gloves, and laid them down on the table. His first rage had burned itself out; he had a problem to grapple now and was not the man to waste time in fruitless anger. "When did my messenger say that Edward died?"

"Upon the fifth day of January," FitzOsbern replied, "the Abbey wherein they laid him having been dedicated at Childermas."

"Two weeks since." The Duke drummed his fingers lightly on the table. "Time enough. If Tostig had spies in London he will have learned the tiding by now, and we shall see him in Rouen ere many days."

Raoul raised his head. "Why?" he asked bluntly.

A smile glimmered in the Duke's eyes. "To ask aid of

me, my friend, or counsel. That last I will surely give him. I think—yea, I think I may count on Harold to deal with Tostig."

"Tostig could not be so great a fool!" Raoul exclaimed.

"I will wager my new destrier against your big bay he is," William said.

"The destrier Giffard brought you from Spain?" demanded Raoul. "And what will old Walter say to that?"

"Nothing. I shall not lose," William said, twinkling.

"Tostig must be mad if he comes to you for aid. Done, seigneur: the Spanish horse to my bay."

But he lost his bay horse. The Duke's envoys had barely left Normandy for England with his first careful letters to Harold when Earl Tostig arrived in Rouen upon a foaming steed and attended by such thegns as had fled Northumbria in his train. He was in a stuttering rage, too bull-headed to guard silence, ready to blurt out all his fury and his ambitions into the ear of the one man he had need to beware.

Not one of those about the Duke let fall a single word that might have enlightened Tostig. He knew nothing of the envoys sent to England, nothing of the Duke's own ambitions. Out came his tale, and, swiftly following it, a request for aid from Normandy to cast Harold down.

The Duke dealt with him easily enough, but to Raoul he said: "How Godwine, who, by all accounts, was a man of some parts, could have bred so big a fool, is a matter passing my comprehension. Aid of Normandy? Rood of Grace, I am the one man he should at all costs leave outside his confidence!"

The Duchess, who was watching her sons at play in the gardens, turned away from the lancet-window to ask whether Tostig thought to get himself crowned King.

"Like a-many others," said the Duke.

"And asks aid of you?" Matilda gave an angry little laugh. "Oh, brave! Normandy to be used to serve Tostig's ends! What will you do?"

"Use Tostig to serve mine own ends," replied the Duke grimly. "I have given him words which he thinks of great worth. He sails for Norway, as soon as he has taken leave of your sister, to interest Harold Hardrada in his cause." He put out his square hand and took Matilda's chin in it. Pushing her head he smiled at her, saying: "Here is strategy to please that subtle mind of yours, my Mald. Tostig may go with my blessing to attack Harold. So is he got out of the way, for I am very sure he will not outlive that venture. He will do no more than prepare the road for me." He glanced up, and saw Raoul looking at him. "My Watcher, I know what you would say. This is such craft as you mislike, but it will bring me to my goal."

Raoul did not say anything. He was looking at the Duchess, wondering how she could approve a strategy that seemed likely to make her sister a widow. He remembered how she and Judith had been wont to go linked arm-in-arm in the old days at Lille, the russet and the gold heads close together, green eyes telling secrets to blue ones.

My lord Robert's voice was heard suddenly, calling to Red William below the window; Raoul saw Matilda turn her head, listening, smiling, and he knew all at once that she was not thinking of Judith. Judith and girlhood's days were far outside her busy mind, forgotten in the misty past. Matilda wanted a crown, perhaps for William, perhaps for herself, but above all for her fair son. Raoul guessed that already she considered it to be his right; probably if her own father were to reach a hand towards the prize she would be as ruthless an enemy to him as she was to Tostig.

She spoke, drawing away from the Duke, fixing her intent eyes on Raoul's face. "Are you against us, Raoul?"

He shook his head. She did not seem satisfied; she was even a little troubled. He said: "No, lady; I am your man." He could not explain to her the qualms that shook him, nor beg her to see how the glory of a crown was already obsessing the Duke. She would scarcely understand; like William she had always a certain goal ahead; less even than he would she, being female, care what means went to its attainment.

He thought all at once: If only I could be as they are, seeing one end alone worth striving for, not torturing my soul with thinking of what might have been, nor finding that my happiness tastes bitter on my lips after all because the price I had to pay for it was too heavy, and tore my heart in twain!

But he knew that he would never be as they were; he must always see the smaller joys and griefs life held, and count them dearer than a distant, splendid goal. There is not one jot of greatness in me, he thought. They were certainly right who called me dreamer. And I wonder to what end, my dreams? None, I suppose. While I am groping in the murk, William will have cleaved a way through, trampling under his feet the obstacles that set me wavering. But I am afraid for him now. O William my master, do not lose all that I have loved in you for the sake of this accursed crown!

As though in answer to his thought the Duke said suddenly: "Trust in me yet, Raoul. You may mislike my dealing, but the end I see you also desire."

"I desired peace in Normandy," Raoul said, meeting his gaze. "Only that—once."

"And safety for all Normans, and a noble heritage," the Duke insisted.

Raoul smiled faintly. "Why, yes, seigneur, that too. But it came out of your head, not mine. I never looked so far until you pointed the way. Even now I think you see a star shining beyond my sight. My vision is filled with the darkness that lies between."

The Duchess opened her eyes at him. "Raoul, you talk as a poet did who once made rhymes for me," she said. She added slyly: "Tell me, is this Elfrida's work? Are you turned poet indeed?"

"No madame," Raoul answered lightly. "I am only one unfortunate who is shaken by doubts. Like Galet I must say, 'Pity the poor fool!' "

CHAPTER II

Upon the return of the envoys from England events began to move swiftly. Harold replied to the Duke's letters very much as William had expected. He admitted that he had sworn an oath at Bayeux, but contended that this having been wrung from him by force, it could not be thought binding. England's crown, he said, was not his to dispose of at will, but belonged to the people, and by them only could be bestowed. As for the Lady Adela, Earl Harold informed the Duke that he might not marry without his Council's advice, and they had begged him to wed an English lady.

The Duke read this answer thoughtfully, and gave it presently into Lanfranc's care. It was destined for Rome, and to that end had been extracted from Harold.

Lanfranc studied the letter for a while in silence. At last he said: "This could not be better. He admits the oath." He put the paper away in a casket, and locked it with a golden key that hung from a chain about his neck. Soothing his cassock with one thin hand he seemed to meditate within himself. He raised his eyes after some time, and said slowly: "I am of the opinion, my son, that you cannot do better than appoint Gilbert, the Archbishop of Lisieux, to be your envoy to Rome."

"I had a mind to send you, Father, as once before."

"N-no." Lanfranc put his finger-tips together very exactly. "It is possible, my son, that I am too well known. Let Gilbert go, under my guidance. The Cardinals will not cry: ''Ware Gilbert! he is too subtle a man for us.'"

The Duke laughed. "Instruct him then; I am ruled by you in this."

Upon which the Prior took his leave, and rising up went out with his stately gait, and the casket tucked safely under his arm.

The Duke next called a council of those nearest to him, but what was said at it no one knew. There were present his half-brothers, Robert and Odo; his sister's spouse, the Viscount of Avranches, and his cousins of Eu and Evreux. Outside his kin were his Seneschal, his Standard, and the Lords of Beaumont, Longueville, Montfort, Warenne, Montgoméri, and Grantmesnil. These gentlemen being of one mind with the Duke it was agreed that a second and general council should be called at Lillebonne, which was a vast new palace some leagues from Rouen, especially designed for such a purpose.

The masons had only just finished work on this palace, so that it reared up stark and white against the blue sky. A huge vaulted hall formed its centre, and leading from it a range of doorways gave on to various chambers. Above, small coupled-windows divided by pillars and arches let in the light. The walls were hung with tapestries worked in bright new threads, murrey, and vert, and azure; rushes were strewn over the stone floor, with rosemary and sweet-gale dropped among them to give a pleasing scent. But the prevailing aroma was of mortar, and in spite of the fires that roared away up the vent-pipes the place still felt dank and chill. Time would weather it, thought Raoul, blinking at the glaring white structure. Certainly, he supposed, the mouldings were very fine.

A throne of state was set up on a dais at one end of the hall, with a canopy of rich cloth stitched in a design of quatrefoil over its head. Before it stood a footstool on legs. The Duchess had embroidered gold lions on the cover with

259

her own hands, so that whenever the Duke placed his foot upon it he had the emblem of Normandy under his heel.

There were chairs on the dais for the Duke's chief councillors, and on the floor of the hall benches were provided for the less exalted persons.

Lillebonne teemed with the vassals who flocked to this meeting-place in answer to the Duke's summons. Gilbert d'Aufay, who, with Raoul, was in attendance on William, said testily that he could find no place wherein to be alone. Gilbert had left his lady heavy with child, and cherished hopes that after six daughters she might be about to present him with a son. He sent off messengers every day to learn how she did, for just before he left her she had had the ill-fortune to catch sight of a hedgehog in the curtilage, and it was well known that nothing could more easily provoke a miscarriage. Further to add to his annoyance he was compelled to sleep in the hall at nights with a hundred others.

Raoul, having taken in the situation at a glance, announced firmly, but with a hidden twinkle, that he proposed, since the Duchess had stayed behind at Rouen, to take up his old sleeping-place on a pallet at the foot of the Duke's bed.

"Holy Face, do you expect to see me murdered?" said William, surprised.

"No," said Raoul frankly, "but I expect to be very damnably housed elsewhere, seigneur."

Upon the day appointed for the Council the barons and vavassours assembled in the hall at an early hour, jostling one another for the best places, and wondering loud and long what could be the Duke's need. Those who knew tried to explain to those who did not, and by the time the Duke entered the hall by a door behind the throne there was so much noise of discussion that it was difficult for any man to make himself heard above the general hubbub.

An usher preceded the Duke. He had a stentorian voice which he used to some purpose. All talk ceased abruptly; the vassals waited in respectful silence for the Duke to address them.

He was escorted by his Council, and by all the chief prelates of the Duchy. At sight of the Bishops' robes those in the body of the hall realized that the affair was to be one of great moment. There was a sound of subdued rustling; necks were craned; short gentlemen stood on tiptoe to peer over the shoulders of their taller friends.

The Duke wore a mail tunic, and a helmet of ceremony on his head, with his coronet round it. This attire was significant; Gilbert de Harcourt, who had come in Hubert's name to the gathering, grunted under his breath: "Ho! Is it war?"

The Duke mounted the steps of the throne, and looked round the hall as though he counted heads. When those who had accompanied him had taken up their places on the dais, he began his speech to the barons.

They heard him in profound silence. His voice was strong, and the echoes caught the ends of his words, and carried them faintly through the vaulting. There was no longer any fidgeting in the hall; it was evident he had taken the vassals by surprise; evident too that most of them listened to him in alarm and disapproval.

Standing to the right of the throne, Raoul could see nearly everyone in the hall. He held his drawn sword before him, with the point resting on the floor, and both his hands clasped on the hilt. Once he stole a look at Gilbert d'Aufay, standing in the same attitude on the left of the throne, but Gilbert would not respond to the amusement in his eyes. Gilbert was not enjoying himself.

The Duke's appeal ended; he sat down, gripping the arms of his throne. For an interminable minute no one spoke or moved. Then someone whispered in his neighbour's ear. More whispering followed; it became a subdued chatter, which grew steadily louder.

The Duke rose to his feet again, and was regarded with suspicion. He said: "Messires, I will withdraw, that you may be free to confer amongst yourselves." He made a sign to his brothers, and went out, followed by them.

No sooner had the door closed behind him than babel broke loose. A score of men tried to demonstrate to the assembly how impossible the Duke's demands were; several of the younger seigneurs, snuffing battle like war-horses, attempted to shout down the general disapproval; and the company naturally separated into groups varying from five to a hundred men round the several spokesmen.

FitzOsbern was the first man to leave the dais. He stepped down from it, and elbowed his way through the press, taking this man by the arm, clapping that one on the shoulder.

De Montfort got up. He winked at Raoul, saying: "Soul of a virgin, how they mislike it! What now?"

"I am going to hear what is being said," Raoul replied. He sheathed his sword, and slipped his hand in De Montfort's arm. "Come, Hugh, we are not like to be so much diverted in another twenty years."

Together they stepped down from the dais, and began to make their way from one to another of the groups.

"Raoul! Stay a minute! Has the Duke gone moon-mad?" The Sieur d'Estouteville caught at Raoul's mantle. Henry de Ferrières elbowed him aside. "Raoul, what does this mean? Journeying outremer to fight a strange people in their own land! Folly!"

"Why, we should all founder at sea!" Geoffrey de Bernay took up the tale indignantly. "Remember what befell Harold off Ponthieu! Crowns! Kingdoms! Holy God, who ever heard so wild a scheme?"

"Unhand me, unhand me, it is not my scheme!" Raoul protested. He was swept from De Montfort's side, and pushed his way through a knot of men to a group gathered round FitzOsbern.

FitzOsbern was liked by all, and could always command a hearing. Raoul grinned unseen as he listened to his convincing address. He had a voice that carried; one by one the barons drew towards him. He met condemnation with jests; he talked his hearers into better humour, and having induced them to see that the affair was not so redeless as they had first imagined, he bade them remember their duty, and meet the Duke in calm discussion. Somebody shouted to him to know what he thought of the Duke's demands; his answer was somewhat evasive, but pleasing. The barons began to think they could do no better than appoint him to be their spokesman.

Raoul slipped away through the crowd to the room where the Duke was waiting. He went in and found that William was standing by the fire, holding his hand up to shield his face from the blaze. Mortain leaned against a chair-back, picking his teeth, and Bishop Odo, always more impatient than these two, was seated at the table, tapping his fingers on it in scarcely curbed restlessness.

The Duke glanced up as Raoul came in and gave a faint rueful smile. Raoul said solemnly: "I thank you for this day, beau sire. I have not been so much entertained since I can remember."

"What are they saying?" demanded Odo, darting a look at him out of his quick dark eyes. "They need a lesson in courtesy, by God!"

"Why, they are saying that the Duke's many victories have made him reckless, my lord," Raoul replied.

"Fools!" said the Duke calmly, without raising his head.

"A fine gathering of nithings!" Odo snapped. "There has

been peace in Normandy too long. Men have grown fat paunches and sluggish livers, and have learnt to love ease more than glory. Bah, I would school them!"

Mortain stopped picking his teeth to ask in his stolid way: "Are they going to give the Duke nay for an answer, Raoul?"

Raoul laughed. "Well, they seemed like to choose FitzOsbern to be their mouthpiece when I left them, so God knows what answer you will get. Nay is in their hearts. They say you cannot command their service outremer, beau sire. I think a-many are afraid to venture on the seas."

The Duke turned his head. "Is Néel of Côtentin there?"

"Not yet. But Tesson is, and will have none of your scheme."

William's teeth gleamed. "I can twist Tesson which way I choose," he said.

Someone scratched on the door; Raoul opened it, and found Gilbert d'Aufay upon the threshold. Gilbert said, looking rather troubled: "Will the Duke be pleased to come back? All are agreed to let FitzOsbern put their objections before him as doucely as may be."

In the hall order had been restored. The Duke sat down on his throne again; his brothers stood beside him, and Raoul stayed by a pillar in the background.

"Well, messires? Have you considered your answer?" said the Duke.

FitzOsbern rose from his chair. "Yea, seigneur, we have considered, and it falls to my lot to speak for all who are here to-day."

A murmur of assent sounded; all the noble gentlemen looked gratefully at their spokesman, and waited to hear how he would soften a blunt refusal.

"Then speak, FitzOsbern," said the Duke. "I am listening."

The Seneschal gave his mantle a hitch on one shoulder, and bowed. "Seigneur, we have heard your proposals, and honour you for that high courage which makes you look upon this emprise as a thing easily to be accomplished."

His followers nodded indulgently. They had no fault to find with this way of beginning; it would be just as well to put the Duke in a good humour before the unpalatable meat of the matter was reached.

"You desire a crown and a kingdom, beau sire; we know you to be worthy of them. You ask us, your loyal vassals, to

263

lend aid on that venture. Seigneur, it must be known to you that by the laws of fealty our service overseas you cannot command."

He paused, but the Duke said nothing. The vassals nodded again: FitzOsbern was managing the affair very creditably.

FitzOsbern went on: "You ask us to follow you to a strange land, peopled by bitter foes—a thing no Duke of Normandy has done before. We are unused to sea-faring, maybe we like it ill, maybe we have lands needing our care here in Normandy, wives who would weep to see us go forth to battle. But this we have in our hearts, my liege: you have ruled over us long fruitful years, leading us to victory upon victory. That thing which you have sworn to do never have you failed in. Seigneur, every leal man's trust in you; every leal man's hands lie between your palms, and this is a leal man's answer to you: We will follow whithersoever you lead, be it to England or to Araby, and he whose duty owes you twenty men-at-arms will give in love for you twice that number." He stopped. The vassals were staring at him as though fascinated. Raoul saw one man open his mouth, shut it again, and swallow hard. The Seneschal took advantage of the appalled silence to say heroically: "Sixty ships will I myself furnish for the emprise! Seigneur, we are your men to command!"

This was too much. The outraged vassals found their tongues at last; decorum was cast to the winds; a roar of "No!" went up from scores of angry voices. Henry, Lord of Saint-Hilaire de Ferrières, thrust forward to the very steps of the dais, and glared up at the Seneschal, saying: "False! false! These are your words, not ours! We do not journey overseas!"

A muscle quivered at the corner of the Duke's mouth; he turned his head to survey the speaker. At the back of the room Richard de Bienfaite sprang upon one of the benches, and called: "Shame! shame on you, Henry de Ferrières! All true men cry Yea to what FitzOsbern has said."

"Not so!" Fulk Du-Pin tried to pull him down. "This is no matter touching our fealty!"

"What, are we afraid?" cried young Hugh d'Avranches. He leaped up beside Richard de Bienfaite on the bench, and waved his sword over his head. "Let the young men answer!"

The Duke took no notice of this; he was looking at Raoul Tesson, who all the time had said no word, but stood aloof from his peers by one of the pillars at the side of the hall. There was a mulish look on his face, he met the Duke's eyes squarely enough, but his own held uncompromising disapproval.

Robert of Picot de Say had followed De Bienfaite's example and hoisted his bulk up on to a bench. "Nay, nay!" he rumbled, "let us not forget the respect we owe the Duke's grace! This is unseemly. Yet I must say in all duty and humility——"

His voice was drowned. The vassals had no patience to waste on his tedious periods. Ives de Vassy elbowed his way to the forefront, and said loudly: "Where our duty calls us be sure we will go, but no duty calls us outremer. What! are our borders to be left open to the French while we go junketing forth upon such an errand?"

Odo took a sudden step forward to the edge of the dais. His eyes flashed; his fingers worked nervously in the folds of his robe. "O Norman dogs!" he said bitterly. "Must a man of peace show you the way?"

The Duke moved. He spoke, but what he said no one heard but the Bishop. Odo gave his shoulders an angry shrug, and sat down plump in a carved chair behind him.

The Duke rose. It was some little while before the clamour abated, for it was considered necessary by those in front that they should order those behind to be silent for the Duke's grace, and three men thought it incumbent upon them to pull Richard de Bienfaite down from his bench.

The Duke waited in unmoved calm for the lull. When it came, and everyone was anxiously watching him, he looked directly at the Lord of Turie-en-Cingueliz, and said on a note of command: "Tesson!"

The Lord of Cingueliz started, and moved forward with a darkening brow. A passage was made for him; he advanced to the foot of the dais, and looked frowningly up at the Duke.

A faint smile hovered on William's mouth; he said blandly: "Give me your escort, Raoul Tesson."

"Beau sire——"

"Your escort, Tesson."

The Lord of Cingueliz stumped up the steps of the dais, and sulkily followed the Duke from the hall. Those left behind looked at one another in surprise, and reflected that it was beyond the power of man to tell what the Duke would do next.

In the room leading from the hall, Tesson took up a

defensive position by the door, and eyed the Duke sideways.

William unclasped the fibula that held his mantle together, swung the heavy fur-lined cloak from his shoulders, and held it out. The Lord of Cingueliz came forward, and took it. "Well, my friend?" said the Duke.

Tesson put the mantle down over a chair-back. "Beau sire, you shall not cozen me into giving you yea," he said bluntly. "You are a young man still, but I have left a young man's rashness behind me."

"Will you stand against me, Tesson, denying me aid?" inquired the Duke.

"In plain words, seigneur, yes. If you go upon this chase you go alone."

"So?" the Duke said softly. "Yet I remember one who rode up to me on the plain of Val-es-Dunes, and struck me on the cheek with his glove, saying: 'Henceforward, seigneur, I will do you no other wrong.'"

Tesson flushed, but shook his head. "Nor will I. If I refuse you now it is for your good, my lord, ill though you may like it. Young hotheads may follow you if they choose——"

"Am I a hothead, Raoul?"

The Lord of Cingueliz glowered. "No, seigneur, I have not thought so. But you have been victorious too often, which makes you reckless now. I who am arm-gaunt and grey-headed tell you I will bear no part in this madness. This I would not say out yonder in that rabble, look you, but now you have asked me, and that is mine answer."

"The years slip by, Tesson." The Duke moved towards the fire. "I had forgot that you have grown too old to venture forth with me."

Tesson began to bristle. "Old? That in your teeth, my good lord! Who says that I am old? I can still bear my part—yea, and something more than my part—in any joust or skirmish. You call me old? What, are my limbs wasted? Do you think my muscles are turned to fat, my strength all sapped, my blood thin as water? Sacred Mother of God!"

"Not I, Tesson."

There was a peculiar meaning in the Duke's voice. A red light shone in Tesson's eye; he said with a splutter: "Bowels of God! Let me hear the name of the rash fool who said that of me! I warrant you I will show him how much my strength has left me! Old? Ha, God!"

The Duke turned, and laid his hands on Tesson's shoulders. "Nay, my friend, no man doubts your hardiment. Yet I think you have grown older in heart, and maybe love ease more than of yore. None shall cry scorn on you for that: your fighting days are spent. Forget I called on you for aid. If I carry my arms into England maybe you will join those whom I leave behind to rule the Duchy."

The Lord of Cingueliz' chest swelled. "Seigneur," he said, fixing the Duke with a smouldering eye, "what is it you demand of me?"

"Nothing," said the Duke.

The Lord of Cingueliz swallowed something in his throat. "Twenty ships I will give, and all the men of Turie! Is it enough?"

"Yea, it is enough. Who shall lead your vassals?"

"Who shall lead them?" repeated Tesson, staring. "Who shall—— Blood of the Saints, I shall lead them! Tell that to my mockers!"

"Be sure I will," said the Duke with the ghost of a laugh. He heard the click of the door-latch, and glanced over his shoulder. "Néel!" he exclaimed, and swung round holding out his hand. "Chef de Faucon, I had begun to despair of you!"

There was mud on the Viscount of Côtentin's boots, and he still held his whip and gloves. Years might have powdered his brown hair with white, but he held himself easily erect, and there was no spare flesh upon his tall person. He came briskly across the room, and clasped the Duke's hand. "Pardon, beau sire. I came as I could, and from far. Your messenger found me from home. Now, what is your need of me? FitzOsbern has told me some but bade me seek you out straightway for the whole."

The Lord of Cingueliz, having cooled somewhat, grumbled: "A madman's errand, no less. Get you hence, before you are cozened as I have been." He shook his head gloomily. "Oh, I know you, seigneur! Cunning you are, seeking to bend all men to your will. But by God, William my lord, you know full well you cannot venture without the men of Turie!"

The Duke laughed. He was still holding Saint-Sauveur's hand in his grip. "Néel, I am bound for England to wrest from Harold Godwineson that kingdom that was promised me. I need you: will you go with me?"

"Yea, with all my heart," Néel answered. "Let us have it on parchment. Ships do you need? Well, I can furnish you with some few. Send for your scrivener, beau sire, and bid him write down my name. Do you come too, Tesson?"

"Ho, do you think I hang back where you press forward, Chef de Faucon?" said Tesson, swaggering a little. "How many men can you muster? I will engage to beat your number."

Preserving a grave demeanour the Duke struck a gong that stood upon the table, and summoned his clerk. The names of Saint-Sauveur and Tesson were duly inscribed under their seals; they went out, and the Duke sent for the Lords of Moyon, Trégoz, and Magneville, severally.

One by one the chief among the barons were closeted with him. The roll of names grew imposing; to refuse the Duke began to savour of disloyalty; willy-nilly the barons set their seals to promises wrung from them, and those who had been won over became anxious that those who still stood out should be forced to share their obligations. The Council of Lillebonne ended at last in a triumph for the Duke. The vassals passed from unwilling consent to a certain degree of enthusiasm. It became a point of honour for a man not to be outdone by his neighbours in promises; preparations for the building of the fleet were discussed; Gilbert, the Archbishop of Lisieux, departed for Rome, well-primed; and the Duke, at an ecclesiastical Council held at Bonneville a few weeks later, raised Lanfranc to be Abbot of that monastery of St. Etienne which had been built at Caen as part of his marriage-penance.

CHAPTER III

A conclave of Cardinals heard Gilbert in Rome. The discussion lasted for many days, but it was plain from the start that the question of perjury weighed the scales heavily against Harold Godwineson. The peculiar sanctity of the relics was considered, and Harold's letter debated upon at length. But Raoul, when he heard of all these dealings, said acidly: "William is a very good son to Holy Church, and Normans build monasteries when Saxons give feasts. Did that sway the Pope's judgment, I wonder?"

"Raoul!" exclaimed Gilbert d'Aufay, shocked.

Raoul jerked up an impatient shoulder. "Well, I am sick of this business. It is all bribery and cunning, and the noise of the shipyards drums in my ears day and night."

"What folly!" said Gilbert, smiling. "You cannot hear anything here in Rouen."

"I think I can," said Raoul. "In my head, in my brain! Oh, let be! I am caught up in this coil, and must go on to the end."

The Archbishop came back to Normandy at last, and a Papal Legate accompanied him in great pomp. The Duke received this exalted churchman with a deference that was not assumed. A blessing was bestowed upon him; a consecrated banner given into his strong hands. Its folds, sewn with gems, and rich with gold thread, hung heavily from the shaft; Ralph de Toeni took it from the Duke, and stood holding it stiffly erect while the Legate produced out of a casket a ring containing a hair of Saint Peter himself. Kneeling the Duke held out his hand. The ring slipped over the knuckle; the Legate pronounced the blessing.

It was learned that the Duke had engaged himself to hold England as a fief of Rome, paying annual tribute, if he should succeed in his conquest. "Is there anyone in this world who is above bribes?" said Raoul de Harcourt.

Hardly had the Legate departed on his journey back to Rome than a strange phenomenon was seen in the sky. A comet visible for many nights rose in the west upon the eighteenth day of April and slowly travelled southward to the wonder and admiration of all who saw it. "It is an omen," men said, but whether for good or ill was a point argued upon by every seer and wise man in Normandy.

There arrived in Normandy exiles from England, those Norman favourites of King Edward whom Harold had banished. They brought tidings that the light in the sky was looked upon by the Saxons as a sign from God. It had made many uneasy, for certain men versed in such matters had declared that God was angry at Harold's usurpation of a throne that belonged in right to Edgar the Atheling.

In Normandy the popular reading of the phenomenon was that it was William's star, travelling to success. Certain Churchmen held by this opinion; others who mistrusted the English expedition stated that it was far otherwise, and that the Duke should regard it as a warning to proceed no further. The Duke himself supported those who considered the sign to be propitious, but remarked to FitzOsbern that if the comet foretold victory in England it was travelling across the sky in the wrong direction.

He had little time to spend upon such celestial problems. His ships were building in the yards; the blows of the woodmen's axes resounded through the forests; the felled trees were borne to the coast on wains dragged by straining oxen.

There the shipwrights and the carpenters fell to work on them, while armourers were busy forging swords and lance-heads, and leather-workers stitched tunics for archers to wear.

The Duke sent letters into France, putting his claims before the wise Regent, and making certain proposals. Count Baldwin read these thoughtfully, and presently showed them to his lady. "Your daughter is like to wear a Queen's crown, wife," was all he said.

The Countess exclaimed at it, and eagerly read the Duke's despatch. She said: "He reaches high, the tanner's grandson! What of Tostig and my other daughter? Now, by my soul, Mald was ever a sly secret little cat! No word of this passed her lips when Judith lately sojourned in Rouen!"

Count Baldwin took the letters back into his own keeping, and locked them away. "I tell you frankly, madame, if I must support one of my sons-in-law, that one will not be Tostig," he said dryly. "But this is no matter for France to dabble her fingers in. Content you, son William: France shall not break your borders while you are from home, but other aid you do not get of her." He put up a hand to his beard and absently smoothed it. "And yet I know not." His gaze dwelt blandly upon his wife's face. He said slowly: "If any should desire to follow Normandy for the chance of plunder in England I believe I shall not say them nay. France is too much troubled by such hungry gentlemen: let them seek advancement otherwhere."

It appeared that many desired to try their fortunes in England. Duke William sent letters into every country, offering lands, money, titles to any man who would join him. Aghast, Raoul saw these perilous documents dispatched. He tried to remonstrate: the Duke would not listen. England he must have, by any means.

His offers brought the scum of Europe to his standard. Needy adventurers came from Burgundy and Lotharingia and the Piedmont hills, making up in swagger for the clouts on their worn hose. Knights from Aquitaine and Poitou came nobly caparisoned into Normandy; little princes brought their levies, ready to hazard their lives on the chance of possessions to be snatched in England. Eustace als Grenons, that Count of Boulogne who had once been flouted by the men of Dover, sent word that he would lead his men in person; Alain Fergant, cousin to Count Conan, swore to raise troops in Brittany; from Flanders Duke William's brother-in-law wrote in cautious terms inquiring what reward he might expect for his services, if he should agree to risk his noble person in the field.

His letter reached the Duke in Rouen. William was in his solar, with two clerks busily writing at his dictation, and a tangle of papers spread before him. He had broken off to study the plans of his ship, the *Mora*, and a ship-wright waited humbly at his elbow. Outside in the ante-chamber two men frowned over lists of stores, which they desired to present to the Duke's notice, and a master-carpenter wondered whether his designs for the wooden castles William had commanded would meet with his approval.

The Duke slit open Baldwin's packet, and ran his eye over its contents. He gave a short laugh, and crumpled the sheet in his hand. "Parchment! Give me a fair scroll of parchment!" he said, and jabbed a quill in the ink-horn. "Raoul, where are you? Roll me that sheet, and set my seal to it. Here is a jest you will like. Read young Baldwin's letter, and you will understand." He began to write upon a label.

"There is nothing writ on the parchment, lord," one of the clerks ventured to remind him.

"No fool, nothing. Is it done, Raoul? Then bind this distich about the scroll, and let it be dispatched to my noble brother with all speed." He gave the label into Raoul's hands, and turned back to his shipwright.

Raoul read the distich, and laughed. The Duke had scrawled two crisp lines only:

> *"Beau frère en Angleterre vous aurez
> Ce qui dedans escript vous trouverez."*

"A right good answer," Raoul said, binding it round the scroll. "I wish that you had made it to all the others of his kidney."

The Duke made no reply, and with a heavy heart Raoul watched him at his work. Few princes, he thought, had earned for themselves greater names for upright dealing. It had been said of him always that he could not be bought, and favoured no man unworthily. The serf got justice from him as easily as the baron, and lawless vagabonds had short shrift under his rule. Yet with this obsession of a crown holding him in its grip he seemed to have grown reckless, even callous. Bad enough, thought Raoul, to lead a Norman army into England; to loose upon the land this horde of foreign

271

mercenaries who had joined his standard urged by no loyalty but by hope of plunder alone, would be a deed to cry shame on through the ages.

To Gilbert d'Aufay he said later: "Unruly, ravening, swine rootling for truffles—God, what an army have we mustered!"

Gilbert said peaceably: "I know, but good Norman blood will stiffen the rabble."

"Yes, you know," Raoul answered. "Full well do you know that it will be beyond even William's power to curb these masterless rogues once plunder is in sight."

"Well, I do not like it," Gilbert said in his calm way. "I am for Normandy, but as I see it I am bound by mine oaths of fealty to fight for the Duke, be it here or outremer. As for you"—he looked up gravely—"you are bound by friendship, and I suppose that is why you hate it so." He wrinkled his brow, trying to find words to explain the vague thought in his mind. "You care so much for William, don't you? Now, I am his man, but I have never been his friend. I have envied you sometimes, but I have come to see yours is no easy path. It is better not to be the friend of such an one as William, Raoul."

"Treason, my friend," said Raoul lightly.

"No, only truth. What profit is there in that friendship? What comfort? None, I think. William thinks of kingdoms and of conquest, not of you, Raoul, nor of any man."

"No." Raoul glanced fleetingly at him, and away again. "I have always known that. William stands alone. I have not looked for profit in his friendship. But years ago, when he and I were boys, I took service with him, believing that he would bring peace and strength into Normandy. Trust I gave, not friendship. That came later."

"He did bring peace, and strength too."

"Yes, both of these. No man ever did more for this Duchy. You might give him fealty of body and soul and not fear to be betrayed."

"Still, Raoul?"

"Always," Raoul said tranquilly.

Gilbert shook his head. "I think ambition is changing that."

"You are wrong. As well as any man can I know him, Gilbert. A crown he may desire, but beyond that is something more. Now you see how great a fool I am, that knowing this I must still grieve to see him pick up weapons—unworthy of his chivalry."

272

Gilbert looked at him curiously. "What made you give your heart to him, Raoul? Often I have wondered."

A smile crept into the grey eyes. "One little corner of it? Is that by your reading my heart? No, Gilbert, William does not deal in such tender stuff. Worship I had for him in my grass-time. Lads feed upon such stuff. It could not last. It changed to respect, as deep and more enduring. Yea, and friendship also: a queer friendship, maybe, but still—enough." He got up, and strolled towards the door. "Hearts are given in exchange one for the other. At least, not otherwise does mine leave my breast."

"But—Raoul, this is strange talk on your lips. I did not know. . . . If he loves any man that one is you, I am very sure."

"Ah!" Raoul looked pensively at the door-latch. "I would rather say: As much as he loves any man he loves me." He looked up; the smile lingered in his eyes. "That, my Gilbert, is why——" He broke off; his smile grew. "Just that," he said, and went out.

All that summer Normandy hummed with activity, and no man talked of anything but the coming expedition. The fleet, numbering nearly seven hundred vessels, both large and small, was built and lay at its moorings at the mouth of the Dives. The army swelled to giant proportions; if many thousands of foreigners joined it, at least two-thirds of the force was composed of Normans, and however the mercenaries might conduct themselves in England, in Normandy they were kept under a discipline that allowed of no rioting, or plundering of the countryside.

At the beginning of August the Duke received the tidings out of Norway for which he had been waiting. Tostig and Harold Hardrada meant to set sail for the North of England towards the middle of September. Their plan was to wrest Northumbria from Morkere's hold, and to march southwards on London with such English auxiliaries as they could prevail upon to join their force.

"You serve me better than you know, friend Tostig," said the Duke. "Harold is not the man I think him if he does not march north to crush that army of yours."

Four days later, upon the twelfth of August, the Duke left Rouen for Dives. Twelve thousand mounted men were gathered there, and twenty thousand foot, and in the river-mouth hundreds of ships swung gently on their anchors with the tide. Chief among them rode the *Mora*, which Matilda had presented to her lord. Crimson sails hung from the masts, and the prow was carved in the form of a child about to loose an arrow from his bow. The boat was caulked with hair, and gilded, and had a cabin built in the stern which was hung with worked curtains, and lit by silver lamps.

Near to the *Mora* floated Mortain's ships, a hundred and twenty in number, beating by twenty his brother Odo's donation. The Count of Evreux had launched eighty vessels, all nobly equipped, and the Count of Eu sixty.

The Duchess and my lord Robert accompanied William to Dives. Robert was feeling important, because his name was joined with Matilda's in the powers of Regency which the Duke had delegated for the period of his absence; but he would have preferred to have gone with the army all the same, and when he visited the camps, and had his eyes dazzled with the sparkle of sunlight on steel, or went aboard the *Mora*, he became so envious that at last he blurted out his wish to his father, and asked to be allowed to go too.

The Duke shook his head. It should have been enough, but Robert was desperate. "I am no child. I am fourteen, my lord. It is my right," he said, staring up sullenly into the Duke's face

The Duke looked him over, not ill-pleased to find him so eager. Behind Robert Matilda clasped her hands suddenly in her lap. "Rest you, wife," the Duke said, with a little laugh. "You are over-young for this encounter, my son, and besides that you are my heir. If I return not, you will be Duke of Normandy in my stead."

"Eh, William!" The Duchess rose quickly, her cheeks grown pale.

The Duke signed to Robert to leave them. "What, Mald, afraid?"

"Why did you say that?" She came up close to him, and laid her hands on his ringed tunic. "You will conquer. You have always conquered. William, my lord!"

"I wonder?" he said, with a kind of detached speculativeness. His arm encircled her, but he was looking beyond her.

She trembled; she had never known him unsure of himself before. "Do you doubt, beau sire? You?" Her hand tugged at his shoulders.

He glanced down at her. "I know, my lass, that this will be my sternest fight. I am risking all upon this venture: life, and fortune, and my Duchy's weal." He knit his brows together. "No, I do not doubt. This was foreseen."

She faltered: "Foreseen?"

"So I believe. My mother dreamed once when she was heavy with child and near her time that a tree grew up out of her womb, and stretched out its branches over Normandy and England till both lay cowering in their shadow. I am that tree, Matilda."

"I have heard tell of this," she said. "I think it was a holy vision, my lord, no sick woman's fancy."

"Maybe." He bent and kissed her. "We shall soon know."

The fleet was detained at the river-mouth for a month. Some of the vessels were found to be unseaworthy; the carpenters had not finished building the wooden castles which the Duke was carrying in separate parts to England, and armourers were still labouring day and night to fashion hauberks, and helmets, and tunics of mail. The soldiers grew restive; there were desertions, and pillaging raids were made upon the neighbouring countryside. The Duke punished malefactors by death, and confined the foot-soldiers to the camps, and the trouble died down.

Upon the twelfth day of September when all was at last in order, and a favourable wind blowing, the Duke bade farewell to Matilda, blessed his son, and went aboard the *Mora* with his Seneschal and his Cup-bearer, and attended by Raoul, Gilbert d'Aufay, and his Standard, Ralph de Toeni.

Watching from the narrow window of the house wherein she lodged ashore, Matilda's straining eyes saw the banners slowly rising to the mastheads. The consecrated emblem of St. Peter unfurled its rich colours against a clear sky; beside it the gold lions of Normandy fluttered bravely in the wind. The Duchess's fingers gripped together, and she drew a deep sobbing breath.

"The anchor is up!" Robert said. "Lady, look! the *Mora* is moving! See how the oars dip in the water! Oh, if I were but aboard!"

She did not answer; the *Mora* was gliding down the stream, with banners flying, and the furled sails showing crimson against the masts.

"My uncle of Mortain is next, on the *Bel Hasard,*" said Robert. "Look, you can see his standard! And that is Count Robert's ship, and that is the Viscount of Avranchin's, close behind. Ho, how Richard and Red William will whine that they did not see this sight!"

Still she did not answer; it is doubtful if she heard him. Her eyes did not waver from the *Mora;* she thought: He is gone. Mary Mother, give aid! give aid!

She stood motionless until the *Mora* had become a speck on the horizon. Robert, kneeling on a bench drawn up under the window, went on chattering and pointing, but she paid no heed to him. She was thinking how she might stitch this scene with threads to make a tapestry worthy of her skill. She would do it, she decided, she and her ladies, while they were left lonely and anxious in quiet Rouen. She began to plan. Pictures flitted across her mind's eye: Harold swearing upon the relics at Bayeux; the Confessor dying; the Confessor buried—a very fine panel, this one, with the noble Abbey on one side, and a coffin borne by eight men upon the other. Her brain ran on; her eyes gleamed. She would have Harold crowned too; she could see it all; how he should sit in the middle of the panel upon a throne, with false Stigand standing beside him with his hands outspread to bless. Stigand's robes would need rich coloured threads; she would embroider them herself, and Harold's face too: her ladies might work on the background, and the throne. And then there would be William's preparations for the invasion, a difficult panel this, with arms, and mail-tunics, and stores being dragged to the ships; and after that she would stitch this day's departure, choosing bright threads to show the glitter of shields, and good blue for the sea, and crimson for the *Mora's* sails. It would take a long time, she thought, but the end should justify the labour. And if God were good there would be more panels to embroider: a battle, a crowning—if God were good.

Her gaze left the horizon; she took Robert's hand in hers, and said in a calm voice: "Come, my son. We journey back to Rouen this day, for I have work to do there."

Standing in the stern of the *Mora*, Raoul was watching the coast of Normandy grow dim in the distance. FitzOsbern came to join him presently. "Well, we are away at last," he said comfortably. "The lodesman fears inclement weather, I am told, but it seems fair enough to me." He leaned on the gilded rail, and stared across the sea at the thin line of coast. "Farewell, Normandy!" he said, jesting.

Raoul shivered.

"Holà, are you cold, my friend?" FitzOsbern inquired.

"No," said Raoul curtly, and moved away.

They were sailing northwards, and at nightfall the wind, which had been rising steadily, was blowing half a gale. Heavy seas broke over the deck; the timbers groaned under the strain, and half-naked men with sweat and sea-water streaming off their backs were struggling to lower and furl the sails. They shouted to one another above the noise of the wind, and thrust better-born people out of their way with no ceremony at all.

FitzOsbern grew limp and strangely silent, and crawled away presently to be private in the throes of his sickness. D'Albini scoffed at him, but a roll larger than the rest sent him off in a hurry to join the Seneschal; Ives, the Duke's page, curled himself into a miserable ball on his pallet in the cabin, and closed his eyes upon the heaving universe. He heard his master laugh, and shuddered, but he would not open his eyes, no, not even if the Duke bade him.

The Duke got up from his bed of skins, and wrapping a cloak of frieze about him made his way out on to the deck. Raoul and Gilbert were standing by the opening into the cabin, holding on to the sides for support. Raoul grasped the Duke's arm. "Have a care, seigneur. Gilbert was all but tipped into this angry sea a minute ago."

The Duke peered into the gloom. Lights bobbed on the water; he said: "We shall lose some of the smaller ships this night."

Spray broke over them in a shower. "Beau sire, stay within the cabin!" begged Raoul.

The Duke shook the wet out of his eyes and hair. "I am staying where I am, Watcher—unless I am washed overboard," he added, clutching at a support.

The wind dropped just before dawn, and the grey light showed the sea the colour of lead, with a sullen swell lifting the *Mora* uneasily. The weary ships drifted towards St Valéry in Ponthieu, and cast anchor there.

It was nightfall before the Duke knew the extent of his loss. Several of the smaller craft had sunk, and some of the horses and stores had been washed overboard, but the damage was not serious. The Duke gave orders that dismal tidings should not be spread, and summoned up the ships' masters and carpenters to learn from them what repairs must be effected before the fleet could put to sea again.

When these were done a fresh delay occurred to set men grumbling. The wind changed, and blew steadily from the north-east, so that no ship could reach to England from Ponthieu. Day followed day, and still the contrary wind blew. Men began to look askance upon the Duke, and to whisper that this voyage was against the will of God.

Foreboding seized many of the barons; there was an attempt at mutiny amongst the men-at-arms, and the uneasy whispers swelled to open condemnation.

The Duke showed no sign either of impatience or anxiety. He dealt with the mutineers in a summary fashion which put an end to overt demonstrations, and met his barons' troubled looks with a cheerfulness that heartened them. But matters were beginning to look ugly, and after ten days spent in port he took the Count of Ponthieu into his confidence, and arranged an impressive ceremony for the benefit of his host.

The bones of the good Saint-Valéry were dug up, and carried in procession round the town. The Bishops of Bayeux and Coutances preceded them in their robes; a service was held, and the Saint invoked, and begged to change the wind, and thus declare the righteousness of the venture.

Hopeful, sceptical, a little awed, the host knelt, awaiting a sign. A hush fell upon the town; men stared towards the fluttering standards in the harbour; fingers were licked, and held up to test the wind. An hour crept by. The sun was a red ball sinking in the west. Men began to murmur; their voices sounded like the growl of some angry monster. Raoul stole a look at the Duke, and saw that he was kneeling with his hands together palm to palm, watching the death of the sun.

The glow faded; a chill of evening spread coldly over the kneeling ranks; the growl was growing louder, and from time to time a single voice could be heard raised in bitter mockery.

Suddenly FitzOsbern sprang up. "See!" he cried, and pointed to the harbour. "The wind has dropped!"

Thousands of heads were turned; a breathless stillness lasted while a man might count to sixty. The standards were hanging slack from the mastheads; the wind had died with the sun.

The Duke took one quick look, and rose. "The Saint has spoken!" he said. "Get to your ships! When tomorrow dawns, you shall find a favourable wind blowing to carry us over the sea to our goal."

It seemed as though the Saint had indeed spoken. The next day was bright and clear, with a wind blowing steadily from the south-west. The fleet weighed anchor betimes, and sailed out of Saint-Valéry in good trim.

The fair weather gave the *Mora* a chance to show her superiority. By sundown she was well ahead of the other ships, and during the night she clean outstripped them.

In the morning an anxious deputation awoke the Duke with the tidings that the *Mora* was alone. He yawned, and said: "I would the Duchess might know how gallantly rode her ship."

"Lord, this is no jesting matter," De Toeni said seriously. "We fear that our ships have been intercepted by Harold's fleet."

The Duke said: "My good Ralph, I had certain tidings at Dives that the English fleet had been forced to put back into London to revictual. Send me my valet, and do not think you see a wolf at every turn."

He came out of his cabin presently to find the barons gathered in an anxious group in the stern, trying to catch some glimpse of the sister vessels. He laughed at them, and they jumped round to find that he was munching his breakfast. He had a hunk of cold venison in one hand, and some cocket-bread in the other, and bit into each alternately.

D'Albini started towards him. "Seigneur, I implore you, let us turn back! We are defenceless here, and indeed we are sure there has been a mischance."

The Duke said with his mouth full: "O faint heart, what abodement do you fear now? There has been no mischance; we have but outstripped the other vessels." His eye fell upon a sailor who was standing at some distance and watching him in great awe. He took another bite of the venison, tearing the meat away from the gristle with his strong teeth, and summoned up the man with a jerk of his head.

Thrust forward by his comrades, the sailor advanced nervously and knelt.

"My man," said the Duke, "you cannot serve me in that posture. Up with you to that masthead, and let me know what you can see." He watched the sailor climb up the rigging, thrust the last morsel of bread into his mouth, and brushed his hands together to be rid of the crumbs.

D'Albini touched his arm. "Beau sire, it pleases you to be merry, but we, your servants, are much alarmed for your safety."

"I perceive that you are," said the Duke. He looked up at the masthead, and called: "Well, fellow. What tidings?"

"Lord, I see only sky and sea!" shouted the sailor.

"Then we will heave-to," said the Duke. He looked up again. "When you see more than that, my man, you shall come and tell me."

"Seigneur!" D'Albini sounded despairing.

"Come to my cabin, Néel," said the Duke, taking Saint-Sauveur by the arm. "We will play a game of chess together, you and I."

At noon the Duke's dinner was spread upon a trestle-table on the deck. Several of his barons had no appetite, but the Duke ate heartily of some freshly-caught eels stewed in brewet, followed by hashed porpoise in frumenty, and brawn served with chibolls and Lombard mustard.

The *Mora* rocked lazily on the swell of the waters; at the masthead the sailor gave a sudden shout, and came clambering down to tell the Duke he could espy four vessels upon the horizon.

The Duke tossed him a gold piece. "You have sharp eyes, my friend. Keep a watch for more of my ships."

FitzOsbern had started up from the table to gaze out across the water. "I can see nothing," he said.

"You will see soon enough," said the Duke, and bordered a pasty with his own hands, and began to eat it.

It was not long before the sailor came down from aloft in a great excitement. "Lord, I see a forest of masts and sails!" he declared.

"Do you indeed?" said the Duke, licking his fingers. "Well, come, FitzOsbern. Let us try the power of our own eyes."

A couple of hours later, the fleet having drawn up close, the *Mora* set sail again, and bore for England.

The line of coast came into sight in the late afternoon, and grew gradually more distinct. Chalk cliffs gleamed very white across the sea; the men who crowded in the bows of the ships could soon see green trees, and a few squat dwellings. No hostile craft appeared to bar the fleet's approach, nor was there any visible sign of life on the shore. The *Mora* pulled in to Pevensey and ran up on the shelving beach.

The men-at-arms would have leaped ashore straightway, but were called to order by their leaders, and drew hastily into two ranks. The Duke passed down the line, set his hand on Raoul de Harcourt's shoulder, and sprang lightly on to the bulwark. He measured the distance, and jumped. A horrified groan went up. He had missed his footing in the shallow water, and fell half-in, half-out of the sea.

"Ill omen! Ill omen! God aid, he has fallen!"

The Duke was up in a flash, and turning showed his hands grasping sand and pebbles. His confident voice checked the dismay. "Normans, I have taken seisin of England!" he cried.

CHAPTER IV

The Normans disembarked at various coves and beaches along the coast between Pevensey and Hastings.

Pevensey was deserted, and fires smouldering in the hearths told that the inhabitants must have fled at sight of the fleet. A camp was formed, surrounded by a ditch and a palisade of stakes driven into the ground. The Duke next ordered one of his wooden castles to be erected on a slight eminence commanding the harbour; and while this was doing he occupied his time in surveying the countryside, to the considerable alarm of his friends. The same fearlessness which had prompted his rashest exploits long years ago at Meulan still possessed him. Accompanied by a mere handful of his knights he would sometimes be absent from his camp for many hours together. He found the country very wild, with treacherously marshy valleys, and hills covered with dense woodland. The roads were often impassable, and so full of ruts and swamps that riding was a danger. There were wolves and bears in the forests, and very often herds of wild cattle could be seen moving across the valleys.

The country was sparsely populated, whole tracts being folc-land, belonging to the state; but a collection of small towns and hamlets were dotted along the coast. These seemed to be void of any soldiery, but the Norman barons, seeing their lord ride out day after day attended by no more than twenty of his knights, lived in constant dread of his death at the hands of the sullen peasantry. Once, when at dusk he had not returned to the camp, a party led by Hugh de Montfort set out to search for him, and met him at last tramping towards them on foot, with FitzOsbern's hauberk as well as his own upon his shoulders, not in the least tired, but laughing at his Seneschal's exhaustion, and as cool as though he walked for his pleasure in his own Norman fields.

Hugh de Montfort relieved him of the extra hauberk, and said severely: "Beau sire, do you never think how the inhabitants of this land might set upon you?"

"No, Hugh, never," the Duke answered cheerfully.

His expeditions soon showed him that a more convenient base than Pevensey would be Hastings, several leagues to the east. This town commanded the London road, and its natural harbour was better fitted for the shelter of the fleet. Leaving a garrison at Pevensey, the Duke led his host eastwards, and ordered the half of his ships to sail round to lie under Hastings' white cliffs. His second castle was then erected upon a mound enclosed by a stockade. It consisted of a single wooden tower. A moat was dug round the foot of the mound, and a large levelled space beyond formed a bailey, where sheds were put up to house men and horses. An outer ditch with a fenced bank upon the counterscarp surrounded the whole, and a smaller tower protected the drawbridge.

Men were still at work on this building when a messenger reached the Duke from one Robert, a man of Norman birth dwelling not far from the coast. He brought greetings, and a letter laboriously written on sheets of cotton-paper. This contained tidings of great import. Tostig and Hardrada, wrote the Duke's well-wisher, had landed in the north, and defeated the young Earls Edwine and Morkere in a pitched battle at Fulford, near to York. Harold, gathering the thegnhood and the huscarles to his standard, had marched north two weeks before the Duke's landing, and meeting the invaders at Stamford Bridge on the twenty-fifty day of September had defeated and slain both Tostig and Hardrada, and practically annihilated the whole of their army. The writer went on to inform Duke William that couriers had fled hot-foot to York, where Harold lay, to convey the tidings that the Normans had landed, and he advised William not to stir from his entrenchments, for King Harold, he assured him, was marching south in force, having sworn to die in battle rather than let the Normans advance a league into England.

"Tell your master," said William, "that I shall give battle as soon as may be." He waited until the messenger had withdrawn, and turned his head to look at Raoul. A grim smile hovered round his mouth. "Marching south," he repeated softly. He glanced at the letter again. "He is advised to hold London, and await me there. Very good rede, Harold Godwineson, but you will not take it." He threw the letter on to the table before him, and leaned back in his chair. He said: "Brave words, but they did not come from his brain. My Raoul, well did I judge Earl Harold when I told you he would act on the impulse of his heart. He will meet me on these coasts, just as I have planned." His brows twitched together. "Eh, but he is a fool!"

"He is also a very brave man," said Raoul, looking at him.

"Brave! Yea, as a lion, but he will lose England by this
282

folly. He will not let me advance one league! Why, spine of God, he should lure me on, further and further from the coast and my ships, into a strange land where mine army might be surrounded. Thus did I when France brake my borders. I made no speeches to fire men's loyalty, but planned how best I could save my country. Harold will not waste the fields he has sworn to protect! There spoke his heart: proud, noble, if you will, full of hardiment, but uncounselled by his head. I tell you, Raoul, had he stayed in London he might have ruined me."

"And yet you braved this chance?"

William gave a laugh. "No. From the day I set eyes on him I knew that I had nothing to fear from his strategy."

When the castle at Hastings was finished, and the ships beached below it, the barons led their men out on foraging parties. The south coast was ravaged for many leagues, and only at Romney did the inhabitants make a stand. Here a force composed of serfs and burghers, armed with what weapons they could come by, beat off Hugh d'Avranches and his men with loss. It was the first taste the Normans had of the Saxon mettle.

A second message reached the Duke from his unknown countryman. On the first day of October the news of the landing had reached Harold at York. Upon the seventh he had arrived in London with his thegns and huscarles, leaving Earls Edwine and Morkere to rally their battered forces and join him with all speed.

William Malet, knowing the distance from York to London, was incredulous. "Seven days with all his army!" he ejaculated. "It is a feat beyond the power of man!"

But corroboration of the tidings soon reached the Duke. Harold had left York immediately upon hearing of the Norman landing, and he had led his army southwards on a nightmare march that allowed of no more than a few hours' sleep snatched upon the road from time to time.

The Saxon in William Malet cried out: "Heart of Christ, they are men, these English thegns! Where can they have rested? When found they time to break their fast? Stubborn, dauntless foes, worthy of our steel!"

He spoke to Raoul, but Raoul did not answer. He was thinking of those legions of fair-headed bearded men, of whom Edgar was one, marching, marching, all through the day and the night, to defend their land from the foreign host. Battle-weary they must be, many of them bearing wounds dealt at Stamford Bridge; foot-sore; perhaps blind with fatigue; but indomitable. He fancied that he could hear the tread of many thousand feet marching nearer and nearer, and see, somewhere in the ghostly ranks, Edgar's face, dogged and tired, the eyes looking straight ahead, the mouth set hard as he had so often seen it.

Harold stayed four days in London, mustering the fyrd to his standard. They flocked in, peasants, burghers, farmers; he left London upon the eleventh day of October, and all along the line of his march more shire-levies joined him, some armed with byrnies and shields, some carrying only stones bound to wooden staves, or the tools of their husbandry.

Two days later word was brought the Duke that the Saxon host had reached the outskirts of the Andredsweald, and was encamped three leagues distant from Hastings where the London road crossed a hill above the Senlac bottom.

The Duke at once dispatched an envoy to the English camp, a monk, Hugh Maigrot, learned in the Saxon tongue. At dusk Hugh returned to Hastings, and waiting upon the Duke in his tent, faithfully recounted all that had befallen.

Tucking his hands into the wide sleeves of his habit, he said: "Beau sire, when I came upon the Saxon encampment, I was led straight before Harold Godwineson, and found him seated at his dinner under the sky with his brothers, Gyrth and Leofwine, and the thegnhood gathered round. The Earl received me with courtesy, lord, and bade me state my business with him. I then did deliver the message entrusted to me, speaking in the Latin tongue, and commanded the Earl in your name to relinquish unto you the Sceptre of England. I did make known your offers to him, saying that all the land north of the Humber would you bestow on him, and that Earldom of Wessex which his father Godwine ruled over. While I spoke the Earl listened, smiling a little; but those about him interrupted me often with mockery, and words injurious to your Grace. When I had ended, the thegns who were seated with Harold at the board lifted up their horns, and shouted Drink-hael! and Skall! to him, and having drunk this toast, cried 'Death to the Norman dogs!' and so drank again. This being spoken in the Saxon tongue the others gathered near heard it, and such a roar went up as might have come from an hundred thousand throats. 'Death! Death to the Normans!' sounded upon all sides, but I, standing firm and unmoved, convinced of the righteousness of my mission, waited in silence for the Earl to answer me."

He paused. "Well, what then?" demanded Mortain impatiently.

The monk cleared his throat. "While the tumult lasted the Earl sat still at the head of the board, with his head a little flung back, looking not at the thegns but at me. He lifted his hand presently, and the shouting ceased. He then said to me: 'You are answered.'" Again he paused. Raoul drew back softly to the opening of the tent, and stood looking out into the gathering darkness. Hugh Maigrot drew a long breath and continued: "Again I spoke with him, urging prudence, and reminding him how he had sworn upon holy relics to support your Grace. At that a growl went up from all who could understand what I said, and black looks were cast at me, and men spake angry words. These I heeded not, but exhorted Harold the more, he sitting very still, and hearkening to me without speaking or turning his head. When I had done he was silent a while, with his eyes upon my face, yet as though they saw me not. He then said so that all might hear him that he would rather die in bloody combat than betray his country to invaders. His oath, he said, was got from him by force, and could not bind him. He bade me bear this message to you, that he would yield him never, and while breath stayed in his body he would bar your passage, so help him God! Whereupon the Saxons broke into cheering, and swords tossed in the air, and men cried with one voice, 'Out, out!' which is the Saxon battlecry. Again I waited for the clamour to abate, observing the while the demeanour of the thegnhood. Hot for battle they seemed to me, fierce dogged men with shaggy heads, and short tunics woven in barbaric colours, hand-locked byrnies, and helmets of wood and bronze. They had eaten and drunk very heartily; many were flushed with mead, and their hands clasped on the hilts of the knives they call their *seax*. Some looked threateningly upon me, but I stood still, and after some minutes Harold again commanded silence, so that I might speak. Then, being assured that all men waited upon my words, I stretched forth my hand towards the Earl and pronounced upon him Holy Church's excommunication for his perjury, saying that the Holy Father had declared his cause unhallowed. No man lifted his voice when I had done. The Earl's hand closed upon the arm of his chair: I saw his knuckles grow white; his eyes were veiled from me; he neither flinched nor spoke. But those about him were sorely troubled, many making the sign of the Cross upon their breasts, and shuddering to hear the Church's ban pronounced. I saw some with blanched cheeks, and some with eyes turned in great alarm towards their lord. But he gave no sign. Then Gyrth Godwineson rose up from his seat, and maybe deeming that I had no knowledge of the Saxon speech, addressed the thegns in a loud voice, saying these words: 'Fellow-countrymen, if the Duke of Normandy feared not our swords, he would not seek to blunt them with a papal anathema; had he confidence in his knights he would not trouble us with envoys. Would he offer us the land north of the Humber if he did not tremble for the consequences of his rash venture? Would he parley if he felt strong in the justice of his cause? Let us not be the dupes of his artifice! He has promised your houses to his own followers; I tell you not one hide of land will he leave to you or to your children. Shall we beg our bread in exile, or shall we defend our rights with our swords? Speak!' And at that, being moved by his brave words and unafraid countenance, the thegns thundered out their battle-cry yet again, and shouted: 'Let us conquer or die!' Then Gyrth, turning to Earl Harold, spoke with him, saying very earnestly: 'Harold, you cannot deny that you swore an oath to William upon holy relics, whether by your own accord or by force it matters not. Why then hazard the fate of war with perjury on your soul? I have not sworn to anything, nor has our brother Leofwine. To us it is a just war, for we fight for our native land. Let us alone encounter these Normans; if we are repulsed you may advance to our aid; if we fail, you shall avenge us.' "

"What answer made Harold?" asked the Duke as the monk paused for breath.

"Lord, he got up from his chair, and taking Gyrth by the shoulders shook him gently to and fro in the way of love, saying, half-chiding: 'Nay, brother: shall Harold fear to engage his person? Though I take the swan's path, and die unshriven in the fight, I will yet lead my men, and it is my standard shall float above their heads, no other man's. Be of good cheer! Right is with us; we shall conquer, and drive the invaders from our coasts. Who follows Harold? Let every man declare his will!' Then Edgar, the Thegn of Marwell, whom your Grace knows, sprang upon a bench, and cried: 'We follow none but Harold! Saxons, out swords!' "

Raoul's fingers clenched suddenly on the folds of the tent-flap. He turned his head, watching the monk with painful eagerness.

Hugh Maigrot picked up his tale again. "They drew their swords with a mighty shout, and waved them aloft, declaring, 'We follow Harold, our true King!' Then Harold, being somewhat moved, as I thought, put his brother aside, and beckoning to me to come closer, spoke with me in good

Latin, bidding me begone and tell your Grace that he would meet you in battle, when God should declare between you. And so I left the camp, pausing only to speak with certain monks from the Abbey of Waltham. My lord, the levies of Edwine and Morkere have not yet come up to join Earl Harold."

He stopped, and bowed. No one spoke for a moment; then the Duke said: "So be it. We march at daybreak."

The Normans spent a great part of the night in confessing their sins; and receiving the Sacrament. The camp was in a bustle of preparation which did not cease until the moon rode high. Men curled up in their cloaks then upon the ground; the sentries paced slowly up and down with the starlight on their helmets; the priests were shriving penitents until the dawn, but Odo, the Bishop of Bayeux, lay sound asleep in his silken tent, with his shirt of mail hung from the pole behind him, and his mace ready to his hand.

The Duke was up until midnight in conference with his barons, but he laid himself down on his couch then, and soon dropped off into an easy slumber. Raoul had a pallet in his tent, but he could not sleep. He went out into the night, and stood looking towards the line of dark hills that lay between Hastings and the Saxon encampment. Somewhere beyond those tree-crowned heights Edgar was lying, perhaps wakeful too, thinking of the morrow. Raoul tried to picture him: was he confessing his sins? or was he spending the night in feasting, as he had once said Saxons were wont to do before a battle?

Tomorrow, thought Raoul, tomorrow. . . . O God, let me not encounter Edgar! Let me not remember him, not see his face confronting me, nor meet his sword on mine, with death in both our hearts!

A howl rose in the stillness, eerie and melancholy. Raoul started, and crossed himself involuntarily, but it was only one of the wolves that prowled round the camp at night, hunting for scraps thrown out on to the garbage heaps.

At daybreak, when Mass had been celebrated, the Duke broke camp, and led his host in three divisions up the road that led to the hill called Telham, and over it to the fringe of the Andredsweald.

The first division, which was composed mainly of French, Flemings, Ponthevins, and the men of Boulogne and Poix, was commanded by Count Eustace of Boulogne, and was to form the right wing of the army. Young Robert de Beaumont led a thousand Normans in this division. It was his first trial of arms, and he was eager to acquit himself worthily. He rode a restive destrier, and the badge of his house was blazoned on his shield.

The second division, Norman to a man, was commanded by the Duke in person, riding the horse brought to him by Walter Giffard from Spain. He wore a plain tunic of steel rings sewn flat on leather, with loose sleeves reaching just below the elbows, and skirts to the mid-leg, slit before and behind to allow him greater freedom of movement. His hauberk and helmet, which were borne by his squire, were both quite plain, the helmet being sharply conical, and having a neck-piece as well as a nasal. The only weapons he carried were his lance, and the mace which hung from his saddle-bow.

Near to him rode his brother and the Bishop of Coutances. The Bishop wore his robes, and held his crozier, but Odo had put on his mail shirt over a long white albe, and had armed himself with a formidable baston.

The Count of Mortain was joined with Néel de Saint-Sauveur, in the leadership of the Côtentin troops. His squire carried the standard of St. Michael before him on the end of a lance.

Close behind them rode Roger de Montgoméri at the head of the vast forces of Belesme, and near at hand were the veterans, Giffard and Gournay, and William FitzOsbern with the men of Breteuil, and of Bec-Crespin. None of the men yet wore their armour, since the weight of hauberks would only add to the fatigue of the march.

The third division was to form the left wing. It was led by Alain Fergant and Count Haimer of Thouars, and was composed of Bretons, Manceaux, Poictevins, and auxiliaries from the banks of the Rhine.

The way led over the foothills above the Pevensey marshes. When the sun grew warmer men sweated freely, and the long line of spears glittered like a metal snake winding along the road.

From the summit of Telham Hill the Saxon army came in sight at last. The Norman host halted, and rested awhile in the shade of giant trees. The Duke had ridden forward a little way with Counts Eustace and Alain, and was closely observing the English position, and the ground that lay between.

Harold had pitched his two standards on the opposite height, a narrow hill about a mile in length, which sloped gently down to the Senlac bottom at its foot. A hoar appletree marked its summit, and by this Harold's own standard of the Fighting Man was planted. Across the valley the Normans could see the sheen of its golden folds; beside it the Dragon of Wessex floated red against the sky.

The hill seemed to be completely covered with armed men. The Normans, straining their eyes to see more closely, whispered amongst themselves that a forest of spears awaited them.

"Hear me, Count Eustace!" the Duke said. "If God grant me victory this day, I will build an Abbey where that standard waves now." He pointed across the valley. "That I swear, before God and the Pheasant." He wheeled his horse, and came cantering back to the lines. He put on his hauberk, and taking his helmet from his squire set it on his head before he realized that he was holding it hind part before. He saw that some who were watching him were inclined to regard this accident as an ill abodement, and he said with a laugh: "A sign! My Dukedom shall be changed to a Kingdom, even as I now change this helm."

The army was in movement by this time, deploying along the sides of the hill, archers to the fore, the heavy foot immediately behind them, and the chivalry drawn up in the rear. Bardings jingled; caltraps caught the sun and flashed points of light; pennons and gonfanons fluttered a medley of devices.

The Duke summoned up De Toeni with a nod, and held out his gonfanon. "Bear my gonfanon, Ralph de Toeni," he said, "for I would not but do you right, and by ancestry your family are Gonfanoniers of Normandy."

De Toeni rode up close. "My thanks to you, beau sire, for the recognition of our right, but by my faith the gonfanon shall not be borne by me this day! Seigneur, I claim quittance of that service for one day alone, for I would serve you in another guise, and fight the English at your side."

The Duke laughed. "As you will, De Toeni." He looked round; his eye alighted on old Walter Giffard; he said: "Lord of Longueville, I know none worthier than you to carry my standard."

Walter shook his head vigorously, and reined back. "For the mercy of God, beau sire, look on my white hairs!" he begged. "My strength is impaired; I am short of breath. Let Toustain here bear your gonfanon: I warrant he will be glad."

Toustain FitzRou Le Blanc, a knight of Caux, coloured up, and looked eagerly at the Duke. William held out the gonfanon. With a gasp Toustain took it in his reverent hold.

Facing the ranks of his army the Duke made a short invigorating speech to the listening soldiers. "Now is the time for you to prove with what courage you are endowed," he said. "Fight like men, and you will have victory and honour and riches! Fail, and you will be swiftly slain or live to serve cruel enemies." His voice lifted; he said strongly: "There is no road for retreat. On one side arms and a hostile country bar the way; on the other the sea and the English ships oppose flight. It is not for men to be afraid. Try only that nothing shall make you retreat, and soon triumph shall rejoice your hearts."

He ended on a confident note; FitzOsbern, who had been fidgeting with his bridle, spurred up to him, and said in his impetuous way: "Beau sire, we tarry here too long. *Allons! allons!*"

The knights now put on their armour; men gripped their spears, and slipped their arms in the enarmes of the big kite-shaped shields; in a few moments the order to advance was given, and the lines moved forward down the slope of the hill.

A rough valley separating Telham Hill from the Senlac height had to be crossed. It was boggy in parts, with bull-rushes growing in great profusion, but on the higher ground there were trees and bushes. Brambles caught in the archers' tunics, and often the riders had to duck their heads to avoid low-hanging branches. As they drew nearer to the foot of the opposite ridge the Normans could distinguish the figure of the Fighting Man upon Harold's waving standard, and see the glint of sunlight on the jewels with which it was sewn. The men-at-arms, observing no mounted soldiers amongst the Saxons, exclaimed at this. Some, better informed than the rest, spread the information down the ranks that no Saxon rode into battle.

"See how they plant their gonfanons firm in the ground!" grunted a spearman, shifting his shield on his arm. "When my father went to fight King Edward's battles under the Lord of Longueville and the King's brother Alfred, thus was it then. The troops whom they call huscarles stand with the noble lords around the standard, and will not move. Ho, ho, we shall teach these Saxons something of warfare this day!"

"What, will they not charge on us?" demanded the next man.

"Nay, nay. Look how they have fortified their position!"

In front of the Saxon lines a hasty ditch had been dug, the loose earth being beaten into an embankment which was crowned the whole length of the hill with a breastwork of osiers and brushwood. In the centre waved the standards, and round them were gathered the thegnhood and the trained huscarles, all fully armed with byrnies, and helmets of bronze, and wood, and iron, and round bucklers daubed with crude colours and devices. Each wing of the army was composed almost entirely of the shire-levies, men belonging to the fyrd of England, not trained to war, some wearing their simple woollen tunics, some the proud possessors of axes, some brandishing hammers, and scythes, and even iron spades.

At a distance of a hundred yards or so the chivalry halted, and the archers, advancing steadily up the slope, discharged their first volley of arrows. They were met by a storm of missiles: javelins, lances, taper-axes. The breastwork of osiers did much to protect the Saxon line from the arrows, and though some found marks, many hit the brushwood, and stayed there quivering. The archers pressed on through the rain of missiles, and loosed a fresh volley. This succeeded little better than the first, and the throwing-spears and axes that hurtled down upon them made them waver on the slope. A man fell with a taper-axe stuck fast in his shoulder; stone and flints whistled past the archers' heads; they shot again. One or two gaps appeared in the Saxon front line, but these were quickly filled. The heavy projectiles were driving the archers back; they retreated, leaving their dead and wounded sprawling on the field; and stumbling over the boulders and flints and javelins with which the ground was by now littered they fled back out of the Saxon range.

The Duke's messengers went galloping down the lines; the heavy foot, spearmen fully armed and carrying shields and gavelocs, moved forward in a formidable line all along the front.

Dodging the hail of missiles, some falling, some stumbling over the dead, they came up the slope with their shields before them, and tried to storm the breastwork. Steel clashed; wild shouts and groans rang out; the Saxon axes whirled in the air, and descended with a force that cut through the Norman hauberks as though they had been made of paper. A man's head jumped from his shoulders, and went hopping and rolling down the slope; the body toppled into the ditch; someone slipped in the blood, and was thrown forward on his face and trodden underfoot by his struggling comrades. Here and there the Saxon line gaped for a moment, but swiftly closed again; in some places the breastwork was beaten down; and all along the line the ditch was filling with dead bodies and blood-boltered debris.

The Norman foot was thrown back, and retreated down the hill in confusion, pursued by a fresh storm of javelins hurled from above; the chivalry, standing motionless at the bottom could see maimed men deserted on the slope and trying to crawl to safety, some armless, some dragging a bleeding stump where a leg had been; others, whole, but hideously gashed, staggering downhill with blood spurting from their wounds and splashing over their tunics and hose.

The leaders managed to check the men-at-arms' precipitous flight, and to marshal them into order. A command ran down the lines of the horsemen: the chivalry was coming up.

The foot retired to the rear between the divisions of the cavalry; a single rider spurred ahead of the line, and began to sing the *Song of Roland*, tossing his sword in the air, and catching it as it fell. Taillefer, it was; he of the golden voice. His full-throated "Aoie!" set the Duke's knights roaring out the refrain with him. He galloped before them up the slope, still juggling with his sword. Behind him thundered the whole weight of the chivalry. He caught his sword a last time, and gripped it, sat well down in the saddle, and dashed straight into the Saxon breastwork. It broke under his charge; he was in amongst the enemy, hacking and slashing; his voice rang high on the triumph of his song; there were swords all round him; he fell, pierced with a dozen wounds.

The knights and the barons behind hurled themselves against the breastwork. Horses floundered in the ditch; cries of *Dex aie*! and *Turie*! rose, answered by the roar of "Out, out!" Away on the right wing Robert de Beaumont was earning laurels for himself for the gallantry of his many attacks; nearer to the centre the Lord of Moulines-la-Marche was fighting with a ferocity that made men call him William Sanglier thereafter.

In the forefront of the battle the gold lions of Normandy waved; Toustain was sticking close to the Duke, gritting his teeth, hanging on desperately to the shaft of the gonfanon. Mortain fought beside his brother; no axe before, no press of horsemen behind could force him from William's side, but a terrific blow aimed at him cleaved his horse's neck nearly through, and the beast sank under him. He sprang clear; Raoul cried: "Take mine, Mortain! Up! up!" He forced his way back out of the press, and slid down from his destrier's back. Mortain grasped the bridle with a brief word of thanks, and hoisted himself up. One of Raoul's own men struggled to reach him, and thrust a bridle into his hand. "Here, master!"

Raoul mounted. "Good lad. Get you back out of this." He drove in his spurs and thrust forward into the mêlée again.

A tremour ran through the line. Away on the left the Bretons and Manceaux under Alain Fergant were wavering. Only the fyrd confronted them, but these men of peace were filled with a courage of bitter hatred, and the ferocity of their blows turned the Bretons' hearts to water. They broke, and fell back; their leaders were yelling at them, and trying to beat them forward with the flats of their swords on the horses' quarters, but a storm of slings and taper-axes settled the matter. The left wing turned and fled down the slope in headlong confusion, sweeping away their own foot which had formed again behind them.

"Seigneur, seigneur, the Bretons have broken!" Raoul struggled to reach William's side. "Back, for God's sake!"

The centre and right were already giving ground before the murderous Saxon axes. The Duke gave orders to draw off, and rode down the slope to a point from where he could observe the whole line of his front. His chivalry retreated in good order, but Toustain's horse had been slain by a spear-thrust through its chest and men could no longer see the gold lions turning and twisting in the ranks. A rumour spread swiftly that the Duke was slain; dismay seized the host; a sort of groan went up.

"He lives, he lives!" Gilbert d'Aufay shouted.

The Duke pulled off his helmet, and galloped down the line, calling: "Behold me! I still live, and by God's aid I will conquer!" A flint sang past his ear; FitzOsbern snatched at his destrier's bridle and dragged him down the slope to safety.

Someone furnished Toustain with a fresh mount; the lions waved on high again, and a cheer went up.

In the rear those in charge of the spare horses and the battle-harness saw the rout of the left wing, and were so filled with dismay that they began to retreat. A white horse dashed after them, a white alb fluttered. "Stand fast! stand fast!" bellowed the Bishop of Bayeux. "We shall conquer yet!" He waved his baston to his own men, and said: "Hold this rabble! Let them not stir!"

There was now a fresh movement on the left. The English

fyrd, seeing their foes fleeing in panic away from them, burst out of their breastworks with yells of triumph, and surged after in a straggling horde.

The Duke saw the blunder, and wheeled his cavalry. Led by Néel of Côtentin, and William, Lord of Moyon, the centre charged over the ground, and falling on the fyrd's flank, rode down the peasantry in their hundreds. The serfs, ill-armed, unprotected by mail, were cut to pieces almost to a man; the Bretons halted in their flight; their leaders got them into some sort of order, and brought them up again to assist in a slaughter that was by then complete. More than half the English right wing was slain in that brief encounter; the Norman horse drew back from a field of dead, and the squadrons, swinging about, cantered back to the centre.

A breathing-space, much needed, was snatched while the Breton lines formed again, and those who had lost their destriers in the first attack mounted the fresh horses which their squires brought up. The Norman ranks were shaken and thinned. William de Vieuxpont had been slain, Tesson's son Raoul, and many others, and their bodies lay spread-eagled on the hill. Gilbert de Harcourt had been wounded in the thigh, but he had bound his scarf tightly round his leg, and seemed little the worse for wear.

Eudes' sorrel destrier pushed up to Raoul's Bertolin; Eudes grunted: "This is a bloody fight, by my head! I suppose you are grown used to such battles, hey?"

"No man alive has seen so stern a fight as this," Raoul answered. He wiped the red stains from his sword; his hand shook slightly; there was a smear of blood on his cheek; and his hauberk was dinted across one shoulder.

Messengers rode down the ranks; the trumpets sounded the signal for the second attack; again the chivalry thundered up the slope. The breastworks, already broken and sagging, were swept away, but a wall of shields met the horsemen. The line swayed; the ditch was full of limbs and shattered helmets and bodies mutilated beyond recognition. Now and then a Saxon fell amongst the Norman dead, but the shields never broke, and the axes swung as fiercely as ever.

A Saxon in the forefront of the battle rushed straight at the Duke and struck with all his might at the big Spanish horse he rode. It fell with a scream of agony; the Duke flung himself clear, still grasping his mace, and turned, and dealt his assailant a blow that smashed through his helmet of bronze and felled him to the ground. He had a brief vision of a fair face, startling in its resemblance to Earl Harold's; an anguished cry rose throbbingly: "Gyrth! Gyrth!" and a young man burst from the Saxon lines, and bestrode the fallen body. A knight rode at him, shouting: "Saint-Marcouf! Sire Saint-Marcouf!" and was cleaved almost in twain by a terrific axe-blow. For a fleeting moment Raoul saw the young Saxon heroically defending Gyrth's body; then the Normans closed round him, and he sank, and the horses swept over him.

A roar of fury came from hundreds of Saxon throats; a single voice howled: "Gyrth and Leofwine! Both, both! Out, Norman butchers! Out!"

The Duke slipped on a repulsive bleeding tangle of horses' guts, and caught at a destrier's bridle. A knight of Maine bestrode it; he tried to thrust past the Duke, shouting: "Loose my bridle! God's eyes, let me go!"

The muscles on the Duke's arm stood out hard as steel. He forced the plunging destrier back. "Splendour of God, know your over-lord!" he said. "Dismount! I am Normandy!"

"It is each man for himself! I will not dismount!" gasped the knight recklessly.

The Duke's eyes blazed suddenly. "Ha, dog!" He seized the man by his belt and heaved him out of the saddle as though he had been a featherweight. The knight fell sprawling; the Duke vaulted on to the destrier's back and pressed forward to the front again.

The martlets of William Malet's gonfanon fluttered before him; somewhere down the line the men of Cingueliz were yelling their fierce battle-cry of Turie! Closer at hand men were calling on Saint-Aubert, their patron saint. The Lord of Longueville's voice rose above the cries. "A Giffard! a Giffard!" Old Walter, fighting hand to hand on foot with three Saxon warriors, was beaten to his knees, and shouted his watchword as he fell.

The Duke forced a way through the pack, and charged down upon the Lord of Longueville's foes. "Up, up, Walter, I am with you!" he called. His mace crashed down upon a wooden helmet; a man's brains spilled on the torn ground; the Duke's horse was plunging and snorting; he held it hard; the Saxons scattered, and Giffard struggled to his feet. "Back, old war-dog!" the Duke commanded above the din of the fight.

"Not while I can still wield a lance!" panted Giffard, and grabbed at a riderless horse, and hoisted his bulk upon into the saddle.

Thousands of Saxons lay dead on the field, but still the wall of shields held. It was long past noon, and the sun beat pitilessly down on the sweltering hosts. The Norman chivalry was limping and spent; they fell back a second time, and saw the Saxon line above them broken but invincible.

The field reeked of blood; the ground was slippery under it, and all over the slope of the hill dreadful relics were strewn: hands still rigid on spear shafts; whole arms cleaved clean away from the shoulder, here and there a gory head battered to a shapeless mass, sometimes no more than a finger, a horse's ear, or the half of a horse's nostril that had been velvet-smooth before and was now sticky with congealing blood.

The weary squadrons drew up out of range of the Saxon missiles, which still continued to hurtle down at them. Men sat their horses like sacks of flour; the horses themselves stood with trembling wide-spread legs, foam at their mouths and on their bardings, their heads hanging down and their flanks torn by the riders' spurs.

All thought of Edgar left Raoul, even as he had prayed it might. The world contained nothing but blood: blood spurting from cut arteries, blood oozing sluggishly from flesh wounds, blood drying on the dismembered corpses that littered the field.

He let the greasy reins fall on Bertolin's neck, and tried to wipe his hands on his gartered hose. He wondered how many of his friends still lived; he thought he had heard FitzOsbern's voice in the press, and he could see Grantmesnil and Saint-Sauveur now, wiping the sweat from their faces.

Someone nudged his arm. "Here, drink some of this," said Eudes in his phlegmatic way.

Raoul looked up. His brother was pushing a costrel into his hand; he looked dirty and blood-stained, but his stolidity was unimpaired. "Saints bless you, Eudes!" Raoul said gratefully, and took a pull at the heady wine. "I was nearly spent. What now? Do you still like warfare?"

"Well enough," said Eudes placidly. "But I have a grudge against some swineshead out of Caux, who jostled me into the ditch in that last skirmish, so that I was like to have foundered. When this affair is ended I shall have a score to settle with him. He bears a pennon with a stag's head caboosed. Do you know him?"

"No," said Raoul, beginning to laugh. "Not I."

A horseman went galloping down the line; the barons who had been conferring with William dispersed and came riding back to their posts. Word ran through the ranks: the squadrons re-formed, and stood waiting.

The right wing now charged up the slope, and what had been done by accident on the left was repeated by the men of Boulogne under Count Eustace. After a wild exchange of blows with the English fyrd the troops wavered, and broke, and fled down the hill with all the appearance of utter rout. On the crest of the hill the thegns scattered among the peasantry sought in vain to hold them back. The serfs were mad with the lust for blood; they had not seen the disaster on their right; all they saw was a beaten foe flying from the field. They broke from their leaders uttering yells of fierce triumph, and swarmed down the hill in pursuit of the enemy. Axes, scythes, clubs, javelins waved in the air; thousands of serfs were screaming: "Victory! Victory! Out, out! We have conquered!"

The Norman centre was again swung round; a deep roar of "*Dex aie!*" drowned the shouts of the fyrd, and the chivalry came crashing down on to the English flank. The lower slopes of the hill were thick all at once with fallen men, writhing and struggling under the chargers' hooves; the Norman feinting-party checked, wheeled about, and rode back to attack the English front. Those on the hill-crest saw the shire-levies mowed down in their hundreds. A few escaped, a few managed to crawl back to their comrades on the hill, but thousands lay dead on the torn ground, weltering in their gore, crushed and battered by the cavalry riding over them.

But the ruse brought disaster upon the Norman right. The foremost of those who had feigned flight, hurtled down the slope in an assumed disorder that soon became real. A deep fosse dug at the foot of the hill and concealed by brushwood and clods of turf lay in their path; they blundered into it, man after man, till the pit was full of living bodies struggling and heaving in one smothered mass. The horsemen behind, unable to check the impetus of their rush, rode over them in scores. Backbones were smashed, heads beaten in, limbs broken, and those at the bottom of the pit perished from asphyxiation, and their bodies were flattened to shapelessness by the weight of men above.

A cheer rose from the Saxon ranks. These were terribly thinned, but round the standards a solid core stood fast. The ditch was filled with dead, the breastworks were beaten underfoot, but a wall of shields comfronted the Norman host.

A series of attacks was now made upon the English front. Charge after charge was led; the Norman horse plunged and trampled over the filled ditch; lance and sword strove against the axes; the Saxon line gave under the sheer force of the impacts, but each time the gain was only temporary, and the chivalry was thrown back with heavy loss.

William's second horse was slain under him; Count Eustace, swept from his post on the right, was beside him, and offered his own destrier. "Take mine, Normandy," he puffed, heaving his bulk from the saddle. "If the host see you not the day is lost. Holy Face, these Saxons are made of iron! Will they never break?"

The Saxon shields danced before Norman eyes, barbaric colours glaring in the sunlight; the ranks stood firm; the axes, red with blood, swung and fell with a force that cleaved hauberk and bone in one murderous blow. The Duke's helmet had been smashed in; a lance-thrust almost unseated him; his third horse was slain by a Saxon *seax* ripping up its belly, and fell with a squeal of agony, nearly pinning him beneath it. He managed to fling himself clear; a destrier reared up suddenly above him, and was wrenched round with violence that came near to pulling it over backwards.

"God on the Cross, beau sire!" Raoul was out of the saddle, even as the Duke reached his feet. "I had nigh ridden you down! Up! Take my bridle!" He thrust it into the Duke's hand, and ran back, dodging and ducking between the riders.

The chivalry fell back again; the Duke ordered his archers up and volleys of arrows were loosed into the Saxon ranks. A fresh storm of missiles drove off the bowmen; they retreated to the rear, and the chivalry charged up the slope again.

For over an hour the cavalry attacks alternated with the volleys of the archers. The store of Saxon missiles was running out; while the archers loosed their bolts the English ranks stood motionless and silent, and the chivalry at the foot of the hill drew up for the next attack.

The sun was setting in a red ball of fire behind the trees to the west. All day the desperate fight had raged, and still showed no sign of abating. The Saxons were holding on till Morkere should come to their relief. Their lines were maimed and crippled; the flanks were swept away, but the standards flaunted obdurately on the highest point of the hill, and the thegnhood formed an unbreakable wall round them.

Ralph de Toeni looked towards the sun, and said: "It will be dusk in an hour, and we are nigh spent. They are devils, these Saxons!"

"Their axes dismay our men," Grantmesnil said, binding his scarf tight about a flesh wound on his arm. "The Duke is wasting his arrows: they stick in the Saxon shields, and do little harm."

The Duke was spurring towards the archers; their captains ran to meet him, and stood at his stirrup listening to what he said. He made a gesture, snatched a bow, and bent it to show the archers what he needed; FitzOsbern rode up to him, anxiously questioning, the captains ran down the line of bowmen, explaining and exhorting.

The archers now aimed their arrows high in the air. The shafts shot upward, over the heads of the front ranks of the Saxons, and fell in a sharp rain right in the heart of the thegnhood.

The Saxons had no more missiles to throw; they could do nothing but stand passive, gritting their teeth, while the dropping arrows thinned their ranks. When the archers' supply of shafts was exhausted they fell back to refill their quivers, and the chivalry charged up the slope to attack the shaken line. Again steel rang on steel, again the ranks surged back, recovered, and stood firm. The chivalry flung itself against the wall; the English were a solid mass through which it was impossible to break, but they were becoming wedged so tightly that it was difficult any longer for them to wield their weapons. The chivalry drew off again; more arrows dropped, carrying noiseless death.

The pauses between the attacks were nerve-racking to the helpless host. Below them the Saxons could see the Norman horse drawn up behind the archers, standing motionless while the arrows weakened the enemy lines. Harder to bear than the shattering cavalry charges were these periods of tense silent waiting. Hardly a movement stirred the Saxon ranks. From under the shade of helmets haggard faces looked out, worn with endurance, and eyes stared westwards to where the last glow of the departed sun was fading. A thousand brains dulled by fatigue drummed with the thought: only a little while longer; only a little while till darkness.

Over the marshes in the valley dank mists were rising; a grey shadow stole over the battlefield, and an evening chill spread through the patient ranks. The arrow-shower ceased; a sigh rose from the English lines; men grasped their shields tighter, and dug their heels into the churned earth in readiness to withstand the attack that would come.

The chivalry thundered up the slope; the whole mass of the Saxons shuddered under the crash of meeting; almost the only movement in the host was the dropping of the dead.

The Normans were nearly as exhausted as the English.

Some still fought with the old dash, notably the Duke himself; his Seneschal; the Lord of Moulines, who was spattered from head to foot with the blood of the scores he had slain; and Robert de Beaumont, whose energy and courage seemed invincible; but the greater part of the army fought like men in a dream, mechanically hacking, cutting, guarding.

Raoul had no longer strength to force his way beside the Duke; Mortain still held his post, the Watcher was swept away down the line, hardly caring, having in his head only one fixed thought: I must kill or be killed. A kind of dull rage possessed him, and lent new strength to his arm. His sword was dripping, the hilt sticky in his hold, and the runes on the blade hidden under the blood that had dried over them. A Saxon, breaking out of the pack, dashed at him; he saw the gleam of the *seux* thrusting up at his horse's belly, and slashed downwards with a snarl of fury, and rode over the still-breathing body. His horse was sliding and plunging on a heap of slain, snorting in terror, with wide nostrils and dilated eyes; Raoul drove it on to the locked shields ahead, shouting: "Harcourt! Harcourt!"

A shield was flung up; a face drawn with weariness swam before his blurred vision; eyes he knew were looking steadily into his. His sword-arm dropped. "Edgar! Edgar!"

A horse jostled his; he was forced on down the line, white as death and shaking. The fight raged about him; a spear glanced along his shield; he parried it mechanically.

The Count of Eu's voice sounded, shouting above the din: "Normandy! Normandy! Smite for Normandy!"

"Yes," Raoul echoed stupidly. "For Normandy! I am a Norman . . . a Norman . . ."

He gripped his sword-hilt tighter; his arm felt heavy as lead. He struck at a hazy figure, and saw it go down.

A scuffle drew his eyes to the right. He saw Roger FitzErneis, flinging his lance away, take sword and shield and ride like a maniac at the Saxon front. He burst through; Raoul saw the flash of his sword, hacking, thrusting. He was up to the standard, his blade slashed at the shaft. A dozen spears surrounded him, and he fell.

His heroic attempt whipped up the flagging spirits of the Normans; again they charged, and the Saxon mass was borne backwards under the fury of the assault, until the ranks were wedged so tightly that the wounded and the dead could not fall to earth, but stayed, jammed between their living comrades in the pack.

Raoul's horse stumbled over the carcass of a destrier, and

came down, pitching him over its head. He was all but trampled under the hooves of the Lord of Bohun's horse, but managed to rise and stagger clear of the danger. He heard the trumpets sounding; the chivalry fell back; he found that he was shaking from head to foot and reeling like a drunken man.

He made his way down the hill, stumbling over the débris that littered the slope. A head lay cupped in a hollow in the ground as though it had grown there; the glassy eyes stared dreadfully, the lips were drawn back from the teeth in a kind of macabre grin. Raoul began to laugh in lunatic gusts. Someone caught at his arm and tried to drag him on; Gilbert d'Aufay's voice reached him. "Raoul! Raoul, stop, for God's pity!"

"But I know him!" Raoul said. He pointed a trembling finger at the gruesome head. "I know him, I tell you, and there he lies. Look, it is Ives de Bellomont!"

Gilbert shook him. "Stop! Stop, you fool! Come away!" He forced him on down the hill.

The archers were moving forward, and again the shafts shot upwards into the air and fell in the midst of thegnhood. The light was now very faint and uncertain and the painted shields had become dark barriers still held against the enemy. Of the twenty thousand men Harold had led into battle very few remained. The fyrd was almost wiped out; more than half the thegns lay stretched on the ground, wounded and dead and dying; and round the standards the remnant of the host made their last gallant stand.

It was not the Norman chivalry that at last broke the shields, but one chance arrow. A bitter cry arose from the Saxon ranks: Harold the King had fallen at the foot of his standard.

Men dropped on their knees beside him, frantically calling his name. He was quite dead, must have died instantly. An arrow dropping through the dusk had pierced through one eye to the brain. They raised him in their arms; they could not believe that he was dead. They pulled out the arrow and tried to staunch the oozing blood; they chafed his hands, imploring him to speak. And all the time the arrows were falling.

"He is dead." A huscarle let fall the limp hand he held. "Dead, and the day is lost!"

"No, no!" Alfwig, the Earl's uncle, clasped the body in his arms. "Not dead! not now, with the end so near! Harold, speak! Speak, I charge you! You have not lived this day

301

through to die thus. What, is all then in vain? Alas, alas!" He let the body fall, and sprang up. "It is over. The King lies dead for whom we have fought and died, and there is no hope left to us, but only flight! What guard we now? Nothing, nothing, for Harold is slain!" He tottered, for he was badly wounded, and would have fallen but for the thegn who caught him.

Down the slope the Normans could see the line above them waver; the archers fell back, a last charge was made. William of Moulines-la-Marche, yelling his battle-cry, led a party of his knights straight for the Saxon shields with a ferocity that cleaved a passage through the ranks right to the foot of the standards themselves.

The Saxons were already flying from the crest of the hill. The Lord of Moulines slashed at the standards, and they fell, and a roar of exultation went up from the Norman ranks. Harold's golden banner lay trodden in blood and mire; two of the knights, mad with a savagery that equalled their lord's, hacked at his body where it lay.

All that remained of the Saxon host were escaping northwards towards the dense forests that lay behind the hill. The descent upon this side was no gentle slope, but a precipitous drop leading to a fosse at the foot. The thegns flitted through the half light down the steep sides; a party of Normans, riding in pursuit, blundered over the edge of the scarp, unable in the dusk to see what lay before them. The treacherous fosse afforded no foothold for the horses; destriers and riders rolled headlong down to the bottom, and there the Saxons, rallying for the last time, turned and slew them in one brief desperate encounter. Then, before reinforcements could come up, they fled on into the darkness, and the forests swallowed them from sight.

CHAPTER V

The noise of the fighting at the foot of the scarp reached those above and inspired one man at least with a lively alarm. Count Eustace Als Grenons, thinking that the levies of Edwine and Morkere must have come up, rode towards the Duke quite pale with dread, and catching at his bridle-arm advised him in the strongest terms to retreat.

The Duke shook off his hand, and turning from him with a look of disdain gave orders that his tent should be set up where Harold's standard had flown all day. "Clear me a space," he commanded. "It is here that I will spend the night."

The camp-varlets were busy with this work when the Lord of Longueville came riding up in a bustle of disapproval. "Beau sire, what are you about?" he demanded. "Surely you are not fitly placed here among the dead? You should lodge elsewhere, guarded by one or two thousand men, for we know now what snares may be laid for us. Moreover, there is many a Saxon lies bleeding but alive amidst the slain, and would be glad to sell his life for the chance of killing you. Come away, seigneur!"

"Are you afraid, Walter? I am not," said the Duke coolly. "Join Als Grenons if that is the mind you are in." His gaze swept the battlefield; he said on a note of anger: "Bid the leaders look to their men. I will have none of this plundering of the slain. Let each side bury its dead, but Earl Harold's body do you find and bring to me presently to my tent with all honour. Raoul, I want you."

It was over an hour later when Raoul at last slipped away from the Duke's side. He had stripped off his battle-harness, and washed the bloodstains and the sweat from his person. His squire, a zealous lad much devoted to him, had brought him water, and a clean tunic of fine wool, and his long scarlet cloak.

Binding the straps around his hose Raoul nodded to where his discarded garments lay in one corner of the tent, and said curtly: "Burn them. Throw that hauberk away; it is smashed across the shoulder. Have you cleaned my helm?"

The squire held it up, and the sword too, both burnished very brightly.

"Good lad. Buckle the sword round me." Raoul stood up and fastened the mantle across his chest while the squire knelt to adjust the sword.

The Duke was at supper with his brothers and the Counts Eustace, Alain, and Haimer. The tent was lit by candles, and the meats were brought to table as though the Duke sat in one of his palaces. No one entering would have dreamed that all round the tent dead and dying men were lying in heaps on the festering ground. The Duke, who showed no other signs of fatigue than a certain taciturnity and a slight furrow between his eyes, ate and drank sparingly, but the noble Counts, smelling the spices that flavoured the dishes, smacked their lips, and made to forget the day's turmoil in feasting.

Raoul escaped as soon as he was able and made his way

between the cluster of tents to the spot along the ridge where he thought he had seen Edgar in the press of battle.

He carried a horn-lantern and a costrel full of wine. All over the hill-side other lanterns were moving to and fro, but the moon was coming up and a faint cold light threw the mounds of slain into silhouette.

Raoul found that already priests and monks were moving amongst the wounded, some Norman, some English. A monk of Bec looked up at him as he passed, and recognizing him advised him not to walk over the field unarmed. "There are many Saxons who still live, Messire Raoul," he said, "and they are dangerous men."

"I am not afraid," Raoul answered. He turned the light of his lantern on to a crumpled figure that lay face downwards at his feet. The big shoulders had something of the look of Edgar's; Raoul bent, and with a shaking hand turned the body over. It was not Edgar. He drew a sigh of relief, and passed on.

His foot slipped in something; he knew what it must be, but he had seen and shed so much blood this day that it no longer had the power to disgust him. Or perhaps he was too tired to care. He did not know, but his eyelids were heavy and his limbs ached. Sleep was all his need, sleep and forgetfulness, but even this held off while Edgar's fate was still uncertain. A faint hope lurked in his breast that Edgar might have been amongst those who escaped into the woods to the north. He had been searching this shadowed field for a long time now, but the task was too great. It seemed as though the world contained nothing but dead men, lying in still, twisted attitudes under the stars. There were thousands of them, tall and short, old and young—thousands of Saxons, but not Edgar.

Some of the mercenaries were sneaking along the sides of the hill to strip their ornaments from the slain. No, thought Raoul, you cannot stop an army such as ours from plundering.

He passed a priest kneeling beside a dying huscarle. The priest looked up at him in vague alarm, but in the glazing eyes of the huscarle hatred gleamed. Raoul saw him drag a hand to his *seax*; a rush of blood poured from his mouth and nostrils; he fell back dead, and the priest gently drew the lids over his eyes.

It was very quiet along the hill, strangely quiet after the day's din and clamour. The only sound was a low moan that seemed to come from the earth itself. Sometimes it would resolve itself into a single voice, sometimes a shattered form would stir, muttering: "Water! water!" but mostly the sound was confused and indistinct, made up of many voices.

A hand clutched at Raoul's ankle, but there was no power in the stiff fingers. He saw the sheen of moonlight on steel, but the knife fell to earth. He hurried on. Something writhed at his feet; the lantern light showed a mangled form, still breathing. He stopped over it; it neither shocked nor revolted him. He remembered how he had turned sick at Val-es-dunes at the sight of far less horrible wounds than these, and supposed that either he had grown callous or his nerves were dulled by fatigue. If he could only be sure that Edgar had escaped he would not care who else lay dead on Senlac field, he thought.

Then he found Edgar. As soon as he saw him he realized that he had known all the time, known since that moment of prescience long, long ago in Rouen, that this was how he would find Edgar, lying at his feet with his golden curls dabbled in blood, and his vigorous limbs sprawling and limp.

He dropped on his knees and raised Edgar in his arms, feeling for the beat of the heart under the shattered byrnie. The lantern standing on the ground beside him showed blood welling from many wounds. Across Edgar's brow a sword had slashed a deep furrow; the blood from it had matted his hair and trickled down his face; his beard was sticky with it.

Under his fingers Raoul thought that he could detect a feeble flutter of the heart. He snatched the costrel from his belt and set it to Edgar's lips. The wine slowly trickled past the shut teeth, some of it running out of the corners of Edgar's mouth and spilling on to his breast.

Raoul set the flask down and quickly unfastened the cloak from his shoulders and managed to fold it with one hand into a pillow for Edgar's head. He lowered him on to it and began to tear strips from his tunic to bind round the gaping wounds.

Edgar stirred, and lifted a hand to his head. Raoul bent over him to catch the words he muttered. "Something in my eyes. . . . I cannot keep it out."

Raoul wiped the blood away, and fashioned a bandage from the strip of woollen fabric. He took Edgar's hands, and chafed them. Under the grief that clogged his tongue a curious sense of fatality possessed him. He picked up the costrel again and forced some more of the wine down Edgar's throat.

The blue eyes opened; Edgar was looking at him. "The fyrd broke," he said.

"I know," Raoul answered. His voice was steady and low. "Don't think of that." He tore another strip from his tunic, and tried to staunch the blood that oozed continuously from a deep shoulder wound.

Recognition crept into Edgar's eyes. "Raoul," he said. "I saw you. You rode at me, your lance to my axe, just as you said once, oh, long ago!"

"I did not know until I was upon you. Ah, Edgar, Edgar!" Raoul bowed his head, shaken by bitter grief.

"Well, it is all over," Edgar said dreamily. "Harold fell." He moved his head as though in pain. "Soon I too shall take the swan's path, following him."

"You shall not!" Raoul was slitting the thongs that fastened Edgar's byrnie. "Edgar, no! You shall not die!" But he knew that he spoke vain words. It was of no use to bind the wounds, no use to force wine between those strong teeth.

Edgar said: "Do you remember how I told you once that Duke William would only reach to the throne across our dead? It was many years ago: I can't recall. But you see it was true." He paused, and his eyes closed. Raoul had cut away the byrnie and was trying to stay the bleeding of three wounds at once. "Let be, Raoul. O God, do you think I want to live?"

Raoul took his hand. "I cannot let you die. I know—oh, I know! What need to tell me? Would to God I too lay dying, for my heart is dead long since!"

"No." Edgar roused himself. "No, you must not die. There is Elfrida. Care for her. Promise me! There is no one else now. My father was slain, my uncles too, both, fighting side by side. I am the last. It was too much, and God was angry. Tostig came with Hardrada. We slew them at Stamford. That was a long time ago." He raised his hand to his face. "My beard is all sticky—oh, it is blood! Well, no matter. I hoped you would come, Raoul. Friendship does endure. When we heard of the landing I thought it did not, but it is different now, or maybe I am too tired to hate." His hand clasped Raoul's feebly; his speech was becoming laboured. "We marched on London, league after league. I cannot remember. After a time we could see only the road, stretching on and on. Then we came south, not waiting longer for Edwine and Morkere. And Harold had prayed in his Abbey at

Waltham, and we knew that God was angered, for when Harold came from the chapel the tower fell to the earth. And Gyrth would have led the army in his stead, but he would not have it so." A trickle of blood ran down from the corner of his mouth. "How cold it is . . . The sun went down so slowly. We needed the darkness, and prayed, each man in his heart, that God would send it in time. But He was angered, and held off the night. If Edwine and Morkere had been true! if Harold had not fallen! We could have held till darkness. We could, Raoul!"

"I know it. No men have ever fought as you did." Raoul raised him again, and holding him against his shoulder wrapped the scarlet mantle round him.

"We were driven back, but the shields did not break, did they? Do you remember Alfric? An arrow slew him at my side, but we stood so close that he could not fall. That was very near the end, round the standard. Thurkill said the day was lost, but it was not. The day was ours while we held the hill and Harold lived, even though we could no longer move in that press." A shudder ran through him. "It was worse when the arrows came. But the light was fading, and we thought—— But Harold fell after all. It was cunning of William to loose the shafts in the air." His eyes closed; he seemed to sink into a sort of stupor. The blood had soaked the bandage round his head, and was running down his face again. Raoul laid him down, and tried to tighten the strip. Edgar gave a fretful moan. He roused himself; Raoul saw that he was smiling. "Harold sent two spies to observe your camp. They brought word the Duke had mustered an army of priests because you had short hair and no beards—shaveling."

Raoul could not speak. After a moment Edgar said: "I saw FitzOsbern. And Néel too. Do they live yet?"

"Yes, they live," Raoul said drearily.

"And Gilbert? I am glad. They were my friends. Not Alfric, nor Thurkill. All those years in Normandy: I wanted to be at home, but then the Duke let me go, and it was all so changed—or maybe I was. I don't know. I shall die very soon now, and it will be ended—all the heartache I have known, and the bitterness, and the strife in my breast." His eyes were wide open, looking into Raoul's. "I would have slain even you if by that I could have saved England from Duke William. But I could not; even Harold could not. I hated you. I hated every Norman I had ever known. I wanted to slay and slay, sparing no man amongst you." He sighed; his voice sank to a whisper. "But I am tired now, and you are by me, and I remember only how we rode to Harcourt, and your father gave me an eyas of his own rearing, and how we hunted at Quévilly, and how you thrust a brat into my arms when we took that town in Brittany." He groped for Raoul's hand; it clasped his, and again he sighed, almost contentedly. "I try to think of England under William's heel, but I cannot. I can only think of the jests we had in Rouen, and the way you used to call me Als Barbe, and Barbarian, you and Gilbert." He gave a little laugh which changed to a cough and brought a rush of blood to his mouth.

Raoul wiped it gently away. "O Edgar, friend of my heart, carry only those thoughts with you down your swan's path!" he said. The hands in his were very cold; he tried to warm them in his breast.

"Elfrida ..." The word fluttered wearily past Edgar's lips.

"I will care for her," Raoul said steadily. "I would give my life for her. That you know."

"Yes. You said you would have her in despite of us all. And you will. Well, I always wanted to be able to call you brother." His breath caught; he tried to struggle on to his elbow. "I shall not do it now: it is too late. But you will be kind to her, and perhaps it is best after all." He heaved himself up still further, struggling for breath; his eyes stared past Raoul, and widened; he made a huge effort, and flung himself clear of Raoul's hold. " 'Ware, Raoul, 'ware!" he cried, and fell back on to the ground.

Involuntarily Raoul looked round. A dark form was crawling towards him; the lantern-light glinted on the blade of a knife. He grabbed at it, felt the steel sear his arm, caught a wrist, and twisted it hard. The knife fell; he threw his assailant off, and quickly picked the knife up. Hardly caring whether the unknown Saxon had strength to come at him again or not, he turned back to Edgar.

He knew before he touched him that Edgar was dead. He had spent his last strength in warning his Norman friend against a danger threatened by one of his own countrymen.

For a long time Raoul sat quite still, holding the lifeless hand. In spite of the bloodstains that disfigured his face Edgar looked very peaceful, he thought.

A great sadness stole into his heart, yet he knew that if it were possible for him to conjure Edgar to life again he would not do it. Nothing remained on earth for Edgar since all that he had striven for had passed with Harold. Saxon England had died on Senlac field; the England of the future would be Norman, and there would be no place in it for such as Edgar.

This was where friendship had led: to bitterness, and bloodshed, and to death. Gently he laid Edgar's hand down, and drew the folds of his own scarlet mantle round the body. He covered the face: it was not thus that he wanted to remember it, gashed and blood-dabbled.

A light was moving towards him; he stood up, and waited with folded arms for it to come closer. It was carried by a Saxon monk who was making his slow way across the field, tending the wounded, and shriving the dying. He seemed, from his black hood and white cassock, to be of the Benedictine Order. When he saw the strange knight standing motionless by the dead he paused, looking a little nervously up at him.

Raoul spoke to him in Latin. "Come forward, Father. I shall not hurt you, nor am I here for plunder."

"I see that you are not, my son," the monk said, drawing nearer. "But alas! there are many among your ranks who do not scruple to rob the dead."

"Many," Raoul agreed. He looked down at Edgar's cloaked form; the monk, watching him curiously, thought that he had never seen so sad a face. "My father, do you know a vill called Marwell? It is by Winchester, I think."

"I know it well," the monk replied.

"Could you carry a man's body there for burial?"

"Surely, my son." The monk sounded grave. Raoul lifted his eyes, and the holy man looked right into them. He came up quite close, holding his lantern so that he could see Raoul's face. "Whose body must I carry to Marwell?" he asked.

"The body that lies at your feet, Father. It is Edgar, Thegn of Marwell." He watched the monk go down on his knees and draw the corner of the cloak away from Edgar's face. "Cover it," he said. "But later wash away those stains." He saw that the monk was praying, and waited till he had risen to his feet again. "You will give the body into his sister's charge," he said. "I do not want her to see those ugly wounds. Will you cleanse them?"

"Rest assured, my son, that we shall do all that you would

wish," the monk answered. His voice was kind; he wondered what lay behind the request, and what interest in a thegn this Norman knight could have.

Raoul took his purse from his belt and held it out. "There will be expenses upon the journey," he said, "and I should like to buy Masses for his soul. Will you take my purse?"

The monk hesitated. "I pray you, take it," Raoul said. He dropped the purse into the monk's hand, and went down on his knee again beside Edgar's body. He lifted the cloak for a moment and looked long. The wound and the blood faded; he saw Edgar sleeping, no more. "Farewell!" he said softly. "There shall be no bitterness, no enmity, nor any grief when we two meet again. Farewell, my best of friends!" He rose; two lay-brothers had come up, and were staring at him stupidly. He said: "Will these take charge of the body?"

"They will carry it to a place of safety, my son, and it shall be taken thence to Marwell." The monk glanced at Raoul's torn tunic, and at the mantle that covered Edgar. "But your cloak?" he said doubtfully.

"Keep it round him," Raoul answered. "I do not want it."

He went slowly back towards the Norman tents. Lights burned there, and men were seated round fires kindled on the ground. He passed two of these groups on his way to his tent. The soldiers seemed tired, but cheerful, making light of their wounds and talking of the rewards they would snatch as soon as the Duke was crowned.

Raoul lifted the flap of the tiny tent he shared with Gilbert, and went in. Gilbert was lying on his pallet, not asleep, but frowning up at the tent-pole. When he saw Raoul he sat up. "So here you are," he said. "Where have you been all this while? Why, you have torn your tunic!" His eyes grew suddenly suspicious. "Where is your mantle? What have you been about?" he asked.

Raoul did not answer. He sat down on the edge of his own pallet and propped his head in his hands, staring down at the crushed grass beneath his feet.

"I see," Gilbert said pitifully. "You have been looking for Edgar. And—you found him?"

"Yes."

"Raoul, does he live?"

"No. Not now."

Gilbert brought his fist down with a crash on to the pallet. "Heart of God, I have had my fill of this accursed war!" he said. "Lands in England? I want none! I have lands in Normandy which need me, and this I tell you, Raoul: when the Duke has done with fighting I will turn to them, and forget these sorrowful shores." He stopped, and peered across the small space that separated them. "What is that on your arm? Why, it is blood!"

Raoul glanced down at it. "Yes. A Saxon crept up behind me as I knelt beside Edgar. Edgar saw, and died warning me." A silence fell between them; Gilbert cleared his throat presently, and Raoul rose stifling a sigh. "I know," he said. "Give me your mantle. I must go back to the Duke."

Gilbert nodded to where it lay. "You gave yours———?"

"Yes," said Raoul unemotionally. "He was so cold." He fastened the heavy cloak round his shoulders, and went out.

At the entrance to the Duke's tent FitzOsbern met him, and grasped him by the arm. "William has been asking for you, but I guessed where you had gone, and told him. Raoul, did you find Edgar?"

"Yes. He is dead."

"Was he dead when you came to him? Tell it me all!"

"No. He was wounded, but he lived still."

FitzOsbern cried out: "Could you not have brought him in? There are surgeons here who might have saved his life!"

"Oh William, don't you see?" Raoul said. "He did not want to live. I think he was too badly wounded, but even had he not been— no, it is better as it is. He spoke to me for a while before he died. He said he had seen you in the battle, and asked whether you had survived. When I told him, yes, he said he was glad, for you were his friend."

FitzOsbern shed tears at that. "I would I had seen him! But the Duke has been busy, and I could not leave him. Ah, poor Edgar! Did he believe I had forgotten him? Did he think my love had changed towards him that I came not?"

"Oh no! Let me go now. Some other time I will tell you how he died; not tonight."

"But stay!" FitzOsbern said. "He must be buried with honour. Do not tell me you have left his body for the wolves and the vultures to devour!"

"No, I have not done that. I gave it into the care of a monk, who has promised to bear it to Marwell."

FitzOsbern was disappointed. "You should have brought it here. The Duke would have granted an honourable grave, and we could have followed his coffin, mourning."

"But he was not a Norman," Raoul said. "Do you think that is what he would have chosen? I have done as I think he would desire." He disengaged himself from FitzOsbern's hold, and passed into the Duke's tent.

William looked up. "Well, my friend?" he said. "You have been absent from my side longer than is your wont." He glanced keenly into Raoul's face. "If Edgar of Marwell is dead I am sorry. But I do not think he would ever have lived at peace with me."

"No," Raoul said. He came further into the tent. "You are alone, beau sire."

"At last. I have had two monks from Waltham here, begging leave to search for Harold's body, and offering me ten marks of gold if I would let them bear it hence. That I cannot do." He pushed a paper across the table. "Here is the first list of those slain. Do you want to see it? We do not know all yet. Engenufe de l'Aigle was one."

"Oh?" Raoul ran his eye down the list.

The Lord of Cingueliz came in. He looked worn, and rather grim. He said: "They have found the body. It has been hacked with swords, which, for my part, I think a deed worthy of sharp punishment."

"Who did it?" William demanded.

"I know not. Two of Moulines' knights, I believe."

"Discover them, and let me know their names. I will have their spurs chopped off for this unknightly deed. Do they want to make my name odious?"

Raoul was looking at the Lord of Cingueliz. He said: "Is all well with you, Tesson?"

Tesson did not meet his eyes. "It is well with me. But my son lies dead. It is no matter. I have others." He turned abruptly as the sound of footsteps came to his ears, and held back the flap of the tent.

Four knights carried Harold's body in upon a rough bier, and set it down carefully in the middle of the tent. The Duke got up and moved forward. "Take off that covering."

William Malet drew back the cloak from the body. It lay very straight and stiff, with feet drawn together, the fearless eyes closed, and the hands crossed on the hilt of a sword.

For a minute or two the Duke stood still, looking down at the man who had fought him with such stubborn courage. His hand went to the ouch that fastened his mantle, and unclasped it. He took off the mantle and held it out to William Malet, still looking down at Harold. "Wrap him in my cloak," he commanded. "Perjured he was, but a great and a brave warrior." He paused and seemed to consider.

"William Malet, since Saxon blood runs in your veins, to you I entrust this corpse. You shall bury Harold with knightly honours by the coasts which he guarded so well. If any should wish to follow his bier they have my leave. Take him up, and bear him hence."

The knights stooped, but before they could raise the bier someone else came into the tent and stood staring wildly round.

There was a surprised silence. The newcomer was a woman, tall and graceful, with a face ravaged by grief, but beautiful even in despair. A cloak covered her; her long golden hair was dishevelled, but she was obviously no common wench, for she wore precious stones round her white neck, and bracelets on her arms.

Behind her two monks, Osegod Cnoppe and Alric the Schoolmaster, stood in nervous support. She put her hair out of her eyes, peering from one to the other of the faces turned towards her. Her mouth hung a little open; she was quite distraught, and kept on wringing her hands together.

Then her gaze fell on the figure wrapped in royal purple on the bier, and she sprang towards it with a cry of anguish, and dropped on her knees, drawing the mantle away from the face.

It was terrible to see her stroking the dead cheeks, terrible to hear her voice whispering in ears that would never heed her again. The Normans stood in horrified wonder. It was William who broke the painful silence. "Who is this woman?" he demanded.

At the sound of his voice she reared up her head and stared at him. She spoke in the Saxon tongue, and William Malet translated. "She says, which is Normandy? for she sees none here habited like a prince."

"Tell her I am Normandy," said William, "and ask her who she is, whether wife or sister, and what she wants."

She heard William Malet in silence, but when he had done speaking she rose up and came towards the Duke and addressed him very passionately.

He looked across at Malet. Malet, who had listened with pity and surprise to the lady's words, said: "Beau sire, she is none other than Editha, called the Swan-neck, who was Harold's *mie*. She has sought for his body to bear it hence to Waltham for Christian burial, and begs this favour of you, that you will relinquish it into her care."

"Harold's *mie*! Tell her that I myself will see Earl Harold honourably interred," William said.

313

But at this she cried out vehemently, like one who is mortally hurt, and tumbled to her knees again, stripping the jewels from her throat and arms and holding them out to him.

"She offers gold, beau sire, a king's ransom," Malet said, greatly moved.

"Splendour of God, does she think I am a merchant to sell the body for gold?" William said irritably. "Tell her she wastes her words, and bid her begone with her priests." He looked down at her, and added in a softer voice: "Is she afraid that I shall not bestow the corpse with honour? Tell her that Harold shall be buried in purple, with his sword beside him, keeping watch for ever over these shores."

When she heard this her eyes flashed, and she began to speak in a fierce shrill voice, twining and untwining her fingers.

"Beau sire, she thinks you mock her."

"I do not. Take her hence." He turned away from her, and she was led out, hanging back and stretching her hands to the still figure on the bier, and calling her lover's name over and over again.

But Harold lay dead, with closed eyes, and his hands crossed on his sword-hilt.

CHAPTER VI

The road that led to Marwell was very rough, and the serf who guided Raoul was afraid of the Normans all round him, so that his fear drove the wits out of his head. He came from Winchester, but he did not seem to know the way very well. It was further than Raoul had expected, and he was glad, since it was unlikely that pillaging soldiers could have penetrated so far.

He was impatient to reach Marwell; it was many weeks since Senlac field, but he had not been able to leave William sooner.

From Hastings the Duke had marched on Romney and Dover. Dover surrendered at once, but some of the foreign levies fired the houses, and there was wanton damage done. To the surprise of the citizens the Duke made good their loss in gold coin. Later he gave further signs of a just disposition, for he had marched on by Canterbury to a point below the reach of Greenhythe on the Thames, and encountered there the men of Kent drawn up in battle array under the leadership of one Agelsine, an Abbot, who demanded in their name the preservation of the ancient liberties of Kent. The Duke confirmed them in these, saying: "I am not come into England to destroy the laws and privileges of the land." The Kentish men, won by this answer, escorted him to Rochester, and proclaimed him their ruler. From Rochester he sent a detachment of his troops to begin the siege of London, which had declared for Edgar the child-Atheling. He himself marched westward to Winchester, but when he came to the town he heard that Queen Eadgytha, that rose born of thorns, lay within the walls, Winchester having been part of her dowry. With one of his sudden unexpected flashes of generosity the Duke promised, out of respect for the Queen, not to enter the town if the citizens would make their submission to him. This they did, and holding to his word he withdrew with all his force, and marched back to besiege London in person.

Raoul had left him at Barking. He was deep in negotiations with the city's intermediary, one Ansgard, a crippled veteran. He let Raoul go, but he pulled a grimace, and said: "Henceforward I suppose I must share you, my Watcher." Then he had said: "All day long men demand their warisons of me, Raoul, but you are silent. What shall I give you?"

"I want nothing," Raoul answered. "If you would be ruled by me, William, you would not give away lands in England to all who clamour for them."

"I am ruled by my word," William said. He regarded his favourite in silence for a moment. "No, you ask nothing; that has always been your way. And I would have given you an Earldom. Well, there is something I can bestow on you which you may be glad to have. Come to me again before you leave: I will give it you then."

When Raoul saw him a few hours later he had a parchment scroll in his hand. He gave it to Raoul with a quizzical smile. "I am not King of England yet, nor have I bestowed grants on any other man. Keep that against the day when it shall be valid. And God speed this errand of yours, my friend."

He had given Raoul the deed granting him the lands of Marwell, with the title of Baron.

Gilbert d'Aufay had ridden a little way with Raoul on his journey. He was troubled; he said a second time: "I want no lands in England. I could have sworn you would have said the same."

"No." Raoul shook his head slightly. "It is true I did not desire this conquest, but it is done, Gilbert, and we cannot hinder it. Oh, I know what you feel, but if all true men such as you refuse lands in this country it will be left to be the prey of Robert the Devil of Belesme, and Hugh the Wolf, and others of their kidney."

"This war has sickened me," Gilbert said obstinately. "England belongs to the Saxons, not to us. I am a Norman, and Normandy suffices me. I have seen a pack of ravening wolves gathered round William, slavering for prizes, and I tell you I will not become one of them."

"Look further," Raoul said. "We must live the future William carves for us. It lies in England. You say you are a Norman. I think in the end we shall be English. Not you nor I, perhaps, but our sons' sons."

"Mine shall not, for they shall be bred in their own land."

"But mine shall be bred in England," Raoul said, "so that when I die I shall leave the lands I snatched to English-born heirs. Stay, Gilbert. There is work to be done in this stricken country."

"Stay to ravage England like any brigand? No, Raoul."

"To bring justice back, and order, which you have loved as much as I. William means this land to be the home of Normans hereafter. He told me once, long ago, that he would win a kingdom for his posterity that should be guarded by the sea, and no fickle border-holds. Well, he has done it, and like it or hate it as you will it makes no odds. Cling to Normandy: perhaps we shall all do that, since it is our country, and we care for it, but let us teach our sons to think England their home. For in the end it will be a struggle between England and Normandy. And I think England will win, and Normandy will die, like the half of that prodigy we saw at St. Jaques." He paused. "Do you remember Galet's words? I have thought of them very often."

"I remember, yes. But they were nonsense."

"I wonder? Both Normandy and England William means to hold, and maybe he will do it, being William. But after him. . . . Well, we shall not live to see, I suppose. Go your ways, Gilbert."

"And you?" Gilbert looked at him rather sadly. "Shall I see you again in Rouen?"

"Why, surely!" Raoul said. "The Duke means to return in

the New Year if all is well, and I expect I shall journey with him, unless——" He stopped, and reddened a little.

"Unless you are wed, do you mean?"

"Perhaps. I expect I shall still go with William. I am his man. If you see my father, Gilbert, bear my duty to him, and tell him—— I don't know. Tell him I have a barony in England. That will please him."

Gilbert nodded. "I will tell him. It is Marwell, I suppose. I daresay Edgar would be glad to know you had his lands, and not a stranger. God speed you, Raoul. You choose the new way; I choose the old. We shall know one day, maybe, which of us chose aright. But I think I do not care very greatly. While Normandy lives I am hers. Fare you well!"

They clasped hands. Gilbert turned and rode back to the camp; Raoul watched him gallop out of sight, and gave the order to his escort to press on.

The way was difficult, and often the road was lost, so that it was not until the third day that Raoul rode into Marwell. He met with no resistance on his route, but black looks there were a-many, and he knew that if he had had fewer men with him he would have been attacked. The peasantry seemed cowed, but hatred gleamed in the meanest serf's eyes. He thought: It will be many years before these people forget that we are invaders. A hard road lies ahead, William my seigneur."

South of Winchester green meadows and thick woods stretched for many leagues. Marwell lay in a hollow, sheltered by gently-rising hills, and watered by a stream that meandered through its fields. Round the house serfs' huts were clustered; the house itself, which was built of wood, with a slate roof, and an outer stairway leading to the upper chambers, stood in a curtilage with a little chapel beside it and several out-buildings. A stockade enclosed it, but the gate stood open, and since no guard watched by it, it was plain that a Norman visitation was not expected. As Raoul rode into the curtilage the sacring-bell was ringing in the chapel. The place seemed deserted, but even as he swung himself down from the saddle heads peeped from the chapel door, and men ran out, snatching at whatever weapons they could reach.

Raoul stood still. He made no attempt to come at his sword, but spoke quickly over his shoulder. His own men rode forward; steel glittered, and the crowd of serfs fell back.

Raoul said in his halting Saxon: "I come in peace. But if

you set upon my men there will be bloodshed." He walked on alone, unconcerned by the glare of a score of menacing eyes, and went into the chapel.

The priest was holding the Host between hands that shook. Raoul stopped, and took off his helmet, bending the knee and making the sign of the Cross.

Elfrida stood by the altar-steps with the serving women clustered about her. All were looking fearfully towards the strange knight; a stout dame threw her arms protectively round Elfrida.

Raoul spoke her name. She had been peering at him as though she doubted, but when she heard his voice the cloud seemed to lift from her brow, and she broke away from the women who shielded her, and stumbled forward, holding out her hands. "Oh, you have come to me!" she said. "I have wanted you so, Raoul!"

The women were amazed to see her go towards the stranger with just that look on her face, but the stout dame seemed to understand the Norman tongue, and spoke a sharp reproof.

Raoul strode to meet Elfrida, but even as his hands clasped hers she shrank away from him. "Ah God, your scarlet mantle!" she whispered. She covered her eyes with her hands. "Oh no! Oh no! not that!"

The priest said quaveringly in Latin: "I charge you, Norman, as you fear God, stand back from this hallowed ground!"

For all the heed Raoul paid to him he might have held his peace. Raoul said gently: "What is it, my little love? You cannot think I come to hurt you! Look up, my heart: I have come to you, as I swore I would."

She backed away from him; her eyes were very wide, fixed on his hands. "You must not touch me. There is blood upon your hands." She pointed with a shaking finger. "Gules, gules!" she whispered in a dreadful voice. "You cannot wash it away. I know. I have tried. O God of mercy!"

He grew rather pale; he spread his hands for her to see. "Look again," he said. "There is no blood upon my hands."

"Yea, but I have seen," she said. "Blood there is, blood that no tears may wash away. Oh, do not touch me!"

"There is no blood," he repeated steadily. "My hands are clean. Not otherwise would I come to you."

She seemed as though she dared not believe him. "Not Edgar's blood? Not his, Raoul?" She began to wring her hands together. "They brought him home to me with a red mantle

318

covering him; and red wounds were on his breast, and a red scar upon his brow. And now I know that it was your mantle."

He stood still, holding her eyes with his. "It was my mantle, but as God lives Edgar met not his death at my hands," he said.

The stout woman tried to come between them. "If you are one Raoul de Harcourt of whom I have heard my nephew speak, answer me now! Sent you his body to us, wrapped in a scarlet cloak?"

"I sent it," Raoul replied.

"But you did not slay him," Elfrida said. She was trembling. "No, Raoul, no! You did not slay Edgar!"

"I have told you. I slew him not, but he died in my arms, and I sent his corpse back to the home he loved, wrapping it in my mantle. I sought him amongst the slain when the battle was done, and found him, and he still lived. Elfrida, between us twain was no blood nor any hatred. I swear it on the Cross. We spoke of old days in Rouen, remembering old jests. I cannot talk of that. Yet he said as he lay dying that friendship had endured."

The tears were running down her cheeks. "You did not slay him. No, you could not. But he lies between us, and you may not take me." She threw out her hands to check his advance. "See what lies between us!" she said. "It is ended, Raoul, the dream we had."

He looked down. A plain paving-stone marked Edgar's grave. He stood still for a moment with bowed head, but presently he said: "You are wrong. He would not wish to lie between us. At the last he spoke your name, giving you into my care."

She shook his head. "You are mine enemy," she said. "Normans have slain all that I held dear. It is ended."

A harsher note crept into Raoul's voice. He said: "Even though I had slain Edgar with mine own hands I would still take you. Through a path of swords I have come to you, because there was no other way." He stepped over the grave and caught her in his arms. "Have you forgot?" he said. "Have you forgot how you promised to trust in me even though I came thus to fetch you?"

She did not struggle, yet neither did she yield. Dame Gytha said angrily: "Do you know where you stand, Chevalier? Is this fitting work for such a place? My niece is not for you."

He held Elfrida closer, till the rings of his tunic dug into her cheek. "Can you say you are not mine? Oh, my heart, I would have died to spare you this bitter grief! Do you think that I wanted to take you as now I do? You know that I did not!"

"There is death all round us," she said in a hushed voice. "Dare you speak of love?"

"Yea, I dare." His hands gripped her arms ungently; he held her away from him and looked down at her. She had never seen his eyes so stern. "You are mine, Elfrida," he said. "I will not let you go."

Dame Gytha pulled at his sleeve. "You shall let her go!" she said. "Do you forget that she has lost father and brother both, Norman wolf? What has she to do with bridals now, poor broken heart? She dedicates herself to Holy Church, Chevalier, a surer haven than your arms!"

He released Elfrida; his face had grown dark. "With your own lips tell me that, Elfrida!" he said. "Come, let me hear it! I will believe it from none other."

She looked at her aunt, and at the silent priest. "I did say it," she faltered. "It is all so dark, and there is death—death! In a nunnery I may find peace again."

"And happiness?" he said.

She gave a little bitter smile. "Never again. I have done with happiness, but peace I may find."

"Yea?" He folded his arms across his chest. His glance swept over her; it held no kindness, no pity. He felt neither. She was his woman, and she was denying his right to take her. The gentle chivalry he had practised all his life was thrust under by some more primitive emotion. "Then break the vows you made to me!" he said harshly. "Forswear your love, Elfrida! Come! if you love me not you can surely say it!"

She stood drooping before him; he saw the tears rolling down her cheeks, but his face did not soften. Dame Gytha would have taken her niece in her arms, but his hand shot out and grasped her wrist, and jerked her roughly back. "Stand away from her!" he commanded.

Elfrida said: "Have pity, Raoul! I have borne so much. Oh, you cannot be cruel now!" She laid a timid hand upon his arm, but he did not move.

"I have no pity," he said, "but only my love for you, which is more real than pity. Though Edgar lies dead we live on, and there is happiness within our grasp. You would spurn it, cloistering yourself. Well, I hold the deed that gives me Marwell in your right; if I am your foe, speak boldly, and tell me you love me not, and I will tear the deed, and be done with you, for though I might take you by force, I will not do it. I want no bride who comes to me against her will."

Dame Gytha was flushed and indignant. "Tell him you hate all Normans, Elfrida! Give him your answer!"

"I cannot. It is not true." Elfrida's fingers twisted together. "I dare not say it."

"Are you afraid?" Raoul said. "Or have you love for one Norman at least?"

She did not answer. He gave a short laugh, and swung round on his heel. "I see. You dare not say it, and you dare not come to me. Then fare you well: I have done."

Her voice followed him, dazed, uncomprehending. "You are going?" she said. "You are leaving me?"

"Rest you, since you have no love for me you shall not see my face again," he answered.

"That is right good hearing!" Dame Gytha declared.

"Raoul! Oh, Raoul, stay!"

The cry was faint, but it stopped him. He looked back. "Well?"

"Do not leave me!" Elfrida begged piteously. "I have lost everyone but you. Oh, Raoul, be kind to me! Only be kind to me!"

"Elfrida, will you wed me?"

Her eyes searched his face, and saw it unyielding. She knew that he would go unless she answered, and she could not let him leave her. "I will wed you," she said helplessly. "I will do what you tell me. Only do not go away!"

He held out his arms. "Then come to me, my heart. I will never leave you."

"Elfrida, you shall not!" Dame Gytha cried. "Are you wood-wild, girl?"

But Elfrida did not seem to hear her. Raoul had said: "Come to me, my heart," and in his eyes the old, dear smile comforted her grief. She went to him; neither aunt nor priest could stop her; and across the grave that lay between her hands clasped his. For a moment they stayed thus, looking down at the grave, then of her own accord Elfrida stepped over it into Raoul's arms. They closed round her; she gave a deep sigh; and Raoul lifted her, and holding her against his heart carried her out of the dim chapel into the court, where the sun was shining.

EPILOGUE
(1066)

"When the trumpet ceases to sound the sword is returned to the
scabbard."
Saxon inscription.

There was snow in London, and thin icicles were hanging
from the gutters of the roofs. Inside the Abbey the cold
made men draw their mantles closely round them, and blow
surreptitiously on benumbed fingers. The Archbishop of
York's hands shook a little; he was nervous, and spoke his
office in a low troubled voice. He thought how the Duke had
repelled Stigand, the Archbishop of Canterbury, and as he
proceeded with the ritual he remembered Harold, whom
Stigand had crowned in this Abbey less than a year before. It
had all been so different then that it seemed like another life.
The Archbishop could not forget how the spring sunlight had
glinted on Harold's golden head. It seemed strange, he
thought, to place England's Crown upon a head as dark as
William's.

The Duke had chosen Christmas Day for his coronation.
The Abbey of St. Peter at Westminster was full of people,
both Norman and Saxon, and outside Norman troops formed
a strong guard to protect the Duke from any attack that
might be made by the populace. But it did not seem as
though an attack would be made. London had withstood no
long siege, but had come to terms with Duke William, after
parleys, and deep discussion, and many journeyings to and
fro by Ansgard, her intermediary. The Duke had shown great
patience, but his huge army encircled the city, cutting her off
from any help, so that although he treated Ansgard with
courtesy, and attempted no assault on the walls, London
knew that he held her in the hollow of his hand and would
close that hand if she defied him. The gates were opened to
him at last, and the Atheling delivered into his power. Edgar
was only ten years old, and when Aldred of York and

Wulfstan of Worcester had led him into William's presence he had been frightened, and had held tightly to the Archbishop's hand. But the Duke took him in his arms, and kissed him, and talked to him a little while of his Norman cousins, Robert, and Richard, and William, so that he soon lost his alarm, and went away with FitzOsbern, quite happy to exchange a Crown for the suckets that were promised him, and the companionship of the Duke's sons.

Earls Edwine and Morkere were the first to render homage to William. Stigand came next, with sleek words, but the Duke was not the man to be won by these. He repelled the Archbishop from office, and chose Aldred to set the Crown upon his head.

His Holiness the Pope had declared for William. Aldred tried to keep that always in mind. As a Churchman he approved William's claim, but the Saxon in him kept on reminding him that William was a Norman, and an invader.

Quite near to William Count Robert of Eu was standing. As he listened to Aldred's Latin phrases it seemed to him that the years slid back and he stood again in a smoky hall in Falaise, looking down at a babe who clutched a sword-hilt in his tiny hands. An echo reached him from that far-off day: "William the Warrior!" had said Count Robert of Normandy. But someone had whispered: "William the King." That must have been Herleva, thinking of the queer dream she had had. "And the tree stretched out its branches until both England and Normandy lay cowering in its shadow." He forgot how it ran. A beautiful woman Herleva had been, he thought. He wondered whether her spirit watched to-day, seeing her dream fulfilled. Someone had said: "William the Bastard." He tried to remember who could have said that, and suddenly the old Lord of Belesme's face rose before him, and he remembered how Talvas had cursed the babe. Bastard, Warrior, King: thus William had been called when he lay in his cradle. Count Robert thought how they had laughed: he, and Edward who had also been a King, and Alfred whom Earl Godwine had murdered. It was a long time ago: it made him feel old to reckon up the years. Strange, he thought, that they should have laughed. But they had not known William then: he was only a bastard brat clutching at a sword-hilt.

The Archbishop was addressing the Saxons in their own tongue. Count Robert came back to the present with a jerk. The Archbishop asked if the people would have William to be their King? They shouted Yea; it sounded spontaneous enough, thought old Hugh de Gournay, shifting his weight from one foot to the other. He wondered how long it would be before the whole land accepted William, and whether there would be much fighting to be done. He looked at William, and noted with approval that the Duke held himself very straight, and stared directly before him. Well, he might be a bastard, thought De Gournay, but he would make a good King.

The Bishop of Coutances stepped forward, and spoke in Norman to the Duke's own subjects. He asked if they were willing that their Duke should accept the Crown. They cried their consent, as the Saxons had done.

Am I really willing? thought Raoul, as the word left his lips. God knows! He saw William Malet frowning: he was not willing, but he gave his consent, of course. FitzOsbern was beaming with triumph; Giffard seemed pleased, and Tesson too. Néel looked rather grave; so did Grantmesnil: perhaps they remembered the prodigy at St. Jaques, and Galet's words.

Prayers followed the two declarations, more ritual. The Archbishop took the golden Crown between his hands, and held it above the Duke's head, and the assembled people burst out into cheering.

The Bishop of London held the sacred oil. He moved towards Aldred, but hesitated all at once, and looked in a startled way towards the doors.

Something was happening outside the Abbey. Shouts were heard, the clash of steel, and a rallying call.

The voice cried: "Treachery, by God!" and men rushed to the doors.

The Duke knelt on. Only by his sudden pallor, and the quick look he sent down the aisle did he betray himself.

For the first time in twenty years, thought Raoul, I have seen him afraid.

He too was afraid, but he did not move. He thought of Elfrida, who was lodged outside the City, and his mind began to grapple a desperate problem. If London has risen against us, how best can I reach to her? he thought.

The noise was growing louder; a smell of burning wood crept into the Abbey. "Spine of God, are we trapped?" muttered the Count of Mortain in Raoul's ear.

The Duke's jaw was set hard; the Archbishop had broken off in the middle of the ritual, and stood trembling and aghast.

Men were struggling to get out of the Abbey to beat back

the supposed assault. None of the Saxons remained, very few of the Normans. Up by the altar FitzOsbern stood his ground, Robert of Eu also, and De Gournay, and Mortain, and Raoul.

The Bishop of Bayeux, who had taken an impetuous step towards the door, caught the Duke's eye, and recovered himself. He whispered something to the Archbishop. Aldred passed his tongue between his lips, and took the sacred oil from William of London.

In the deserted Abbey, with sounds of strife raging outside, William was anointed. He stretched out his hand to take the gospel-book. Aldred held out the Cross, it shook in his grasp. The Duke kissed it, kneeling, and swore the oath in a clear unfaltering voice. The Crown was set upon his head, the Sceptre placed in his hand. He stood up, and the heavy robes he wore brushed the stone pavement.

FitzOsbern cried out: "Hail, William, King of England!" and the words echoed through the empty church.

The Duke's eyes met Raoul's; he made a faint sign with his head towards the door, and his brows lifted in a mute question.

Raoul slipped out of the Abbey. Several houses were blazing near at hand; the open place was crowded with people, but though there were signs of recent strife it seemed to have ended.

Raoul caught sight of Ralph de Toeni, and made his way towards him, and grasped his arm. "For God's sake, what is it?" he demanded.

De Toeni looked round. "Nothing. I thought the Londoners had planned an attack, did not you? But it was no such thing. Our men seem to have been at fault, but there is not much harm done: a few slain, but no more than a score, I think. From what I can understand, the guards thought the Saxons within the Abbey had set upon William when they heard the noise of our cheering, and they straightway fired the houses round, and fell on the poeple gathered here. Tesson and Néel stayed the riot. Holy God, Raoul, I will confess I was sore afraid! Did William leave the Abbey? Where is he?"

"Crowned! And none there to see it done!" De Toeni pushed a way through the uneasy crowd, calling out the tidings.

Raoul went back into the Abbey. The Duke was at his prayers, but presently he rose up, and a glance passed between him and Raoul of question and of answer.

The sound of cheering reached them from outside the

Abbey. The Lord of Cingueliz came through the doorway, crying: "Long live the King!" and the barons standing round William echoed the shout.

An old memory flitted through the Count of Eu's head. He thought he could hear Duke Robert's voice saying: "He is little, but he will grow." It was odd that he should remember that, for Robert had only been jesting, after all.

He looked at William again, wondering what thoughts were in his mind. But he could not tell: the King was staring straight ahead, his dark face inscrutable, and England's Sceptre firm in his grasp.